M000288180

ANDERSONVILLE

MIGUEL LOPEZ

Copyright © 2022 by Miguel Lopez.

ISBN 978-1-958128-86-2 (softcover)
ISBN 978-1-958128-87-9 (ebook)
Library of Congress Control Number: 2022910408

All rights reserved. No part of this book may be reproduced or transmitted in any form or by any means, electronic or mechanical, including photocopying, recording, or by any information storage and retrieval system without express written permission from the author, except in the case of brief quotations embodied in critical reviews and certain other noncommercial uses permitted by copyright law.

This book is a work of fiction. Names, characters, places, and incidents are the product of the author's imagination or are used fictitiously. Any resemblance to actual locales, events, or persons, living or dead, is purely coincidental.

Printed in the United States of America.

Book Vine Press
2516 Highland Dr.
Palatine, IL 60067

DEDICATION

"To my Lord Jesus Christ for creating me and
giving me life in his glorious works"
"To my mother. How believed in me when
others didn't. I love you mom."
"To my sister. For always telling me how it is
in life as she sees it. I love you sis."
"To my father who taught me how to be the man
I didn't want to be. I miss you dad."
"To the Rizzo family for accepting me for who
I was and who I became to be."
"To The Johnson's family. For teaching me its more
about GOD more they can understand."
"To Bishop Hibbert, for his preaching and being
totally genuine with all his Flock."
"To Paster Balcerak. For being who you are and how
you persist to follow the lord's word to the letter.
And to inspire people to follow the word of Jesus Christ."

CHAPTER 1

Prologue

In 1865 the American civil war has ended in a truce. Said truce was established by the Canadian government on the behalf of the Confederate states of America. As per the treaty both sides retain of their borders. The north or union now consists of the Northeastern states, Ohio, Michigan, Pennsylvania, Delaware, Wisconsin, and Maine. New Hampshire, Vermont, Rhode Island, Massachusetts, Connecticut, New Jersey, Illinois, Minnesota, and New York. The States of California, Nevada, And Oregon succeeded form the union. They didn't join the confederacy. However, they joined the Canadian government with the federal territories. This was official in 1867 and ratified completely in 1868. The remaining Confederate states of Texas, Arkansas, Alabama, Georgia, Florida, Tennessee, Mississippi, Louisiana, South and North Carolina and Virginia remain intact as the Confederacy.

In 1870, Robert E Lee became the second president of the CSA. He abolished slavery in accordance with a new Canadian treaty that allowed free trade with the former western Union territories. In spite of what his population thought about property rights, He was able to transition the slave population to a freed stated. Despite domestic terrorism form the Kul Klux Klan. He was president for the confederacy until a heart attack took his life at the end of his term in 1890. Thus, the truce with the union and Canadian remained intact for another 23 years.

The outbreak of WW1 plunged the union and Canadian and Confederate forces. This joint collation with the inventions of the Wright brothers and ford was successful in defeating the Austro-Hungarian empires. With Germany paying the debt it owed in the Treaty of Paris. The roaring twenties was roaring until the depression came upon us all. This greatest depression lasted until the Nazi party rose and engulfed us all into another world war. At the end of this war the unification of Canada and the C.S.A. was done. Even though the confederacy was allowed to maintain its Capitol at Richmond Virginia, the national capitol in Ottawa is still known as the nation's capital. The cold war did affect us all. The Berlin wall fell 1983. Thus, the state of the world is in rather sad state of affairs. With the desert wars, raging with ideologies running rampant through the world. We are in a state of constant watch. Ever imposing our eyes on things that shouldn't be, alas all is quiet in a nice southern Georgian coast in a nice small little quaint town know as Andersonville. Andersonville is a nice little jewel, with a rich history in the Canadian confederation where it resides. The weather is temperate year-round, and yet just north from there you do have a nice ski resort that is part of the town itself. But this is an exclusive town. Only the truly affluent and special can live here. This town's history is rather unique. Due to this you can be only invited to this town as one of its members. It has the most prestigious schools in most nations. Name any school in the world that has pre-k through PHD levels in all subjects known to the world. And this school is names after the glorious Jefferson Davis and Robert E Lee. The best of the best can only enter to the institute for higher learning. It's rich history for a hundred years for medical advances through technological advances. This center of academia is the best in the world. Robert E lee himself was the president of this fine institution for Military and other pursuits for the students that graced the fine halls and the streets of this town. Robert E Lee donated his land to become a monument. The land was turned in to cemetery for all the fallen in the civil war once he became the second president of the Confederacy.

CHAPTER 2

The Broacher

In Nowhere OK there are rumblings of strange things going on. Nowhere it's a small spot that has nothing. Small town with a few buildings but in either direction there is fields of grass, or fields of barren areas. A few buildings in the center of the main drag, which is a mile long, then nothing, as far as the eye can see. They say nothing happens in Nowhere. Sad thing is something always happens in nowhere. But everyone knows, and everyone stays quite about it all. The year is 1998. And a party of sots is happening in Nowhere. Here you have Rodney. He is a man of medium build. Solid not to cut but not fat either. 5'11 225 lbs. brown hair with red highlights. He looks in his early Forties.

"Now look Tania. It's been so long, and I need just one more chance to find her. Just one more shot. We are out of Andersonville. So, the rules don't really apply here. I'm only asking if you can make an exception for one night only for him. You know that he can't see any of them, and there is full left of the others like him."

Tania is a slender woman with the with long red hair 5'11 and green eyes. You can she is Norwegian in her appearance.

"Alright, I'll make an exception here and now for him. Because it's for him and others like him I do this for. And I do pity him because his last love wasn't worthy of his kindness and generosity."

Rodney "Thank you Tania. We all appreciate this."

Tania "Don't thank me yet. He will go through a different type of hell before all of this is over."

Rodney "We all know that But, why after all this time? Why did they want to go after him and others like him now?"

Tania" That's unfortunately on my head. I pulled a practical joke. And it didn't go over well. And a person who shall not be named at this time, decided to stir the pot further. Then there are the other parties involved that make this all poor, poor timing."

Rodney "OH great! Now we must wait for the dust to settle. No wonder why everyone is in here in Nowhere! This isn't the place anyone wants to be!"

Tania" Precisely! That is why we have gathered here to remedy the situation. No, go get stoner boy and his other stuff. I know once everyone tokes up it will all be pleasant!"

Rodney "Alright. Where does e find and grow his crap?"

Tania "I don't know? All I know he has all the best stuff ever made. And that is no wild boast!"

Through the crowd there is a man with blonde hair, and they are dreadlocks and thick. He is wearing a Grateful Dead t-shirt. With ravaged jean shorts. With a stench that you can smell miles away, the contact high of what he smokes makes you feel lightheaded as you approach him. With his John Lennon sunglasses. Rodney approached feeling the joy from that he imbues from his radiant aura.

Rodney "Why don't you ever tell me your full name. Why do you prefer Stoner Boy, Or Peace maker?

Stoner Boy "Once you have my stuff all you want is peace. Or at least have peace of mind. What do you want Rodney?

Rodney "Well Tania sent me. She needs one of your special herbs to enhance an experience for a friend of ours.'

Stoner Boy "Does this person have a penchant for causing trouble with the full moon club?"

Rodney sighs "Yes, he does."

Stoner Boy "Well why didn't just say so. Anything I can do to help to give that clubhouse a mind full of dramas. Now where is the person in question? I got the bong and the herb ready to go!"''

Rodney thinks, now he I excited to do this. I wonder what he is up to. We left for a furlough three days ago. That dam club has started up enough crap to last five lifetimes this time around. So How is he in the up and up. We had to leave Orville behind. But then again Orville only has that god forsaken bench of his and nothing else.

Stoner Boy "So where is he? I really have something for him to enjoy. Is there anyone else with him to partake in this as well? The blend is made just for two after all."

Rodney "Ah yes there is another one. How did you know there would be two?

Stoner Boy "I know all, best to remember that. So where are they in this crowd? I usually prefer them know before they inhale. It's always better that way. No unpleasant surprises."

Rodney "Well here they are."

Stoner Boy "Ah the local and him. Well, I do hope they both appreciate what they are about to get. It's the most potent stuff in the world. This surpasses the red dragon itself.

Rodney 'What!"

Stoner Boy "Yup! It has to be that strong to overcome certain obstacles in his head after all. The young lady will be fine. But eh potency of this really rocks. This will keep them happy for about hmmm, six months?"

Rodney face palms, and says "Really having them that happy for six months? Are you crazy?! Wait a cotton-picking minute. Please! Don't you dare, answer that question!"

Stoner Boy simply smiles "ok, do not to start the music and get them to take a hit just yet. I don't like doing this. But you all insisted; through a lot of complaints, talks, and prayers too."

Rodney "I understand, as you always say. Remember you all wanted this. Be careful what you wish for. You might just get it."

Stoner Boy "Exactly, sometimes wanting is better than having. In this case. It will be both. But alas, time will tell. Time will tell."

Now flutes, harps, banjos and drums are being play. The music is soft yet loud. So Serene in the melodies that play, it relaxes the people in the crowd. This crowd is a lot bigger than Woodstock. A lot of happenings are going on here. People dancing, drinking smoking and having a good time after the rush that was made to get them out of town for about a month. As they approach the couple. The bong was smacked out of Stoner Boy's hands. The bong rolls on the ground. A person picks it up and discovers that it's lit up. Now the bong is now passed around the crowd. Stoner Boy is now trying to get his bong back. Meanwhile, Rodney is running through the crowd. He is tackling people attempting to get the bong as well. A person picks up the bong and throws it deep in the crowd. As the bong is tossed, smacked and flung around the crowd. After hours of this Stoner Boy gets his bong back.

Stoner Boy "Well looks like everyone toked up. Only thing left is the water. And that will get them high for about a year."

Rodney "What do you mean for about a year!?"

Stoner Boy "it will only take one shot each to do it. Good thing I do have three shot glasses. Now that I know what they look like it can be done. They are still talking to each other. I shouldn't be a problem."

As Stoner walks to the couple, he sees Tania.

Tania "Oh, you're resorting to that. I didn't want them to have that. But it looks like everyone is high here and having fun."

Stoner Boy "Well things happen. At least it's going to right people. So, they will experience the high."

Rodney "Why does it always turn red in any cup or glass."

Stoner Boy "There are mysteries you shouldn't know."

Stoner Boy gives them the shot glasses. And sees the desired effect. He notices the male took longer than usual. He also noticed that the female took longer than usual. He simply smiled and said "Enjoy yourselves. I know everyone else is."

Tania "I didn't know this was for him!?"

Stoner Boy "Why yes, it is for him and his happiness. Now he can come back and have a home of his own now and a few other liberties he hasn't had for a while. Unlike Orville whose hasn't had jack shit."

Tania simply laughs and smiles "Yes Orville is a stubborn coon. Always rummaging through the trash to find his happiness."

Rodney "Yeah but, He will get it all back. You know how he likes to bide his time."

Tania" Sure he likes to bide his time. However, if he screws up ever so little, he will be there for another few years. And I'm going to make sure he does screw up!"

Stoner Boy" Now Tania, you'll have to forgive him at some point. Besides, we all have a purpose. And unlike you he still serves his purpose. And he will be redeemed in everyone's eyes. After all he takes it for the team all the time. That is why he does what he does."

Tania "we shall see. We shall see."

CHAPTER 3

A Fresh Start? Or a death sentence?

Present day, London Ontario. A small Canadian city, with its own air of excitement and just on its out skirts. Nothing but plains and farms. It has it all so to speak. And yet a youth is comprehending why he is going to moving from here to Andersonville Georgia in the CSA territories. He is not too skinny nor thick either. But just right overall. He is 6'1 slightly tall for his age of 16. But he is about to embark on a journey of a lifetime so to speak. As he is walking home, he scans the neighborhood. Despite all the times he has been hazed, teased, fought bullies here. He hates to admit, that he'll miss this place despite the pain it caused him. He was given the name Orin Ezekiel McNeil. He going to miss winter and the changing of seasons. He has heard that in Georgia there isn't any snow. Just hot and steamy weather down in the southern tier of the North American Continent. As he walks into the apartment complex. Looking it over and sighs. Thinking to himself I'm going to miss this dump. Yes, it's a dump but at least its my dump. As he approaches the door. He sees his mother talking everything over with the landlord. Orin thinking to himself. The sick sadistic man. Cheats on his wife with half the women in here. And still, he wants to get it on with my mother. And I know mom doesn't like him. But how can she stand him and play nice like that.

After coming close enough he can hear what his mother and soon to be ex landlord are talking about.

Landlord "Now Cher, we can make more accommodations if you wish. All I need is a little respite so to speak."

The Young woman here is about 35. Not too slender and yet not to thick. Curves in all the right places and in incredibly shape. Most women younger than her are a awe. Because it's been stated if you call her a hag. The ladies have stated I want to be that hag. Long sandy blonde hair down to her back. Wonderfully deep green eyes. And a smile that can light up a crowded room. This is Erin Marybeth McNeil. She always puts up with flirts and unwanted advances. As for her Landlord. She always knows how to say no with a punch.

Erin "Now. Now, you know I play bridge with your wife tonight. And the rest of the gals are going to be there. You do know how possessive your wife gets when she suspects that you been fooling around again. Like how you and the young misses Sanchez three hours ago. After all she did make a lot of noise. And most of the neighborhood heard her? And there was that nice young lady who was collecting for charity this morning? Now she was all aghast after the session you gave her. Now you wouldn't want anything to accidently slip while you go bowling tonight."

Landlord "Absolutely not. Since it's a league night.

Erin "Oh, that is right you're bowling against the women's league champion tonight. You should conserve your energy for them. After all they prefer their men to have stamina." She simply winks and nods. Her landlord simply takes the hint and leaves."

Orin "Why do you put up with that?"

Erin "No son when you reach a certain age. You don't mind complements at all. And yes, he is a pig. But that pig knows how to charm a lady of any age. And besides, that total cheating hag of a wife of his saddle him with more kids that aren't his than he ever made with anyone else. And for the record only three are his. The rest he supports and nurtures. So, he is a good man for the most part. But he is far from perfect. Now if your father was here. He would tell you about things that would make your skin crawl."

Orin "Yeah that deadbeat who never comes for my birthday. Never shows up for any my games piano recitals. Oh, wait what about my art shows! You would think he would have time for those too!"

Erin simply frowns. "I know you love him. Or you wouldn't be angry. But he had to leave us. He didn't want to leave you alone. He didn't want to leave me alone either. Now we have to say our goodbyes. Because we are getting a fresh start in Georgia. I'll enjoy my game tonight. Why don't you go to the Knights game tonight? I will make sure Anna will come with you. It's your last game together. I'm sure she'll appreciate it."

Orin simply shrugs a bit and says "Sure, that was the plan. But I'm not sure I should do that. I'm not good at goodbyes. I simply don't want to break her heart."

Erin "It's been far too late for that young man. She has been crazy for you for a long while. The only reason why she is giving up. Is that fact that she can't come with us. If she could, you know we would have a lot of things to do. But since it's the both of us. It makes this trip easier so to speak. And a lot harder for us too. Saying goodbye is never easy. You should be straight to the point and tell her goodbye. Tell her how you feel. And hope she doesn't cry."

Orin "Thanks, I needed that. Just say Anna I love you and miss you. And she wont cry. She will just say see you on the flip side Zek! Smile and then moon me if I am a good boy."

Erin simply smiles. "She won't do that. But I hope she doesn't do anything rash."

Orin "Yeah but I think she will. I Just... I don't know what to do. She is a nice girl. It's just......."

Erin "I know your just good friends. You do love her. But not in the way she wants you to love her. But you do love her like a sister. So now go hang out with your friend we leave tomorrow. And don't worry about staying late. It's going to be a while.

Now Orin goes to Anna's place. It's a condo. Nothing fancy. As he approaches the door, it opens. Standing there is a young woman with red hair brown eyes. Wearing jeans and a London Knights jersey with her favorite player on it. Smiling and waving Anna "Come here zek! You got to see this!"

Orin walks closer to the door and sees the living room is a mess with water. The pipes apparently burst. Looks at Anna with a questioning look.

Orin "You didn't cause this?"

Anna smiles "Maybe?" looking innocent. Hands behind her back. Smiling.

Orin "What else did you do?"

Anna "Just wait for it."

Orin 'Wait for what?" He hears a crash and a slip from outside. And a voice where the fuck is all the water!

Orin "Your still not angry with Cecilia over the dye?"

Anna "I don't get mad. I get even now look"

Orin cringes to see what Anna did this time. He looks out of the window and see Cecilia cover with dye. Walking naked across the back yards of the condos. He simply smirks and speaks. "We better get the fuck out of here now! I don't want to know how or the rest of it. The game is our cover.

At the game....

Anna simply nods in agreement. As the walk to the bus stop for the arena for the game. Anna looks and simply asks "Are you going to miss it here?"

Orin "Yeah I guess I am going to miss the Hockey games and other things here. But It's one of the most prestigious schools in the world. So, mom made sure I got accepted to their accelerated classes."

Anna cynically smirks "Since when your mom is interested in the high-class life. The proper schools and such. You don't have the money to go there. Do you know the coast of living in there?

Orin "Well she even arranged for me to have a job down there. She has everything setup. Plus, a good job down there too for me. Working at a game shop. So At least I can have some fun, I guess." Looking down at the ground looking a bit depressed.

Ann Looking quizzically "You're going to miss this awful little city of ours?"

Orin" Yes"

Anna gives Orin a hug. "Now let's see the knights Kick the Pete's butts tonight. And remember that Hockey players are a breed apart from those stupid football players!"

Orin 'True and pro wrestlers. At least up here there is plenty of them. Hmm they just dropped the puck."

Anna looking at Orin says "Why aren't you paying attention to me right now. You would be talking up a storm right about now?

Orin "Anna, I just can't say it. I just can't say it. I don't want to say it. You made it bearable for me to be here. In spite of my autism, you never treated me cruelly. Now I have to say goodbye to you. I'll miss the pranks. How you smile your way out of the messes. Yes, I will miss that. You're my only friend I've had." Orin is in the tears. "I just want to enjoy the last game here for a while."

Anna "It would have been crueler if we didn't have this last game night. Instead, let's enjoy it."

Orin simply nods sniffles and dries his tears. Says "Look Anna, I am going to miss you a lot. You know I am terrible with things like this."

Anna "yeah we moved around a lot together since we were babies. And we stayed together a lot. We were barley apart. But that commune still takes the take of weird places. But still, we'll be back together soon." Anna hugs Orin "You will always be mine Zek. Now and forever in my heart."

Orin smiles with a look of disappointment in his eyes "I wish you would move on and get someone that adores you like you adore me."

Anna smiles "You First!"

Orin "I just may be the first." Smiling with a teasing look in his eyes.

A puck zips past them and Orin grabs it! Now he looks at it. With a puzzled look. "Out of all the times they cleared the puck in the seats. The night before I leave, I get one. Go figure this out?"

Anna "Yeah and now you're going to see a fight break out right about now! Look!"

You see the players drop their gloves. And the crowd roars. As the enforcers throw punches ay each other. The Knights player manages to knock the Pete's player down to the ice. The referees now pull the players apart. As the crowd cheers. The players are now in their respective team's penalty boxes. As the game lingers on into overtime.

Anna "So now you have to watch football?"

Orin "I hope I can get an NHL game down there. You know how I hate Basketball."

Anna "You're moving down south. You are going to assimilate with at least one of their sports down there."

Orin "Nope, I'm never going to enjoy those sports. Maybe I'll teach them how to play Lacrosse."

Anna frowns at the idea. But smiles when thinking on the prospect of Orin introducing a spring summer sport like that down there. She giggles to herself and says "Hmmm, I think you are going to have a good time down there explaining what real men play down there. Also, what you think what type of losers that play sports without any real skills."

Orin "I bet they are clamoring at the seats to see a Lacroix game."

Anna "Well it's better than football. I can tolerate soccer."

Orin "The fight has been settled. Dam it was a good one too."

Anna "Yeah it was and dam he did knock the teeth out of that guy!"

Orin "Well the period is almost over. Why, don't we get drinks at the concessions while the Zamboni resurfaces the ice."

Anna simply nods. "Sure, It's my treat."

Orin "Okay, but I'll buy next time."

Anna smiles "Yes, there will be a next time. But It's going to be warm down there."

Orin "Yeah I know. I hate hot weather. I sweat like a pig as soon as the heat hits me."

Anna laughs "yeah you are going to be miserable in the heat."

As the London Knights end the game with a 2-1 win. They walk to Anna's place. Orin Looks around and it dawns on him that he is going to miss these walks with Anna. As slight tears in the eyes. As he is walking to her home, he hears screaming and other commotion as they approach the door.

Old man "That demon spawn of a daughter of yours did this much damage to the complex! No either you're going to pay, or she is going to pay for the water damage she has caused."

Anna Mother "Now how about your refusal to fix anything when we paid the rent the homeowner's association fees on time mind you every month. And this damage is the fact you haven't done any maintenance on the place. Anna kisses him on the cheek and says "I'll miss you Zeke. But don't worry I'll be there sooner than you think."

Orin walks to the old apartment crying as he looks at the place at night one last time. He feels a sense of foreboding. As he approaches the car. He sees his mother checking the last of the things and says She asks, "Well are you ready?"

Orin "I thought we would be leaving in the morning?"

Erin "I changed my mind, and I got your bags. Also, he changed the locks while I was at the game and left our bags out."

Orin "Dam son of a bitch, maybe we should rat him out to his wife?"

Erin "No need, I cleaned her out and everyone else tonight. So, we have petty cash for the trip a lot more than expected. So, we can afford a motel or two now"

Orin "Well let's go before, I start crying my eyes out. You know How I hate saying goodbye."

Erin looks sad and smirks" Yeah your right let's blow this popsicle stand and head south. At least we have money and a good drive. So, you'll see Nowhere OK first! Nothing much to see but it will be good to see where I met your father."

Orin just rolls his eyes, "Yeah that wild party and you dinking out of the bong water and you two were so high that you still haven't come down from that."

Erin" Yes, and that was really good shit!"

Orin "Okay, fine let's go to Nowhere, and then to Andersonville Georgia!" sarcastically.

CHAPTER 4

The Road to Nowhere

Going through customs on the Union side of the fence. They weren't particularly happy about he Canadian and The Confederacy uniting as one country. Seeing that now that two thirds of the continent is under Confederacy control. The union soldiers sneering at us as they went through everything o make sure nothing was illegal. Then the personal searches they made to Erin and Orin. Erin was really disgusted because they were just short of a strip search. They though better about it because Orin just gave them the dirtiest of looks. Once everything had been repacked. Moving along the northern Mississippi river to the CSA border crossing wasn't that horrific. However instead of making that left to go towards Georgia. Mom decided to visit Nowhere OK because it was a 2-hour detour from where we were on the drive. It ended up being more of a 5-hour detour. As they enter, Nowhere OK. Orin looks around and just sees miles of miles of plains. Nothing there at all. Just a small drag if you call it a drag and nothing but fields of grass.

Orin "Now I know why the call this place Nowhere! It's literally nowhere! I can figure why people would want to throw a huge party here. You can get drunk high and anything else you want in here."

Erin "Yeah it was a fun night here. Hmm I met him right about here. Now the dinner is there. They make the best Rubens here. They cord beef is stellar. But the dry rub steaks from the brisket is to die for!"

Orin "Hmm…. I think I'll have the brisket. And have a Ruben for later."

Erin "You know what your right about that. The collared-greens are great too!"

Orin "Sounds like a plan. You think they will let me get away with a beer down here?"

Erin "Probably not, but you're not old enough to drink yet as far as I'm concerned."

Orin 'Ok mom, I won't ask again while I'm here. But what else is there to see. We took a 5-hour detour to get here. I don't think it was worth it."

Erin "It's worth the trouble. Let's see ahh there it is. The rock we kissed each other for the first time. And oh…The bunk house is still for rent and has vacancies! I still wonder if we can rent a room for the night." Erin walks to the house and sees a familiar face. Orin running behind her trying to stop her before the elderly lady answers with a great gasp!

Loni "Oh it's you! You said you would visit me on your way to the Andersonville school!"

Erin "Yes, her is my son Orin Ezekiel McNeil. He got accepted to the prestigious school."

Loni "Wow, he is the spitting image of his father! He was a handsome young man. To be that young again. Now where is his father?"

Orin "He bailed out on us when I was four."

Erin "Please forgive him, he's never gotten over the fact he had to go away. He's doesn't realize that he was born forty miles from here. And doesn't understand he grew up here."

Loni "Oh…Dear boy your father is a complicated man. He had to leave you two. It wasn't by choice. But where your going is a fine place. There are people who lived there here. It's a wonderful place. Also, your father was from there originally. His family still has pull down there too."

Orin looks at his mother with a disapproving look "Really, did you know this mother?"

Erin "Well… Yes, but I never contacted them. It's complicated with family on both sides. So, I made sure we got in based on our own merits. Family members can get a free pass in to that school. Nothing more. But they will find out eventually."

Loni "Come, let me feed you to at my dinner and don't worry it's all on the house and you two get to sleep in your old place one more time. I want to hear all that you two been up too for the last 12 years now?"

Erin says "Yes, it's been too long. Come let's have the best food on this side of the Mississippi."

Loni simply nods and smiles and gives Orin a great bear hug. Loni "Your looking good Zek!"

Orin simply smiles and heads to the dinner. After five hours between Loni and his mother talking up a storm and caching up. As the night went on. He visits for one last night his old abode. He remembers so little and yet so much of this place. Sleeping on the couch as mom sleeps in the bed. He looks around and wonders if it's still there. He goes into his old room. The furniture is still here for a toddler. As he looks underneath the bed and finds a silver pendant with a wolf's head. Orin takes a long look at it. He feels tears running down his eyes. Because he remembers that his father gave him this pendant and the sorrow over the fact, he lost it. The day he left them. He simply puts it in his pocket. And as he walks to the couch, he sees a slight shadow out of the corner of his eye. Now he sees his mother crying.

Orin "What is wrong mom?"

Erin "You were right she shouldn't have stayed here this night."

Orin "We would've had to stop over at some point."

Erin "True, but not here. As you say I hate saying goodbye. I found a few things still here. Some things I though forever lost and other things I didn't want to find. I see tears in your eyes. You found your pendant?"

Orin "Yes I did as a matter of fact. What did you find?"

Erin "Some old pictures of us as a family. Loni kept everything intact so we would recover them. I told her se can sell the furniture. She says she never rents this part of the house because she understood your father all too well. Also, what type of trouble he was in as well. So she can rent it out now. But she says it doesn't matter. Because this was your father's place. And the money he gave her in the first place has yet to run out. So, you see, this will always be our home away from home here." As Erin sobs.

Orin "How much money did dad have?"

Erin "He has a lot because we missed him by three days. He was here…"

Orin starts crying more "We missed him by three days! Three whole days! Where was he going?"

Erin "He went up north tracking down where we were. She did say he was going to the greater Toronto Area to look for us. But she will tell him that we were here and where we are going. She keeps tabs on him. She knows the transfer for this time of year there is rough as it is. So, he will make his way back soon. Hopefully without incident."

Orin with more tears in his eyes, with a bit of rage and more disappointment and sadness. "What type of man is my father? Why is he on the run so to speak?"

Erin "I just can't tell you that yet. But this is a good sign that we are on the right track."

Orin simply nods and says, "I think we better get moving then, right?"

Erin" No, we'll leave the day after tomorrow. There are a few more things to pick up here."

Orin simply nods and gives his mother the pendant, she takes it and smiles. And they go back to sleep.

The next day going through the things to take on. Orin looks around and thinks to himself. This is the last place to look. But then again it may be the first place to look. Now he asks Loni a question.

Orin "Loni, what does my father do for work?"

Loni "He's from an old family with money. Unfortunately, your mother has the same background too. Unlike your mother. Unlike your mother he didn't alienate her family. But your mother's family didn't take kindly to your birth being successful."

Orin looking shocked and surprised and depressed with the news. Looks at his mom. And asks, "Grandma and Grandpa that one time to see me is because the rest of the family doesn't approve of me?"

Erin "More like they didn't approve of your father. And they wanted to know how much of your father was in you. And they said you have too much of him in you. So, they held you once and left us hanging. I know through special means your father has helped us out. It's my family we are running away from. So, there are a few places where they can't touch us nor find us. And finding things is the family's specialty. So, we come from very old money. I hope that when we get to Andersonville. We will be safe and sound. And then I can begin to answer your questions. Loni knows some of the answers but not all of them. And she can't tell you what she doesn't know."

Orin "When will I know?"

Erin "I'm not sure when. But I know when the time is right. And now it isn't the time."

As they go through some more things. And the packing is done. They look around the place. Orin has tears in his eyes. Knowing that he just missed his dad by a few days. And his anger that he is on the run due to his grandparents' beliefs. Things he doesn't understand. All he knows that his next few days he is on the run. For the first time he understands why his mother cries at night. How she wants to hold on to things but can't. Knowing that for some reason dad had to draw mom's family away from us. Even through they found us that one time the in the nudist colony when I was 9. That was interesting time there. But we had to leave after we were found. What makes Andersonville Georgia so different? Orin now as to hide how he feels before anyone notices it. He looks over and see his mother with a frown. He knows now she suspects how he is feeling. Good thing they are staying the night in the old place for one more day. But he asks one more question of Loni. "Can you get in touch with my father before he goes too far away for nothing?"

Loni "Well I can make an inquiry. But I won't be able to get back to you before you reach Georgia. Also, if it doesn't tip off who is chasing him. He does know how to avoid people for the most part. However, I have letters from your mothers' family addressed to her simply. And none for you. I feel that is a good thing. However, you will be caught up in a lot of nasty things if you dig too deep there. So, I would rather let things be on that front. But he supposed to check in with me in a few days. Since I got your mom's cell number, I can tell him to contact her right away. That is the best I can do. I know you have questions. But he and your mother have all the answers you seek. But telling you where you are safe is a big part of it."

Orin looks down and is sad. However, this is the first time in eleven years he gotten straight answers from anyone about his father. So, he simply nods in acknowledgement of understanding and goes over a few more things he may like to take with him. As he looks over, he hears his mother "Loni, I think you told him too much. More than I would've."

Loni "Erin, he has to know at one point. Your families didn't approve of the marriage. Also, one side accepted it. And that was your husband's family. I bet dollars to doughnuts that his family set you two up nice and neat over there in Andersonville. Also, things calmed down a bit there for him too. So, Orin will be seeing more of his father. He spends time here weeks at a time then moves on.'

Erin "Well, I never met any of his family. But I hope they do except Orin instead of rejecting him behind his back. I fear for him, all the time."

Loni "I get it. I do get it. You should have more faith in your husband's plan this time around. He was hoping you would stop by here. Too bad you missed him. But everything is set for you both there."

Erin "I would love to be in the loop for a change. Well, I better quit complaining. I don't want Zeke to hear."

As the rest of packing was done. The last night in Nowhere and its quiet. It's Orin walks outside and sees a white Rasta with blonde dread locks smoking on his bong. As Orin approaches him. He smiles and waves him to come over. "Now I haven't seen you since you were a small child here. Fancy seeing you here.'

Orin "Who are you?"

Stoner Boy "My nick name I go by is Stoner Boy. White Rasta of Andersonville Georgia. Philosopher and poet. Want to toke up a bit."

Orin 'I don't think my mother would approve?"

Stoner Boy "Now Zeke, your mom at least drank the bong water with your dad. At least drink that."

Orin drinks the water. He feels the rush to his head as he feels his vertigo. Seeing pretty colors of rainbows with the star field being totally clear and nothing obscured at all. As he feels the nausea and yet doesn't puke. The water was sweet. To his surprise it was red when he drank it. The weed most be potent stuff. And he feels the full rush to his head and sees a vison of a woman. She is naked and is circling around himself. He notices that the person is him that she is circling. Then the vison fades as he starts laughing like a jackal. As he is laughing, he hears his mom come out. And she points at stoner boy. And says, 'What are YOU doing HERE?!'"

Stoner Boy "Just gave him a swig of the water. He's higher than the two of you were the night I gave you the water. Got some intense visons too, I reckon. Wow the eyes are really lighting up as well. It's been a while for him hasn't it. Good thing you're coming to Andersonville. He'll fit in just fine. He is almost there. Hell, even Orville will like him. I know Tania is excited to see him. So, I am going to walk up the road a bit and be back by sunrise to see you two off. Nice seeing you before you hit town Erin. Don't worry it will last a few hours. It wasn't the same stuff I gave you two 23 years ago." Then stoner boy simply walks in the direction he was heading to. As Orin's eyes are now rolling as the trip, he is taking starts to wears off. He looks at his mother. Erin simply smiles and says "You'll be seeing more of him when we get there. But he will have to ask for permission from now on. I know how good that stuff is good. We had it the first night we met. And it was the real good shit, to boot. He gave you a different blend." Erin simply smiles and helps Orin back to the to the abode and lays him down on the couch. As he falls asleep. He hears him mom "say sweet dreams my handsome boy. Don't dream too much. With what you drank your dreams might be really, weird. But then again, they might be more visions. I had them for about three or four years. Then I was pregnant with you. No sleep well."

Sunrise, and Orin and Erin wake up later than expected. They look outside and sure enough they see Stoner Boy talking up a storm with Loni. As they wash up and get ready. Loni waves them over.

Loni 'I have breakfast for all of you ready. Boy you too slept well. I tried to wake you tow. But you were out like a light.'

Erin "well we are having a late start, but we can make up time in the road. Stoner, why are you out all this way?"

Stoner Boy "Well I was supposed to meet Owen out here. In the event I missed him I was going to hitch hike all the way to California. But since I ran into you two. I was hoping if you two didn't mind driving me back to Andersonville. I can drive a good way and take shifts. I just like walking more than driving."

Orin is about to say something, and Erin speaks "Okay we can do that for you. Do you have money to cover gas and food?"

Stoner Boy "Of course, I do. Owen also gave me cash just in case If I bump into you two."

Store shows the rolls of cash in the rubber bands. And Erin guides his hands back to his pocket. And smiles "Okay, I should've known you would be around here.

Stoner Boy "I haven't seen him since he was four. He sure has grown in twelve years. Looks like his dad at that age. It occurred to me that he hasn't been to Andersonville in his life, has he? Also doesn't know anything about the history of the town itself. Outside of the historical facts left behind in history texts."

Orin simply nods in acknowledgement. Stoner Boy "It's ok son. I can tell you the rich history of the town. It dates back as a civil war internment camp. But after the release of the prisoners. Most stayed and built homes and expanded it. And the great Robert E Lee built the school. Some of the facts. But you know that the schoolhouse for the first eight grades was at the church itself?" Orin nod no and Loni "Breakfast is getting cold. Stoner you have plenty of time to go over the historical facts about the town. And I got lunch packed for all of you for the next week as well. So, you can save your cash as you go on."

Stoner Boy "Loni, god less Jesus for making your sweet soul! And god blees you for your kindness."

Loni "Why thank you Stoner Boy. So, the eggs are getting cold with the hashbrowns. So, you 'awl better, get in and eat. You have a long journey ahead of you."

They all simply nod and sit in the dinner for the meal. As they are eating Orin notices that stoner Boy is barely eating and yet he is just watching Orin. As he is eating the hashbrowns with ethe corned beef has and the eggs. Stoner Boy asks his mother a question "What took you two so long coming into Andersonville?

Erin "Well it's a long story about running from my family. And your father's family was crazy about the idea. But at least they accepted me. But my family didn't take it so well about your farther marrying me."

Stoner Boy "I think there is plenty of time for that for another time. Now you want to know the beauty of the nice town you're going to. It's more like a city in the sense of the population of a city with a area of a town. From the humble civil war museums to the best place for fire cooked peanuts. The best place to make chocolate to the ice creams parlors, we have it all here and then some depending on what you are looking for."

Erin "He is more of a hockey and lacrosse player at heart. He doesn't like football. He tolerates soccer. Besides he deep in reflection on how this are right now with he answers he just received."

Stoner Boy "That is why I'm here to answers his questions about the town and its history."

Erin "True but he wants to find out by himself. It ruins the surprise."

Stoner Boy 'Oh... He will find surprises in every street and in every corner. If I may who approved the letters of recommendations?"

Orin "From an Orville and Tatiana Ulberg. One Mayor and the President of the town's historical and student activities societies."

Stoner Boy "So Orville Himself approved this. And Tania as well. Hmm... You must e honored that they approved this and your transfer to the school. They rarely do this for anyone. This is a rare honor you have. Oh, and what about the work papers you have?"

Orin passes the work papers where he is going to work to Stoner Boy.

Stoner Boy "Wow! You're working in her game shop! Oh...boy you're going to have a fun time with Rory. He loves to try the new games out. Also, the patrons in that shop. You'll have a fun time there. Its just Roy can get carried away a lot. So, best be mindful. Also be mindful that Rory Lund tends to be a bit mischievous. So, he will be a bit to handle. Then again Tania does have him handled for the most part. Also, there is the gentlemen's club a block and a half away. That place is off limits to you. And be careful of the ladies who run it. They can be a bit feisty. They do go to the school too, by the way. But they are a very proud bunch."

Orin "Yeah I get it. Been there and done that. No big deal."

Stoner Boy "Well with an attitude like that you'll get nowhere fast in the town. Then again Jacob and Horatio will straighten you out. They both teach military history in the school. They take young ones and shape them into hard nose recruits."

Erin "Stoner please he going to ignore you for the rest of the way. At least I'm not the preacher in the night. But I have yet to meet him. Let us just enjoy the sights for now.

Stoner Boy "sure, not a problem. Some people just, must learn the hard way. Then again it would ruin all the fun if you knew everything. All I have to say you can talk to me anytime."

CHAPTER 5

The Arrival at Andersonville

As Erin drives up to the edge of town. Orin eyes soaks up the view. After of hours of Stoner's Stories about the town and the dos and don'ts that would put anyone to sleep. Funny thing was it didn't put him to sleep. He sees the view from afar and whistle's and realizes that Stoner Boy was right. This is a place to be. He could see the school, The museums, The shops, the developments, and the parks and the rotaries. Orin also see the fields and the sports complexes in the area. Stoner told him everything and it pales from what he described. And all he wants to do is get a shower and relax a bit. But He will track Stoner later apparently. Erin is talking with him "What do you mean you're going on a 26 mile walk down. We took you this far why not all the way to town?"

Stoner Boy "Well, you have to understand.... I never leave town in a car. Also, I never come back in a car either. I have a reputation to uphold. And that is that I am never driven around. But guess I accept rides. But I don't want confirmations of the rides. I had people take a full hour doing five miles an hour talking to me to hitch a ride and walk all the way into town."

Erin "Oh, Orin did enjoy the information and the talks. Even though I think you ram it all down his throat."

Stoner Boy "He was curious, and I didn't bore him at all. I know he enjoyed it. Just look on how he is soaking up the town from here. In utter awe of the sights before his eyes. He wants to get cleaned up and relax a bit before he starts. But I doubt he will get the rest. But his eyes are gazed at the center of town. And its where he is going to get a lot of his answers too. Weather he believes it or not. Zeke don't cause to much of a ruckus now. I'll be around always if you need a ear. Also, when you meet him, Tell Orville I said hi." Waves and starts walking down the road whistling a tune he didn't recognize. As Stoner walked down the hill until he simply disappeared. It looks as he blended into, he the forest. As that happened, he looks to his mom and said, "Did he just melded with the forest?"

Erin "Nope your just seeing things. After all the ac did run out and no one could've recharged it. The heat is getting to you. After all its hotter down here. Also, we have to make it into the check in on time with the school and the town acceptance committee. And we must get down there as is. It's in center of town. Right where you were apparently staring at."

Orin simply nods and asks "why did you name me Ezekiel?"

Erin laughs "It's your grandfathers name on your father's side. Also, Orin is your great grandfather's name on my family's side."

Orin "Okay, I get it. But why those names? You used Thomas, Johnathan. To say a few names.

Erin "Your father's family name is Ulberg after all."

Orin "Orville and Tatianna might be relatives of mine?"

Erin "Possibly, I've never met them before. But I have heard of Orville and Tania in passing. In Conversations with Stoner Boy and your father. But if you paid attention Orrville is always running around town doing something. So, he is going to be tough to track. Then again, he told me this while you got some sleep in. Now your fully awake and aware of your surroundings."

As Orin looks around the forest and sees the sprawling trees and other rock faces. He wonders how Stoner-boy got away so fast. As he looks around and sees the town. He scratches his head. It looks more like a city than a town from here. As he looks around, he notices the signs for different locations in the town. Also, the tourist info center with the maps of all the locations. He grabs the maps knowing it will be useful. As Orin grabs the maps. He Notices that there is a group of people walking by waving. He waves back and one of the ask "Have you seen Stoner boy?"

Orin "Only a few seconds ago! He went over that way. But I lost sight of him pretty fast why?"

The man "Ahh up to his ole tricks again. No worries he'll always be around when you least expect him. You're new here. Welcome to Andersonville. The Town that is a city and yet it still a town! Enjoy your stay!"

Orin simply waves in acknowledgement and looks puzzled as the group simply laughs and walks to the general direction, we he pointed out where stoner-boy went off too. He looks as if the whole group disappeared in the same general direction. Orin does a triple take and looks to his mother.

"Did you just see that!"

Erin responds, "See what?"

Orin "The whole group disappeared!"

Erin Chuckles "Now your imagining things. Let's get back to the car and drive on down into town and see what the whole hub hub is about?"

Orin "Mom, this is weird? People just don't vanish like that?"

Erin "No son, you're making something out of nothing here."

Orin 'Mother I saw people just vanish before my eyes."

Erin simply smiles "Now Orin, this place in unlike what most people see. There is a lot of things you need to catch up on. Also, this place has been known to have strange phenomena from time to time. So please don't make too much of a scene here. This place has year-round tourism. Meaning that is how they make the money here."

Orin "Okay, I won't make it a point out call out the unusual. But you must admit it is pretty strange to see these things. Not only in the flesh but for others to dismiss it?"

Erin 'Now, Now, Zeke. Everything is strange in the beginning. You are just tired and woke up from a long ride. You'll be alright once we hit, the house in town. Now git into the car and let's roll down into town now."

Orin simply complies as he climbs into the front seat. And looks forward sighs, squinting his eyes trying to see anything unusual. So far, he's seen nothing, but he scans the area as they drive into the main parts of the openings of the area. He looks around and sees an old confederate prison and a fort as well. As they pass by the historic site. He sees something floating around the cabins that look somewhat familiar. As they pass by, he sees deer jumps around the area. The car stops as the deer run in front of the car. Then the deer bounces across the road. Orin just looks odd. The town that was big as a city and deer just outside the town. He does a double take. As they see the fields turn into suburbs, then starting to turn into close buildings almost one building on top of each other. The blocks were tight, but the streets were divided by names or letters instead of numbers. As they navigate to the center of town. As they hit the center of town. The surprise that it is an open area. With a rotary with a park bench in the center of it with walkways cut through the four channels to hit specific areas in the town. They see a hobo sleeping in the bench. The take the north entrance to the avenue m. While entering avenue m. They pass a gentleman's club and two blocks past that it's the game shop. Then one block over it's the house they got as part of the lottery. The house is three stories high with two balconies on the left and right side. With a driveway that has a huge curve and so you can park easier and a garage with a room on top. Orin looks and sees that the yard leads to the other side of the block. And he notices that he is two blocks away from the school. He thinks to himself. Dam if I get into any trouble, it isn't that far of a walk. As he is looking around, he sees a slender man. He is 6 feet even black hair with emerald, green eyes. He walks closer to Orin and smiles. He says "You must be Orin! My name is Rodney Brit. I run the game shop with Tania. Now where is your mother, Erin. Please forgive me, I forgot to shake your hand." He extends his hand, and he shakes it vigorously. And Comments "you have a firm grip Orin. I noticed that your middle name is Ezekiel. Do you prefer Zeke?"

Orin is taken aback by the whole situation and simply nods not in acknowledgement but more of being defensive. Rodney notices the defensive posture and says I live in the game shop with my Auntie Tania. We are going to be working a lot together. Others are running for now. But I think Tania is waiting inside for the both of us. As Rodney gestures Orin to follow him. Orin does it slowly and scans around and notices the second gentlemen's club in the town is across the street from his house? As he looks over there and wonders why it is so black when the other one is so vibrant in comparison. He notices that the other was rather flamboyant.

Rodney shouts 'Come on Orin Tania can't wait to meet you!"

CHAPTER 6

A New Home 15 Lupus way Andersonville

As Orin enters through the back door, he sees Tania and his jaw drops. A Slender woman about 5'8 with hips that would make most women envious with hatred. That's If he remembers correctly from some women, he did sketches in the nudist colony. With the Platinum blonde (Silver Hair) hair with emerald, green eyes. With a very busy chest. He just doesn't want to make a guess on the size just yet. He starts to mutter a bit before he says "Hello, nice to meet you." All he could muster from the shock.

Tania simply laughs a bit while Erin smiles "Most men of any age would've mumbled for a few minutes before saying hello. I'm impressed young man. Only those who know me a while would be able to speak clearly. Why are the good ones ever so young? Why taking a good look at you? I know a few young ladies that would absolutely want to make your acquaintance. If your mother doesn't mind me fixing you up with a date or too."

Orin tries to give his mother a signal before she chimes in the following.

Erin "Sorry he left a close friend behind. She wasn't exactly crazy she would have to wait a whole two years before she could come down here. So, he tends to be picky of who he socializes with. So please forgive me

If I say no that isn't necessary for now." Tania simply smiles and asks, "So why did you check out the yard first?"

Orin "It's just a habit looking for the exits and entrances so in case of a fire I know my way out."

Tania "Oh my, most people don't check that out when they first go for a home. My, my you are a smart fella. Looking after yourself and your mother that way."

Orin "I have a lot of stuff that is flammable. So yeah, I do check things out like that."

Tania "What do you mean?"

Orin "All the paints I have for my models and other stuff I mod into new creations for War Scythe 90K. And the city and other landscapes I've made through the years."

Tania "Oh you know how to play that game. It's one of our best sellers. Rodney, you got the help you always wanted! Now you have someone to tell you how to paint those pieces right!"

Rodney "You know I'm all thumbs with pants! Besides, I prefer the maps premade out and a bunch of dice too…."

Tania "Now you know those games are forbidden in these parts, with good reason Rodney!"

Rodney "I know, I know no rolling up character sheets either. But that is the fun part of the game. We get to…." Before he could finish the sentence. He sees Tania's look of now hush you idiot look all over her face. Now Roney changes the subject rather fast and quick. "How did they get this plum picking of a house Tania?"

Tania "Well the good lord Orville wanted them to have something nice. And I dare say he was right about giving this place to them rather than letting one of those harlots across the street."

Erin "There is a club across the street!"

Tania "yes there is, and I don't get along with the management of that establishment."

Orin "Oh…That is the building across the street? I found it strange that it's all black."

Tania "Good eye, and yes the are rather goth in there. If you're into that sort of thing."

Erin "He is into the unusual. Be that mostly out of curiosity? Not as a lifestyle."

Tania "Oh…You best be careful with that. Around here curiosity can get you into very deep trouble. So please do not try to pry. Even if you see what seems out of the ordinary. We have a lot of different customs around her brought over from the mother land. Most of us are from the Norway via family lines. So, you will see some odd things and customs."

Orin "Oh… I do like learning about new cultures and how people lived."

Tania "Hmmm…. A history buff. You and Rodney will get along shamelessly."

Erin "Orin you get the room with the back Balcony of the yard. It's setup with the lighting you need for your artwork."

Tania "Oh wow an artist. In my game shop? Now young man I must see your work. And I need to see it right now!"

Orin it's going take a few days to unpack and get ready for school and such…"

Tania 'Now hush, I can get a crew to help in five minutes no fuss. But there is a rush. Things do move fast around her day and night. Too many night owls in this town. Too many dam night owls for its own good I dare say."

Erin "That's unnecessary, we would like to take our time and do it right to our tastes."

Tania "It's no trouble at all. Now let me make a few calls here and get you settled right away." As Tania snaps her fingers her fingers she gazes into Orin's eyes. And looks very, very puzzled. She raises an eyebrow and gives a quick glance at his mother Erin. From what she was able to perceive from the look. Tania simply pulls out her cell phone and makes a few calls.

Tania "Enos, is your dimwit bother Cletus and Billie and Joel there? I don't care if they are having that swill you call moonshine. I need them here now. The McNeil's have arrived, and they need help with moving in. Don't worry I'll have the grill here to. No huss no fuss there. I'll be doing the grilling of course. Yes, Rodney is here too. And no shenanigans you all, I want this to be a civil gathering. Whatever you do don't tell Orville we're doing this. He's cranky as it is about that pack of jackals pulling those pranks again. I swear all the practical jokers in this humble city, and I know it's a town but please all the people that are here. I know he refuses to give this place the designation of a city. We have a population of a dam city. Just git your arses down here and Get Jo-bob and Roy here too. We'll have them unpacked and settled in no time." Tania Looks at Erin and Orin "They'll be in in about ten minutes. Now Orin, be a good boy and go to the grocery store, Here's 300 bucks. Here is a list of things you need to buy. As for Trevor. He'll know what to do it's three blocks to the right from your back entrance. The Asian pacific Tea company market. It's still having the long spelling of that corporation. Now git while I'll talk with your mom about her job and will talk about your job as well. The school and other things will have to wait for a few days. Now get going, the grill will be here any minute from the shop." As Orin nods with acknowledgement and walks out the back door he sees a couple of women dressed in black entering the blacked building with the red neon lights that are still on. One of them just stares at Orin. He notices that her eyes are gold. That is unusual color to sees and another woman grabs arm, and she turns around and enters the building. He looks puzzled and walks to the market. As Orin walks the two blocks, he now sees why Tania said use the back door. Going through the front would be a mad house passing the main rotary. Also, the sheer traffic in that circle and the hobo that is sleeping there. As he enters the market. When you see one market you seen them all. But once he enters his eyes widen and all he can muster is what the hell is going on here? As he thinks to himself.

CHAPTER 7

The Biggest market in the CSA!

From the outside it looks like a rundown feed dispensary. Once you get inside it looks better than the state-of-the-art markets. There are tons of mini shops at the ends and within the walkways too. He looks around a bit that the isle ways have registers at each end that most define a particular business transaction. He Looks at the sign, and it says Fuck Bullseye and Fuck Walton Markets corporation. He laughs out loud. He is thinking wow this place is getting a lot curious by the moment. Then he remembers to find Trevor. He asks what seems to be a working in the market. He is stocky but built. A man red hair with hazel eyes, as he approached him, he feels a hand on his shoulder. And turns around and see it's the hobo in the park bench.

Hobo "Young man your new here. What is your name? Sorry I apologize My name is Orville."

Orin "My name is Orin. I'm looking for Trevor."

Orville "Hmm…McNeil?"

Orin 'Ah yes McNeil."

Orville simply smiles "So my pistol of a wife sent you here to the market as soon as you got in the house?"

Orin simply nods but Orville "I asked a question and I expect a verbal answer young man."

Orin "Yes she sent me here. And you're not supposed to know."

Orville laughs "After all these years she still thinks she can slip passed me. Now those young jackals I need to teach a lesson or two. Why is she in such a rush?"

Orin 'She wants to see my artwork."

Orville "Oh… Now that is a big deal here in these parts. Artists and musicians are rare. If you have talent, then a lot of people will want commissions from you. Tania wanted an artist in the game shop for a while now. Do you have talent boy?"

Orin 'I do stuff pleasing to the eye." As he scratches his head.

Orville 'Ah…You are good, and talented. The best ones usually know they are good and don't brag about it. Let me guess you have the good stuff locked away because you think you can still do it better?"

Orin simply nods a yes.

Orville "Now son you don't have to be shy with me about it. I'll take you to Trevor. The Stocky man there is Liam. He's good at moving things around but doesn't know when to shut the hell up."

Orin simply Follows Orville's lead and ask "Why are you not err… At your home?"

Orville "I was sentenced to live outside my home for hmmm… Mumm… Fifteen years. I have two more to go and I can go back to my wife! But my wife likes the arrangement now and she is trying to prevent me from going back. I basically do all the town's business in the center of town on the bench in the middle of the rotary. I know it's weird and unusual. Be we do things right and mighty different from what you are used to. You'll pick up. You can talk to me any time. Ahh… there is Trevor Von Braun. I'll leave you to him. And one more thing. My wife can detect a line of bull right away. So, if she asks if you bumped into me. You tell her that you did. And that I'm leaving well enough alone. Also, one more thing! Watch Rodney like a hawk. He is always up to some sort of hijinks."

So, Orin simply says "Yes I will remember all of that." As he walks to Trevor. Trevor sizes Orin up

Trevor "Do you have tania's list?"

Orin "Yes I do." Orin hands him the list. Trevor reads the list of what to get.

Trevor "Your first BBQ with her?"

Orin "Yes"

Trevor "Oh... You're the new kid that is in Lupus way, right? Two blocks from here?"

Orin replies "Yes, just got in today."

Trevor "Welcome to the biggest and best market in the CSA! We have everything here. As you can see. Just some things Tania sells for a more specialized games and toys and comic books. But have that stuff here. You also see the toys isle from Child world corp. The rent space here. Also, the two Guys hardware is also here." Orin looks at Trevor with an odd look.

Trevor "You understand that the chains had to restructure. So, they restructured with us in the Asian Pacific Tea company. They rent the space with us with the mergers. So, they are still alive. But under our banners. So, you got everything that the Waltons and Bullseye market has but better service and better selections. We have Hanigan's furniture. Crazy Lenard's electronics where prices are insane too, for your Movie and PC, console games too. We have a few other chains as our partnerships grow."

Orin asks, "You wouldn't have an old chain called moon dogs comics and cards here?"

Trevor simply snickers "Yes we do only 8 stores have them now. But they have the complete database from all 180 stores. They became the super hobby stores. But they are tania's main competition here. But if she can't get it, they can. So, it's a friendly competition between them. They are printing up their own comic books now. So, Tania is looking for artist to work for her shop. Also, we have Cock Buster Video store, with West Hollywood side video. The Latter has the unmentionable videos for rental. That is how they stay in business." As Orin looks around Trevor leads him to the where he has the items on the list. Orin eyes open wide. And thinks to himself how the hell he is going to transport all this stuff two blocks away. Trevor gestures to come over here. As Orin walks over, he sees a small lawn tractor. With a cart attached to the back.

Trevor" So all you have to do is drive over and drive it back."

Orin "Cool!"

Trevor "Ok just be careful. If you don't know how to drive."

Orin "I've driven mini tractors before. This is cool. I can drive it without a license?"

Trevor "Nope, none needed here. All you need to do is hop in and drive."

Orin "Ok cool. Can't wait to hit the road with the this and the stuff!"

Trevor "All the stuff will be loaded in about fifteen minutes. Go check out the store while it gets loaded. Also know that you can use this anytime. Tania just keeps it here when she wants to entertain some guests at the shop."

Orin "Ok cool 15 minutes where to look?" As Orin pounders on where he should look. He wanders in the Market. He likes the idea that the Asian Pacific tea company decided to partner with all the local chains under an umbrella. He sees the benefits for all in this. The Walton's and Bullseye markets are nice but very limited. In here is the best of both worlds. Its like a mall and at the same time not. There is even a clothing department and a few ristorantes here as well. He looks at this over-the-top Spanish place called Mucho Macho Taco's the best Spanish cuisine in all the southeast and west. The signs also state's, unlike Paco's Hell across two. We guarantee you won't have the runs. So, you won't have to run to the nearest borders." Orin laughs at the claims and thinks I must eat here and Paco's just to compare the taste of the food. Because I need to check out Crazy Lenard's for the TV's movies and other electronics and appliances for the house. Ahh there is an art supply center too. And Moon Dog's comics and cards and games. I wonder if my account is still in the active state. I have shopped here numerous times. As he enters the isles looking at the boxes of comics in either side of the isle. Seeing old toys that were on shelves with posters and numerous games. As he approaches to the counter. Orin sees a Black man with deep blue eyes. As he approached the register the man Stands tall and introduces himself. "My name is Horatio Tiberius LeClair. Humble owner of this establishment within the establishment. I control the last eight Moon Dog's collectable shoppes. My I have your name to see if you are still in our database?"

Orin "My name is Orin Ezekiel McNeil. You may find me in your old London Ontario location."

Horatio looks up the account "My, my... Young man I owe you quite a bit or merchandise. From there we closed there and couldn't give you your money back nor the things you requested because you move around a lot. I have all the items here. It will take me about 45 minutes to get it all together. Also, I will give you 1,000 dollars in credit. Is that satisfactory young man."

Orin simply nods and says 'Yes"

Horatio "If I may inquire? Where, are you working young man?"

Orin "I just arrived today but I am employed by your competition. Tania House of Games? I believe the shops name is?"

Horatio "That was the name of the shop five years ago. It's changes names every few years. You must be the new family the McNeil's if I am correct according to the data base."

Orin says "Yes"

Horatio "Well that is all fine and dandy. Most of her employee do shop here too. What she can't get I have. Then again what I can't get she gets. Its' more of a friendly competition." Then they hear "That's boulder dash and you know it Horatio!" They both turn their heads and see a Native American wearing a union uniform. It's a naval uniform. With the three stripes with the full under bands with the stripes on the forearm meaning his is a master chief. "Horatio why are you lying to that young man who doesn't know any better about his current surroundings. Sorry son I forgot my manners. My name is Jacob Gator-star. At your service. He is a bitter rival of tania on my matters. The shop is where they both are embittered in a tie."

Horatio "Now listen here Savage, I don't hound your clients when I'm at your disreputable establishments."

Jacob "Now you listen here you dumb ignorant son of a bitch. You got nothing on me. Besides, you can't swim as I recall correctly."

Horatio "Now listen here savage you betrayed your sovereign state of Florida for those dam Yankees in Massachusetts!

Jacob "Hey they appreciate my nautical skills especially when it comes submarines!"

Horatio "god dam you and your gifts at sailing you savage dumb mule!"

Jacob simply laughs" Now you do know over half o f this land is on...."

Horatio "Don't rub that crap in my nose. I know half of this town was given back to your tribe! I Just don't understand why my house is surrounded by your tribe!"

Jacob "Well I did that just to make you angry. I may be a savage. But I am a well-educated savage in your honky ways you dumb cry baby bitch!"

Horatio "I forgive my colleague for his rude behavior. He just knows how to needle everyone he meets. I give you a lot of credit. Most people would laugh by now?"

Jacob "Well it's been what an old friend of ours would say…A coons age since I picked him apart in public like this. But I hate insulting raccoons. Such resourceful animals."

Horatio "I agree with that sentiment. But you are right, Robert would use such terms."

Jacob 'May I have your name young man?"

Orin "My name is Orin Ezekiel McNeil"

Jacob "Oh you're the new family that moved to the house on 15 Lupus way, correct?"

Orin "Yes how many people know we are moving here?"

Horatio "Young man, very few get the scholarship to our humble yet well regarded and established school. Then, secondly fewer still get the prime house. You are literally on the main campus and at most three blocks at every education hall on the campus. If there is a parent in the house, the alcohol is allowed in the house. It is assumed it's for the parents."

Jacob "The fraternities' here are for people who pay and over 21 years of age. The also includes the Sorority houses too. But if your 20 years of age and under. All party functions are monitored with chaperones."

Horatio smiles "Yes… That is true. We have the honors when we are both around to monitor such things. Kids will be kids after all."

Jacob "Isn't tania doing a barbeque today at the 15 Lupus way?"

Orin "Yeah that is where I am now."

Jacob and Horatio" Oh…that house?!"

Orin "What is the big deal about that house?"

Horatio "Well… That is one of the faculty's homes that they don't use. That is all I can tell you until you meet that person in school."

Jacob "Oh… I didn't know that. Has people used the house for other activities?"

Horatio "Well that house people have tried using the back Balcony to get the view of the outdoor stage across the street. Sometimes the workers do manage to climb up there to get the view from there or the stars. If you have a telescope, it's great view on the celestial sky."

Orin "Oh...Well, I do have one. But I am a star gazer. The heavens and the majesty of the cosmos."

Horatio "Well said young man. Well said, is there anything you might want?"

Orin "I'm not sure yet. I have to start the job first and get unpacked."

Jacob "Boy, If you are here. Then she has the crew unpacking everything for you now. If she feels you're going to be difficult. She sends you here in this market to shop. And she makes sure that you meet Trevor. Did you happen to see Orville here?"

Orin 'Yeah...You missed him a few minutes ago? I was surprised that he is the town hobo. Also, he stated if my wife asks tell her the truth that you did meet me."

Horatio "That woman can smell bull crap miles away. So, you better take that advice to heart and mighty fast too. She doesn't understand that you had an account with my establishment. And I decided to give you your stuff as promised with the store credit. So, you will tell here that. This way she won't take it personally that I am doing right by you. This way she doesn't have to negotiate for you. Anyways, I'm always happy I put Jacob's enterprise in hobbies out of business!' As Horatio chuckles.

Jacob "You there are plenty of your family I can convince to join a nice organization."

Horatio "Shut the fuck up you dammed savage. I kicked most of those fuckers out and they went up north!"

Jacob "But they did start down here. Your name might be Thomas. But you are sure fine Uncle to your nephews and nieces." As Jacob smiles.

Horatio simply sneers at Jacob after that comment is made. Gritting his teeth and glares. He simply asks this question before Jacob. "Are you challenging me to a dule young man?"

Smiling Jacob replies" No, fine sir. I wouldn't dream of it. Considering the last time, you fell horribly short. Because you thought I used a double side coin for a coin toss. Might I remind you I won both fair and square. Also, might I remind you. That I always tell you to walk your punk ass home. Now you don't want to embarrass yourself in front of this fine young but naive man?" smiling.

Horatio collects himself and regains his composure "Your right now isn't the time nor the place for such things. But remember Gator-star, every dog does have his day." Smiling.

Jacob "True, your dog days have left far behind himself for quite some time. Then again, another dog we know. We want his day to end fast. At least we can agree on that."

Horatio "Now Orin, may I call you Zeke?"

Orin/Zeke "Ordinarily I would say no to the both of you. But I'll let you two have that honor and pleasure. Because you two tend to be yourselves around me." Both Jacob and Horatio smile and say in unison "Thank you Zeke. Now we have to run off."

Jacob 'Now you better delivery the groceries like your boss wanted. Now get going"

Horatio "Best not to keep that lady waiting now go Zeke!"

As Orin gets back to where Trevor showed him and sees the tractor. And he sees it filled in the cart. Orin's eyes widen as Trevor asked if he ever driven a tractor before? Orin gave the impression that he has driven one before. Orin convinced Trevor he has driven one before. As Orin slips in the seat and then turns the key. He has his foot in the clutch. When he releases the clutch, and the tractor rolls forward. As the tractor rolls forward, he notices that the wheel is stiff. He had to use twice as much force to make a simply turn. As Orin makes the turn barely out of the gate. As he is driving down the block. He was able to run the tractor as 15 miles an hour. So, as he is driving the tractor to the back yard. As he is pulling into the backyard. He sees that grill is setup and he pulls into the yard. He notices that there is a crew of fifty people coming in and out of the house. Orin goes in his mind oh shit! As he looks dumb founded as the people. Erin run up to Orin.

Erin "Honey, I'm sorry it was a crowd before I knew it."

Orin "You mean there is a crew over fifty in our house."

Erin "Yes Zeke, I know how protective about your works. But we do need the help. But…Tania is one of the people that is setting us up with the jobs and well. She managed to get to your whole collections in general. And well you find it weird. They are placing everything exactly the way you want it."

Orin 'What!" He runs into the house. As his mother stated. They are placing everything as if it was supposed to be there. "Something that doesn't meet with your approval?" a woman's voice shouts. As Orin turns around, he sees a young lady with purple and red streaks with her black hair. "Please forgive me. My name is Billie Jean. You must be Orin." Billie Jean is very leggy with a medium chest. Wearing super short shorts. What most people would say a young southern belle.

Orin responds "Err…. Umm Yes. By the looks of it. I am rather surprised everything looks up to my mother's standards. But I tend to be very picky about my stuff. It's just thy way I am."

Billie Jean shows the hobby rooms and Orin's has a hard time preventing his jaw is dropping. And is astounded that everything is placed the way he would want it. With the room to spare. As he inspects the rooms and the basement everything looks right. As he ascends to the top floor where the bedrooms are. Each room has a Balcony. He noticed that His mother's room is next to the walled side of the building where no can see. The opposite balcony is empty and setup as the guest room. The he sees what is to be his room. To his surprise it has everything setup and hears Rodney and Tania speaking. As they turn around and say in unison "Hello Orin!"

Orin looks at his room. Also, a bit dismayed that his works are out in the open for people to see. As if a show was going to happen sooner that he anticipated. But is more shocked that everything has been placed perfectly. Also, the telescope on the balcony. As he inspects where everything is. He notices that the clothes are in the drawers and other places. For the whole setup was done in a matter of minutes. He wonders how they were able to do this. But his emotional state due to his asperges kicking in with a vengeance about people touching his stuff. As his anxiety rises.

Tania asks" Did we do something wrong?"

Orin "Look I really appreciate this, but I would've had more time and privacy in doing this. That is all I am saying."

Rodney "Oh…Sorry we didn't mean no disrespect. We figured sooner was better so you could enjoy the town a bit before you start the trimester and work."

Tania "I apologize, I didn't realize that you were that protective of your works. I really like a lot of them. I was hoping to display them during working hours at the shop or the gallery in the school itself."

As Orin stats to shake his head a bit. His mother arrives.

Erin "He is a bit overwhelmed at the moment. Because everything is happening a little too fast right now. I suggest that he stays outside and get his composure." As he takes the hint from his mother Orin walks down the stairs of his new home. As he is walking outside, he hears Billie Jean walk behind him.

Billie "Look we are just trying to help. No harm meant by it. We tend to be a very welcoming bunch."

Orin "A little too welcoming. I find that people are way too polite. They tend to be hiding something. All my red flags just went off all at once. I tend to trust my gut about it." As they walk outside, Billie following closely he sees Jacob. Jacob notices that he is irritated.

Jacob "What is wrong young sir?"

Orin "Well Mr. Gator-Star, everything is moving too fast too soon. It's a sea of chaos in there. It looks ordered but it's pure chaos."

Jacob "You may call me Jake. May I call you Zeke?" As Jacob winks to Orin.

Orin "Yes you may call me Zeke."

Jacob "Well Zeke, Tania moves things at her own pace. And her pace is always fast and tight. It's never loose. When she realizes the mishap. It's usually far too late. All I suggest is that you don't treat anyone too harshly for that here. We love to welcome new commers to our nice humble yet large town. If she sees real talent. She tends to be too aggressive about displaying it. Has she mentioned how to display whatever your talents are already?"

Orin "Ah… yes she has. She even set aside pieces of my works to be displayed in her wing of the school I think." Jacob looks directly at Billie Jean for confirmations.

Billie "Yes he has wonderful works in there. She really wants to display them right away."

Jacob scowls at Billie Jean "Now we have to talk to Orville about that young lady. Make no mistake moving a little too fast too soon."

Billie "Look I think that is unnecessary to drag Orville into this."

Jacob "It's either Orville or Horatio. Take your pick. Moving them in this fast is a bit overwhelming. Now you have to convince me not to do that. You all know how much I hate to ask that dam son of a bitch for help." Billie gives Jacob a glaring angry look. With nothing good in her eyes.

Billie Jean "Alright I'll get her now Jacob. But Know she won't like the idea that you mentioned getting either Orville or Horatio to back down." As Billie Jean walk to the house, she sees Tania looking disapprovingly at Billie Jean. Billie Jean looks puzzled.

Tania "That won't be a problem. I got a polite mouthful from his mother. We are excited that they finally arrived here. Explaining that most of us are extended family. Also, that we are happy that they are here. I forget his father was the same way at his age. Cranky when people would go through his stuff. Sorry for being overzealous. We just wanted to get things into full swing. That is all we wanted." Orin calms down a bit. He looks around and the grill is going. And he wonders how many more people are going to be here. Then he asks, "How many more people are coming that are my relations?"

Billie Jean "Well that depends on how…"

Tania "A good chunk of town are your relations. Have you me Orville yet?"

Orin replies "he said if you asked to tell you yes. And not to try to lie about it either. I met him in the market. Jake here and Horatio told me to best follow his advice about it."

Tania smiles "Well he gave you good advice. He figured out about the barbeque with you being there. Why were you at Horatio's part of the shop."

Orin "There was a Moon dog's in London Ontario until it closed down. He was able to bring up my old account and he offered to give me the merchandise that I order plus a thousand dollars in store credit."

Tania eyes widen" He gave you that much back! How much did you spend at his store in the past!"

Orin "Well… I did order a lot of high ticketed items. And they were on the no refunds sections of the orders. So, I did pay for them. He just offered me the credit. Because he still has the items I did paid for. And the years he calculated the coast. Just to keep me in good standing."

Tania "what did you order from him?"

Orin "Oh… the Whole hardcover masterpiece works of the Eliminators and the Cowl with slipcase poster and the full statue set. Plus a few other high collectables that he still has in stock."

Tania "He did promise the people who paid in full their stuff plus the credit worthy of keeping them customers. I Know he had one set left. Now I am wondering if the stuff Rodney and I wanted to get other customers was your stuff he has?"

Rodney "Oh I would be a safe bet that you have a lot of that stuff. And I wouldn't brag about it too much. Because there are collectors here that would do some unscrupulous stuff to get it. And other forms of skullduggery."

Jacob "Now Zeke, let me help you load the stuff on the tractor and bring it over here. If tania doesn't mind. And If we may do a box opening for all the things you deserved." Orin simply smiles as he takes Jacob on his offer. As they walk back to the now empty tractor with the trailer. Jacob turns his head and smiles as Tania is smiling and gives Billie Jean a scornful look. Then, he turns is attention to Orin.

Jacob "Now look son, calm down and relax. We will go in and talk shop a bit. After that we will bring your new stuff in to the home. And we will bring Orville and Horatio over. I don't care if Tania is mad at me or Horatio for bringing Orville over. It's about your anxiety attacks that we are taking care of. Do you remember your father's name Zeke?"

Orin "Yes his name is Owen. I just don't know the last name because they thought it best for me to have my mother's name."

Jacob "That is good to know some of it. Your true last name is Ulberg. But the Ulberg's are a huge part of the population here. You have about 300 relations here." Orin's eyes widen.

Jacob "Yeah if your used to being isolated. Which by the way your reacting? You are very used to being isolated. You now in the middle of a pack. So, I took it upon myself to give you temporary relief. But it won't last here. Your father is away on business of sorts. On the behalf of the Union and Confederate states of America. That is why he had to leave you at a young age. However, if you need guidance. He asked for me, Horatio, and Orville to keep an eye on you. So the 1000$ credit well.

That is what Horatio did owe you plus the merchandise. Your father knew working with Tania would be stressful for you."

Orin "When is he coming back?"

Jacob "He is taking the route back the way you came in here. You've been on the run for so long. Because of the fact your father helped Horatio and I on serval occasions. He helps keep the peace between the nations. You can travel anywhere from here. Getting back here tends to be a problem. Putting you two in that nudist colony was a brilliant move on his part for five years until he had to move you two again."

Orin jaw drops "He's been around a lot in my life, and I didn't know it?"

Jacob "Yes he has, unfortunately that responsibility falls on myself and Horatio and Orville. Please be easy on him and us. Also, the preacher is a close friend of his. But he tends to keep unusual hours." As they make it back to the market and the tractor is there with the last of the goods carefully placed. Horatio sees them both approaching. Horatio had a questioning look at Jacob and sees the look on Orin/Zeke's face.

Horatio "The woman gone and done it again, overwhelmed a person into an anxiety attack?"

Jacob and Orin/Zeke "Yes"

Horatio "I got the right thing to fix that with you. Come on over to my isles." As the approach where the counter is. Horatio pulls out a bottle of Whiskey. He mixes it with C&C cola.

Horatio "This settles down your father. It should work on you just fine. Just the one shot. If your mother has a problem with that Zeke. She will have to talk to me about it. Jacob gave you what you needed to know I take it." Zeke/Orin nods in acknowledgment.

Horatio "Good, makes our lives a little easier." Then a shout form behind "Yes it does!"

Orville wanders into the market "Now my boy you should be at the impending feast."

Jacob "He has an anxiety issue like his pa."

Orville "Now, why am I not surprised." Sighs

Orville "We don't like crowds in general. Smaller the better. But We need to talk to Tania about that, for future endeavors." As Orville grabs the bottle and a glass from behind the counters pours himself a drink. Orville "Everything should be perfect. As per your father's specs. He did know where everything would be placed in advanced. But he did Tell my wife to take it slow deliberate but concise. Let me guess she did it at her ungodly speed again didn't she?"

Orin "'Hmm... Err... ah yes"

Orville laughs "Yes boy I would use that as a proper response too. So, what else did she do that you thought was unthoughtful of her?"

Orin "Picking my artwork out to be displayed in showing without my consent."

Orville "Oh.... Sorry about that. But she tends to be a freak when it comes to artwork and young artists that have yet to fulfill their potential. So, she tends to be desperate when she sees new works. I tend to be more patient about it." As he finishes his drink.

Orville "Let me show you around and let these gentlemen finish up the business of moving that stuff you ordered a while back into the house. And you two tell Tania I am taking a walk with him and expect him with the first round of food. Also, that I am partaking in the event because she almost scared the be Jesus out of him by going too fast again." Both Jacob and Horatio nod in agreement.

Horatio "Zeke if you need help placing everything just right just let Jacob and I know. We will do it right by you okay.

Orin/Zeke "Sure thank you both."

Jacob "'Don't worry we will keep the teasing at a minimum for your mom's sake. She has met us before. She doesn't quite get why we are so harsh with each other."

Orville escorts Orin/Zeke out of the market. And says, "Now young man let me show you the splendors of Andersonville."

CHAPTER 8

The tour of the town With Orville!

Orville starts with the gentlemen's club on the opposite side of town. Showing the seedy areas first as to avoid them. The club is light day and night like a rainbow and all its colors neon lights. And the pink and pastel colors all over it. Nothing like the one across the street from Orin's house in the back. Orin never really noticed how fast they got to the other side of town. As Orville is making him take the sites as he is soaking up the locations. And paying attention to specific, paths to take. He pointed out the hockey and curling rinks. Orin was surprised these sports were don this far south with the lacrosse fields as well. The baseball fields and the local rivalries with the other local towns that make up the greater Andersonville area. Here is Walton's markets with eh Bullseye markets as well. They were a bit far off. But they are in an area that the Copperfield and Glover's Field Ga were accessible. So, understanding the layout was east to understand. It's a huge wagon wheel. So, if invaders came the wider parts are in the outer edges. But as you get closer inwards. The narrower the streets are. So, it becomes close quarters fighting. It's a real headache when traffic and cars were introduced. As Orin takes in the paths taken and how fast things became. He was wondering when they were going to his place. He asks Orville "So When do we show up to my home again?"

Orville "When we are good, and god dammed ready. I love my wife. But there are times when she drives me nuts. She should've been gentler with her rush getting you all set up. So, we are going to make her wait. I'll take the blame. Then again, I'm the one who usually takes the hit for the team when it comes to her temper."

Orin "Ah… I get it. Making sure the bare minimum of people I need to meet will only be there."

Orville "Precisely, and by now your mother has covered the more than half the people that weren't invited. So, we walk a bit more. Now we are Robert E Lee national park. Now there is a fine son of a bitch if you ever meet one. Yes, and honorable and yet kind son of a bitch. None the less a son of a bitch indeed."

Orin "You sound like you knew the man?"

Orville "Well let's say our family had many of dealings with him back in the day. I still have the journals with the accounts that never made it to the books. In his younger days he was a real piece of work. As he grew older, he softens up a bit. Realized that he was fighting for the wrong cause well before shots were fired. The sad problem was, he couldn't hold a gun to his neighbor's heads. Davis and Lincoln refused in their own way to understand that. That is why Davis was impeached and removed from office in 1866. As per the request of our Canadian allies."

Orin "Yeah I've read that. That period was rather dark and conveniently lost?"

Orville "Well Robert had to give up his plantation to become the international cemetery for the union and confederate troops. You know that they used a name he chose. Arlington. Anyways, his late wife was appalled in what the union did initially to spite the confederacy. Burying the dead in all the gardens she had planted with the help of her slaves. Since the rights of succession was brand in in both countries. The confederate congress decided Robert E Lee to become the second President of the CSA. And that is when the peace was made. And his first act was to abolish slavery. Also, he convinced doing business with Canada was a better proposition than with the north at the time. The other states went about the change slowly. But they knew better to challenge Robert E lee. Unlike them, he lost far more than the rest. Was the president of the CAS until his death in 1896? Too much family history involving too many mattes in the past four hundred years. From your ancestor Leif Erickson through the joint moon landing in 1965."

Orin's eyes widen "Dam that is a lot of history that didn't make it to the books."

Orville "Yes, and a lot more. Jacob and Horatio are experts in that period of history. But once they get to know you better. Besides there are people in their families they just don't like to talk about."

Then you hear a scream behind the statue of Robert E Lee. "Halt! Who goes there! Identify yourself now! By the grace of the lord Jesus, I am charged to protect this place with my life!"

CHAPTER 9

Miguel De le Guy the 36th!

The man Is 6 foot even and ripped. Muscles upon muscles. Sandy blonde hair with dark blue eyes. With a scar down his right cheek. Armed with a long bow, knives, and a sword. He also has firearms and a bullet belt and a badge. He is wearing a dark gray pants and a jacket.

Miguel De le Guy the 36th "Oh it's you lord Orville. Sorry about that. I caught a few fornications around the statue again and bust a few pimps and drug dealers here. Nothing too crazy. But I would like to get extra help once Owen comes back. Oh, please forgive me young sir. My name is Miguel De Le Guy the 36th. At your service."

Orin "Ahh…My name is Orin Ezekiel McNeil."

Miguel De le Guy the 36th" oh…pleasure to meet you, young sire" Shakes Orin's hands firm and vigorously.

Orin "Young sire?"

Orville "He just got into town today Miguelito. He didn't know until today he is related to half the town. It's a bit overwhelming for him right now. So, I decided to take him for a walk to calm down and get his composure back."

Miguel De le Guy "Oh, that is alright. May I accompany the two of you back then. I haven't eaten a thing since breakfast this morning."

Orin "Yeah that is ok with me. How about you Orville?"

Orville smiles "Yes it's perfectly fine. Listen Orin, we are going to talk a lot of shop. So, try to keep up and any questions you might have. Save them for later and we will fill you in. If anyone asks, just play dumb and say you are truly ignorant of such matters. Not even my wife will question that. But she will ask of what you remember. Tell her the truth and the fact you don't understand the significance of the matters. You got it?"

Orin" Yes I go it."

Orville "Now Miguelito what can I do for you today other than the meal and getting to know Orin here?"

Miguel De le Guy the 36th" Well, we have spotted our favorite Apache Indian again a few towns over. I told Jacob and he told Horatio by now. I am understandably worried if he comes here and starts a whole lot of trouble."

Orville "Don't worry, stoner boy is here with Jacob and Horatio. He won't be causing any trouble here because of them. But I understand your worries about such things. He's one of the reasons Owen left and get a lot of things going with the satellite schools and annexes across the country."

Miguel De le Guy the 36[t h] "Ah...So, keeping a track of his movements. He is on everyone's most wanted list. True, but he must be cornered where the population is nil. So, he is being monitored for now. As in, do not approach at any costs."

Orville "Yes, that is precisely it. I fear he may get our good Reverend in trouble if they were to bump heads."

Miguel De le guy the 36th "True, less people around the better. Besides..."

Miguel sees at the conner of his eye three winos and a couple people with a film crew shooting an adult film scene on the benches. As he turns and runs a flicker of like. And a clear ripple starts to form as he runs towards them. Before Orin gets to ask a question. He realizes that he I at the Asin Pacific market a block and a half away from his new home.

Orin to Orville "What just happened?"

Orville "What do you mean?

Orin "Orville we were just at the park Miguel de le Guy the 36th ran towards a spot and we ended up here?"

Orville "You must be imagining things Orin. We were walking back home. I'll let tania know to leave Miguelito a plate or three of food. He does work to dam hard." Making a blank stare at Orin.

Orin walks to his house with Orville. And he notices that the is a crowd, but not as bad as it was probably. Then He sees his mother and Tania walking up.

Tania "My husband showed you around I see?"

Orin "Yes, but I am wondering how, did me make so much......."

Rodney slaps Orin on the back. "Hey! You finally made it! I bet you're happy that you missed the worst people in the lot. But that is ok for now. You'll get to meet them in the school. By the way Tania showed some of your works. With your mother's permission."

Orin is about to glare and sees his mother stern look and sighs" How much of it did you show Tania?"

Tania "Only the pieces I'm going to put in the wing of the school and the few things I wanted to be displayed at the game shop. I also allowed Horatio to have a few pieces as well. Your mother was kind to allow us this small favor of gratitude."

Orin Looks at his mother and sighs "As long you didn't pick up the pieces that were finished. I am fine with that."

Rodney 'They were pieces that weren't finished?"

Erin "yes a quite a few of them. I made sure they didn't get those dear. At least the ones I was aware of. Sometimes there are works I think he did finish. To discover that he was still working on them. So that is why he tends to be so protective? Did you meet anyone on your walk?"

Orin "Miguel De le Guy mom. He is very rambunctious is what I would say."

Tania and Rodney laugh hysterically. As they laugh the ground shakes a bit and they fall down to the ground and, a mini quake starts and subsides as fast as it came. Orin looks around as how people are not noticing this. Orin is looking around and it seems normal to them and looks at his mother. And she isn't making any kind of reactions of this being unusual. And a voice makes this comment "You look rather confused?"

CHAPTER 10

The Madame across the Street

She is 5'7 black hair with hazel eyes. Very busty. But has a stare that looks dep into your soul. She is wearing super jean shorts a tank top that you can see the lower shape of her breasts but no nipple showing. Also, Orin finally notices this is sunset now.

He responds back" Er uhm…yes I am."

She laughs a bit "Don't worry young man. We get small tremors a lot more often than people think. So, you are ethe new neighbors in this house?"

Orin simply nods. And sees tania's and Rodney's face glare with anger and a few other emotions he can't place his fingers on. As they glare at here. She smiles and says "Now Tania, you have such a big party so close to my establishment. And not thinking to knock on our door to invite us? Oh…forgive my manners young man. My name is Rebecca Von Weib. At your service young man?"

Tania "Does your mother know you're not working?"

Rebecca Von Weib" Why Tania, tonight is my day off. But the other ladies including the Madame would have been enjoyed an invite to the festivities here. We do invite all the people to ours, after all." As she smiles."

Tania "If you mean how the Madame get her customers in to her establishment. By offering the free food is one thing. But they do have to pay for a lot of services. And it's all by word of mouth."

Orin looks at Tania's stance and Rebecca's stance. He notices that Tania's hands are chalk white with adrenaline, and fists clenched. While Rebecca is calm relaxed. Now he hears Miguelito's voice shout "Just wait a dam minute, ladies!" As Miguel De le Guy approaches the women.

Another voice "Becky come over right here now. How many times I've told you not to start up trouble!"

The other lady Looks exactly like Rebecca's, but she is a bit taller. Leggier and even 5'11 with silver streaks in her hair as if be design. She is wearing a micro min skirt with a white blouse and black stockings and black shoes. As she speaks "Now Miguelito, sorry to make your job harder tonight. My Daughter was just leaving. Young lady, you are working tonight! I won't hear a dam thing about it. Go back to the club now!"

Rebecca "But.."

Rebecca's Mother "But nothing! You get inside now! You caused enough trouble this week. I'm so sorry about this Tania. I will make sure she is dealt with for this one and the other stuff this week. Oh…I forget my manners. My name is Wilhelmine von Weib."

Erin extends her hand "It's nice to meet you. I am Erin."

Wihelmine shakes Erin's hand "So you're my new Neighbors. Sorry for my little girl. She tends to start a ruckus everywhere she goes."

Erin "It's fine, I've dealt with types like that before. It is a very hard thing to phase me. I have a thick skin."

Tania "They'll wear it down in no time Erin. Trust me on that one."

Wihelmine laughs "Well once we get to know each other better. We can be a pain. All five of my little girls."

Rodney rolls his eyes" Little early to be this charming Wihelmine."

Wihelmine "Rodney, I would shut your mouth right about now."

Rodney "Your four She-Devils are not to be trifled with. Your one Angel isn't either. Then again you have five daughters. Most of them shorter than you. With, the exception of your angel. She is the same height."

While this is happening, a quarter bounces of Rebecca's ass. "Who the fuck did that!" As the crowd chuckles. As she approached the crowd in the back yard. Orville steps in and says "Young lady you're in enough trouble as it is. Also, I'm the one who did it because you dropped your

58

wallet. I believe this is yours. Because you never listen to me in general. I used the only method available to get your attention."

Rebecca frowns and snarls slightly" I'm sorry Lord Orville. I should listen to you more often. You are right about that. But you must have a better way?"

Orville "Unfortunately child you seldom leave me with little choice." As he stares at Wihelmine with a disapproving look.

Wihelmine just looks at Orville "Becca he's right you and most of your sister leave us with very little choice. No go to work. I'll deal with you later."

Rebecca "But mom".

Wihelmine "No buts get back to the club. Before some else decides cause you trouble as pay back for your pranks." As she turns her head and gives a good look over Orin.

Wihelmine "You do look so familiar. Do I know your father?"

Before Orin provides an answer Orville answers "He doesn't know his father. But he is family and related to us. Hence the house plus a few other things here and there Wihelmine. No need to ask any more questions of the lad. Or his mother for such matters." As he looks at Tania with a help me out here glance.

Tania "Yes… That is true. His father is always running about the world. After all he is a busy man. He just wanted his only child to have a good education and a better place to live." As tania smiles at Orin with a loving look but sadness in her eyes.

Wihelmine "Oh… You have that in common with my quintuplets. Their father is also running around the world way too much. But then again, it's how he does pay the alimony and other things when he isn't running things here. I'll let my girls know to treat you right and proper. Meaning no practical jokes on you nor other forms of mischief. Is that fair tania?"

As Tania smiles 'Yes that is perfectly fine. I know you will do your upmost on this matter. The others are working tonight?"

Wihelmine "Yes they are. So Am I. We will stop by after the parishioners leave." At the corner rounds the block. Walking up with pamphlets making their way to the back yard. Orin thinking wow there are a lot of night owls here. Maybe this place has more than you think. After all, during the walk he remembers Orville saying there is plenty to do. He must have met this town is open twenty-four by seven days a week.

Wihelmine" I must take my leave. If you all are still up, I'll stop by. Just forgive my attire. I'll be in my work clothes."

Tania "Well at least wear the robe when you come out!"

Wihelmine "Excuse me Tania! I'm just crossing the dam street." A Voice says, "Tania you know she has a point there according to a few laws passed by Orville."

You see a priest. He is about 6'3 with a wiry build. With a short sleeve black shirt white collar. Brown hair with baby blue eyes. As he approaches into the e yard. Shakes Orin Hand. "Pleasure to meet you, young man. You have a firm grip by the way." Orin feels the priests grip and I's like steel. As he shakes back. The Priest "You look very familiar? Do I...."

Wihelmine answers "He doesn't know his earthly father preacher!" With an angry scowl.

The Preacher smiles and answers "Jesus will forgive you too Wihelmine. All you got to do is ask for it. And actually, put a effort for repentance. Young man where is your mother? You two should come over for services at 10pm. We are an unusual Parish. We do everything at night hours. We feel it's the perfect time to get to know the lord." As he smiles Orin feels a bit uncormfortable. And the anxiety is coming around again. Then he feels a hand on his shoulder and turn its Horatio.

Horatio "Now father the boy is rather overwhelmed tonight. Give the boy a little room to breathe in a bit. You can discuss the great works of Jesus another time when he is truly settled in."

The Priest "You are right of course Horatio. I didn't know he got in today, right?"

Horatio "That is correct father. I'll bring them in sometime this week. Just don't pressure the boy and his mother please. I have, to make sure they get settles in. Also, Jacob and Orville are handling the matters in this. So, we would appreciate a little measured responses to all that is going on. It's a lot to take in all at once."

The Preacher "Of course... I meant no offense young man."

Orin "None taken. And thank you for your understanding."

The Preacher "Oh… I forgot my manners my name is Reverend Jonathan Robert Kingsley. It's my pleasure to meet you. And if you need an ear. You can talk to me always. Day or night. But nighttime is preferred."

Orin "My name is Orin Ezekiel McNeil. It's a pleasure to meet you Reverend."

Rev. Johnathan R Kingsley "Nice to meet you Orin. Hmm As e scans and sees Erin at the corner of his eye. Erin is that you! It's been a dogs age!" As Erin walks up to Rev Johnathan R Kingsley. And gives him a great big hug.

Erin "Nice to see you again John. You finally turned into a night owl? Back in the day you used to wake up in the crack of dawn and go out and preach. Now you're doing it at the crack of sunset?"

Rev. Jonathan R Kingsley "Well things changed for a while now. I've been doing the reverse schedule for about a full score now. Then again Wihelmine has a lot to do with that. Since I don't fall for her wilds easily." As he smirks

Wihelmine frowns "Well Reverend you do represent a challenge. A challenge I intend to master!"

Erin laughs "Good luck with that. John and I go way back. I had my chance at 16 and I know I blew it! I should've talked, him to go to a specific seminary school that allows marriage!" As she spanks him on the ass.

Rev, Jonathan Kingsley" Now Erin! Stop that. I am a priest! Please show the proper respect!" As the crowd laughs hard.

Orin sighs "You too huh…?"

Rev. Jonathan R Kingsley "Sighs…Yeah some things never change, I guess. The again your mother and I knew each since we were kids. So, you're going to hear stories that are going to make her blush." As he smiles.

Erin "Johnny don't you dare!"

Wihelmine "I agree with the young lady on this point Reverend. Aren't you supposed to keep secrets?"

Rev, Jonathan R Kingsley "This is stuff before I was ordained. Meaning I can have a little fun for a change!" As he laughs.

Both women look at each other and Wihelmine "Well he got us there. He can run his mouth. What sort of mischief you got into back then?"

Erin "Way too much. And I don't talk about those stories. I would appreciate it if you don't tell my son Johnny!"

Rev Jonathan R Kingsley "Well it really depends on the situation Erin. Don't worry I won't tell him everything. Just the embarrassing stuff to make you blush." As he smiles.

Erin just hits him on the shoulder and light smacks on his arms as he laughs it off "Feisty as ever Erin."

Erin "You're dam straight about that one Johnny!" As she smiles.

Rev. Jonathan R Kingsley "Don't worry Erin it's going to be fun here. He will adjust to a lot of things. Also, how competitive the school is with the grades as well as with other extracurricular activities here. I run the night activities now."

Erin raises an eyebrow "You're a night owl now? I remember the days you would wake up at the crack of dawn. You would be fast asleep by 7pm. And you used to call that a late night. You slept through half of prom. All because you had to wake up at dawn to do the Lord's work as you always put it. Now Orin he was always going to be a priest. But his parents made him wake up at the crack of dawn. And home by sunset to eat sleep and repeat the same cycle all over again. Wow nights creep up fast around here." She also noticed that Orin noticed that too.

Erin" Orin how long was that walk around town?"

Orville "I just showed him a small sliver of the town. And the spots he best avoids at all coasts. The rest of the tour I'll Leave for Horatio or Jacob. I really don't trust Rodney with that. But I do trust Tania with it that. Or Miguel De le Guy. This way he will know how to run around town with ease. Things happen fast around here. Also, there is shindig every week. This is one of the rare weeks that nothing was happening. Until you two arrived. The welcome mat is always open with the community."

Erin's eyes widen and narrows" So there is some type of local party every week?"

Rev. Jonathan R Kingsley "Erin, there are events every week here. For five weeks. There isn't an event here. We have either football games, or the big basketball games at the university level. With the rivals in the state as well within the conference. We even have hockey games down here with lacrosse games as well. I know you're a big fan of those sports. Since the school has trimesters vs semesters. The sporting events are year-round with baseball as well. So, people come in and out. The economy is fueled by the school having grades k through PhD doctorate level degrees. So, it's a big thing getting accepted in the elementary through middle or high school levels here. Because once we accept you get first dibs on the university level courses here." As Orin's eyes widen with his jaw dropping.

Orin "Meaning as soon as I graduate, I get to go to college here?"

Tania "Yes with an average of 3.0 meaning B's or better. 2.9 and below you have to wait a year or do the courses over again to get in the following Trimester."

Orin whistle a long "Well my grades are good right?"

REV. Jonathan R Kingsley "Oh, yes they were exceptional. One of the reasons why you were accepted and qualified for the housing and the job. It's rare that the president gives up this house for anyone. So, I will be seeing a lot of you in the hallways. I'm also the pastor for the school as well."

Orin "What do you mean by that?"

Rev. Jonathan R Kingsley "Meaning I do a lot of the education as well. With the religion courses that are mandatory here as your grades. I teach them twice a week at night. I made arrangements with Tania for those nights off at your part time job." Orin's head begins to explode. School doesn't start up for another week. And he's being told how stressful it's going to be. Well before it starts up. As he is shaking his head, he feels the cold hands of the preacher on his shoulders. As he looks into the blue eyes.

Rev. Jonathan R. Kingsley "Don't over think it things. You'll be fine. Just take it one day at a time. The Lord will provide." Orin notices at a closer look the preacher is rather pale as the hands begin to warm up while his shoulders get colder. As he pulls away slowly as Orin calms down. As Orin scans around. He notices that the night caem upon him and his mother rather fast. As he looks around, and he see another young lady next to Rebeca. She is the same height. And they look almost exactly alike. As he is staring at them another one strolls up behind them. With more of a scolding look at the other two. Then a fourth strolls up. On the far left one speaks "Now Becca your causing commotion again?"

Becca "Now Rachel, I'm doing nothing."

Rachel" Really then why I see quarters around your feet?" smiling

Becca "Now I am trying to figure that out." Her other sister starts laughing to her right.

Rachel "Now Colleen, that isn't nice."

Colleen "I never piss anyone off to have the audacity to actually bounce quarters off my perfect pristine ass." The other sister laughing even harder says "All too true."

Becca "Now Rory I don't need your comments. Nor your opinions on how to handle things!"

Rory "Well I do move my hips better than you." As she smiles teasingly.

Becca 'Well good thing Saundra is too busy working. She knows how to shake everything better than all of us put together!" Now the other three ladies give glares that could kill anyone in a second. The rest of the crowd laughs as Rev Jonathan R. Kingsley "Now you met four out of the five Von Wieb sisters. The self-professed ultimate dancers on the planet. Know to all senses of perversions. And other earthly pleasure of the flesh Orin." As the four sisters now glare at the Reverend. He smiles and says "Young ladies, your souls still can be saved. At least Cassandra is far ahead of you in that department."

Wihelmine "Now Reverend. How many times I've told you not to incite my daughters?"

REV. Jonathan R, Kingsley "Now madame, All I stated like them as it is the same for you too. It's never too late to repent and go into Jesus's embrace. For the remission of sins. For his glory and honor. You all can be saved!"

Wihelmine "Isn't god the reason why you're at how we shall say, current state of being?"

Rev. Jonathan R. Kingsley "The Lord always tests us in way that are unimaginable. I simply instructed my flock that this too was a test of our metal. And that Jesus will provide godly solutions to our plight. And for those who caused our predicament. Have mercy love compassion and above all else pity. Why you ask because pity? That they don't know their heavenly father yet. But they still have time to make a profound relationship with him. Also pity that they truly don't know any better. That is why we are such a noisy soulful lot. Amongst other flocks we do make the most joyful noise in the name of Jesus. Which reminds me I have to call a few of them and tell this house, I'll take care of the administering the work of Jesus and the rest of his gospel personally!"

Wihelmine "He doesn't exist! If he did why would he let such things happen!"

Rev. Jonathan R. Kingsley "Well then why don't you just come into the church a few blocks up and put it to the test?" Rev. Jonathan R. Kingsley simply smiles after issuing the challenge.

Wihelmine looks around and the people saying in unison "OOOOOOOOOOOOOOOOOO"

As she looks around and her daughters having a bit of a scared looks on their faces. As the crowd is at an awe of the challenge. As she surveys the crowd, she sees Erin glaring at the Reverend and the crowd. The look on her face says it all. Wihelmine simply smiles at this point and looks to her daughters and simply says. "Well played as always Jonathan. Well, played as usual. But that mother particularly didn't like how you made this challenge on her property. As she smiles.

Rev. Jonathan R. Kingsley "Erin will forgive me for this one. But I know it will take a moment or too. Long moments. But the invite is always true and honest. Your souls can be saved too. If you wish to believe and repent." Wihelmine simply smiles and nods. And she says "Tania. The BBQ's are always fun. But they do have the habit for causing a bit of drama. These newcomers, I like them a lot. For some reason they have me intrigued. I also like they do have a set of manners beyond reproach. All my girls will love that about them. Especially the fine handsome young man before them." She smiles and takes her leave with her daughters. Walking across the street. Slowly looking over their shoulders as the walk across hearing muttering about a few things. All Orin could get is how they let the preacher get away with this.

Tania" Sorry about that. The Weib girls tend to start trouble amongst themselves. But it usually spills to the neighbors and the other students. Casandra is the best one of the lot. To her friends she will let you call her Saundra by the way. But her mother and sisters have a wicked sense of humor. Also, they tend to be a bit on the mischievous side with their humor as well."

Erin "They cause that much trouble?"

Tania "Dollars to doughnuts, it was one of her sisters that bounced that quarter off her ass. And if that isn't the case, I know the man that did it." As she stares at Rodney. As he put his hands up and emphatically gesturing, he didn't do a dam thing this time. As the crowd disperses slowly but surely. Erin invites Orville inside to stay the night. After Tania left and the yard is cleaned as fast as it was setup. Orin is looking around and at the corner of his eye he sees a young woman wearing a black see-through shirt smiling at him. As he turns around, she is gone. As this happened. The reverend calls to Orin to come inside to begin bible study. Orville has a concerned look on his face as Orin walks back. As he looks up He sees something on his balcony. A shadow of sorts. Orville walks towards him as he glances at Orville. He notices the shadow is now gone.

Orville "Those ladies are a bit of a handful. They have been at each other's throats for ages. Don't get involved if you can son. I will handle things with my wife about this. Also let the Reverend handle the Weibs' girls. All six of them. Don't let your mother or you be alone with them. They can be quite persuasive. And above all else, the one you can trust is Saundra. But she is a bit cold and aloof. Because she has seen it and heard it all. So, lets come in and get that bible study under way. By the way you have the Christian religion as one of your classes. But hey are held in your home. So, you will be seeing a lot of Johnny. And you will be part of the precious few that will be allowed to call him that. Because your mother and he go way back."

As Orin scans the area and know he has questions. He looks to Orville's eyes saying not tonight. Let it go for tonight. Tomorrow is a new day. And you'll need all the strength and help for tomorrow. As they walk into the house, Orin hears snicking and laughter. He scans the area and hears more giggling. Orville simply frowns and the giggling stops.

CHAPTER 11A

Night 1 through Day one T-minus 6 days before the first day of school for the trimester days before start of trimester The first full day at Andersonville:

After The reverend finished up with the bible study. He recommended that Orin read the books of Acts, and Psalms in its entirety. To teach him how to pray and praise the lord properly and to witness the miracle for the Holy spirit to be delivered to humanity. As Orin decides to read the bible that Jonathan gave him. As he is reading the book of Acts, he hears giggling outside on the balcony, that overlooks to the strip club across the street. He hears laughter now. AS he approaches the sliding door of the balcony. As he closes into the door, he gently draws the curtain, and he sees five women on the balcony. Just wearing panties and all see through PJ tops. He hears them talking about customers. AS he decides to slide the door open. As he slides the door open a small squeak from the door. AS the door opens, he looks, and they are gone. He walks on the balcony and looks around the only clue that someone was there is a purse filled with loonies and toonies with dollar bills of fives, tens and 20's. As he picks up the purse, he hears a hiss behind him. Then he sees four of the five across the street looking worried. As he simply gestures for them to come over. The four, look surprised. The hissing stops, but he feels his hair stand on end. As one of the girls makes a frown. As the hissing stops. He simply puts the purse on the railing.

Orin asks, "How did the five of you get up here so fast?" The ladies across the street jaws drop.

Colleen Looking stunned "Well most people don't notice how fast we are. How did you pick up on this?"

Orin "Look I don't mind you all on the balcony. I just want a heads up, so I don't disturb you in any way. From how Becca presented herself, this is your spot to hang out when work is way too much trouble. Having my mother and I move in here. It looks that would ruin your favorite spot. We don't mind. Just a heads up for the insurance and how did you get up here would be nice to know. We tend to look for home invasion purposes. When I was a child people tried to kidnap me when I was four. So, we would like a heads up on all the ways in and out of the house we don't know about." He notices as the women across the street have a hand over their mouths. As he turns around and see Colleen. See had tears in her eyes. As he hands the purse to her.

Collen simply hits a railing to her immediate left that would on Orin's right and a ladder slide down. As Orin looks down and smirks.

Orin asks, "Let me guess there is a switch that will lower and collapse the ladder just as fast?"

Colleen "Says yes that is true. I can show you if you like?"

Orin" I would like that. I am guessing the other balconies have the same feature?"

Colleen "Yes, they do different spots."

Orin "When can you show me?"

Colleen "Not tonight but tomorrow night when we come up here. We didn't mean to disturb you nor your mother."

Orin "That is alright, just don't drop anything that you might not want me picking up."

Orin hands colleen her purse with the money in it. She simply smiles

Colleen "You are rather unusual young man?"

Orin "I prefer the term odd. But I have lived a life less ordinary. Do you go to the school?"

Colleen laughs" Of course we go to the school. But we are in the university portion of the school. What part are you in?"

Orin "I have the advanced course list in my bedroom. If you will allow me to grab it?" As he looks over his shoulder. He sees three of the ladies there. They are looking rather curious about him. Some of them scratching their heads. And looks at Colleen and she is simply smiles.

Colleen "Of course, I would like to see your schedule. It's not every night I get to meet one of the advanced class members before they enter the school. "As Orin goes into the bedroom and picks up his schedule. He notices that that Becca is now on the balcony. AS he approaches the balcony Becca just looks at him and smiles.

Becca "You're going to be okay with us hanging out on the balcony here?"

Orin "As long as my mom and I know about it. It will be okay."

Colleen is Checking the schedule "Wow, you must be talented. To have these teachers for the art courses alone with the math and engineering courses as well."

Becca "Colleen, you're going to be up next."

Colleen "He is going to be running in our circles Becca."

Becca "Really! Oh my, he must be really talented. No wonder Tania has claimed his services already."

Orin "I was given the job at her game shop actually. It was arranged as part of my enrollment."

Becca "Oh my, you're going to be working with Rodney! I do feel for you. He tends to be a handful. Did you get a good look on who bounced a quarter off my ass?"

Orin "Please forgive me. I didn't notice. But I was having a panic attack for the overwhelming amount of people going through my things moving us in today."

Becca simply smiles "It's okay. At least I know you have manners. Forgive us for the lack of them. And thank you for letting us still have our spot here. But now we must go back to work. Also, one more request. When you're in. Please have the curtains drawn so we know you're here in your room?"

Colleen looks at Becca with a strange look. "Why would we have that as a request?" And Becca smacks Colleen on her ass.

Colleen "Ow! You didn't have to do that!"

Becca "If you don't mind of course."

Orin has a quizzical look on his face "Sure, But If my mother disapproves of that request for any reason. We have to come up with something else alright."

Colleen and Becca in unison" That is perfectly fine now we have to go. Is that an Isle in your room?" As Orin turn his head and turns his head back, they are gone. And he sees one of the Wieb girls across the street now. He still can't make her face out completely. However, he sees a smile on her face tilting her head back and giggling a bit as she turns around and decides to shake her but a little bit and looks over her shoulders with a shocked look on her face. Orin simply waves with an awkward look on his face with a thin smile. She simply looks and smiles back and walks back into the club. And then he hears a bit of laughter as if it was on the roof of the house. Orin looks up and see nothing and he feels a smack on his ass. He turns around and sees Becca and Collen giggling. With Rory and Rachel smiling and waving at him. As they walk back inside. He leaves the curtains drawn open as agreed. As he finishes halfway through the book of Psalms. Orin passes out, as he sleeps, he hears whispers and giggling. He opens an eye and sees the four women simply watching him sleep through the window. And hears Wihelmine says to her girls.

Wihelmine" Will you four stop it. You are drooling over the boy, at least. he did let you all still hang out here. I know he is handsome and way too understanding. But Tania laid claim to this man. So please don't start up crap that we are all going to regret. Orville has taken a very special interest in the boy too. So at least be respectful of him and his mother. I really like them both. So, no trouble the lot of you. At least Casandra has the sense not to cause trouble. So, get off the balcony now!"

The girls "Oh mom he looks so cute laying in there."

Wihelmine "Did he invite you all in?"

The girls answer in unison "No, not yet. But we were going to ask?"

Wihelmine "So get off the balcony! The club is full of customers. And the rest of the ladies are earning their money good and proper."

Rachel "Mom he is very special. He returned Colleen's purse when she dropped it."

Rory "Mom, he also was understanding about us using this spot. Most men would have started at our breast. But he looked into our eyes instead. We find that unusual."

Wihelmine "Oh my, look get out of here now before he decides to ask too many questions. I'll handle it if Tania asks too many questions too."

Becca 'Come on all, mom is right about this. It's a good idea to leave now. We will have plenty of other opportunities to find out what we want to know. Let's go before he fully wakes up." Then a whoosh of wind they were gone. Orin now thinking to himself about how his nights are going to be. Hearing the girls giggling and talking all night long as he sleeps. At least he now knows about the ladders. But still, it doesn't explain the speed of there entrances and exits. But the way time speed up with Orville earlier today during the walk around the town. Even though the town is a size of a city with the school as the center piece. All Orin knows is that there are a lot of strange things in this place. These little things that are out of place. And it all seems normal. People walking invisible dogs or talking to thin air he can handle. Well, he saw that in Toronto and Ottawa. But he now sees that this place is different in a way that only rivals Nowhere Oklahoma. He remembers that small town with things that are vivid. However, the people he did and yet didn't recognize. He misses Anna now. She would find a way to make these things make sense to his sensibilities. But since she isn't here. It leaves him feeling a bit out of place here. He knows he is going to get use to the goings on here. However, everyone doesn't seem to trust Rodney nor the young ladies across the street from his new home. He misses Lupus-Ville North Dakota. Some fun years were spent there. He did meet Anna there too. They were inseparable since, unit now. But she will be here in a few months. So, it's not that bad. As he slowly drifts into sleep. He notices one lady at the door. She is smiling and leaves a kiss on the sliding door. With blood red lipstick. All he knows is that only six women come up here. He isn't sure who did this. But all he knows that he is going to have an interesting time here. He now wonders if he is going to see his father here. After all this time. He has a lot of questions to ask him. Now meeting some of his family relations. Also, some of his father's friends. At least he will have answers now. But now more questions he has. But at least he will have his answers now. As he drifts into sleep, he opens an eye again and this time he sees Orville staring down at him. Orville is smiling and says one thing. "You were smart about letting them have their spot on the balcony. Also, you were smarter telling them that you and mom know how the ladders work. But what especially impressed me is that how you made a wonderful impression that even their mother wont fuck with you as well. Young man you are lucky they like you. But that can be a curse too. Good thing your mom is letting me spend the night three times a week. My wife won't like it initially. But she will respect it. Good night boy. I'll see you in the morning when I cook breakfast for both of you. You have your father's habit with sleeping with one eye open. Your safe here son. Now just relax and go to sleep" As he closes the eye. He sees Orville talking to Wihelmine on the balcony. He hears her say something about his parentage questioning it. And how Orville knows the family. All he can hear is that it isn't any of her concern for now. Also knowing that Orin is a smart kid. He notices too many things but will keep quiet once all is known to him. As he now drifts to sleep. He hears a rather interesting rendition of rock a by baby. With rather explicit things they would do to me. As he drifts off to sleep, he hears Rory mumbling a bit, for something odd about him. As he sets off to dream land. He sees his father smiling at him with a bunch of animals. And this time he hears him speak.

Owen "So you are finally home. So, you met a lot of people today. Don't worry they will all care about you. Even the madame across the street. But they don't know who you are yet. But once they do. Your life will be interesting. As the Chinese curse. May you live in interesting times. You'll have a pleasant time here. However, do not trust Rodney and Becca at all costs. They are not to be trusted at all. These two causes, the most trouble in the town. So be careful. Don't trust those two. The others you can trust. But Rodney and Becca are bad news. If they get their way. Also, they are constantly at odds with each other. So don't get dragged into their mess. I am so proud of you. That you're home now. But home has its issue as well. So, I'll be home soon. Now that I can dream-walk easier now to the both of you. Now these things will start off fast and hard. Also, one more thing don't invite them in any time soon. It will happen but don't do it too soon. But they will watch over you for a lot of reasons. I will tell you why, another time. Oh, by the way the alarm is about to go off in a minute. So, enjoy your day."

Orin then wakes up and says, "Wait you just can't go like that!" as he looks around and he sess. The room empty except all his stuff and notices one of the girls is at the door and notices the first ray of light. All he hears is from her 'Oh shit! I stayed too late!" Orin blinks and she was gone. Interesting, what came to his mind. Why are they afraid of sunlight? Then he thinks oh. They are people who just can't handle UV light. Those cases are small in number, and Andersonville have the leading treatments for it. Hence the idea of having school at night for k- university level. Some people have developed the syndrome in their adult life as well. The hospital has treatments for these people. As Orin ponders on this. So, these people have enclaves here. That must be why the reverend does his preaching's at night. There is a community of people with this syndrome. And Andersonville has treatments for this. As Orin looks around his room. He sees nothing out of place. However, he sees things on the balcony. He opens the door and looks. He sees makeup and compacts around the railings and a few coin purses filled to the brim. He decides to bring the stuff inside and leaves a note on the railing that nothing was stolen. That he just put it inside his room for safe keeping. As he looks over his shoulder, he sees Whihelmine smiling. With the note faced outwards towards the club. She laughs out loud and smiles. As he turns, he notices that she was wearing a night shirt and a thing. He also noticed two marks on her butt. As she walks into the club.

A few hours later Orin walks around the blocks. After seeing the Asian Pacific Tea market. He walks to the center of town and see Orville. Orville smiles and says Hello Lad. Enjoying the sun?

Orin "Yes I am. Just asking how many people are here for the sun allergy treatments?"

Orville frowns for a second and smiles" You don't miss much, do you?"

Orin "Not really, I don't need names just a general figure."

Orville "Well that is a big number here actually. There is a lot of people who suffer from it. There are a lot of extreme cases of it."

Orin "Oh, like Johnny?"

Orville sighs "Yes like Johnny…"

Orin "Don't worry I won't pry. I just wanted to know. So, the few things I thought were strange or odd now makes sense."

Orville smiles with relief "Really? How so?"

Orin "Well depending on the treatments and how the body's reaction varies from individual to individual. So, some treatments work. While others don't work at all. The sad thing is the later is the norm versus the prior."

Orville sighs "That is the gist of it. I go out of my way to treat it as normal. However, Rodney and Tania tend to be less tolerant of it. That is a sad thing. So, I would be careful around them. On the matters of this subject, okay?"

Orin simply smiles "Okay, no worries. I'll try not to mention it too much. I am a curious kind of young man. So, I've been told by many people in the past."

Orville "Where are you going now?"

Orin "School bookstore, to get my books for the trimester that is going to start."

Orville "May I accompany you?"

Orin "Sure why not?"

Orville smiles like an excited young schoolboy going to school for the first time.

Orville says, "My boy, your parents did raise you right."

Orin "Would be nice to have a dad around more often." And he sighs and lowers his head down.

Oroville looking sad and smiles and pats Orin on the head and Says "He does love you. The problem with your father and mother is the trouble they go into. And the other problem is how people are funny about certain things in life too. He had to leave. And it hurt him more than you think. And he had to keep running until he got here recently. Then he had to get permission for the both of you to live here. And yes, he's not here now. But he will be here soon. He has to take care of a few last details about the security of this fine place. And I just told you too much. Just leave it be, ok?"

Orin simply nods in acknowledgement. "When do you think he will be back? Wasn't he married once? Do I have other brothers and sisters?"

Orville laughs" Well… That is a tad bit of a predicament that your father totally takes most of the responsibility for. Then again, my wife has a lot to do with the rest of it too. And it's a bit of a pickle. But know you are well off. But Things are still a bit hectic now too. Now give me your schedule and let's see what books you need." Orin gives Orville his schedule. Orville looks over the schedule. He simply hums and whistle's and his eyes widen. And looks over everything. And he simply looks the boy over. And Orville says "Wow, you are really book smart. You do have street smarts too. This is according to Jacob and Horatio. Letting those girls have their favorite hangout spot on that balcony. Young man these are university level courses. Your mother made sure you were educated correctly." Orin simply shrugs and says "Mom wanted me to have every advantage. She says that being smart in all facets available in life."

Orville "I agree with that in principle. But it doesn't allow the dangers of power getting to your head."

Orin "The more knowledge, equals power. Power equals the ability to abuse it and arrogance in behavior as well."

Orville "Correct."

Orin "I tend to view those type of people a nuisance at best. Then again I guess I am surrounded by stupid people."

Orville 'You're not kidding about that. It's all I deal with a day in and day out business, but then again, all the loons we have here is something to talk about, I guess. That is why I want to go with you to the school. You will need the full tour. I see you have a mid-day gap for the shop and other rest periods for the night classes."

Orin "What do you mean by loons?"

Orville "Why young sir. We have the best school of super geniuses in the whole wide world. Depending on the wings of the school itself. You will find all sorts of happenings. Right now, with the rush of getting the books, supplies, clothes, and food. Also, there are bunches of students starting their courses of studies earlier that the professors would hope for. Depending on the wing of the school. Now here is a current map of the school. It has seven wings and the center of it is the administration building and the chapel for the main church. That is where Johnathan resides. You'll see him there most of the time. Also, the wings deal with a specialty of studies. The Jackson wing, that for the studies of humanities and Politics. The Jefferson Davis wing ironically is for law, civics, policing as magistrates. It doubles as out police academy and the training center for the confederate bureau of investigation training facilities. One would expect it to be the opposite. I assure you that the biggest wing is the Robert E Lee wing. That is our military college. We train our army, navy, air-force, marines, coast guard, national guard officers here. Including our space administration as well. It's a joint operation with the dam Yankees up north so to speak."

Orin" That is the just the first three wings?!"

Orville "Yes there is more. You have the Wright wing. The name tells all. That is the wing of engineering, sciences, chemistry. But the wing merges with another one at the opposite end. That wing is the Ross wing for the medical sciences. But they are fiercely competitive. The LeClair wing is for the arts and poetry. And yes, Horatio has a lot to do with this wing. Also, the Gator-Star wing deals with history. From the viewpoint of the victors and losers. So, it's a true history. So, to speak of the events that has passed to obscurity."

Orin simple whistles. "So, Horatio and Jacob pretty much own half the town?"

Orville "Not really, they however have plenty of say what goes on the school here?"

Orin "How about Miguel De le Guy?"

Orville "Well he graduated top of his class in the CBI."

Orin "Confederate Bureau of Investigation main HQ is here?"

Orville "Right you are about that. Miguel graduated top of his class and choose to train others instead in the practical of law enforcement. Not many do that after they graduate. But Miguel was a former Military Police officer as well. So, they agreed to his request. Patrolling the school is part of his domain so to speak."

Orin "How does he manage to get to one place to the other so fast?"

Orville "Let's say he knows al the ins and outs of this place. It's the main reason why he catches most of his perps."

Orin "Oh..."

Orville "So we're heading through the engineering quad right now. It's the shortest route to the main building in the middle. That is Davis Hall. "As Orville finished the statement, they hear a whistle and

Orville yells "Incoming!" and forces Orin down to the ground. And an explosion happens near them. And a voice yells "Oh shite we nearly got the mayor!" Another voice "God dam it! It didn't bounce off the walls like it was supposed to. Now we have to reconstruct the projectile and get the chemicals from the lab. And fuck get the materials to make the launcher more portable for use. We have to go back to the entire drawing board. It was supposed to bounce six times and land in front of the Jackson wing! Not here in the middle of our quad!"

Orville "God dam it you idiots! All the book smarts in the fucking world and not one once of common sense in the lot of you!"

Engineering student "I said you almost got the mayor you idiot!"

Orville "Young man I give you credit for having some common sense! Now mind telling me what the fuck is going on!"

Engineering student "The yearly science wars has officially started with the stink bomb in the cafeteria this morning sir!"

Orville 'Oh... great! Now I guess you were on the losing side of that. Which club started this this year?"

Engineering students "The club that meets in the Jackson wing sir."

Orrville "Oh great, Rodney's club of double-talking roll top gaming and sciences of alchemy and super science."

Orin "How much trouble they cause?"

Orville "Well he starts the wars of practical jokes here. The Weib sisters usually finish and win it. However, the other clubs are always caught in the middle. I would have hoped Rodney, would show a bit of restraint and waiting to the beginning of the trimester. But no such luck. What club are you from now children? Because you did almost kill us by the way?"

The students "We are of the Science alchemy resource and physics and sorcery club sir."

Orville "Great, you lot. Are you the ones trying to figure out how to open a worm hole to navigate once place to another on a planet?"

The engineering students "Ahh yes teleportation whin an atmosphere. Think of the uses for traveling? Instantaneous travel to one point of the map to another. Think of all the uses of such feats!"

Orin dusting himself off "Isn't that pure conjecture at the moment. Laws of conservation and the Einstein Rosenberg bridge to consider as well, possible time dilation. You need an active super collider making a fusion reaction in a zero g environment to provide the power for such a thing?"

The head of the club steps froth. He looks at Orin and say's "Hey new kid, you think you pretty smart?"

Orin replies" Nope, I just have a lot of common sense. How about yourself?"

The club head" My name is Matt Jones. Nice to meet you?"

Orin "My name is Orin McNeil at your service." As he does a small but noticeable bow.

Matt "Sorry aboot the projectile. Now we are in it are we not Lord Orville?"

Orville "I'll let it go Mathew. Because you treated this young man with respect."

Matt "It's rare I find someone who is humble aboot their intelligence level here. I like that. He didn't even question If I was stupid. And he did make a point. About having more sense in doing this. So, I am looking forward to seeing you around in this school. Getting your books today?"

Orin "Yes" Before he was about to finish.

Matt "I suggest you two take the long way around to the store. Go through the Jackson wing then cut through the Einstein Rosenberg center to get there. As far as I know no one has setup any pranks that way."

Orin "ahh thanks, what part of Canada are you from? I just moved from London Ontario."

Matt "Quebec City Quebec. Dam another Kanuck here! Sweet! We are really sorry about the mess. And thank you both for not turning us in just yet too." Orin and Matt smile and matt points the way. Orville brushes himself off and says "let's go before they think we are involved in this. Orin nod in agreement.

Orin "How many people from the new unification are here? And how many people from other countries are here too?"

Orville "The unification is a good thing. The countries of California and Canada merging with the confederation is great. The money is what is going to be a problem. Converting from Dollars to Loonies for the coins. The bills for denominations for 5, 10, 20, 50, 100, 500, 1000 bills. The agreement of having coins for a penny through the 2 dollars is what California and Canada agreed to. But then again, they agreed to have our flag. So, it was a fair trade. Having the nation's flower be the maple leaf is going to be a change to deal with. We are going to miss having the yellow rose. But having the bear as our nations animal. Now that is going to be rough. Since it used to be a hawk."

Orin "Hey it could be worse it could've been a Nordiques."

Orville started to laugh hard with that answer.

Orville "Yes you are right about that."

Orin "Yearly wars of the clubs here?"

Orville "Well either Rodney or Becca start them. Because it happened this morning. The I would put even money on either one of them. But the smart money is of Rodney for this one. Maybe Becca had things in place, and it went wrong or right. But since she was working last night into this morning. Well, I had to say she didn't start this one. But now all the clubs are in it to win it. The club we had the unfortunate and yet fortunate luck running into their unsuccessful prank has the nicer lot of students in it. But by no means start a fight with them. And they do openly like you. Because not only did you speak their langue. You also didn't treat them like simpletons either. Reminding them to be careful of others without insulting them."

Orin "Meaning?"

Orville "They are going to recruit you into their club by hook and by crook. Once they find out you work at the shop. They are never going to let you go anywhere else. They have a long-standing feud with Rodney since grade school. And that is going to cause a big amount of trouble between the both of you. May I suggest you join no clubs at the moment. Once you are truly settled in the school and at home. Alight?"

Orin "Yeah, I get it. And I agree with you. I don't do the club thing. So, I will try not to get involved if I don't have too."

Orville "Okay, now let's go the safe way that Matt suggested. Now we will see all the pranksters at work today."

As they walk through the wings and cut through the areas Matt has suggested. Orin sees the pranks for the Dormitories from each of the clubs in full scale. Seeing things from fireworks through graffiti in certain dorms. People running out of the buildings half naked to full nude. People dyed in colors that would make others laugh. Orville just simply sighs as the shenanigans go on.

Orville 'Don't worry they will be too busy to pull these stunts once the Trimester starts. And the other festivities as well. Such as the college season of Hockey, football, tennis, and basketball. The school has multiple mascots too. The tennis mascot is interesting one at that. Also, the Weib girls are on that team too. People tend to notice of tight and revealing their uniforms are. You play hockey?

Orin "I do but, I'm not that good. I didn't make it to the jv team in London Ontario."

Orville "Couldn't throw a punch?"

Orin "Nope, I could barely skate at the level required for the JV team let alone the Varsity team."

Orville "Oh…I can fix that up easily. I can talk to the speed skating coach we have here. He can teach you how to skate. He's done wonders with people with no foot eye coordination. I bet your hand eye is really good."

Orin sighs "Yeah.. I can pass and shoot like it's nothing. I just can't skate worth a dam and no one willing to teach me."

Orville "Don't worry, If, he can't do it. I know I can do it too. So don't worry too much. You'll get in shape to join the JV team at least by the las quarter of the season."

Orin "Thanks, but I down own the equipment for a fitting let alone…." Orville Interrupts Orin.

Orville "I said don't worry about such things. You have a lot of money now. But your mother doesn't want it going through your head. The child support and a few other things. The fact is. You are staying in your father house. He usually uses the apartment in the main administration building here. But since he rarely uses the house. Your mother is now getting around to the things he left behind and all the things getting you two settles here. And yes, there are way too many people that are sticking their noses in to it as well. The Wiebs are on top of that list. Rodney wants to know more as well. Also, other that you didn't meet. Your panic attack really helped you out of a uncomfortable situation. These people Jacob and Horatio handles when your father isn't here. Tania knows what is going on and she is keeping her trap usually shut for a change. Which is a good thing too. So now understand you finally have means to accomplish a lot here." As the walk to the main building in the center of the campus. Orin notices that the bookstore has no windows and is in the center of the building itself. Same with the cafeteria. While scanning around the store he sees five young ladies' wave for him to come over there.

Colleen "Hey Orin come over here!"

Rory "Orville is with him. Are you sure that is a good idea?

Rachel "Don't worry, the kind old man won't say too much. Also, Mom really likes him a lot too. Besides Becca is to be in her best behavior. Isn't that right Becca?"

Becca "He can finally meet Saundra now."

As the two approaches the women. The final one walks up front of them with a quizzical look at Orin. Her eyes are sizing him up and down. He looks exactly like Wihelmine. This must be Cassandra; Orin thinks to himself. Ten he hears a voice, "you're a quiet one even in thought. No wonder mom likes you."

Orin looks puzzled. And sees Saundra smiling like a cat who eat a canary. She walks towards them and introduces herself.

Saundra "Hello I am Cassandra. I prefer Saundra. You must be Orin?"

Before he gets to answer Orville makes his presence know.

Orville "Hello ladies funny meeting you al here?"

Colleen "Hello your lordship. Orin has been really kind to us. He left a note about how we left some things behind, and he has put it for safe keeping."

Orville "Oh he is kind like his mother that way. I presume nothing missing?"

Orin "Nope not that I am aware of. I don't like to go through other people's stuff. Like I don't like to go through my stuff. I am respectful that way." He hears snickering from behind him and sees Rodney waving to everyone. The Ladies simply glare. If looks could kill. There looks at Rodney would kill regiments of soldiers. Then he hears in his head "Oh…You have no idea about that." Orville Looks around and stares at Saundra. She gives a puzzled look at him. As he is about to ask a question Rodney clears his throat.

Rodney 'What are you doing you crotchy old man?" as he smiles.

Orville "I offered my services to this young lad. Unlike like you he knows how to treat his elders with manner!" With an excited but cold tone.

Rodney 'Aren't supposed to have the town meeting about; I don't know how the cleaning up of sanitation or, how the funds get to the schools here. I don't know how about the law enforcement and crime rates. Why are you here showing this young man around? Isn't this beneath your station here you dammed hobo?" As the ladies' hiss in unison. Orin's face looks blank. He hears another voice 'Dam you are very calm. I've baited everyone here and your cool as a fucking cucumber. You present a challenge. I know why Matt and the others want you. They don't know where you work yet. And I sense the old man told you to stay out of it all together. Hmm will you do that I wonder." Everyone looks at Orin blank yet calm demeanor. As Orin begins to speak. He hears Saundra utter something low and calm.

Saundra 'You know Rodney. It takes a few weeks usually to show how rude you can be. Why start tis early?"

Rodney "Well, he did bump into a rival of mine. Nd that rival wants to recruit him to his club. Since we both are going to work in the same shop. I'm either going to claim him into my club or make sure he doesn't join a club. But the hockey team I will abide by. We need a few more would be backup players on the team." As he looks at Orin as a thing not a person.

Orville "Boy, you're overstepping your bounds here. You have to contend with Horatio, Jacob, Miguel De le Guy the 36 and lastly, I, in these matters. The boy has been through a lot already." Then they hear a voice "Ahh Rodney he also forgot about me as well before him." As they turn around. The see Rev Jonathan R. Kingsley.

Rev Kingsley "Starting up trouble with your grandfather I see as usual. I don't care what your grandmother says about her husband. It gives you no right to judge him this harshly. Also, no one can claim this young boy for anything either. Tania has overstepped her bounds in this case already. And I already had a really, really, long chat about that too. And another thing young man. He changed the schedule last night and informed everyone about it. Also, young man. The commotion you have already started up with the first prank till now is unacceptable!"

Rodney "Are you going to give me another sermon about being kind to others. Not to be mean to others again blah, blah. Blah blah" Orville is flustered now and the Weib girls are equally flustered as well. The Becca walk front and center.

Becca 'Now, you grandfather is a kind and gentle man. When he needs to be. Even I have enough respect to the power he wields. And I cause even less trouble than you!" The crowd that is gathering say Wahoo!" Orville simply smiles at Becca and Says 'You're taking this punishment heart this time?

Becca 'Yes you funny silly old man. I am sorry for what I did after I calmed down. But I'm not as bad as he is!" pointing at Rodney.

Colleen "If I didn't know any better, I say you were jealous Rodney" Kingsley simply snickers at the comment. Rodney now glares at the preacher. And then smiles and motions where the sun is shining through the window.

Rodney "Why don't you and the Weibs walk through the sunlight?" And laughs about it with a mean spirited look on his face. Yet he is charming enough that everyone else laugh as it as well.

Orville "You know welp, I can make your life really miserable here. Ordinarily I would show restraint about it too. But because you're itching for a fight that badly. I'm well nice enough to oblige you for it. However, thew rules of engagement are all mine and you have to abide by them or forfeit whatever I dam well please." Rodney eyes narrow as e is about to say something. A voice shouts "Rodney! What are you doing this time in here!" As everyone looks is Pauline. A Slender looking woman with blonde hair with purple eyes. People assuming contact lenses for that...

Orville "Saved by the dammed bell boy. Another time perhaps. But I remind you. Tania and Pauline's other sisters are well going to hear about this. And I'll make sure they will tan your hide. If I don't find a way to do it first mind you. And I'll have the help of five certain young ladies to boot." As he smiles. The Weib sisters look at Rodney with grins and the eyes tell the rest of how they are going to enjoy whipping Rodney to his place. And the girls in unison "Bye Rodney, let Pauline save you for now. However, when our mother hears of this too. You'll be sorry!" Rev Kingsley just laughs out loud and hard. And walks to Pauline.

Rev Kingsley "Pauline. Rodney has now been banned from the club he created and is banned from all extra circular activities until the President returns from his Trip. Also, he is to clean up all the messes made on the grounds and the walls and the holes that were made. From this moment on until the end of the trimester. If you do not like it. Well too bad you'll have to take it up with Jacob, Horatio myself, Orville, and the president. Knowing he will be busy when he returns. I wouldn't hold your breath for a quick meeting anytime soon." Orville simply smiles.

Orville "Tank you Johnny. I do appreciate this a whole lot." The Weib girls are laughing hysterically. Rodney is incensed and attempts to speak. But another voice "Now young man. You did start a fight you couldn't finish." And you see another slender woman with rd hair and green eyes.

"Please forgive me young man my name is Kathy." Looking to Orin.

Orin Nice to meet you Kathy."

Orville "Orin this is Pauline Goodspeed and her Sister Kathy McLean. Where is Donna?"

Pauline answers "She is with Tania right now at the shop. We were seeing what the commotion is about. And we do agree with Johnny's assessment and disciplinary actions in this case." As she scowls at Rodney. Rodney jaw drops and before he speaks.

Kathy "Utter one more syllable and I'll have you tared and feather in front of the whole school. The pour molasses for good measure. Having you squawk like a chicken to boot. Never, ever start a fight you're not prepared to finish. And just you wait till Tania hears of this from us. Meaning all of us. She just might let the old man here get some satisfaction. You're not to cause this type of commotion. Do you hear me!" as she yells it out.

Rodney puts his head and lets out a sigh and Looks at Orville "Yes, sir and mam. I'd better get start now, right?"

Rev Kingsley "Not quite yet young man. As manners demand. You must apologize to everyone here. Before Your two Aunts take you out of here and tell your grandmother." Rodney now sneers at the Rev. Kingsley as Johnny smiles.

Rodney looks at his aunts. They simply give him cold looks.

Rodney "I'm sorry everyone I went too far. As for the punishment. It's a fair one too."

Orville "Good, but everyone will enjoy themselves within reason. Now I'll escort the boy and the ladies to purchase their books." As Orville gather them all around. Orien hears in his head. "This isn't over. Not by a long shot old man. Nor your new golden child either. The Weibs are not stupid they will figure it out. Sooner or later. And I'll have the last laugh about this. I am a patient. All, I have to do is wait. Just wait it out. Another voice states "You are losing control Rodney. You did go too far this time. Also, the others can hear you. I'm not sure if the boy can hear you. If he can then he is more dangerous than his father. He knows when to speak and when not to speak." The Voice "Well he has been on the run since he was four. He pay attention to things that don't add up. So I would be very careful around him. You tipped your hand way to early with him. His artwork isn't that good, is it? Oh…It's really good. Grandma is still raving over the works he didn't finish yet." The Voice "Now dear, you can't hold number one forever. Then again, the boy isn't interested in proving himself. He just wants to get educated and get to know his relations. After all, he is one of few left, of his kind if he can hear this." Orin just stares blankly playing stupid keeping his head clear. As the girls look over his schedule and theirs'. Saundra looks at Orin with a questioning look. As her eyes narrow, he hears" Wow you are a really cool customer. You heard all that and didn't blink nor made a face to give it away. You are not going to clue me in either. That is okay by me. I've met only one other that got under his skin like that. But I must confess you are a far cry from Totowa. Then again you just surprise us all. You know how to keep cool. We have a lot of the same classes by the way." Saundra simply smiles now. Orin still gives a blank look not letting on he heard the whole thing. Saundra simply smiles more and ask aloud.

Saundra "So where are you from?" Orville laughs a bit.

Orin "London Ontario. I've bounced around the California territories as well as the wester Nord territories." Saundra simple smiles and then says "Oh…you have been around."

Orin "Yes I have been around. Have you traveled before?"

Saundra "Yes, I have travelled through out Europe. We've all have travelled through out Europe and Asia. We were very young when that happened." Rory giggles.

Saundra "What is it my sister?"

Rory "we told you he was different. But you didn't believe us?"

Saundra "Becca endorsements ruins everything for most people. Especially if they don't know er very well."

Orin "When we met, she was more concerned on who bounced a quarter off her ass. During a panic attack."

Saundra laughs out loud. "Oh…. That explains a lot. You honestly didn't know who did do that?"

Orin "No."

Saundra "Oh, well I would've liked to have met the person to do that. It's rare when someone, hits the target with her. The rest of us usually gets the daggers for her antics." Glaring at Becca.

Becca 'How many times do I have to apologize about those things to all of you?" The rest of her sisters in unison "Not enough! After all the trouble, you usual cause!".

Becca simply frowns looking at Orin and she says, "Well at least I didn't cause trouble with this one."

Rory "Well at least not yet. He doesn't know you like everyone else around here does."

Orin "It's sound like I'm an interloper in an argument here?"

Colleen "Well said Orin. Well said, girls I think we better lower it a few notches here. Agreed?"

Saundra "I agree with them on this. Airing out dirty laundry isn't always a good thing. Especially when there are too many ears around. Wouldn't you agree Rory, Becca?"

They nod in agreement. As looking to Colleen for help. Colleen nods in agreement with Rory and Saundra. The girls now know its' a three two split against Becca and Rory. Meaning now they have to keep quite for now. Becca simply smiles with a narrowed eye. Orin hears in his head "Wow Saundra is really protective of him. I haven't seen her this territorial since Totowa?"

Colleen is looking at Orin with a quizzical look and wonders if he can hear all their thoughts now? Colleen thinks about projecting. She really hates doing this without permission. But decides better not to do this for now. AS she nods towards the bookstore. She begins to speak to Orin.

Colleen 'So what is your schedule again? I'm sure Orville was trying to give you the whole tour before the interruptions." As Orin hands the schedule over to Colleen. Orville interjects.

Orville "Colleen, can you be a dear and get three of the totes over here. Also the a bottle water. I haven't seen his schedule yet."

Colleen 'Oh…of course!" She hints to Orin to give Orville the schedule. Orin hands over the schedule to Orville. As Orville scans the schedule. Collen comes back with he totes and the water.

Orville 'Thank you Colleen. I wish people wouldn't underate your kindness to others." Colleen simply smiles and kisses Orville on his forehead. Orville smiles. "Thank You Child."

As Orville looks over the schedule. He makes a few interesting noises.

Orville "Now ladies, and Orin. I want this to go through with ease. Good news all the books are here. Bad news the crowd is starting to filter in here." As the crowd is forming inside the bookstore. The girls get all the books fast. Also, Orin watches in amazement how orderly the ladies work in getting all the books. Also, they have his books too. Down to all the extra stuff for his supplies for his art courses and paper and notebooks as well. Then Orin notices the time. It's been barley fifteen minutes. Orin looks around puzzled. When he came to pay for the books. He realized with his vouchers he was able to just walk out wit the things he came to buy. As he and Orville are leaving the school bookstore. He Bumps into Matt again. But this time he smirks at Orin and Orville and the Wieb girls. Looks directly at Orin and then he about to ask a question until Saundra interrupts his train of thought.

Saundra "Hi, Matt how are you doing this fine morning?"

Matt "Well my experiment went wrong again this morning. The I found out that your new neighbor is working in Tania's shop. And he is very bright as well, by the way."

Colleen "Really, how would you know about that?"

Matt "He was able to explain an energy source in layman's terms. And also stating that he isn't the smartest man in the room. However, he has the most common sense in the room. I really like that about him. Has he looked through the clubs yet?"

Becca "He may join the hockey team. Once he finds a good skating coaches."

Matt "Oh…I know a few here and there. I would be happy to help out. Are you sure he will have time for a club or two?"

Orville "I would like hi to settle in before he decides on a club or two."

Matt "I wouldn't dream to take away from his studies nor his job either. It's just Rodney is starting the clubs wars this trimester already. Now the rest of the clubs are ready to make his club and other he's associated with."

Orin "Outside of hockey. I tend to keep to myself really. I apricate it the help for the skating coaches."

Matt "Sure, not a problem. I would follow Orville's advice about staying out of the way for the clubs. However, the Hockey team and the rest of the sports teams are considered clubs here. Just to let you know. They tend to stay away from the rest of the drama of the clubs."

Orin "Thanks, for the heads up. I appreciate it."

Matt "One more thing the tutors here are part of the clubs too. So, If you unaffiliated. It may be harder to get one. If you're going for a team, However It would be easier to get a tutor."

Orin "Well I have a lot of work to do then. I guess I'll start with a skating coach."

Orville "In order to get a coach. You have to make it to a team. Meaning the bench warming part at the very least."

Matt "Well we could get him on the spade squad in the JV team. They get the coaching easier than most. But Getting Slava Fetisov to take you in would be rough. But he does like developing players from the ground up."

Orville "I can talk to him about it easily. He owes me a few favors, but besides. Giving him a chance to mold a young player from the ground up would be nice. He usually gets player that have been taught wrong. Orin here would be a bit of a relief instead of the rest of the characters he gets."

Matt "I agree, you're going to learn form one of the greatest players Russia has ever produced. He has won multiple Gold Olympic medals and a silver one too. But he doesn't like talking about the silver medal.

He almost went to a gulag for bringing home the silver medal that year with the rest of the team."

Orin "Oh...I guess never mentioned that game?"

Orville "It would be best if he mentions the game and that you don't bring it up."

Matt "I would let him bring it up. But he is a good man. Left the right way. SO he isn't on the crap list of players form Russia. At least he became a citizen after he entered the NHL."

Orin "Oh...he's that Slava Fetisov! Wow that is going to be rough. But worth the time learning under him!"

Orville "Yes, it is. He's a tough man. But then again, he did play for the red army team in Russia. So, remember, he didn't grow up here. He'll remind you how lucky you have it here. Also, he is a very kind and loving man. But he will be rough with you to toughen you up."

Orin "That is okay. I am used to people trying to make me tough. However, for that game you have to be toughen up to survive the punishment you get on and off the ice."

Matt and Orville simply smile. Then Becca runs up to them. "You're not going to believe this!"

Matt and Orville say, "What is it now?!"

Becca "Rodney signed Orin to twelve of the clubs he is involved with!"

Orville with a very cold look. "Where is that devil now!"

Rory and Rachel "He's with Katy and Pauline. But... Xenia is in the building as well!"

Orville "Rachel go get the three ladies and tell them if they value what little they have there are to see me now!"

Rachel and Rory simply nod in agreement "We'll go now my lord." In unison.

As they runoff quickly Orin feels a cold touch on his arm and its Colleen giving him a very sad look. "I'm surprised you are not having an attack yet?" Orin is trying to keep it at bay and gives a nervous smile. And that was all the information Colleen needed to affirm that he is having one. But with the support around him. He is keeping it together barely. Now Becca walks up to them. "What sort of mischief is that nut up to this time?

Colleen "I don't know. But I wouldn't want to be him right now. Orville is really mad this time around."

Saundra comes up to them. "What do you expect from Rodney. He causes more trouble than you Becca. And he tends to bring a lot of chaos with him. He is always up to something. Now the problem is what is he up to? With Kathy, Pauline, and Xenia here. We know something is really, up. They are coming here to make sure everything is alright?"

Becca "Yeah, I have a talent for small level pranks and practical jokes. But Rodney ad I loathe to admit ti. Is on a totally different playing field. He's just mad that we don't help him with his schemes and mischief."

Colleen 'More like that you don't help with those ideas and plans of his sister."

Becca 'True, but you know he is just mean spirited in general. But he is their favorite for some reason."

Orin "Who favors him?"

Saundra "Kathy, Pauline, Xenis and…drum roll please Tania!"

Becca 'It seems you knocked him out of a pecking order in a day. He doesn't take well to that."

Orin 'oh…Is that a good thing?"

The three ladies smile and in unison say "Depends on your definition of good."

Orin 'Terrific. Now I need is something to drink while Orville takes care of this right?"

Saundra "That is if he can take care of it. They are chatting with his lordship now. And its seem it doesn't bode well with the two of you in this case. Seeing Rory and Rachel trying to be peace makers in this. They are failing miserably. I wonder why?"

Orin "Let me guess they a usually very successful?"

Becca 'usually they are but when it comes to those three sisters. They are at a lost. Even with our mother in tow it's tough. Yeah, but they back off completely once we mention Nana will have a word with them about this!" Saying loud enough that Kathy, Pauline, and Xenia look at Becca with a sneer. Orville simply smiles when that happens. And the ladies apparently back down. However, Xenia simply states to Rory and Rachel" Your nana isn't going to be around forever you know. She is getting up there. Also, I wouldn't be too proud about having around also. Well, all have to go. But Rodney is yours to deal with Orville. But understand he did have approval from Tania to do all of what he did. But you are right more of a heads up would've been appreciated." As Orville and the girls walk back towards matt and Orin. They all looked stressed.

Orin "So what happened now/"

Orville "Becca, thanks but you shouldn't have done that."

Becca "I only wanted to put an end to it."

Orville 'I know… So, I'm not going to scold you. But… It makes it more difficult to deal with later on. Especially when she makes her quarterly visits here. And she is about due for one."

The ladies in unison "Oh…."

Orville "Now let's take this young man around and show him the rest of the school. With all the sub levels it has too. He will need to know all the ins and outs of this place."

Orin eyes widen with the knowledge of that fact there are sub levels to the school itself.

As the tour continues Orin see the hallways with natural light and the ones with artificial sunlight without the UV rays. It seems they calming and soothing entering hallways with a vanilla color. As they go through the hallways. Orin notices that there are sublevels. When he sees street names with the sub level. Orin does a triple take.

Orin "What is it with the street names?"

Colleen "We have a condition that we burn easily with UV light. So there is a subset of tunnels with entrances to very street in the town. Much like New York City's subway system. You must have seen them with the tour?"

Orin "Oh… Yeah I saw them was wondering about all that. Aren't all of you worried that someone can use these tunnels to sneak in and out unnoticed?"

Orville "That is whey the CBI main headquarters are here. That is one of their highest priorities. To monitor the use of the tunnels. Those with the UV light allergy. Well, they can use the tunnels with the students in law enforcement. Also, the people they take along. However, you need permits to use them. Good thig you were given access to the tunnels as well as part of your enrollment. As long if an official show you around."

Orin "Good thing I have the town mayor showing me around."

Orville smiles "Right you are about that young man. There are a lot of people here who have allergies to UV light. Some born with them. Other developed them as they got older in life in this town. Because of that we have these tunnels and the best medical school in the country dedicated to the research of ending this allergy to Ultraviolet rays."

Orin "That is why Rodney made the crack about walking in front for the window."

Matt "Yeah but I think I came up with a polymer to allow the sunlight in but not the ultraviolet light through. It's in the developmental stages."

Rory "Really Matt! That means if it works right? I can finally see a …."

Saundra "Don't get your hopes up. He will need a test subject to see if it works right?"

Matt sighs "Yeah…I will need someone to test it. That why I don't really talk abut the stuff I'm working on that much. I don't want to get a lot of people's hopes up. Just to fail those hopes."

Orville 'I don't blame you, at all son. Not all your inventions work on the first try. That projectile this morning was a perfect example of things."

Matt "Thanks for understanding."

Orville "Nothing to worry about. Who did volunteer?"

Matt "Rev Kingsley."

Orville "Why am I not surprised that he would do that. Then again before he developed his condition. He did like to go surfing on the beach. He does miss that."

Orin "Yes he does. After the conversation we had last night. He and my mother are old friends. Boy did they catch up on a lot of things last night."

Rachel "Really, your mom knew him before he became a preacher? I bet she has a lot of good juicy stories about the man?"

Orin "Let's say that they have so much blackmail on each other. The rest of the people involved would silence them both. But getting either of them to talk. Well, that is going to take a lot of effort." Orin then wonders how much effort he is going to need. Mom never once talked about John Kingsley. Then he feels a strange sensation in his head. His vision is getting blurred. And then the hallway stretches longer to infinity. The everything starts to spin. Then he sees a man at the end of the hallway He just smiles. Ands says "Orville, you know most people can't come through this section without explicit permission?" As Orville glares at the man. The sensation stops. The man has a wiry build and fit. Then he notices a rank insignia on one of his shoulders. The patch on his chest states Suicide Bolts. With the rank of Sargent.

Orville "Listen they have all the proper credentials right here and the new young man here as well."

The Sargent looks over everything "I'll have to check everything out here Orville. We are running a few war games down here today. Don't worry it's just a few drills. I don't want you and the kids to get caught up in one of the drills."

Orville "It is okay Clyde. I understand, he is new. And he is a customer of moon dogs as well."

Clyde "Oh...I understand perfectly. He is the newcomer everyone is talking about. The one that moved into Owen's House, right?"

Orville "Yes he is. I would like not to bother everyone in your group. Nor anyone asking too many questions of you and the others."

Clyde "Let me check this out first stay here."

Orin "Orville what is going on here?"

Orville "Well, my boy thing is. This is a military college as well, right?" Orin nods in acknowledgement.

Orville "Well militaries tend to recruit officers from here. Hence there are things here that are matters of national and international security. So, every now and then there are spot security checks. All the credentials are valid. Matt has some, the girls have them too. I have them. They are just checking you out now. Clyde and Miguel De Le Guy, the 36th works with securing the place in general. Miguel handles topside. Clyde handles down below. So once he is satisfied, we can go on our way." AS Orville finished up with that Clyde approaches them.

Clyde "Orville why didn't you tell this was...." Orville gives Clyde a look.

Clyde "Ahh ahem. Forgive my manner. My name is Clyde Armstrong. As you can se my rank is Sargent. I run security for the tunnels here. Young man did you know you have a tunnel straight to your residence? To the basement to be precise." Orin nods with a no.

Clyde "Well I think Orville, or the ladies take you home that way. It's usually the fastest way here for you. Also, because this is also a military installation as well. You have clearance of a cadet here in the college. Due to your living situation. SO, I suggest you learn to travel down here as well. When the snowstorms hit. And they do hit hard. Everyone uses the tunnels to get around. You will see others in the college using these tunnels. I am one of the many that keep them secure. We also ask for the civilians for help of projects from time to time in your classes. May I have your schedule as well? Just so everyone knows, down here not to bother you if they see you here." Orin hand over his schedule to Clyde. Clyde scans it and upload it to the tablet he had on hand.

Orin "If it's not too much trouble? How often do you see Owen down here?"

Clyde smiles "Actually a lot often than he likes. Part of his duties is managing the military part of the college and all the information and developmental projects here as well, One of the reasons why there is a vast tunnel system that the public and the military uses. His quarters are her as well. But I can't show you around unless he wishes it." As he looks at the girls who have a very sad face hearing about this.

Clyde "Ladies, he gets sent out a lot of the military invites from our war college division. That is why he away a lot. Then again So Is Horatio or Jacob when he is in town to take his place. So, Orville sow him around with everything. If you don't have time, send him to me. And I'll show him around. It's the least I can do. But I can't do it today. A lot of things are going on down here now. So, please no arguments go up a few levels and take the west substation around. I know it's the long way around." All nod in agreement and follow the directions as Clyde suggested. As they walk up a few levels up and go for the substation. Saundra looks sad with Becca, Rory Colleen and Rachel.

Orin "Ahh…. Ladies what is wrong?"

Orville is about t interject and Colleen "Our father always works down there too. Mom never talk about it. So, the closest thig we have in the balcony at night. So, we were hoping to catch a glimpse of him down here. And we didn't. SO, we are disappointed. It's not your fault Orin. You didn't know. So don't feel sorry you brought this up. You don't know your father as well, right?"

Orin "Just a few memories, and images. But you're right no full remembrance as of yet. But I do feel lonely when I think of him. I know I miss him on a very primal level. How about all of you and your father?"

Rory "We feel the same way. Even though we care not to openly admit to it. Ad I am feeling the glares sisters. But let's be honest with ourselves. We do miss our father." The rest of the Wieb girls nod in agreement.

AS the rest of the tour goes through without a hitch. Orin walks back topside to the house and hears Tanis voice "Young man come over here!" AS he walks towards the direction of the vice and sees the game shop. Noticing it's nighttime. Wondering if he had to cook for himself again. AS he walks into the shop.

CHAPTER 11B

Second Night through day before school begins. Lessons from Tania and how to be a gentleman in Andersonville. T-minus Five days before the trimester begins.

Orin enters the shop behind Tania. He sees Rodney cleaning up the shelves and he simply sneers at him. Tania gives a disapproving look to Rodney, and he stops. But if looks could kill. Orin believes he would be dead by now if not worse. The he hears in his hears "Boy you got that right. You and the old man spoiled a lot of my fun." As Orin dismisses what he heard in his head. Tania turns around and smiles. And says "You are a very cool customer, like your father. He never lets anyone know that he hears them too. Such a very smart lad you are."

Orin Simply looks dumbfounded at Tania. Trying to pass off ignorance. Tania simply laughs. "Now, Now my boy. My weird sisters know that you can hear them. They told me as such. But you have such manners that you stay quite about it. That is good to a point. However, it's rude not to let anyone know you can hear us. So, what have you heard today?"

Orin is now nervous. Understanding that Tania can smell bull crap a mile away. He decides to tell half the truth. "All I heard was a loud high pitch noise. I do suffer from occasional migraines. I never make a big deal about them. But the lights in the sub levels in the school did bother me a lot today. I experienced vertigo for a bit too."

Tania "Oh my... You, poor dear, so you heard nothing at all?"

Orin "Nothing I could ascertain as a distinguished voice. Nothing I could call coherent."

Tania "Ah...I see, well maybe we are pushing things a bit too fast for you. I've had run ins with your mother's family relations before. They aren't the nicest of people. Down, right rude and obnoxious. Worse than Rodney here. And he has met them before." Rodney smiles and he's thing about something as he looks at Orin directly.

Rodney "So what would you use in a War Scythe 90K city landscape with 8 Battalions of the myme-mox fodder. Thee Colossus's with a armored battalion of dragon wings as back up?"

Orin "Well I would use the Asgardian spear laser basic for the fodder. But I would use 2 battalions. Due to the special ability to throw plasma waves 5 times per soldier. Then I would have 12 Frost giants for the Colossus's, and they would over run the dragon battalions easily. For the mop up % sets of Valkyrie Calvary to wipe the mess clean. With that basic setup. You can clear the field within 10 moves of less. If you know how to use that setup correctly. It's one of the hardest to get right let alone role correctly. Good thing you can role ones and still win with it."

Rodney whistles "Dam, I never thought of using that combo like that. They all have extra roles once something hits. If you do the combo right. You can clear over half the field in one turn!" Now Rodney looks worried and impressed at the same time. Now Orin hears his voice in his head "Dam, why I didn't think of that earlier. No wonder he is a cool customer. He constantly strategizes everything in his head. He observes way too much. No wonder the girls are fascinated by him. Also, Tania and her three sisters as well." Rodney then smiles.

Rodney speaking "Have you ever done a total field sweep in one turn with this setup?"

Orin "I've done it twice. But the players were overconfident about their defenses. Also, they couldn't think using the so call useless pieces to make a one turn board sweep. The again I did this twice in Moon Dog's in London Ontario twice in the same day to win that tournament. The shortly after that my prizes were sent to the local location that was too far away. I just got my prizes the other day for that." Rodney and Tania jaws dropped.

Tania "Horatio gave you your prizes and the credit. Because you were the top player that could do that. Yeah, but I needed all the new expansions and scrapes to figure out hot to make the one turn board wipe a automatic thing. And those expansions are expensive now. And they were expensive when they came out." As Tania look at Rodney and smiles back to Orin.

Tania "Now I know why Rodney started way too much trouble about having you in all his clubs. Just like your father a tactical genius! I've seen him do things in strategy games that would make the most battle-hardened soldiers jaws drop."

Orin "I didn't know he did that."

Tania "Oh.. I keep forgetting. You didn't spend much time with him. And you noting of your family on either side of the tree. SO how was your fist day looking around campus?"

Orin "Where is my mom?"

Tania "She is at work. It's her first night. And she didn't want you to be alone. So, I offered to make you dinner in the shop here and talk about your day. And apologize for Rodney's rather abrasive behavior today. He was supposed to help you out. Not draft you in his hijinks with the rest of the school."

Rodney 'He made friends with my nemesis Matt at the club circuit today."

Tania "Now will you drop it that he finally beat you at your own game last trimester."

Orin "What game was this?" and Tania chuckles.

Tania 'You just gave him the answers to that. Rodney was the reigning champ of War Scythe 90K. For five years straight. The Now that you will be playing. Rodney is going to watch how you play. And if he does beat you fair and square. No shenanigans for losing to him alright Rodney! The shop having a champion in this game is a good thing." Rodney throws his hands up and says "Alright Tania. Alright I won't throw a hissy fit if I lose to Orin here!"

Orin "So, what smells so good here?"

Tania "Now I have dumplings with southern friend streak and potatoes. With gravy and a side of mixed vegetables. With raspberry herbal teas." He smells the food and sees the table set up for three.

Orin "Wow this looks great. Eating during store hours?"

Tania "I usually have people and customers bring food here. It's not a big deal for us to have food here. It makes it easier for customers have a sense of community here. So, they make themselves at home so to speak. The customer really loves it here. But Moon Dogs have legacy customers that go there. But Horatio does get items I need. And I get items he needs. OS it's a friendly competition."

Orin sits at the table, set himself to eat. "Well, this looks great. Can't wait to dig in. If I may."

Tania "By all means. I know most nights will be like this. So don't be shy. Now eat up. How did you like the school?"

Orin "Well what I saw was interesting. We happened stance into the military portion of the sub levels. Hat is for the college and other programs, right? I don't want to know the details. I just want to know where not to stick my nose in the wrong areas."

Tania "Oh...who did you bump into?"

Orin "Clyde Armstrong."

Rodney "Whoa! I don't fuck with Clyde. He's part of a spec ops group that is run from there. He did check your credentials out?"

Orin As he is chewing on the steak with a gulp. "Yes, he did. He was about to mention a few things about my father. But Orville just gave him a look and he decided not to go into it. He also stated that there was a door in our house that leads to the tunnels. Hat I have access to open and close it if necessary. I didn't know about the tunnels. It isn't in any of the public literature about this place? Why do you keep it a secret?"

Tania looks a bit flustered with the questions. However, she regains her composure and states the following "Well, it goes back to the Civil War. This was a prison camp originally. So, a lot of atrocities were committed here. Also, the first set of tunnels were escape tunnels. After time as new buildings were bult up we made more. Ten built up some more. Much like San Francisco, with the old city underneath the current city. After the earthquake. We in the community kept building more. Until the School was built to be the central point of all the tunnels and ways to go to the streets. We were going to make it a sub rail system. Much like New York Chicago, Detroit even L.A…Afterwards with the first and second world wars. WE kept building the tunnel network. We decided that the locals would know about these networks. Also, our military and the union military would know about them as well. Because our confederate bureau of investigation main training center is the school. With our main Military college too. We boast we are better than west point. But we are their equal up north. However, they do war games in the tunnels for strategic exercises. Most likely they were conducting one and didn't want any of the students to get hurt. That is why you saw the spec ops trainer lurking around today."

Orin "Whoa… I can see why he told us exactly were to, go to avoid the trouble with he exercises today."

Rodney 'Yeah it's a good thing. Did he try to mention your dad at all?"

Orin "Yeah he did. He states that other colleges have him visit their facilities often."

Tania "Well it's true. After all he is the president of the school. One thing you don't want to brag about. He tends to be harsh with relations in the school in general. Your father has t represent the school and all it's specialties to the world. Way too often. Jacob and Horatio rotate the responsibilities. Then He has to run Moon Dogs for a while. HE likes running the game and comics and card shops. He even runs here when I need a break." As Orin finishes up the steak and dumplings Feeling full. Tania pours some tea in his cup. And she looks skeptically at him.

Tania 'Your Mother hasn't taught you manners or do you have a Northerner's sense of manners?"

Orin "I have a midwestern etiquette. But I know different regions have different standards. What are the standards here?" Rodney Laughs as Stoner Boy enters the shop.

Stoner Boy "Well, well, well! If it isn't the newcomer to our humble town that has a population of a city! Care for a drag good boy?" As Tania looks rather uncomfortable with Stoner Boy arriving.

Rodney "Aren't you supposed to be holding a gathering of sorts right about now?"

Stoner Boy "Why yes I am. But I wanted this young man to experience on of my teachings fist hand. That is if you don't mind tania? Were you in the middle of something with him? After feeding him and all."

Tania "Well we were going over the manners set in this fine town."

Stoner Boy "Oh...Yeah, that is important. Tell you what Tania. I'll come back after you finish with that. If that is okay with you, young man?" Orin is looking at Tania. She simply smiles and says "That will be fine stoner boy. I wouldn't offer him anything just yet. He's not ready for a full taste of your wares." As Stoner Boy laughs "Yes, Tania, I will let him be of age before I offer him anything. But I will pass it by his mother first."

Tania laughs "Okay, sure I get you there. But let Erin think it over really carefully."

Stoner Boy "Well his mother can confirm I have the really good shit!" and laughs

Orin feeling uncomfortable" Want any food?"

Stoner Boy "Why thank you young sire. I'll have a few things here and there."

Tania smiles "Now you do have common etiquette. But there is a lot more in Andersonville about our manners set."

Stoner Boy "Best listen to Tania here. A lot of children of diplomats study here and visit here. Due to that. There are the Andersonville manners you will have to learn quickly. Because international incidents have been known to happen here. Because someone forgot their manners set."

Orin Oh... We I hope it isn't hard to learn?"

Tania "Not really its mostly the same. However, there are things that only the political science majors would know. Those are the things I will teach you over the next few days. Did you get your syllabus for your classes?"

Orin "Yes I do have them with me." As he hands it over to Tania.

Tania "Oh...you have a lot of practical classes. But none with any political slant. This won't, due at all. I'm going to have to teach you form the ground up. Then have you take, the test during the finals. I know you'll pass it without fail. Even my sisters will help." Stiner Boy looks at Orin and says "Boy you're going to have too much work on your hands. When her sisters get involved. SO, I would best pay attention. Too many things revolve around your manners here. Even though our mayor is considered, to be a witless oaf when it comes to manners. When in reality the witless oaf is Rodney over there." Rodney just gives a dirty look to Stoner Boy.

Rodney "If it were up to me. These rules would be gone luckily split. But I don't run anything in this town. Not even this shop."

Stoner Boy "That is a good thing, Rodney. You still don't have the maturity to run anything yet. Every time you run something. It goes horrible wrong. You just have to let a lot of things go. This way you will get batter at what you want out of life."

Rodney "That is what you and the Reverend say. As always."

Stoner Boy "But, do we tend to be right? You know what the answer is Rodney."

Rodney" yes your two tend to be right way too often. But why doesn't he accept the bong you have and toke up."

Stoner Boy "He will when it's his time. Not before or after his appointed time."

Tania and Rodney look at Stoner Boy and in unison "Okay!"

Tania "Now Stoner Boy if you don't mind. I need to check all his manners are up to par with some of our higher end customers?"

Stoner Boy "Sure, not a problem. Thanks for the delicious meal by the way." As he gathers himself up and his things. As he is about to leave. He hands Orin the bong. "Go ahead hold it."

Orin holds the bong. He notices its very warm and has a fuzzy feeling. He wonders what is making this warm and fuzzy. And as he is about to asks a question. Stoner Boy smiles "Don't worry, your time is coming soon. But you have to hear me speak in the wilds in the outskirts of town. Also, you better show up to the bible study from Rev Johnathan R Kingsley. Make sure make those studies." Orin simply nods his head in acknowledgement. Stoner Boy continues "Also, the study is tomorrow night. Don't be late. Just open your notebook and just listen."

Orin "Alright, just want to know why he does everything at night? If that isn't too much of a personal question?"

Tania "Well the parish. The Majority of it has the allergy to UV light. So, they can only things at night. Due to that, Johnny has to do things at night. He also developed the same allergy as well."

Orin "Oh… He's seemed rather upbeat rather for his condition?"

Tania "Yes, his faith carries him through. Even though he misses the sun and surfing in the sun as well."

Orin looks at Rodney and Orin says, "That was downright mean of you Rodney."

Rodney "I've already heard enough from Orville already. And tania gave me a good thrashing verbally too. Her sisters did a good job on me too."

Orin "Well, that was mean of you. Also, my day was good. Trying to memorize the maze so to speak of the corridors and the other entry ways."

Tania "Yes that is a bit much for one day. But you need to know how to talk with all our clientele. Because we have people that are rather eccentric about how they should be addresses and served."

Orin "Oh…Okay. I get it. So, what do I have to learn about?"

Tanis "Well… It has to do with a lot of family history of the area. Which families have the political power but no wealth. Versus the families that have the wealth but no political power. It's a rather interesting detente here. Between the families and the Societies, they run. Meaning the club houses, they run. Like the Knights of Galahad. To name one. That is where Miguel De le Guy, the 36th is a charter member. The members are the families that still exist. These societies have been around a long time. The Free Mason are another one of these societies. They have building and donate to the school here. They also activity recruit in the school as well from the secondary level through the university level."

Orin simply whistles "Wow, how many are here?"

Tania "Well, there are one hundred and forty-five of them shop here. And they all shop here as well. So, tutoring you while you work here is going to be my job with you. I hope you are a better study than Rodney. But you are expected to know how they would like to be treated with respect. Because you are a newcomer here. They will give you slack in the beginning. But they won't put up with your ignorance long because you are working here!"

Orin "Is there a book o the history of thee societies in the town I could read? Knowing it's going to add to my reading in general." Tania Laughs a bit.

Tania "Well to read about them you have to join them. So, all of this is passed word to mouth. With Stories and information. Because this all goes down as usual town gossip. You must know all the major players in these social clubs to navigate around here safely."

As Tania starts off with the Knights of Galahad. Explaining that Miguel De Le Guy the first started it. During the French and Indian war. With the first settlers in the new world. But never mention the battles in Saratoga New York. It's just a situation even Jacob doesn't want to talk about. Also, you never want to me Old Crow of that tribe either. He is a bit out there. That according to Mr. Gator-Star. The Knights of Galahad are ex templars and their families. They were relocated all over Europe. They have set up this society since 1760. They've fought in all wars pertaining to the Americas in modern history. What they call modern history is wars fought by the white man coming to the Americas."

Orin "Oh… His family goes way back."

Tania "Yes it does young man. I do like dealing with the Knights of Galahad personally. So you will see their kids shopping here. Some tend to be on the rfined side."

Rodney "That is a nice way of saying that are a bunch of snobs."

Tanis "Rodney now hush. You are in enough trouble for one day. And hearing Becca didn't cause trouble today. It's been good a day. For the most part. Anyways, dealing with Miguel's relatives can be a bit taxing to one's nerves. I will attest to that. But all in all, a good bunch of people overall. As for the other families in the society. Well, that is a different story. They tend to be either rathe warm or cold. In the worse senses of the words by the way."

Orin "What are the family names to watch out for?"

Tania "No need they will identify themselves with the social clubs they are associated themselves with. As for the Knights of Galahad. It's their handshake of sorts is what identifies them. Also, the signet pin they wear as well. Bot the men and women in the clubs. The is the great Order of the Racoons. Yes, I know using a racoon, really? Anyways then have a racoon hat or the pin. The order is not bad. But rather testosterone driven society. They just hangout once a week in the hall and plays cards and watch interesting movies and complain about their wives. Those kids are a rowdy sort. But the men have the hats or the pins. The daughter of the great order of the Racoons. Well, you have to deal with a lot of hazing and vetting to date one let alone marry one. I deal with the wives and children. They are not a bad bunch. But can get on your nerves right and mighty quick." Orin simply nods his head in acknowledgement.

As Tania continues with the first forty families. Orin head is about to explode with all the new information he wrote down. With his hands cramping to keep up with all the information. Orville walks into the shop. He notices how the table was set up. And notices the notebook filled with fresh writings. And asks Tania "So he did pass with flying colors I see."

Tania "Yes he did, and he is a good study as well. Got the first forty families down pat. But I was going to start on The Forty-first family. Then you came in to ruin my fun so to speak."

Orville "Trying to see his frying point. Then I walked in." As he is smiling.

Tania "Yes, and you ruined it for me…husband!" Orville laughs.

Orville "Now I need to convince him never to get married. And make sure you don't pick the wife! Then I'll call that a good day indeed!" Orville laughs harder.

Tania "Now you old coot. What are you doing here?" Orville laughs.

Orville "Now, now young lady. Manners makith woman. Be nice, I'm here to pick up the boy and escort him to his home. The Rev. Jonathan R Kingsley wishes to do a private bible study with him. Also explain a few things about his condition that he shares with the Wieb sisters." Tania simply gives a very cold look to him and sighs.

Tania "You're right it's a lot for information for one night. And he is going to get more the next few days. Going over all the social clubs in this town and their histories. But I need him to get this before weeks end Orville." Orville simply groans and then looks at Rodney.

Orville "Tania, don't get any bright ideas now. Best not to cram too much information too soon. He needs time to acclimate to his situation. Let him learn at his own pace. Nice and slow. The others will understand.

They already know too much too soon is bad for him. Besides he needs to get home and begin his Bible study with Johnny."

Tania just scowls at Orville and says "Yes you can take him now. I do know a few people he should meet. I would like this man to be around the proper sort. Orville, how about you?"

Orville answers "I agree with you whole heartly. However, you and I have drastically different ideas on the proper sort of people."

Rodney "Oh…Boy, here we go again?"

Orville "Rodney, no comments from you would be apricated between Tania and I on these matters."

Tania "Now, Rodney please stay out of this. Orville and I need to talk about things with what we have in mind. Now Orin pledge about what we ae trying to do here. Making your transition smooth."

Orin "II understand man. But it's way too much too soon. Plus, my early studies in the bible before classes actually start is a bit much. Don't you think so Orville?"

Orville "Well… Usually That would be true. However, since your mother and Johnny are old friends. You'll have to take that up with her. She happy having positive male figures in your life right now. I'm trying to make sure you're not overwhelmed here." As he gives an apologetic look.

Orin "I would like to slow down a little bit. It's way too much at once here. I have very little time to get things started with my classes and all the prep work from the professors. I need to get settled in my own way. Because all of you are moving way too fast for me. I need to settle down. I know I have six days before the trimester starts."

Rodney "Kiddo, what you call too fast now. Its slow around here. It gets faster than this. So, you really don't have the time you are requesting. There are a lot of well-endowed families come here and shop here. So…I know both of them are being considerate. But it's going to be bad for business."

Orin "Look, I just moved in. I appreciate all of this. But it's too dam fast for me. I need to be still and settle a bit." Orville puts his hands on Orin's shoulder. And he says 'Look, I know it's too fast for you. Usually, it takes three weeks for someone to acclimate to this place. That is why, I am suggesting no clubs. However, you to get him into the hockey JV team. Then he would get all the exercise and team building spirt. The he would be more available to branch out to the clubs then. So which families did you manage to cover?"

Tania "Oh… The Darquefelou's and, all of the families connected to them. I haven't started with our on wine just yet. Because he has meet many of his relations close to distant. Going over all the Ukrainian and Romanian and Russian customs. Also, other custom of the deep south developed by German and English crown traditions. Also, Scottish and Irish traditions we adopted here as well. You know the games are in a few months. If he going to play hockey. I would enroll him to the games. The caber toss would be nice to win for once. Just saying. You know how many of the women here love men in skirts so to speak."

Orville "It's a dam kilt! Not a skirt!" As Tania Laughs.

Rodney "Great and the dam bagpipes too."

Orville sneers "Rodney! Would you like me to have you clean the sewage here indefinitely?" Rodney turns pale with hat statemen and says "I'm sorry sir"

Orville "that is much better. Now if you please. I am taking the boy with me so he can decompress of all the family linages here. He really strained." As both Orville and Orin leave. Orin looks at Orville. Orville has an annoyed look and before he gets to ask Orville holds his hand up and lets out a really deep sigh of frustration.

Orville "The dam women is going to be the death of me. My mother told me this when I first laid eyes on here. I should have listened to her back them. But no, I had to be a stubborn idiot. That is why I have taken an interest to you boy. You do listen to your elders. But going into the Darquefelou's legacy is tad bit much. Considering they run half the town. And I being the Eldest Ulberg's run the other half of this wonderful place. I keep forgetting that the manner sets of the derivatives of the families gets rather complicated." As He walks Orin to this home. Orin is about to ask a question until he sees Rev Johnathan R Kingsley Waving to come over in to the picnic bench oat the back of the house. As they approach. He sees a BBQ dinner made by Jacob and Horatio. With he Von Weibs at the table. Noticing they are dress a little bit on the risque side. Orin thinking, they are about ready to go to work. Horatio puts a healthy heaping of ribs burgers and sausages on his plate with the skibobs on another plate with the grilled vegetables. AS Orin arranges the food. Rev Jonathan starts to stretch his ands out.

Rev Jonathan "Orin will you please say grace."

Orin "God bless the food and the company here at this fine table. Bless s in the meal we are about to partake. Bless us all that we may find our way through these difficult times. As we always ask for your guidance. We seek your wisdom, and you praise and your will. Amen."

Horatio and Jacob "Well said young man well said."

Orin "Thank you all for the help. I do appreciate it." As he decides what to eat first. Jacob asks the following of Orin. "What were you all doing the military experimental wing of the school?"

Orin "Well I was shown the tunnels that some of the population use to get around during the day. Apparently, a significant amount of the population suffers from Xeroderma Pigmentosum. Meaning they instantly burn under direct sunlight. So, I was shown the tunnels so, I won't be too alarmed how certain people get around here. So, I won't wonder how and why they tend to move so fast around. With the subway system here and other monorail type of rail ways underground here." As Jacob looks at Orville with a raised eyebrow.

Horatio "Now young man. How did you come by this notion?"

Orin "This is the top medical school for that type of research. So, there would be a population of people willing to try the experimental treatments. Depending on the stage they are some levels of cures but not all of them. The school's brochure brags that it's one of the top research programs for it." Wihelmine simply smiles devilishly and looks at the girls who seem to be cats who caught eating the proverbial canary.

Orville "Yes there are many cases of that here actually. And that they come here for treatments. Meaning why you don't see many of them out during the day. That's why the school is open 24/7. Also, the programs are geared to people habits and sleep patterns. This makes it one of the top schools in the world." Looking at both Horatio and Jacob with a sympathetic look.

Horatio "Oh…Sorry we were running a special ops exercise today. So, we wanted to know why you were all down there?"

Rory "It was the fastest way to get to the school bookstore from where we were. We just wanted to keep out of the sunlight due to our condition."

Horatio" It's okay, we now know why. This way no other questions have to be asked. You al please stay away from that part of the tunnels if you can help it. But since you were with Orville. It was okay. Since we do answer to a civilian authority." They all simply shake their heads in acknowledgement. As Orin starts to dig in the ladies on the table just simply watch him eat. This made Orin rather unconfutable. However, Jacob and Horatio were at their usually banter of needling each other. Orin is about to ask a question when Rev Johnny asks the following of Orin.

Johnny "Orin which family did Tania talk about with you for her clientele. She shares with Horatio?"

Orin "Well she was talking about he main family of the Darquefelou's and the lines they have of the family tree." As Johnny eyes narrow with a grim look on his face.

Rev Johnny" Really? I would've thought she would with he Ulberg's first. Since that is who are related to here?"

Orin "Well I did find that curious. I just don't know why with that. Knowing their family lines are Ukrainian, Romanian, and Russian. With all the customs. Then with all the Scottish families and Irish families here as well. With the manner set of each culture. She also managed to squeeze in Japanese and Chinese cultures sets too. It's just too much information all at once."

Jacob" Ah... the information overload. I see it in your eyes now. Yeah, I can see why she would start there actually. Newcomers made a big splash here wen they arrive. Since your arrival is so close to the start of the first Trimester of the calendar year. Well, it's the festivities going through the winter through spring tends to be tough. And there the summer months here. Where it's dreadfully hot and humid too. Now there is a new set of gossip going around here. Since you're starting in the first trimester. Of the calendar year. Most other people find it unusual. But ten again this is a peculiar place of it's own." AS Orin looks at Jacob's expression rather curiously.

Rory "So Orin, did you actually enjoy the tour we gave you?" Smiling.

Colleen "We know we gave you the quick tour. But there is a lot to see. Like the observatory!"

Rachael "Oh…Don't forget about the ball field. Where the football and soccer and baseball is played. We love the night games. For obvious reasons. But the indoor arena is where we tend to watch most of the games live. Basketball is so boring. But we do love hockey!"

Saundra "Well, we can't wait to see you play. What position are you going for in hockey?"

Becca "You look too skinny to play."

Wihelmine "Now hush Becca. He'll do just fine. He just has a wiry build. Nothing wrong with that. Besides Slava will whip him into shape in no time. I took the liberty to make the arrangements for him to coach you personally. To get you up to speed. I hope you don't mind me doing that Orville?"

Orville "You are being down right kind to this boy Wihelmine. And I do apricate it."

Wihelmine "Orville you are more reasonable than your wife. Also, you are kind to my girls. Even Johnny here is kind to them despite how much trouble they cause as a whole. More than others." As Wihelmine eye Becca. Becca simply glares at her mother at this point. Saundra simply looks into Orin's eyes with a quizzical look. As she sees him eating the food. She wonders many things. She sees something unusual in the boy. Like what her sisters noticed last night.

Saundra "Why did you let us have out spot?"

Orin "It was the neighborly thing to do."

Saundra "Oh…You seemed out of sorts yesterday? Why?"

Orin "I'm simply not used to a lot of attentio9n. When I do get a lot of attention. I tend to get heavy anxiety attacks."

Saundra, Becca Wihelmine say "Oh my!"

Wihelmine "So the that overwhelming welcome party was plain too much for you to handle all at once."

Orin "Yes, it was. Now knowing the whole family histories of the customers. All I need know is their purchase history and what they like. Then I can take it from there." Orville, Jacob, Horatio simply cough a lot at this point.

Orin "Okay, I'll bite how much of these manners set are needed to close the deal?"

Horatio "All of them. No exceptions. You need to know who and what you're dealing with the families here. She wasn't trying to overload you. But the War Scythe 90 k world championships being hosted here in three months. Most of your opponents will be from the Darquefelou's and their derivative family lines here. And since your membership has been reactivated. I'm sponsoring you for my shop. Rodney already has his permit from ania's shop. I have no one from mine. So, I am asking if you would do me the honor of representing Moons Dogg's hobbies in this venture?"

Orville Chimes "Well, that is if she decides to change people up?"

Horatio "Nope Rodney is locked in already as a month ago. I don't have time to find a new player for my shop Orville."

Orville "I'll smooth it over Horatio. No issue with that. But a lot of things are happening this spring."

Horatio "True Orville. Very true indeed."

Orin notices that Cassandra was really interested in the War Scythe 90K tournament. He a quizzical look.

Orin "Do you play War Scythe 90K Cassandra?"

Cassandra "Well no. But a close friend of mine did. He was an interesting young man. He was a lot like you Orin. But Shin Motto Totowa Fujimaki is a formidable player.".

Orin "Did you know his online tag for the game?"

Saundra "Why yes it was DragonScytheryuken1974. Why do you ask?"

Orin "Oh... I've played against him before a few times. I was able to get draws on him. But that wasn't easy. Then I got a win because his internet connection was dropped. I don't call it a win per say."

Saundra "What was your game tag/"

Orin "Ahh I decided for an adult film star name for the tag. So, it was Little_Pony. Found it odd it wasn't taken yet. My friend Anna thought it would be funny" The whole table laugh very hard.

Jacob "So you're that obnoxious whelp. He hates your guts because he couldn't defeat you. But then again there are other players here would go nuts to find out you are here to play! Horatio, I am making bets. And I'm betting heavily on this young man. Not many can go toe to toe with Totowa!" As the laughter goes down a bit. Horatio simply glares at Jacob.

Horatio "Now Jake. No gambling involving this young man!"

Jacob "Now, now I always bet on your guy to lose usually. This year I can finally bet to win!"

Orville "Speaking for the boy's father and mother here. And especially my wife. You are not to place bets on this boy whatsoever!"

Wihelmine "Now gentlemen. I know my fine establishment will get attention for this in pics. And other advice how to bet. Why don't we just ask the lad where he placed in the digital finals last year?" As the rest of the lady's smile.

Orin "Well, I place 1rst place in my region. 1rst place in Canada. 1rst place in north America. And I placed first in the world championship. But it was the fluke of the internet connection going down is why I won. So even though I was awarded the trophy. I refused to accept it because of the internet going down on Totowa."

Saundra "That caused quite a stir except for Totowa. He really respects you for that. However, another player thinks you should have taken it and ran off the scene with it. Totowa constantly beats him. And he is here for the tournament for regionals through the countries and the championships. But now that it's going to two countries in north America instead of four. The regions will be split into territories. Totowa plays for the Union. As in the United States of America." As the ladies and gentlemen look at Saundra with a impressed look.

Horatio "The other player she speaks of is here in town. Believe it or not. He consistently wipes the floor with Rodney. And he is from the Darquefelou clan. Main branch family of Darquefelou's. Mean disposition that young man has too."

Wihelmine "Yes, he is a handful. And he has eyes on all my girls. I would just fly under the radar as much as I can around him. He is very possessive of myself and the girls for a lot of family political reasons here. So, Tania actually giving the local family histories was a good idea. And for the time being let's not say who they are to each other. I would prefer the surprise when he loses to Orin here." As everyone whistles in agreement except one. Now Rev Jonathan R Kingsley has a very dark stark look upon his face.

Rev Johnny" Wihelmine, that clan doesn't like to be embarrassed at all. I remember the last time they felt an embarrassed. And specifically, how they took it out on a group of people here. I say we all are playing with fire here!"

Wihelmine "The betting on this tournament is a tradition reverend. Between the houses and covens here. Like it or not. People will bet on this boy. There isn't no way around it. I'm making sure the boy doesn't bet himself nor his mother. His father that is a different story. Depending what odds Jacob is going to give."

Horatio "That is true. I agree with the terms and conditions in advanced. Knowing there isn't a thing we can do to stop it. Wil Tania honor my request, Orville?"

Orville "I'll make sure it's honored. And it will be easy. Because the boy has an account and probably still used your stats board to keep playing the online matches. Isn't that right Orin?"

Orin "Yes, I did. Still have to login to make a few matches for the qualifiers online and tabletop. At least now I got my pieces."

Horatio "Don't worry if you need more. I'll provide it at no coast to me. I want to sponsor a winner in my shops. It's been a while since I have doe that. Besides, I want to see the faces when they lose. Jacob I will make a few bets. Our boy here for 1rst and 2nd place."

Jacob "Well I can do that for you. But I insist that his grades don't drop because of this. His dad will kill us if that happens."

Jacob laughs "Yeah, he sure will. But I have to take Orin here on a river boat ride one f these days. Even though it's wintertime it's still hot down here boy. But not as hot as spring and summer!"

Orin simply nods "So what else do I have to learn about the clans and covens here?"

Orville "Mostly they split amicably into their own family lines. Some not so amicably. Because of that the contests are how we keep the peace between the families and covens and clans. But the contests are rough here. Stoner-Boy really hates it when they start. Jonathan also doesn't like these tournaments either."

Reve Johnny "We prefer that the time spent worshiping the lord rather in these so-called contests. The Lord deserves the glory in his name. I just don't approve Stoner-Boy's bong!"

Orville "Differences in opinion on how to worship the lord here boy. Just leave it be."

Orin "So when did you develop your skin condition Rev Johnny?"

Rev Johnny "It started to happen after two years I stayed here. So, one day I was burning up. So, I had to pack away my surfboard. And all my other summer stuff. I was a beach bum so to speak. Jesus knows how much I loved the sun and surfing. But now of this skin condition. Which is genetic, can appear early or later in life. In my case it appeared later in life."

Orin 'So the cold to the touch is the lack of blood circulation in your body?"

Rev Johnny "Yes, that is part of it. Your mother noticed it. And asked me these questions when I appeared on the doorstep. She held back a lot of tears. Because she remembers me as the Surfing Preacher of our hometown in Los Angles. Now I am forced to live a life of a mole at best."

Orin looks upon Rev Johnny "I'm so sorry. How can you all live like vampires like this?"

Wihelmine "Well, there is a lot of us; Who have the same condition? So, the underground tunnels. And the railways and having easier access to the stores and municipal building and such. But those who remember the sun really miss the warmth of it." Rev Johnny gives her a cold look with anger in his eyes.

Rev Johnny "Yeah those of us that remember the lord's warmth through the Star he created in the center of our solar systems. But the lord challenges us all. Even if we are innocent of the actions, we end up paying for. But this is how the lord shows us his love. Jesus promised us a better life. He never promised us an easy life." As he looks at Orin with a sympathetic look.

Orin "So what is it with this town and manner and etiquette?"

Orville answers "Well we have clans here and branches of the clans. With subsets with different spellings of the names. So, because of the offshoots. They have a different set what they deem acceptable etiquette. Since their children shop everywhere in town. There is an expect protocol on how they should be handled. And they attend weekly, monthly, and quarterly and half year and once a year meeting. Since they control a lot of business in the town and the school. So when you deal with the clientele. You have to approach them with a degree of caution. Which families did she go over with you Orin?"

Orin "Well She stated with the Wolfson's and the Wolfsan's, and the Wolfsen's. The continued with Uldberg's. Then the Gator-star family. Then with LeClair family. Then she started with the Darkmoon's. Then I started to really get lost with that. Because she gave me the lower tier name of the family, I believe?" Giving a very puzzled look.

Rev Jonathan R Kingsley "Young man. I can understand why you have that puzzled look. I've been here longer than you. And I still can't phantom all the reasons of the breaks in each family branch. They are all related by blood or marriage. But the hierarchy is confusing as sin. Lord knows how tania and Orville can keep it straight in their heads. Also, Wihelmine Von Wieb's is related to a lot of them and the Ulberg's as well. Due to the volatile nature of the grudges. It's way too easy to offend them. That is why she bombarded you with the information all at once. Which books of the bible did your manger to read today Orin?" As Tania steps to the picnic table.

Tania "Yes Orin which books did you manager to read today?" As she looks fondly at Rev Johnny.

Wihelmine "Now, now Tania. You're still married to that man over there. And besides if anyone is going to corrupt the good reverend here. It's going to me be." As Rev Johnny laughs out loud at both of them. Tania laughs harder, with Orville. While Wihelmine and her daughters give an icy cold stare at the priest.

Orin "It would be most likely mom would have the snowball's chance in hell first" As he giggles the answer.

The Von Weib sisters all laugh in unison. This gives Orin a very uneasy feeling. While Horatio and Jacob laugh as hard as Johnny at this point. AS he started to notice that not everyone has a plate of food in front of them. As he looks at his plate. Then he looks at the table and all of a sudden, they all have food scraps on the plates. Orin blinks a few times. As he is looking around. He sees that Orville has a look of concern on his face. As he glances over to Tania and Johnny. As they dismiss his notions. They do look perturb as if he saw something he shouldn't have. As He decides to focus on Tania's original question As, he is about to speak. His mother arrives at the table. She runs over and gives him a huge hug. She greets the rest of the small gathering around. They pass a few plates for Erin. She decides to sit between Orin and Johnny. As she settles herself in the space. She bats her eyes to both men. Johnny and Orin laugh with the joke. As Wihelmine just stares in disbelief with her daughters. As Tania laughing harder to the point of hiccups. As Orville, Horatio, and Jacob laughing the hardest now. This was all in a matter of seconds. As Colleen, Rebecca, Rory, Rachel, and Cassandra stare in disbelief. Seeing that Orin can tease people properly. As they decide to hover over him. Erin simply smiles and begins to clear her throat as she swallows some of her food. She smiles at the little girls in her minds eye. And yet Wihelmine and her daughters noticed this look. Erin simply smiles at them. And then she decides to smirk at Tania. Tania looks shocked. As Erin simply laughs at all the commotion at the table. Rev Jonathan R Kingsley simply laughs harder as the scene plays out.

Erin "Now which of you lousy men is babysitting my son?"

Orville 'This Lousy man. However, he married and equally lousy woman." Smiling at Tania.

Tania "Orville! How dare you call me lousy in front of Wihelmine!"

Jacob "Now, now, Tania you need to be teased every now and then."

Horatio "Well, I see why she can get a lot of attention. And yet she doesn't crave it from others." As he smiles at Erin. Erin simply smiles in acknowledgement.

Erin "How was your day Orin?" Orin simply smiles as starts off with ....

CHAPTER 11C

The Second night at the new home. Also, what is to come with having five ladies on your balcony.

After the dinner was cleaned up and the trash disposed of. As Orin recounts the days events with his mother. Erin decides to question and press Tania a bit about too much too soon. As she presses Tania. Wihelmine laughs hysterically over the site. Wihelmine, simply smiles as she has never seen cringing in terror before her eyes.

Erin "Look it's his second day. I said he was a fast learner. But to cram a whole town's history down his throat. Also, if these families don't understand he is new. And it takes time to acclimate to his new surroundings. The they can go to hell as far as I'm concerned!" Erin decides to glare at Wihelmine. Wihelmine simply backs down with an apologetic look. As her daughters see this. Which is a rarity to see their mother back down to someone. They follow suit instinctively.

Erin "Now young ladies. No need to follow your mother's suit in this case. But I do appreciate that you respect me this way." The Von Wieb sisters just smile and wave and see their mother smile back at them giving them the okay signal.

Wihelmine "Erin I meant no disrespect to you." Giving an apologetic look.

Erin "You are forgiven Wihelmine. I just didn't expect Tania to go overboard here."

Tania "Now young lady. I meant no offense. He is a quick study. And he is going to run into these movers and shakers in the local society circles. But they do shop in my stores. They also shop in Horatio's businesses and Jacob's businesses as well. Because we depend on each other for our livelihoods. I can't run the risk of getting them angry. Because all hell will break lose if they do get angry." As Erin looks to Orville about these points his wife had made. Orville simply gives and understanding look.

Orville "Erin, tania would have to educate him eventually about the families. But even I did scold her over it. But she really can't leave Rodney to run the shop. He tends to screw a lot of things up unsupervised. Or when there isn't anyone around to keep tabs on him. But I do agree with you too fast too soon Tania. Back down a little bit. It's a good thing that the families show a little understanding and restraint every now and then. Don't you agree?"

Jacob "Tania, you went too fast as usual. Good thing you didn't picked out a girlfriend for him yet." As Orville looks at his wife. As she narrows her eyes to her husband. He realizes that she has a few prospects for the young man. And doesn't like the fact the Weib's took an interest in the boy.

Orville "Tania... You didn't make any plans without consulting these two? Have you done that?"

Tania 'Well I may have gotten him invited to a few of the big social gatherings before the tournaments begin. There are a lot of people interested in knowing the boy and yourself Erin. After all you are in this house of all houses in the town. Everyone knows it's the presidents house of the school. He doesn't just let anyone stay here. Only high value guests and functions are done here. So, introductions had to been made in advance. The BBQ was just one of them that had to be done. I didn't realize his panic attacks would be an issue. He has to be kept up to speed in these matters. And there is plenty of them you work for directly Erin. So I would be a little bit more careful about these matters." As Erin looks at Horatio and Jacob who nod with a pleading looks.

Erin "I suppose you are right about a few things. But the timetable is a bit interrogable."

Tania 'Sorry about that, but the timetable is the best I could do. They are not a patient bunch of people. And they have the ability to kick him out anytime they want. Which means, I had to make and book a few things and deals in advance. In spite what my husband says. We do answer to these families as well. In spite that fact he is in charge of the town." Looking at Orville

Orville "I'll deal with them in the morning Tania. You better spill the beans to me. So, I can set them straight. And I will make sure that the consequences are. I will get the time he needs to adjust accordingly. Or they will have to answer to my wrath. You hear me beloved!" Tania now bows to Orville upon hearing this.

Orville "I'll find out what deals she wasn't supposed to make without the President's and my approval Erin."

Erin "Thank you Orville."

Orin "If you don't mind if I go to my room now?"

Horation Jacob and Johnny look at each other and nod in agreement.

Saying n agreement "We will escort you to your room."

Orin looks puzzled and nods in agreement. As they escort him to this room They sit in the chairs available and Johnny has some more things to say as he starts the bible study.

Johnny 'How far have you read in acts or psalms?"

Orin "I got halfway through acts until I passed out of exhaustion. But I'm not sure what you want out of me with this?"

Rev Johnny "What does the day of Pentecost mean to you?

Orin "What do you mean by that sir?"

Johnny "Look I know your mother has received the gift of the holy ghost. I'm asking you if you ever received said gift. If you what does this day mean to you? The day of Pentecost? If you haven't received the gift of the holy ghost. I still want to know what this day means to you? For one who hasn't received said gift. There isn't a right or wrong answer per say. I am asking you for a truth as you see, hear, speak, and feel it. The cardinal mind always plays tricks on you. And around here, it really plays havoc on your brain. Where all you have is the holy ghost to get you through most days." As Orin looks to Horatio and Jacob. Jacob simply shrugs his shoulders. While Horatio simply smiles.

Horatio "Now young sir, please don't behave like the savage here. And answer the question as you see the truth in the here and now."

Orin "Well I haven't received the gift of the holy ghost. Because I never spoken in tongues that I am aware of. I heard of the phenomenon. But I never experienced it myself. Nor did I observe the true speaking in tongues." As Horatio and Rev Johnny look at him with sadness. Jacob looks upon him with a look of sympathy.

Johnny "So what does it mean to you Orin?" With a quizzical look.

Orin "Well I feel in a historical sense it's a third birth of a religion. The first birth was when john the Baptist prophesies and baptism was the first birth. The second birth was the crucifixion itself. This would be the third birth. The day of Pentecost is the day of the faithful where the promise was delivered. Where Jesus released the holy ghost from the hidden ark of the covenant. And set it free to humanity as a gift they can call upon it. But do I believe in it? I'll say that I'm skeptical. But then again I was never baptized either according to my mother." Horatio and Johnny just look at Orin in shock. While Jacob simply face palms about this revelation.

Horatio "I knew you had it rough. But I didn't realize it was this rough. You have no belief in Jesus? Or in the concept that a God exist?"

Orin "Well we kept moving around so much. I didn't get to go out and round much."

Jacob 'Boy, that is going to change big time now. With the religion classes you are going to take the next three years. So, you're 'going to see a lot of church going people in the streets on Sundays alone. Let alone the bible studies and prayer meetings. Also, some families her base their whole social lives around the church they attend. Others not so much. But you are going to se a lot of this going around."

Orin "Well, this is okay. Mom is going to take me to your parish. I'm not sure why besides that she knows you sir." Looking at Rev Johnny.

Rev Johnny "Look Orin, I know your mother and you had to move around a lot. So, I'm not surprise you don't have a relationship with Jesus Christ. It refreshes me that you are open to having a relationship with him. As far as your theory of the ark of the covenant housing he holy spirit. When the Jews were wondering the wilderness until Moses's death. And how the during the day it was a pillar of smoke. And at knight it was a pillar of fire. How did you come up with that theory?"

Orin "Ah… Ummu…Well Stoner Boy was preaching the gospel to me while we came down from Nowhere Oklahoma."

Rev Johnny "Hmmm…. Well, I can see how that would inspire you to think that way. Stoner Boy is rather unusual with his sermons. He tends to offer you a smoke out of his bong or the water from it. I don't prefer the use of drugs. So that is my issue with him.

Orin "Well, I can understand why you feel that way. But I haven't had any real reason to go to church at all. Does that make me a bad person?" Then a knock from the glass sliding door from his balcony. As Orin walks towards the door. Horatio grabs his shoulder and whispers in his ear.

Horatio "Don't let them in. Do not invite them. It's too soon for them to enter." Orin looks at Horatio and nods in approval. As he approaches the sliding door. He see it's Becca and Colleen at the door.

Becca "How about if you allow us to enter the abode?"

Colleen smacks her sister in the back of the head and say "It's rather soon for that. We have to wait a bit. Could you allow us to hold our stuff here in your room Orin, please?"

Orin simply nods "So what do you ladies want me to hold for you?"

Then he hears Rory say "Just our purses and other stuff. If you don't mind. We trust you not to rob us. It's just the other girls we don't trust. Oh, Reverend you're here doing the bible study with him?" As they see Rev Johnny look at them with a curious look.

Rev Jonathan "It's alright Rory. I can see why that the three of you are here. As Orin turns his head and whips it back. He sees Rachael and Cassandra on the balcony now. Now Orin wonders how the devil did they get up here so fast? As he is about to ask a few questions.

Rev Johnny "Now Orin, would you mind getting Horati and Jacob a few drinks please?" He notices that this wasn't a request. But more like a subtle order. Orin decides to obey as he leaves his room. He sees the three men take a defensive posture. AS he travels down the stair. He hears arguing between Tania and his mother. As he draws closer to the commotion. A hand slaps him on the shoulder and it's Orville. Holding a finger to his lips. The signal to keep quiet.

Whispering Orville 'What are you doing down here?"

Orin whispers back "I came down to get Jacob and Horatio something to drink. While Johnny is having a conversation wit the Weib's on the balcony. I did allow them to have their spot on the balcony."

Orville 'Oh...Okay, that makes sense. Sorry Tania and your mother are having it out still. Wihelmine went to her club to open it up. But my wife has made too many plans about your future here. And your mother didn't take it too kindly about it. So they are arguing very quietly. SO you wont hear what is going on. The fact they are practically ignoring me. I think it's safer to go to the other kitchen in the house." Orin nod in agreement. As the make their way to the second kitchen. Orin ask Orville a few more questions about his and his mother arrival here.

Orin "So What is the real big deal here Orville? About our arrival here?"

Orville "Well, your father is the school president. Because of that, you're being vetted by all the families that have political and business power over everything here. The spiritual power base is on Stoner Boy, whom most of the families want to get rid of. But for some undefined reason can't get rid of him. And of course, you have Rev Johnny parish to contend with. This makes it harder for Tania and I to do maintain order here. Having the Weib girls on your balcony as nightly visitors. Doesn't sit well with anyone around here. Except for your father. So, people are understanding curious about he both of you. They have heard stories about the two of you. Now they want to know the truth about your parents. Why you came here now. Also, the how to dig up dirt on the three of you. Because there is a lot you simply don't know. And I gather that your mother hates gossip. But around here gossip is as good as gold. Information is the key to a lot of things. Secrets are kept here. Some older than you think. Also, it's about getting ahead at all costs. So, finding out some deals that can't be broken up. And Tania made a lot of them. So, this way your application to the school, and your mother's new job and housing was done. I wouldn't have made those deals personally. But unfortunately. There wasn't any other way getting you two here." Orin simply frowns and rolls his eyes with the expression of great. He gets Horatio's and Jacob's two glasses of whiskey on the rock. As per Orville instructions. As he finished up with the pouring of the drinks. He sees his mother simply storm into the second kitchen with a very angry and sad face. She looks at him and begins to cry. Orin puts the drinks down and gives his mother a hug.

Erin "I'm so, so, so, sorry. But I really did I this time. It's going to be her way for a little while. I know Orville tried everything to get out of this. But there are some deals he can't break either." Orin just simply smiles and hugs his mother and wipes her tears away. Orville simply looks and smiles. Wishing his children would do that for him. Let alone their mother. As tania walks in and sees the sight. Her heart warms up a lot and she begins, to cry.

Tania "Now I'll have to take my leave. But we'll see more of each other. And as the discussed pace. We'll try to slow it down a little."

Orville "No Tania. I will slow it down by a lot! In spite what they think. I'm still in charge here. Or I'll fine the crap out of them into compliance. You hear me woman!"

Tanis "Yes, loud and clear. But... No! You wouldn't do that!"

Orville "Yes I will. Now tell them where they can stick it! Even Owen will understand!"

Tania sighs "Alright... But I'll need dam it, Wihelmine's help with this."

Orville "Don't worry, I'll convince the madame easily. Her girls adore this young man. So it will be easier than you think. But be nice to her in these upcoming matters!"

Tania "I'm taking my leave now. C'ya all tomorrow! And I'm taking him to the school this time around Orville!"

Orville "Nope, we are taking him to school. I'll make sure Miguel De le Guy the 36th will escort us through out the buildings this time around. The matter is settles Tania C'ya in the morning." As she leaves the home. Orin brings the drink up. And still sees Johnny talking to the girls and they look at Orin as if they know something he doesn't. As he hands the drinks to Jacob and Horatio. Johnny walks in the room as the girls stay outside in the balcony. He sees three of them there. Saundra, Rory and Colleen.

Rev Johnny "Some grounds rules were established here. Also, I know you are now going to have a rougher time than I thought. It appears our madame Mayor made a few deals. That these ladies and other interested partied made on your mother's behalf."

Orin "Orville is going to but a kibosh to most of it."

Rev Johnny "Good as he should. Well Orin, I have to take care of a few things. Keep reading Acts and psalms. We need to have you go to Judges next with Job. Now I have to take my leave. We will talk later in the week about your pathway to Jesus. But for now just pray. Also, if you bump into Stoner-Boy. Listen to what he has to say. As well as any advice about your journey with Jesus. He is good with that." As Rev Johnny walk out of the room so does Jacob and Horatio. AS Orin walks to the balcony the other three sisters are still there.

Orin "Mind telling me what is really going on here?"

Rory "Well, the hub bub is about you rally. I'm not sure why though."

Collen "I've yet to make any inquiries. But I know our mother have made a few of them."

Saundra "I've made a few myself. And the answer I got were vague at best. It's not every day a prodigy comes into this school and town. Also, one that no one has ever heard of. Since I noticed you like keeping a low profile. It makes people curious in general. In this town. You might have well screamed. I'm here folks give me all your attention you want."

Orin "Oh…Great, now everyone wants a piece of my hide at best?"

Rory "More like you whole hide in the local politics. The school clubs and other societies that are run here. Having Horatio and Jacob taking an interest in you. Well that also raises eyebrows too here. So, the commotion is just getting started here. And as you found out last night. We are not exactly well thought of here. Because of Becca's and Rachel's antics. Mostly Becca's. However, we like to people watch. And observe behaviors. It's mostly due to our psychology classes we all take."

Saundra "I think it will go well for you. There are a lot of good people interested in you. But if you don't like the spotlight. Well, you better get used to it now. There is a hug commotion about you. Oh.. Dam It's my time to go up." As Orin is about to see Saundra leave. Rory taps him on the shoulder, and he turns to look at Rory. As he snaps his head back; he sees Rachel is on the balcony. Orin raises an eyebrow. As he about to ask a question.

Colleen chimes "So how is the artwork going?

Orin "It's going but what did just happen here?'

Rachel 'I've been here the whole time." Looking innocently at Orin. But Orin isn't buying it one bit. As he seen a blur and Rory was replaced by Becca now. He decides to play along a bit.

Orin "Right, the five of you have been here the whole time." As he looks at Becca. She is smiling as if she knows what is on his mind. Then the smile turns in to a grim as she looks deep into his eyes. He feels a slight pain in his temples. As he hears in his head "You didn't see anything." As he hears the voice and it's Becca's voice. The pain is unbearable for most people. He is just working through the pain as he smiles. And sings an old commercial and sings the tune over, and repeatedly. Becca's face changes with a look of determination as she tries to get through and dissuade him with accepting of what just happened. As this is going on. Collen taps Orin on the shoulder again. And Orin breaks eye contact with Becca.

Colleen "So what work are you doing for tonight? You're not going to read the book of acts tonight?"

Orin "Yes, I will. But I have other stuff I got to get ready for and studying. Apparently, I have a lot of material to go through." He still notices the pain in his head. As If something was scratching his skull. But he just ignores the pain. However, he feels another presence behind him. As he turns again and sees that Rory is back with a puzzeled look.

Rory "What is going on Orin."

Orin "Not sure. I think I'm just stressed out with all the information I took in today. My brains may be fried now. Nothing much. Why do you ask Rory?" As Rory narrows her eye slightly, she smiles and caress his cheek.

Rory "Nothing, just worried that you may be having another panic attack. Knowing that Tania can be overbearing. With all the societies she runs and social gatherings. She loves to show off new prodigies to the town. And there is a lot of people really interested in knowing you. Especially with your artwork. You are quite gifted there." As she smiles. Orin still feels the pain. However, it's less intense now for some reason. He decides to keep singing his tune and change it every few repeats to another song. Rory simply smiles and giggles caressing his face.

Rory "Now what families did she tell you about?"

Orin "Well she started with the Darquefelou's"

Colleen "Dam, she didn't waste any time there. You know that there are 4 branches of that family with the different spellings, right?"

Orin "Yeah, and the Darkmoon's with the five different spellings of that clan."

As Becca rolls her eyes "Well them Darkmune's a funny lot. I bet she went over the Wolfsen's too?" AS she shakes her head Orin's headache stops.

Orin simply says, "Yes Becca, Now Rory why are you surprised that she started with one of the Darquemune's?"

Rory "Well most people stray away from that family in general. They don't think highly of us. Yet they want our mother to marry most of us into that family tree. As you can guess we declined. Especially our mother. Tania figures since we've taken a liking to you. Best start off with that family. Because some of the men will challenge you a bit. So that family with the Darkmoon's can be rough as hell. Forty times as mean as well. So, they like to place their dominion on the Von Weib's. Mother tells them to fuck off most of the tie. Just like that too. Once upon a time she was nice about it. Now she is crude and crass about it. My suggestion, be nice and kind with them. Use whatever manners Tania expects out of you. We are at the point of telling them go to hell all the time. When we see one of them, we sneer at them now."

Orin whistle's "Okay, but I am going to deal with them at the hobby shop, right?"

Becca and now Sandra in unison "Oh, yeah, they shop there and Moon Dogs all the time. You are going to meet them. Alright, and they will try to bait you into something stupid."

Orin" I'll be careful. But is it really that bad between how to use a different set of manners per split off branch?"

Saundra "They are still pissed that I confused a lower branch with a higher branch. I was five years old at the time."

Becca "People wonder why I cause trouble. Those families start up more crap in an hour that I do in a day."

Rory "Isn't that the truth sister."

Becca "You're dam straight about that. Remember the time where the honorary member from Fort Lee New Jersey came down."

Rory "Yeah, and how they treated him. As an honorary member of the clan too. And his adopted protégé'"

Saundra "Yes, he is an honorable man. And a friend of Totowa. But they did treat him like crap. And, when it came time to offer assistance to them. He still did it as a matter of honor. But the boon he required for them to do first before he did the favor. Made sure that they would never dare do that to him again. Because his demands were worse than surrender. They are still wondering if that was a good idea to piss him off."

Colleen "Yeah, they are still paying that off. And believe me. It's still costing them. So, they have been nasty with the other families about pulling their weight around here."

Orin "So that is a small once of information. And there ae more? As in active rivalries?"

Rachel "Yes, there ae more rivalries between the inner families and outer families as well. Things are way to competitive here. When nana visits. It gets worse then better. Because no one messes with our nana. She has another nick name. However, she puts up with nan a lot. Our Grandmother is the head of some of the societies here. And she the one with the most power next to Tania. However, Nana and Tania do get along. But they don't exactly play nice with each other." As Orin sees the expressions on their faces. He sees a whisp and suddenly Wihelmine is in front of him. He decides to play it off as if he sees nothing out of the ordinary. Wihelmine decides to size him up for a second and believes that he was too busy in conversation for him to notice something unusual.

Wihelmine "Girls, a few of the dancers decided to leave early. Meaning I need you all to come back to the club now." As the girls look at each other. Orin decides to turn around.

Orin "Colleen, I forgot to give you the at card you wanted." All he hears is five whisps of air disappear. And he turns around and sees only Wihelmine standing on the balcony.

Orin "I'm just tired. Can you please give this to her?" Handing over the card that Colleen did want. She simply smiles. And he hears in his head "You're such a good young man. Knowing when to back down and knowing when to stand.

Wihelmine "Sure, not a problem. They are going to on the balcony later tonight. Get some rest. Also, thank you for being receptive to our plight in town. Not many people are as understanding as you and your mother."

Orin "You're welcome. Now if you'll excuse me I have to get back to my studies. I'm going to be doing that a lot now." Wihelmine smiles and lets him turn around and he hears a whip of air. Orin doesn't bother turning around. He knows the ladies across the street are not in the balcony now. They are inside the club. As he sets the curtains as requested. He picks up where he left off in Acts and read until he goes to sleep. As he drifts into dream lad. He sees his father. "So, the girls gave you a once over I see. Sorry about Tania. She really did it this time. Your mom will be okay. But yeah, the families want to know what is really going down with my absences this year." As Orin speaks, he stops. The asks "What is it with their speed. Its unusual.?" Owen "Well, that is a story for another day. But you are picking up on things. That you are not quite ready for yet. In a few months' time you will be. Then everything will make sense. Otherwise, when you meet the Darquemune's and the Darquefelou's. Be very careful. They are pleasant with protocol. But they are vicious as they are nice. It depends on the day. But if Tania told you about them first. That means your going to run into them sooner than later. We would all preferred later. So be careful, and don't cause a stare down like you did with Becca today. You made them notice you. And it's not in a good way. And I know Johnny, Horatio, Jacob, and Orville can keep an eye on you for few hours at a time a week at best." The Orin hears a woman's voice. "So now your concerned about all of us!" Owen "Dam they are picking this up. It's too soon. I have to go Orin just wake up." The woman's voice getting clearer now "Where do you think you are going Owen. We've have to talk about a lot of things now." The Orin wakes up. He notices it's around 3 am. As ge gets up he sees all six of the on the balcony staring at him. Five with a curious wonder about him. However, Wihelmine has a bit of an angry look to her. As If something just happened. As Orin walks to the sliding door and opens it.

Orin "You could have knocked. I would've opened it up?" The girls smile along with their mother.

Saundra "We were commenting how peaceful you were sleeping."

Colleen" Yes, you look cute that way. We were wondering if we should wake you or wait until tomorrow night."

Becca" I voted on waking you now by the way."

Rachel elbows Becca "Really Becca, we all need sleep. Besides we can trust him not to go through our stuff."

Rory 'It's so nice to see a person with such a kind and peaceful mind enjoying sleep."

Orin "Oh.. Thanks… So let me give you al your stuff." As he gathers the ladies things.

Wihelmine "I was wondering. Have you ever seen you father after he left you and your mother?" Orin looks at Wihelmine and nods no. But his face seems to be a little discolored.

Wihelmine "Are you sure?"

Orin "Pretty sure. I do have dreams of him talking. But I can never make out the words. If that counts for anything?"

Wihelmine "Oh…Well lest say the girls had their father abandoned them at a young age. He came by to visit them. But the other families got in the way." The girls looked at their mother with a look of shock about what she just told Orin. As if this is the first time hearing of this.

Saundra "Mother? Why are you telling him and us together like this?

Wihelmine "To let the boy know he isn't alone with this kind of hurt. These families you are going to meet. Can make anyone's life miserable. So be careful. And also, one more thing. There are seers amongst them. They pretty dam good at it. Don't act too sure. But at the same time don't act unsecure either. They tend o tear those in either extreme apart for that." As the rain and mist rises Orin was about to ask if they wanted an umbrella. And they were gone. He goes downstairs to the kitchen and gets something to drink. He sees Rev Johnny in the house looking over some pictures. He turns around.

Rev Johnny "Your mom gave me a key. I dropped some pictures of happier days off to her. Have you read more of the book of Acts?'

Orin "Yes, I did. It was easy and yet hard to follow. I usually get the author's intent right away. But when it comes to the bible. I treat is as a historical record. And I attempt to think what it was like in those times. Before the internet, cars, plane, trains. Ships were around. No modern luxuries that we take for granted. And these miracles that were performed. The scientific explanation states that they were never really sick. The again, there are diseases that are dormant for years before they get activated by some freak event. I find it hard to believe these things happen. Yet I can't discount that they didn't happen. Because all things are possible due to the unknown."

Rev Johnny "So, what do you believe happened?"

Orin "To my understanding that Jesus is GOD. While I know people who will state that he was merely an ascendant being on a higher plain of existence. That decided to slum it down here for a few minutes so to speak. I choose to believe that he is GOD. And came down to fulfill promises that he would come. And he made more promises again upon his return. Stating that he wouldn't be a nice guy about it." Johnny smiles and pats Orin on the shoulder.

Rev Johnny "What is making you believe in GOD?"

Orin "The strange things I see at the corner of my eye. There isn't any viable explanation then GOD. So, I am prepared to take things by faith. What is going around here Johnny? What is really going on around here?"

Rev Johnny" I can't tell you that now. But keep that keen eye of yours open. But don't let anyone know that it is open. That is what is going to cause you a lot of trouble. Noticing too many things. The more you notice, the more people want to pry into your life around here. I failed to do that. And it cost me a lot. It also cost my parish a lot in the process too. I do what I cannot attract too much attention. So, I would try not to question the weird things you see out of the conner of the eyes?" As he puts the pictures down. "What did you see that trouble you?" Johnny said with a authoritative look. Orin decided to tell him what happened in the balcony. Rev Jonny had a shocked looked on his face. Then he looked at him after what was said.

Rev Johnny "Just one question. You can hear them in your head, right?"

Orin with a shock of panic responds "Yes, I can. But sometimes I get massive headaches and migraines. But they pass, because I get the sense that they are using way too much force and it's giving them a migraine instead. That I am feeling slight pain compared to them?"

Rev Johnny "Let me get this straight you were able to block them out?"

Orin "Ah...yes. It was Becca that was doing most of the pushing. But I think I heard Collen, Rory, Rachel, And Cassandra in school earlier today. I'm not sure why? However, I just played stupid so they wouldn't catch on too quickly. I'm not sure if I heard Wihelmine in my head."

Rev Johnny "So, let me get this straight they were all on the balcony and you saw the smoke dissipate before you and they were gone."

Orin "Yeah, I believe I smelled some sort of charcoal or sulfur. You use those to make smoke bombs."

Rev Jonathan Kingsley "Yeah, perhaps your right." And he hears Wihelmine's voice in his head "Now Reverend. Aren't going to tell the boy something is truly amiss? Or are you going to let him purposely stumble along his stay here in its entirety. I know it's a longer stay, or shorter stay. But my girls are really fond of him. But they can only hold back for so long. Did he hears us today? I would like to know. Because if he did. The others would want to know. Or do I have to question your flock on such matters?" As Johnny shakes off what he just heard. And looks at Orin now.

Rev Johnny "Look Orin, never mention this to anyone. This includes Tania and Orville. You can mention this to your mother. However, I would prefer you don't. Let's say in this sort of thing. She is a bit out of practice. Keeping her thoughts to herself. Or she is pretending to be a push over. If she is, then that is good. There is a lot of things you need to be brought up to speed. I Agree with both Tania and Orville bringing you into school tomorrow. As a favor o your father. But don't mention his name to anyone. Because that will make you life miserable right now. We are trying o hold off any more questions in general. But tania got you into a real mess. A mess Orville and your father were trying to prevent at all costs. With the families in this town. So be careful. And get to sleep. You have to be really aware of your surroundings in the morning."

Orin "Okay, Reve Johnny. One more question. Do you know why mom was crying?"

Rev Johnny "Yes, very old hurst that were brought up. Also, old grudges that were brought up too. And now people are determined to drag you kicking and screaming into the fold so to speak."

Orin rolling his eyes "Great, that is all I need. Next you are going to tell me that my mother's family is here."

Rev Johnny "Well...Actually, yes they are here. A small fraction of them. That is why she was crying earlier to you today."

Orin eyes widen "You mean those fuckers who attempted to kidnap me multiple times are here!"

Rev Johnny "Well... Yes, they are here. However, too many people here don't like them. But they know you two are here. However, if you look outside; you'll see something interesting."

As Orin looks outside the window. He sees people watching the house He recognizes the uniforms of the military college cadets. With regulars in the CBI agents in training. And he sees Miguel De Le Guy the 36th talking with the cadets. As he sees Jacob and Horatio walking around the blocks. As he sees the areas that are covered. He sees parishioners singing in this hour. As he sees people looking to see a break in the lines. As they appear to get closer. The cadets and the CBI trainees stop them. As one appears to slip by. The other cadets stop him. As the he sees the commotion cease. He sees Orville directing traffic. As this goes on the area. He sees Wihelmine and her daughters waking around the property. But Orin knows they know the area better than most people. As this is going on he feels Johnny hand his shoulder.

Rev Johnny "Go to bed now Orin. You both are well protected. Besides, I'm staying here the rest of the night. Don't worry the meeting tomorrow will put this to an end. But you might have to do more classes about your mother's family contributions to things in life here. I just hope they agree to what Orville has in mind." With that Orin walks upstairs and heads to bed. As he is about to turn off the lights. He sees Saundra on the balcony looking down at the club. Which is still open. As Orin opens the sliding door. Cassandra turns around and Orin notices that her eyes are flickered from gold to blue. She smiles at Orin.

Saundra "You just couldn't sleep, I see."

Orin "Yeah."

Saundra "Well I was a kidnap victim multiple times in life."

Orin "Oh my... Sorry to hear that. I know how it feels to be insecure in your own home."

Saundra "Thanks... Not many people would figure that I have suffered such things. You are a kind young man Orin. We five can tell these things. We know our mom wanted a boy. But she got stuck with quintuplets of girls. But she is taking a liking to you as well. You are going to cause a few fights. My sisters like you too. Even Becca likes you. She doesn't like most men in general. But she really likes you a lot." Orin notices that she is blushing. Noticing the redness in specific area of her body. He realizes that she is just in her panties and a black see through bouse with out a bra. He notices that she has a liter and a pack of cigarettes.

Orin "So, you were looking at me last night? If so, why didn't you come up with the rest of your sister?" She just laughs hysterically.

Saundra "The way people were crowding you. I figured I would introduce myself at a later time. Good thing I know how to wait. But hearing from my sisters that you had home invasion issue. I just couldn't help but have a good feeling about you. To hear that your artwork is good too. That sparked all of our interests."

Orin "Oh, well I hoe that I'm not an inconvenience to you and your sisters?"

Saundra "Well, we were thinking how we were going to get our spot back. Then you said it was still ours. That was really kind of you. Also, that we can trust you with our tips. That really made us happy. Even Becca who loves to prank people as much as Rodney. Doesn't want to prank you yet. But she will. So, watch out. She can be very vindictive." As she places her hand on his face. "Wow you are warm! I suggest you get to sleep. We like seeing people sleep. We believe we see your true face asleep. Do not worry about your relations here. They're not going to get near this place. Everything will be covered. Including the tunnels are well protected." As he turns around and walks to his bed. Because he is tired as he walks back to his bed. He hears a swoosh. As he turns his head, he hears Wihelmine voice.

Wihelmine "Shouldn't you be sleeping now?

Orin "I was getting back to bed now. Isn't sunrise going to be in an hour?"

Cassandra "We'll be okay. No need to worry. Just get some sleep. You're going to have a long day."

Orin "no worries." As he slips into bed. He shuts off the lights. AS he closes his eyes. He hears Sandra's voice and Wihelmine's voice in his head. Wihelmine "Did you successfully compel him." Saundra's Voice in his head "Nope, I just simply convinced him to go to sleep. But Becca's fail attempt to compel him was a bad idea. However, I did notice that he was taught how to hide his thoughts. So, I don't know if he can hear us. Because I get a blank sheet. And Becca's description was a blank area in a room. Nothing else. Just him looking through how to get pass the blank space." Wihelmine "So he can block people out. Is he on your level?" Saundra "I'm not sure. You know I don't like doing that. It depends on the situation. I don't like doing it when it's unneeded." Wihelmine "That is true. You do respect people's privacy. I guess I'll have too make nice with our pal preacher that is friends with his mother for more information about them." Saundra "Mom, it could be that we are broadcasting and nt realizing it." Wihelmine "Are you saying he is that sensitive?" Saundra "He may be that sensitive. It's all I am saying. Didn't you hear him again? Meaning it's been twice in the same week?" Wihelmine" Yes, I find that unusual. However, he is in a bind he calls out to Orville. But this doesn't appear to be Orville he was talking too. I just want to know what he is up to this time. Other than the mission Jacob and Horatio roped him into this time." Saundra "Mother I suggest we go back to the club. More customers are coming in." Wihelmine "Yes, your right we better get going. It's a few hours until dawn." Then he hears silence. No more voices. As Orin drifts into a deep sleep. As he dreams, he sees images in his head. Of the town beneath his feet. With a woman he is dancing with. As they are dancing above the town. He is looking around to see the whole area. He knows this woman is wearing a sleek white dress with a corsage with white rose and jasmine in it. As he drifts deeper into the dream. He hears a voice in his head "Now young man you had a vison of your love. Tis a good vison. You will have more dreams and visons of things to come. But you will be tried and tested in the coming months. But you will pas them all. Your true nae will be revealed. Also, your father will have time for his children. At long last he will have time for his children. Now dream some more. And the visons will come. Oh…by the way it's morning now." The he wakes up. With the sun light through the curtains. As Orin walks to the balcony. He sees people watching the club the market and patrolling around the house. As he decides to go to take a shower. As he goes to the hallway. He sees Orville.

Orville "I was about to wake you. How did you sleep?"

Orin "So, so…What is with all the people here?"

Orville "Well, the people who want to meet you. Decided to change the meeting place here instead of the school."

Orin "Oh…great. When are they coming over?"

Orville "Well Tania and your mother are setting up the living room area. They will be here in about an hour. They are going to be here in an hour. So now clean yourself up fast and proper. Also, young man you're going to wear a suit too. You're going to be tested n how may family manners. So any other questions?" As he gives a apologetic look.

Orin "Which family or families are coming over?"

Orville sighs "I was hoping you wouldn't as that. It's the following heads Darquefelou, Darkfellow, Darquemoon, Darkmun, Lupus, Lupon, Wolfsen, Wolfsan. This is the tip of the iceberg."

Orin "Why all the hub bub?"

Orville "Well your mother's is an exiled from her family. However, they wanted to take you from her. As you well know. Now they're coming here in this get together. You need to know that these families are at a cease of hostilities with each other and your mother's family. Apparently, one of the deals is that you two were never to live here. Now that you're here. They have to weigh in is it worth keeping you two?"

Orin rolls his eyes "All I want is to go to school and a good education and live life a bit. Isn't that too much to ask?"

Orville "Apparently it is. Because that is all I want out of life too!"

Orin "How are we getting out of this mess?"

Orville "Well that is up to Tania and well… Wihelmine, Pauline, Xenia and Kathy do in your behalf. I never seen all of them take such a liking to a young man in some time." AS he gives a wry smile to Orville. As he holds up the suit he picked for Orin with the proper tie.

Orin "Okay, now let me get ready and get into that suit."

Orville "I'll tie the tie-on you son. And remember let the ladies do all the taking."

Orin "Alright. I hate ties. But I'll let you do it."

Orville "Now go, I'll stop holding you up." As he lets Orin go tot eh bathroom. AS Orin turns up the water and the stream in the bathroom. As he steps in the shower. He hears a voice

Voice "Wow, you are a big boy. Hmm Can't wait until you become a full-grown man. If you're not one yet." As Orin whips his head around. He sees a Sandy brown hair woman with a fancy sleek green dress. She has green eyes as she licks her lips.

Voice "Forgive me, my name is Virginia Tepes Darkmun."

Orin "Virginia, would you please leave my bathroom now!"

Virginia "Well, you can't help a curious girl for wanting a peeeeek!!" As hand is pulling her ear. As they see it's his Mothe Pulling her hair.

Virginia "Opps, sorry!"

Erin "Not as sorry as you're going to be if you stay in this bathroom!"

Virginia "I wouldn't make threats I couldn't back up."

Tania "Young lady she has more than enough backing her up. Please leave the poor boy alone. He needs to get ready good and proper! Unless you want to directly deal with me!" Virginia just slips out of the bathroom.

Erin "Sorry honey we are letting them in early. I was forced to do this."

Tania "Now I'm regretting it. Now I have to get people to watch the inside the house."

Orin "Just have Orville guard the door. And I'll let hm dress me so to speak. Is that Okay with the two of you?" Both Ladies nod in agreement.

Erin "I'll get him." They Hear Orville outside screaming at people. As the ladies get out of the bathroom. Orville enters really quick.

Orville "Those dam women letting them in early! I should hog tie them all to a few posts. You need to get ready faster now. You still wear the suit. I tie the tie for you." As Orin finishes up cleaning and a shave. As he puts on the suit. And he feels the fact the shirt and the pants and jacket. Orin wonders how this fits so well. As he comes out of the bathroom. Orville ties up the tie good and proper for a southern gentleman. As they go downstairs, He sees the lower floors with the families arrived. As he looks around. These society people are inspecting the house as if they own it. The Orin wonders if they do own it as the landlords. AS they look around, they look upon him and smile.

Orin "My name is Orin Ezekiel McNeil, at your service." As he bows his head to the crowd. Remembering the basic lessons so he wouldn't make them angry. One young man walks up to him and say "Hello, my name is Luke Tepes Darkmun." As he extends his hand for a shake. Orin responds with the handshake as he bows his head while shaking hands. Making eye contact as he shakes the hand of this man.

Luke Tepes Darkmun" Wow, you have a firm grip. Have you met one of our family before today before?"

Orin "Nope just today. I will be working in the game shoppe. It's my third day in town."

Luke Tepes Darkmun "Oh...And wow, I can guess who gave a crash course of the manners that are to be expected Not many would remember to do that right away." Before Orin gets a chance to answer. Horatio enters the room.

Horatio "Orin come over here now. Sorry to interrupt you, Luke. But the heads want a good look over him." As Horatio saves Orin from Luke's questions.

Orin "Thank you' whispering it.

Horatio "Well it isn't over yet. Your mother's clan arrive here. The Belmonte's are here with eh McNeil off shoot of them. They are very pissed that you made it here passed their check points. The Head of the clan, your grandfather is here." Orin turns pale white and shakes uncontrollably.

Orin "He's here!"

Horatio "Yes, he is. Why are you shaking like that?"

Orin "He is the one who took me. And my father had to give him a few scars to get me back to my other."

Horatio "Oh...Well, he is here. But the rest have to feel your worth the effort for keeping. But the Darkmun's are not to be trifled with. They are cunning as they are dangerous. And Luke is one of the more cunning vipers you will ever meet. He gives Rodney a run for his money."

Orin simply nods in agreement. Still shaking and trying to control it. As he approaches the table. The Family Heads are there. He sees his grandfather and the other side of the table. He about to rise. When Orville signals him to sit down. Orville nods at Orin to sit down next to Tania and his mother. The other ladies in the house simply star down his grandfather. He also sees his enforcer a rather large man, with long hair and sunglasses. You can see a few scars on his face. His grandfather has silver hair now. With a few wrinkles now. He stares Orin down and smiles at his grandson.

Grandfather "Now boy you have grown a bit. Don't be afraid of Regan here. He wont bite. I promise you all that. I prefer to be called Grand Ferret. My grandson may call me grandpa." Orin just rolls his eyes.

Grandpa "He has your sarcastic manners, Erin. I would've hoped he wouldn't inherit those habits. But I was hoping he would have some of his father manner's. I t pains me to admit that he has manners."

Regan "I would love to repay him for his manners."

Jacob "Regan, play nice. Or I will scalp you for your lack of manners boy."

Horatio "Normally, I would disagree with the savage. But in this case, I'll help him by holding your cracker ass down Regan." Regan sneers at both and the other side of the table.

Grand Ferret "Now, Regan we ae here to discuss this young man's future here. Now no old grudges to be had here. I just want my say in this matter. I am amazed that the Darkfellow's and the Darkmoon's with the Wolfsen's and Wolfsan's all in one place. You are here a whole two days. And I wonder if you are set for his education?"

Erin "As I recall correctly. I could come here with him for his education. And I did it without your help. If he could help me. Then it was very indirect means."

Regan "Now sweetheart, I would show more respect to your father?"

Erin "Listen asshole, I go two men willing to scalp you. All I ask is to have that pleasure for myself. Or losing your balls and forced to eat them wasn't goo enough for you last time?"

As Grand Ferret hold his arm back "Now Erin, I wouldn't want to cause any trouble."

Xenia "It's too late for that Grand Ferret. What are your demands. And I'll see if we can accommodate you. But I highly doubt it. At this rate your cohort is going. Your not getting anything. So, let's make this quick?"

Grandpa "Very well, Erin I want to take over the education of your boy. And I will educate him here. But I want better lodging for him. And him to put in the west end as to this spot of town. I feel he is too close to unsavory types. Really across the street from a strip club?"

Tania "Well, there is huge problems with that. He already started his work program as of last night. Once that happens, he is locked in for three years to the full package. Also, your daughter started the job. So, they are locked into the contracts."

Grand Ferret "I request humbly to you to break it. So, I can provide for my grandson. I would like to get to know him as well. I feel as far as the rest of you. This will no longer concern you. So, I humbly request that all deals are to be made null and void."

Erin "Over my rotting cold hands father. Maybe I should scalp your as well."

Tania "Erin, now please be civil. I know after his multiple attempts of taking him. But there are other considerations here."

Grand Ferret "Why thank you lady Tania."

Tania "Don't thank me yet Ferret."

Grand Ferret" It's.."

Orville "Young man I would stop while you're behind."

Grand Ferret "Okay, But I will. But I will not stand for this request to be denied."

Luke Tepes Darkmun "Grand Ferret, I must say the artwork your grandson has created is a treasure. I would rather see his education furthered here. However, I suggest he stays where he is. The west end is rather a dull place. Nothing there to inspire him. After seeing the pieces. He's more of a person that gets inspired with lively places. Nothing nature based as I can tell."

Grand Ferret "Tepes Darkmun?"

Luke "Yes, that is my family name."

Regan "Aren't you young to speak for your family?"

Grand Ferret "Now Regan, let the young man speak for his family. And their interests, if he can."

A man step behind Luke. He is the same height as Luke. Medium build with long silver hair. He says "So this is the Grand Ferret and his Enforcer Regan. I'm not impressed honkeys."

Grand Ferret "May I have the Pleasure of your name?"

The man says "My name is Malcom Darkfellow. As my relation said. What you propose isn't worth it. Are you trying to stifle this boy before he hits his potential? If so, why?"

Grand Ferret "Well he is the last male heir to my line. He holds the McNeil name. Plus, Belmonte's family of my late wife's line. So, I would like him remanded to my care as of right now."

Malcom "Well sir, you can make the request. It doesn't mean it will be granted. It will have to be made by the families here. As for now sir. I will have to deny the request you have made. Due to how the ruckus you made coming here. And the fact you resorted to kidnapping on multiple occasions to this young man. Also, the fact we had to help get him passed your people to get him here. It's one of the reasons why we moved them in right away. And the contracts that are made can't be undone until the renewal. So you have to bow to them."

Grand Ferret "Well, we have an issue friend. I can't back down. Neither can the Belmonte's."

Kathy "The boy stays put. You can no longer dictate anything anymore about your daughter nor her child life. She has been on the run from you for twelve years. I'd say you have no real authority. And you never have since she got married."

Pauline "Before you go over the name changes. She had to change names constantly because you hunted them down. And you are still disappointed in her. You aren't in a position to dictate terms. So as for now your initial request is denied. The rest of the families here will agree. Anything else?"

Regan "This isn't over!"

Grandpa "Regan, I just lost a round but not the fight. I'll be staying a while. I can shoppe anywhere I want. Also, I can visit the school too?"

Orville. "It depends on what you are doing. If either of them feels your harassment. I will throw you out f this town faster than you can say Kennedy's chicken!"

Regan "Now you old coot. I can make you go away real fast and quick."

Grandpa "Regan! Knock it off. They won the round. But not the war. All I have to do is petition more than just the families here. And I shall do that." As he gets up to take his leave. He stares down at his daughter and grandson. He smiles and leave the house. As he is leaving. He is stopped by Miguel De le Guy the 36th.

Miguel "Grand Ferret, his is a restraining order that states that you can't be closer than ten thousand yards from his daughter or his Grandson. Also, any proxies you may have to act on your behalf. Aer under the same conditions. Meaning we've collected all the names of every living member of your clan as well. With all known Blood lines. You have been now served." As Grandpa reads his restraining order. His face turns very angry with tears. He looks at Orville with such contempt.

Grandpa "So, Orville how did you get all the names?"

Horatio "He didn't, you stupid savage. I did. Because they started up a lot of ruckuses last night. That is how I got the names. Your so, called chase people were having too much fun at Jacob's clubs." Grandpa simply sneers at the crowd. As they leave the house starts to empty out. Tanis was impressed that Erin and Orin stayed quiet. Once the house emptied out.

Erin "I thought we gave them the slip."

Orin "What price did we pay now?"

Erin "You must open three shows in three different galleries. With the finished works you have."

Orin "Great!"

Erin "I'm sorry baby. I had to give them something or you are joining twenty different societies. So, choosing the art shows was the east painful. Well, I thought it was the least painful."

Orin "Yeah, you are right about that. So, what do I have to dig through for each gallery?"

Erin "Tania already picked the pieces. So, they were moved out to the galleries. Ready to go and impress everyone in town." Giving a sorry look to her son. Orin decide to change clothes. AS he walks upstairs to his room. He sees Miguel on the balcony. Miguel just waves and he comes to the balcony.

Miguel "Your grandfather was rather well connected. However, Wihelmine is better connected with the right people. So, you thank her, the next time you se her. Got that?"

Orin "Yes, I do. Anything else I should know?"

Miguel "Yes, the patrols with be quadrupled. I don't trust your grandfather's word about being a good loser. He isn't leaving even though he should." As they check a few things out.. Orin looks around where the tunnels entrance is. Miguel De Le Guy.

Miguel "Don't worry about that entrance there. It's lock is quadruple the military locks. But that is because your father does handle a lot of sensitive information. And your grandfather wanted to check out this house for a while. But you should've seen what happened at your grandfather stepped out of the house. It was a sight to behold."

Orin "What do you mean about that?"

Miguel "Well he and Regan slipped on the stairs and fell on their asses. And then as they got back up they slipped again and slide into the fruit cart and then fell into the candy cart. Then they slipped into eh ice cream stand. They are covered in ice cream and candy and fruits and vegetable. I heard they flew into the three carts. Also bounced in the air a few times as well."

Orin simply laughs and says, "Yeah I wished I could have seen that."

Erin "Yeah me to! Now you apparently passed your manners test too after the he was escorted out of the town. Now we have to get you settled into he school life. Your uniforms have arrived. So, I would get ready soon. I heard because of this event. School will start three days early for some of the grades. Meaning you start tomorrow." Orin rolls his eyes and gets the books ready for the first day of school. As the afternoon slides to evening. He hears the ladies whisper on the balcony. As he approached the balcony, he hears the Von Wieb sister arguing with Virginia Tepes Darkmun.

Saundra "Now Virginia, really, he was just taking a fucking shower. Now you really ruined it for anyone else that comes into this house!"

Virginia "Now, don't get those poor excuses of panties in a bunch. Not everyone have a perfect set of breast that don't require a bra for support. Also, he is way too young for me. And if I may say way too young for the rest of you. Remember I was invited in the home. The lot of you don't have the invite." Sticking her tongue out at the sisters.

Rory "Keep it up Gina, and I'll make that pretty little head of yours worse for wear."

Colleen "Yeah Gina, and just maybe we will brand you while we're at it."

Virginia "You'll know I hate that name of Gina!" With an angry look on her face.

Becca "You know this is our spot. Orin knows and still accepted that this is our spot. He leaves us alone. And we let him join in. When we deem fit. You're not welcomed on our spots. Now get out of the spot."

Rachel "Now get off the balcony Virginia. Because I'll beat that prissy Lil ass out of the balcony. And don't come back again." As Orin walks on the porch.

Orin "Now Ladies, I would suggest a peaceful way out. Virginia, would you please leave now. I need to have a bit of fresh air. And I don't need hard times with my neighbors right now."

Virginia "Okay, Orin I'll leave for now. But I will enjoy the hospitality of your home another day." As she winks in front of the Weib sisters. As she walks through the room and shows her way out the home. Orin just rolls his eye. Feeling overwhelmed. The he hears a loud yell as a commotion of bumps down the stairs. They hear Gina's voice.

Virginia "Who the fuck pushed me down the stairs!"

Erin "Young lady you tripped the alarms here I guess why are you walking down the stairs inside my home?"

Virginia "Well. I"

Erin "Get the fuck out now! Your Lucky you are leaving with the bumps and bruises on that bony lil ass!" Orin and the girls laugh as they heard that. As they hear Erin walk to the room on to the balcony. Erin sees the kids as they regain their composure.

Erin" I guess she decided to tell all of you who is boss by doing that?" The girls simply nodded in agreement. Erin simply smiles at them. Looking around the balcony. She sees the view from the house to the club. Then looks around and enjoying the view. She notices the things you can see from here. Also, the how scrupulous or how unscrupulous you can be wit the view.

Erin "You five like to people watch too?"

Rory "Yes, also it's a nice view because you can see half the town from here if you have binoculars or a telescope. I noticed they your son has both?"

Erin "Yes, force of habit. But since most of you people here know what my father is famous for. You can understand why we have them." As she gives an apologetic look to the girls. The girls simply wave it off and smile. Also, they give Erin a hug.

Becca "Don't worry, Miguel De le Guy the 36th is on the job. Yes, we make jokes about him being a screw up. But that is how he disarms you in to thinking he is a simpleton. He really annoys Rodney that way. Playing the fool, and seeing you screw up. He does that all the time. Kindhearted man, and a real believer in what he does. Then again, what do you expect from a descendant of a templar." Erin's eyes widen by that.

Erin "Wait a minute, he is the 36th descendant of Miguel De le Guy the first?" As the girls nod in acknowledgement.

Erin "Whoa…I guess we are in great hands. It's said each new generation of that line is tougher wiser than the last?"

Colleen "Yes, they are. Twelve Generations were taught here. The 2t4h is buried here. Also, they have a wing dedicated to the family line. The De Le Guy's are really good people. The 35th and the 35th are still kicking. The 33rd was laid to rest last years. Boy the stories told of his exploits are fun. So, to speak." As Colleen smiles.

Saundra "Also, the 36th is also the head of the local militia. So, he has a rank of Major in the CSA reserve army. He will go for the test to become Cornel soon. I hope he passes it. He also runs a few classes in the military college and is a CBI field agent trainer now. He was on the field for a short while. He likes educating the next generation."

Erin "So, he pretty much ran my old man out of town. Yeah, with Rodney's help. He can't help but to pull practical jokes. Also, Becca here likes to do that. So, I wouldn't put it pass you to have helped him this time around?" Raising an eyebrow.

Becca "Nope I didn't have time to prepare a good one. Also, mom did want us to stay out of this one too. Virginia has a way of throwing us underneath a bus. After all, she did screw us out of other gainful employment in the Asian 7 Pacific Tea company market. You know I like suggesting makeup to other women. Or the fact I do like painting nails."

Rory "True, or how Luke messed up the job interview at the boutique for clothes. In the west end of town. I do like dressing people up. Men and women. It doesn't matter to me."

Colleen "Or how both of them ruined my library interviews. With the internship at the town hall. Tania was running those. Which didn't help any." As Colleen frowns about that.

Rachel "Lest we not forget. The coming out party we were supposed to have. They decided to book the entire hall and force us out. Also ruining all the dresses, we had too. Nana is still angry about that. Also running Totowa out of town with the Owen too. Talk about men that were worthy and didn't have a chance in life." As the girls put their heads down and sighs.

Erin "Wow, The Darkmun's are a powerful family."

Colleen "You don't know the half of it. I hear Luke really likes you Orin?"

Orin "He tended to vouch for my artwork. And how I wouldn't be a good fit living with my grandpa. I wouldn't say that I made a friend out of him. I don't really know what to make of him. Now that school I am starting a few days early now." As the girls giggle a lot.

Becca "Ah... Don't worry about starting early. They always start early when the practical joke wars start. And those wars last all trimester. If there isn't a prank a day. Watch your back. One is coming for you soon. Also, the gossip about who is going to out prank who. Which club is going to win the trimester cup this time around? And all the other fun events that are held in daytime or nighttime." As Becca smiles mischievously

Erin raises an eyebrow "Now, young lady. I hope my boy isn't a target of yours. Or an willing or unwilling accomplice. If you have bright ideas, now put an end to them."

Rory looking innocently "Nope, no designs on him per say. However, I fear she may ask him for suggestions. And please do not give out harmless information Orin. In here gossip is as good as gold. So keep your trap shut. Especially around Becca here." Becca glares at Rory.

Cassandra "Now, Rebecca you know you're always up to something. Please don't drag him into your shenanigans. We don't want to lose our view here. Especially that this fine woman and fine young man allows us to hang here for our breaks." Becca raises here hand as in submitting with okay I get look in her face.

As Rory asks Erin "So what is your father trying to do here?"

Erin "Well he has no worthy heirs to his title so to speak. And I don't want Orin mixed up in that mess. If I can help it. But most of you know about that don't you?"

Saundra "Yes, we do. We have heard that there was a renegade in his family. We didn't expect it would be his prized daughter. That he was so proud of. His boy didn't produce worthy heirs?"

Erin "Nope, all of them women. And none of them showing any type of aptitude for what he wants out of them. I guess he was hoping that Orin here would show aptitude for what he is looking for. I'm praying that he doesn't have any of those gifts." With a hope look on her face.

Orin "I just want to be an artist, writer, and a good businessman. Making enough to live comfortably. Not too rich, and not too poor. Hence all my interests in games, comics, scientific discoveries. History, and other subjects."

Becca "Why not war?"

Orin "I saw a man die preventing my abduction that my grandpa attempted. I think it was the third?"

Erin "Yes, it was. He was a good friend to us in the colony."

Orin "Yeah, he was cool. He taught me how to draw. I miss him a lot."

The girls put their hands over their mouth and let out in unison "Oh…"

Colleen 'Sorry to hear that. I'm sure he was a good man."

Orin and Erin in unison "Yes he was."

Wihelmine from behind Orin and Erin "What are all of you up to here? Sorry for the intrusion Erin."

Erin "No worries Wihelmine, just let Virginia Tepes Darkmun out the hard way." Wihelmine laughs hard to the point of hiccups. Now all the girls start laughing as hard until the hiccups start with them as well. After five minutes of straight laughter. They manage to get their compusre. After gewtting their composure.

Wihelmine asks "Now how bad did that snotty git it?"

Erin "Well, I made sure, that she isn't the boss of this house. That is for sure. Tania and I are very angry with here right now."

Wihelmine "Why is that?"

Erin "My boy is and isn't kind of shy. Depending on the situation that is. In this case She snuck into the bathroom as he was showering taking a good long peak. Tania and I pull her by the ears out of the bathroom. That is why Orville was eyeing the rest of the area out today in the house." Wihelmine looks outraged, and sneers and snorts.

Wihelmine "Why that little......" As she composes herself.

Erin "that is how I felt., yes."

Wihelmine "As you should. She and her cousin Luke think they run the place. Very well-spoken people. But they are as nasty as they come. However, depending on the situation. Either you want their help. Or you should politely reject their help. It all depends on the situation. I would be wary of their involvement in anything."

Orin "Just asking, does he play War Sytche 90k?"

The girls in unison say "Yes, he is the regional champion here!"

Orin "Oh...Well I guess I'll play him at Moon-Dog's. AT Horatio runs a good establishment. Right?"

Colleen "Horatio will only let him in for qualifying rounds. Because he caught him cheating one time too many. Tania lets him play because of his family name. And also, the fact other members buy and play that game in her shoppe."

Rory "You are registered in Moon-Dog's Orin?"

Orin "Ahh.. Yes, there was one of his shoppes in London Ontario. Before he had to close it down. I have a lot of credit there. And he had all my orders of stuff in stock still. Why do you ask?"

Rory "We are only allowed in Tania's shoppe when invited. But Horatio's Moon-Dog's we can come in all the time. He doesn't mind us too much. He finds it funny how we dig into Jacob when he is there."

Orin "Oh.."

Wihelmine "Now girls you are all in five minutes. Sorry to interrupt this fin conversation. But we have to go back to work. The night is so young. And don't worry your pretty little heads. This place is more than secure. Besides, the fun will only get better. Once you get used to it here. Oh, by the way. It's going to b loud tonight. If you hear gun shots. Don't be alarmed. The nighttime shooting competition will begin in about an hour. So don't worry about it."

Erin "Thank you! Is the community calander always this booked?"

Wihelmine "Why yes, it is. It's how most of the revenue of the town. SO, it's busy like this all the time. But don't worry about unsavory types sneaking in. We have one of the best magistrates in charge of security here. He does not look like much. But he is scary competent at his job."

Erin "Are you talking about Miguel?"

Wihelmine "Yes, I am. Very hard to allure so to speak. Trust me we've tried on multiple occasions. The boy has a mind like a steele trap. And once you set off that trap. Boy you are going to regret it. So, please don't give him a hard time. He is that good. So is the rest of his family too."

Erin "It's okay I won't do that. I would like to chat with his and his family. I ama fan of his descendants."

Wihelmine "That can be easily arranged. Just to Orville about it. He will be more than glad to arrange it. Now we have to go. Cay later you two."

As Wihelmine and the and the girls turn around a loud bang sounds off in the front of the house. As hey turn. Orin hears a whoosh again. This time he saw a slight glimmer at the conner of his eye. As he turns, they are gone. The noise in the front was a few firecrackers going off. This worries Orin a bit. Grandfather knows where they are. He has a house here. Which is worse and was ran out of town to boot. Now he wonders if he has anyone here to take him away. As he walks to his bed, he hears a voice in his head. The voice he hears is Stoner-Boy's "Now, young man don't worry. He can't get back in without the say of the town council, The Mayor and the league of societies. Now read your bible and study the word. I would suggest Job and Judges for what is on your mind. And do read the rest Johnny gave you as well. I'll be by later. Once you relax. I have a lot of things to do. And don't worry I wont toke up in the house. But I will have the bong with me." As Orin turns around and sees nothing but the room the way it is. He now pounders about hearing the voices in his head. He never had this happen to him before. And he wonders who to talk to about this? As he opens the bible and stars reading judges and taking the notes. He wonders what this all means to him. The voices of the girls and their mother. Stoner-boy's voice. He pounders in silence then he speaks aloud his prayer.

Orin "God, it's been a while. I just got to another town. A really, wonderful but strange town. I made new acquaintances. But I do not know who to trust or believe in. My Grandfather knows where I am. I really don't like that. I really like Cassandra, but I know she prefers Saundra. I do like her sisters. At least they are being themselves. I'm wondering when my dad will finally show up in person. I'm scared for a lot of things. These people don't know what my grandfather is capable of doing. SO, I fear for their lives and livelihoods. I don't want to be the center of attention. I just want to live my life without heavy troubles. I just want a peaceful life for a change. And be what I am meant to be." As he is reading judges he sees Stoner-Boy in the balcony.

Stoner-Boy 'Hello, did I just hear you pray?" As he walks into the room.

Orin 'Yes…You did hear me pray. What brings you here now?"

Stoner-Boy "I hear you had a lot commotion today?"

Orin "Yeah, I did. Does everyone know how to get up hear?"

Stoner-Boy "Not everyone. Virginia has to come in through the front door. The poor girl is afraid of heights. So, the way the other girls come in is rather funny compared to her entrances and exits. Then again, you're supposed to not notice things at all. If your mother has here way. Unfortunately, it won't be that way for her. In some regards. It will be okay for her. In other regards. It won't be. She is trying to make life happy for you. But the families are now involved with your life. Which means you have to join a few of the societies here. I Suggest you go into the ones Jacob and Horatio belong to. Those are rather fun and interesting. I do belong to them as your father does as well. And Rev Jonathan Rodrick Kingsley. We do things for the community. We are all one body here. We're all one soul too. And especially we are all one mind too. We try to make everyone who lives here family. So, you'll end up picking them for yourself. Also, you will annoy everyone too. But you will have to choose what you will go into. As for Luke and Virginia. They are troubled and burdened with family obligations. Also desires that never came into proper fruition in their minds. That is why they're the way they act. It's annoying. But the War Scythe 90 k game you both play. Well, he is one of the tougher customers here. You did defeat him a couple times. He doesn't know it yet. But you did beat him a few times. So, I suggest when you do play him keep it on the down low. People do want to see the surprise on his face when he is defeated. The tournament is in a few months. I know you will beat him. You think outside the box, like your grandfather and father. But don't worry, The Grand Ferret has no hold nor sway here. All he can do is impede people for coming here. He can't actually block them from entering and leaving. My boy you have nothing to worry about. So what else is on your mind?' Orin is surprised that he let him talk all the way without asking a single question.

Orin "Do you think God is watching us now?" Stoner-Boy simply laughs.

Stoner-Boy "Yes, he is always watching. However, the watchful eye and running t he universe as we know it is a hard task. Especially that rascal of a first born of his. Always causing mischief. Always ruining their souls. Always biding his time before the end. I swear the devil loves to attempt turn Jesus's hair green. And in the end the devil loses his hair. All he wants is everyone to be good to one another. He wants to come home play with his kids a little. Enjoy his life too. And share the glory with his flock."

Orin "What is with the bong and the removable water collector in it?"

Stoner-Boy" Ahh...it's how this is special compared to other bongs. I'll show you one day. But that is when you're ready." Orin nods in agreement.

Orin "So anything good happen to you today?"

Stoner-Boy "Why thank you for asking that. You know you are one of the very few who asks me how a I doing? The assume that I'm so stoned I don't know they are bad mouthing me when I offer them to toke up?" Orin simply nods in agreement.

Orin "I didn't know people trat you this badly?"

Stoner-Boy "Well, they talk behind my back. They assume I don't hear them. It just hurts me that they are so vain. If they realized that they are really doing to each other. Maybe they can be kinder to each other."

Orin "Well humanity is perfect in its flaws."

Stoner-Boy "True, but that isn't the perfection God A.K.A Jesus never intended. That is Jesus's heart ache. That day he has to bring the rod to the rest of humanity isn't going to be a pretty site. Those that obey will be spared. That is why the gift of free will can be used properly or abuse properly depending on your chosen point of view. You can succumb to darkness. Or you can bask in the light through obedience. Which do you prefer?"

Orin "I would rather bask in the light. My issue is that I'm not perfect. And I feel unworthy.

Stoner-Boy "There is no way you can be God or Jesus. You're not supposed to be God or Jesus. You are supposed to be yourself. The best version of yourself. Let's look at Peter. The rock he based his who ministry after he was crucified. Very crass individual. One night on his boat he sees Jesus walk on water like if it was an everyday act. But for a human it's a feat unimaginable. He invites him to walk on it. With the promise that he won't sink. He starts walking on the water. At first, he isn't sinking. But as he drew closer and realized what he was doing. He loses his faith momentarily. And he starts to sink. Until Jesus reaches out his hand and pull him up on to the water and walks him back to the boat. Seeing miracle after miracle. Peter's faith was built up. Brick by brick. With layer of mortar in his spirit. And yet when he was going to be arrested. He told Peter that he will lose faith in him again like that night on the boat. Be saying he, Peter would deny him three times before the rooster crows. When Peter did this. And the people that once knew him saw the radically changed man he became. His walk had a lot to do with him losing faith one more time. Attaining the enlighten sate is easy. Maintaining it, now that is the hard part. You have to put the work. Most churches sell it's easy thing to do. But you do have to work for it. Jesus promised that things would get better. But he didn't promise it would be easy. He always said that we as in humanity, would have to work for it." Orin is just at awe of what was just said.

Orin "So there is just too many people doing lip service, when they should be practicing?"

Stoner-Boy "Unfortunately yes, once humanity decided to twist the work. As always things got worse. Before it gets better. But I try to push forward. It's always a struggle to teach the meaning of the word. As compared to memorizing the word. I find there a frightening number that quote the word. But have nor really belief in the word. It's about understanding the true intent of the word. The surprising thing about the word itself. Is that the intent changes as you grow into your relationship with Jesus. One verse meant something today. That same verse ten years from now will evolve to even more profound meaning. Because the word is always profound. It always holds deep meaning. The word in immutable. How your mind perceives things is what is evolving with the deepest meaning of the word. This is the growth of the cardinal mind to the spiritual mind. The more the spiritual mind. The more you will be able to success beyond your dreams. By allowing the lord to work at his schedule. Instead of your is the hardest yet rewarding step. Because you have to show patience with the lord as he shows with you. That is one of the keys. Do no harm. That is the most important thing to do. Veryone you meet is your brother and sister. If not by blood, in evr other way. You will have fights, squabbles disagreements. But if you don't show the love and respect. You and the other will loose way too much in life." Stoner-Boy now tokes up. As Orin looks upon with a dazed yet profound look.

Stoner-Boy "Now I'll leave you to your reading assignments of the work. Don't worry about what happened today. Just rest tonight, you have a big day tomorrow. It' a brand-new life you have here. Boy, and it's going to be a fun ride. I Prophesize you find everything you wished for and more. You will find love, acceptance, appreciation, honor, and happiness here. And a few other surprises that will make you laugh. After all, the lord did create humor too."

CHAPTER 12

The first day at the Andersonville School of the Confederacy

Orin wakes up. It's the twilight be fore dawn. As he looks at the balcony, he sees Saundra looking at him. She smiles to see him rested and finally awake. Even though it's about fifteen minutes before sunrise. As he walks to he balcony and slides the door open.

Saundra "Finally awake. You were so peaceful in your sleep."

Orin "Yes, I was sleeping peacefully. Why were you watching me?"

Saundra "You intrigue us a lot. Finding out that you're the grandson of the Grand Ferret. Well, it's just added more layers to you. And a lot of people want to know about you now. You're the grandson he doesn't know of. You stay n the shadows in his community. Some members of his community live here. But they don't have power here. And here you are. A mystery to be solved. What is your mother hiding from you and us? These are the many questions about you people want answered. We know you are unaware of these answers. Your mother knows some of the answers. But your father has the rest of the answers we believe. I myself and my sisters have no contact with our father. So, we know the feeling all too well. Our mother hides stuff from us. Our nana, however, says we are not ready yet. And she keeps it at that. You might have the privilege of meeting her one day." AS she stands up and see the the first peek of day light coming through and sees the sky turning form black to light black with a hint of blue. She smiles and says "My time is almost up. I have to go in a few minutes. I wonder why I am so curious about the sun when I can enjoy it's warmth. Can you go to the bathroom and get me a cut of water please?"

Orin "If you want me to turn around and walk off. Just say so. I'll respect why. Is that okay?" Saundra simply smiles.

Saundra "Orin until we figure a few things out. You have to play along, okay?" smiling

Orin sighs "Okay, I'll turn around and walk. But I'm not getting the water, okay?"

Saundra smiling "okay…" As he turns around, he hears a swoosh. But he sees a glimmer at the corner of his eye. About halfway to his bed. He decides to turn around again. Now she is gone. He walks over to the balcony. And when he is outside. He sees all five young women under the cover on the awning of the club. Speaking with each other. They see him and simply wave good morning. He sees them smiling as they walk back inside the club. Now he has a funny feeling the next few months are going to be interesting. As he concentrated on the words Stoner-Boy said. I will find all that I wish and much more. As he wonders about everything. He hears a voice of Rev Johnny.

Rev Johnny "I see that you're up now?" As he turns around and sees him in a suit.

Orin "Oh. I keep forgetting this is like bedtime for you?" AS Johnny laughs.

Rev Johnny "Yeah, it is so to speak. But unlike most people. You are used to unusual circumstances. So, this isn't new to you. I did speak to your grandfather, however. And I did explain that his input was unwanted and unnecessary. But to appease him, since he and I do go way back. He is merely satisfied. That I will be a profound influence on your education here. So, he did leave. But not in the manner he envisioned. He really wanted to live here. But since he has caused a lot of trouble. He had to leave. But he will find his way back to live in the other side of town. He does own the building there. But he can visit occasionally on vacation or holidays." Orin simply sighs.

Orin "When is the first holiday here?"

Rev Johnny "Well that will be in six weeks. However, it's a long waiting list to enter town in this holiday. Because it's the day of our college football championship and college hockey playoffs too start too."

Orin "Well at least he can't get into the town, right?"

Rev Johnny 'Well he can if he has a valid ticket. With the corresponding reservation. And I won't give him that. Your mother and him were never on great terms to begin with. He only acknowledged her when she gave birth to you Orin."

Orin "oh… Great, since I'm the only male heir of his."

Rev Johnny "Yeah…He is Old Testament that way. He wanted me to marry his daughter. But respected that I made my commitment to God. So he is happy that I'm one of the teachers in the school."

Orin "So, when is class?"

Rev Johnny "That will be later tonight. I just wanted to visit you before your first day. Orville and Tania is taking you in today. And it's a rarity that they both escort one student. Let alone both of them doing it. The Families here are now way too interested in you. Thanks to your grandfather. I'll take my leave. But I don't agree with your grandfather. So, he won't have the influence he thinks. Your mother is relieved about that. But you enjoy life a bit. And one more thing. I suggest you don't get to close to the Von Weib sisters. Wihelmine has a very nasty temper. She tends to overreact when she is angry. The girls have the same problem. Either is a huge explosion. Or it's a slow burn. Either way this is bad. So be very careful. Now I'll take my leave. You need to get ready for school." As Johnny leaves the room. AS Orin looks around and sees his uniform laid out with a note on it. He reads the note. It's from Orville. Son don't worry about nothing. Just concentrate on your studies and you will be fine. Sorry about the dirty laundry you are going to hear today. But the wife and I are always at each other's throats. See you at 7 am. Orin goes to the bathroom. He checks all the entrances and exits before he showers. After the shower he puts on his school uniform. It's a suit with the vest in naval dark blue. It's almost black, with a white shirt and red tie. He hates ties, but he will wear it. The jacket has the emblem of the school. So does the vest. The emblem has the picture of the central building with a dragon curled around it with a dove in the left. With a a bat on the right with a tiger in the center of the patch. He did notice this in the tour. But

155

never asked what was, the significance of this type of coat of arms. All he knows is that he is hungry now. As he walks down to the kitchen. He notices it's a bustle with activity. He sees Orville cooking breakfast. He sees Tania, his mother. And Virginia and Luke Tepes Darkmun. He isn't happy about this either. But can tell Orville isn't happy. As he is platting the food for the guest. As Orin comes down. He finds his seat.

Orin "Good morning all of you"

Tania "Sorry for the last-minute guests Orin. But both of them rather insisted that they have breakfast with you. I'm surprised that Orville is cooking for everyone here without a fuss."

As Orin walks to Orville "Do you need help?"

Orville smiles "No, thank you for the offer by the way. It's nice that you are helpful. Now sit down and eat up. The French toast is great if I say so myself." There is plated bacon and sausages with scrambled eggs and gravy. As Orin sits down as he attempts to settle himself. Virginia and Luke pass him the plates of French toast and eggs.

Orin 'Thank you. What brings you here today?"

Luke "I wanted to get to know you better. Also, Virginia came by to apologize to your mother and you for her behavior." As he looks at his cousin Virginia. She smiles and waves.

Virginia "Sorry about my behavior. I tend to be a little too playful for my own good."

Orin "Apology accepted. Just don't do that again. I bet my mother gave you hell and back already. If not, you too are in deeper trouble."

Tania is about to kick Orin until she sees Orville's glare "Tania, yes of course, it's her house after all now."

Orville smiles "Yes, it's hers now. No complaints or reprisals from your elders. Or, I will make them see the error of their ways." As he glares at the three of them.

Orin "Orville you are a culinary genius. The French toast is perfect, and the eggs and bacon and sausages are perfect with the gravy." As he grabs the flask of orange juice and pours the orange juice and passes the glasses around serving the others. AS Orville sits down and serves himself.

Orville "Eat hardly, you have a long morning and the midday break in the early afternoon. Then the evening classes you have too. Plus, the work in the Shopee this afternoon. Also, the studying you have too as well."

Tania "Sure, that is right your first day will be today there. And today is shipment. So, it's perfect way to get your feet wet. Now finish up, and let's get going?"

Orville "Yes let us get going now. The first day is always the busiest."

As they leave and walk to the school. Orin feels very nervous as they walk to the school. AS Tania with the Darkmun's in tow. He feels that Luke is sizing him while Virginia is trying to get closer to him. As he sees the way to the school. He realizes why they started a few days early. The clubs went to war alright. Hearing the projectiles blowing up with paints fireworks explosions. And all sorts exploding trash cans. Papers every where all over campus. The campus is a mess. Seeing all of this while the Darkmun's looking around and with looks unimpressed. As he goes to the auditorium for orientation. Luke walks up.

Luke "It's the basic rules for all the new students. If you need anything don't hesitate to ask okay. And also, don't be too harsh with Virginia. You mom didn't do that yet. But Tania tried to talk her down. But Orville obviously sided with her. And the family fallout is pretty."

Orin "Luke, I do value my privacy. I have nothing to hide. But I don't like it being invaded as well. So, she doesn't own the town. There are boundaries and you all need to respect them." Luke just nods in acknowledgement, with a very apologetic look. As they go tot eh auditorium Orin finds his seat. As he sees Tania and Orville arguing about a few things. He sees the Von Weibs in the gathering. As Colleen walks up to Orin. And pulls him aside.

Colleen 'What is happening?"

Orville "Tania brought Luke and Virginia over for breakfast. Orville wasn't happy about it."

Collen with a worried look "Yeah you are right about that. Orville can't stand both of them."

Orville 'They apologized about their behavior."

Colleen "Dam, you're lucky you got that." As Virginia gives a death glare to Colleen and the rest of the Von Weib sisters.

Rory "Hey, Orin why don't you come over here!"

Orin says "Hi Rory! What is up ladies?"

Virginia "Now, I wouldn't hang with that lot. There nothing but trouble."

Luke 'Virginia, don't cause trouble. He needs to know the hard way apparently. No fuss over the choices. Besides he has a good head on his shoulders. He will be fine. He has too many mentors to assist him." As he nods to Orin. Orin simply nods back.

Rachel "Wow, that is a first. And I thought I would never see the day."

Becca "Now this is a sight."

Saundra 'I wouldn't get too excited. I'm awaiting the cut down. After the cut down. This will be worthless."

Luke "Ever the optimist eh.. Cassie?"

Saundra "Don't call me Cassie ever again!"

Luke "See here Orin. These five do have a mean streak. It gets the better of them. It always does."

Saundra "Our crime was being a little too trusting. I'll never forgive you for what you did to those two."

Luke "They were unworthy of your and anyone else's attention."

Stoner-Boy "That young man I doubt with all my heart. What you did to those poor men was wrong. And there will be a boon to pay if you don't truly repent."

Virginia "Ah.. the hippie preacher. I almost didn't recognize you without your bong."

Stoner-Boy "Now that you mention it." And he pulls out the bong.

Stoner-Boy "But I won't toke up here. After all it's in poor tastes."

Luke and Virginia just sneer at him. Luke "It's bad that the town hobo has power. It's worse that the town's drug addict has manners and etiquette. What is worse that the only preacher we like is friend with the both of you." As that was said. Reve Jonathan Rodrick Kingsley arrives.

Rev Johnny "Now you two. Meaning Luke and Virginia. Knock it off. Le the young man converse without any issues. Stop crowding him too. He doesn't like to be the center of attention."

Stoner-Boy "You very right about that Reverend. These children need to repent of their many sins. Also, should get the opportunity for their remissions of sin as well."

Becca "That they should. But I fear a lot of us have no soul."

Stoner-Boy "Now Becca, why do you have to say that. It's a wonderful soul you have. Too bad you let it grow dark and twisted into your current state. I must credit Saundra. She tires not to let her pain twist hers into the same condition. Also, Colleen and Rory as well. But no one is as forgiving as Rachel." As he smiles A young man walks up to the site that is developing. He is about 6'6 and looks fit and is about 275 lbs of muscle. And walks towards Orin.

The young an "Allow me to introduce myself. I am Michael Joseph Wolfsen. Junior in the high school. And you are?" Extending his hand.

Orin "My nae is Orin Ezekiel McNeil. It's a pleasure to meet you." As Orville walks up to the boys and nods to Johnny and Stoner-Boy.

Orville "Nice that you all seem to be getting along?"

Orin "All is going fine here."

Michael laughs "Wow you have a snarky sense of humor. You will get along well here. Virginia I'm surprised this one hasn't made a pass at you yet?"

Orin "Ah…she made one at me. And I turned her down. But she was out of line too. I simply no longer wish to discuss it."

Michael laughs harder "Wow, and dam. I wished I was there to see that. Someone actually turned down Virginia! I would've thought that was possible." As he laughs. The Weib girls laugh with him.

Virginia just sneers with her look. "Orin, they didn't need to know that. Or are you just way to honest for you're good?"

Orin "Honesty is my only excuse. Because it's the best policy. Even when you are wrong."

Rory laughs aloud "Yeah, Becca you should follow that! Then again, it's best that Virginia, Rodney and even Luke here follows that! I know Saundra follows that too!" The rest of the Von Weib girls kackle like hyenas with the comments. Even though Becca has a look of how to dodge that comment or a better rebuke to it. As more people fill the Auditorium. Orin finds his seat. Those who don't have to b here are here. He wonder's if there are more newcomers here than expected. It wouldn't surprise him. Then He notices that Wihelmine is sitting next to him. He raises an eyebrow and then he wonders what he should say.

Wihelmine "Now young man, you picked the best row in the house. I'm saving the seats for the girls here. I must say you ae causing a big stir here. The Wolfsen's are a good family. They tend to be openly territorial. Mike there is the most territorial of the young men of that clan. And he likes you too. By simply showing that you have proper manner and respect. Good lot. Even Tania would agree with that. And I see the old hag and the old coot arguing up a storm. We have a guest speaker for the commencement. I wonder who it is? Your mom really works hard."

Rev Johnny "Now Wihelmine, isn't a bit young for you? I know he is too young for Tania. But you have Orville seat. And I know your not warming Tani's seat."

Wihelmine "Well if I tried that the set would shatter. Now for Orville it would crak but not break" As she laughs.

Reve Johnny "Yes, sadly but true that would happen. But I know the guest speaker. And it's not going to be good."

Wihelmine "What do you mean it's not going to be good."

Rev Johnny "Well… It's this young mans Grandfather. The Grand Ferret of the McNeil's. With Regan in tow as usual. You can never trust a man who doesn't like his first two names. Too much hatred pent up that it overflows. So, this why everyone is here from all the classes. I just found out that Eugene made a whole lot of donations and set new things up And he hates being called Eugene the most. He'll except Gene. So that is why I don't call him that. He hates Silas as well. Make sure people know that. He tends to be a spiteful man. Calling him tby his given names out of respect drives him mad." As he smiles

Wihelmine "Why, thank you Reverend, I'll make sure the girls and people I trust know that. Should I tell Tania and Orville too?" He nods as in meaning yes.

Saundra "What did I miss?"

Wihelmine "Oh. there are going to fireworks today. Get the girls here. We're sitting with Tania and Orville. A whole lot of crap is about to go down in the next few minutes. And I don't want to miss it at all." Saundra and in acknowledgement.

As the girls and the Ulberg's sit around with Stoner-Boy and Rev Johnny behind them. Orin's Mother came over and sits next to Johnny.

Erin "What is going on Johnny?"

Stoner-Boy "We are about to find out. Silas is the speaker."

Erin "oh… Great! Here comes the pain and hatred people. It's going to be fun."

Wihelmine "Well It isn't that bad now, is it?"

Orville "It just may. I hope not."

Tania "Well the Darkmun's seem happy?"

Rev Johnny "That doesn't give any comfort. When they are happy. There is lot of intolerable crap is about to happen." AS the final batch of people arrived. They see Miguel De Le Guy the 36th arrive. He is ensuring security. He sees Regan approaching him as the two meet they lock in a staring contest. Something happens where Regan flinches. Miguel simply smiles and tells him some instructions. Regan wasn't happy about that. Now everyone sees Rodney approaches the podium.

Rodney "Now I'm not used to announcing new speaker. But things happened where it has to be done. And the usual early start. Because the joke wars have to be stopped. Due to this our guest speaker will go over the rules as they should be followed. Give a hand to the Grand Ferret McNeil." Aa the crowd claps the Gand Ferret walks up to the mic.

Grand Ferret "Now young ladies and gentlemen of the school. Professors, teachers, counselors, and the rest of the staff. It troubles me that the President of the school. Has been gone for three months. What also troubles me that the Vice president has no control of this fin establishment. Now with the help of the board of directors. The board of governors. AND the Board of education here. That a Temporary president will be here to oversee the running of this school." You hear an uproar from the students and staff therefore mentioned.

Wihelmine" Oh…Great, if he is speaking were are in it now."

Tania "I totally agree with you Wihelmine. This doesn't bode well for anyone here."

Orville "I'm going to hang them all by their fingers nail before I'm through wit them."

Horatio sitting behind them with Jacob. Horatio speaks "I got to talk with Miguel and the military portion of the school.

Jacob "I'll get the tribal leaders involved now. They were never consented at per the land rights here. I can count on your support Orville?"

Orville "I got your back here Jacob. It saves me the trouble of asking them directly for help with this case." That Regan fellow is standing behind him looking around.

Grand ferret "Now, I know you are used to your liberties. But I fell this fine institution should present itself better from now on. So As your temporary President of the college. I am going to go over what changes will be made at this point on." As the corwd boos the speaker. Erin is shaking nervously.

Erin "By hook and by Crook he going to make his presence known in your life son."

Orville "Not if I have anything to do with it." As Orville walks to the podium. As the crowd boos the Grand Ferret. Regan attempts to stop Orville to the Podium. However, Miguel De Le Guy stops Regan. And Miguel takes Regan by the arm with escorts him off the premises.

Grand Ferret "I am the temporary man in charge of the school Orville. Regan stays."

Orville "Nope, you're wrong there. It states in the charter that you have to be a resident for 9 years. Not nine days, nine minutes nor nine seconds. Also, the local Indian tribes have to have a say in this matter. And I know they didn't. And finally, all of these changes have to go through myself and the town council meetings in a open forum. So, I don't know what deals you though you made here. What assurances you were given. But I have the final power to overrule everything if need be. And right now, I a exercising it. Miguel arrests this man and his thugs as per the agreement. Also find and round up all who were involved here now. Get Horatio and Jacob to help ya with that. I want them n the brig for safe keeping in the stockade. Now Eugen, you have to go now. Please make a fuss. It'll make my life easier. And all the money you invested. Well, that is confiscated too. Orville smiling as Eugen sneers at him.

As Miguel and his people escort everyone to the stockade. Orville takes t the podium.

Orville "Sorry about the mess folks. I will handle it as usual. Now we have a lot of newcomers this trimester. Nothing new here, now all I have to say a broken clock is right twice a day. The student body has taken yet again too many liberties with he campus. The newcomers are exempt from this. But the rest of you now, have to clean this place up good and proper. I'll hear nothing of it. Or that man will have his way by hook and by crook. So enjoy the classes. The orientation will be split into groups of my choosing. Also I will be running a group myself. SO go to your sections and we'll get this started." As the crowd claps and cheers. As Orville leaves the stage. And walks towards where he was last seated.

Tania "The Darkmun's and the rest of them aren't happy right now dear."

Orville "I don't give a rats ass hat they think. They can't do that. It's against the charter. So, I am hog tying them if I have to make sure this is done right. Knowing that they will lose this. I hope. But Owen has been gone way too often Horatio. Jacob, you need to bring him back in. I hate the fact the college presidents are still active assets." They both nod in agreement.

Wihelmine "What do you mean active assets?" AS the girls look surprised with shock.

Erin "Oh…that is why there is such a high military presence here amongst the staff?"

Orville sighs "Yes, now I've done it and spoke out of turn."

Wihelmine "No, you haven't right girls." As the ladies' nod in agreement.

Tania "Don't worry, they tend to rotate a lot. However, they seem to always call the main president way too much. Jacob tends to be the union liaison for such matters as Horatio is the Confederacy's liaison. The Canadian liaison has yet to be appointed. The new one at least. The last one died in the line of duty." Looking at Orin and Erin with a sympathetic look as well with eh Weib sisters.

Wihelmine "How what happened this time. Or its better that we don't know?"

Horatio "It's better that you don't know. We receive active reports. But after this stunt. He will be pulled out of what he is doing to run the school. No one wants The Grand Ferret to run this school. He was arrested by the MPs of all the branches here. With the cadets helping regulars and the Graduates too." As Horatio snickers

Jacob "And he's not going to like the fact the tribal leaders will have a lot to say about his attempts to take over the school. I mean the students are a rowdy bunch. But that is why we have the best doctors, teachers, engineers, chemists, physicists, and researchers on the whole planet. They are a mischievous bunch no doubt. But he was going to stifle them. And don't get me started on the best artist, writes, sculptors as well. And we have the best trained soldiers in the world next to the Israeli armed services. We get a lot of special training here. Across the board. This school is unique because we start from pre-K through university levels. The girls here are in the university level now. Orin you are in the advanced placement high school levels. Meaning that your grades will convert to college credits everywhere here."

Rev Jonathan R Kingsley "This also host five seminary schools for Judaism and four for the Christian religions. Best nursing school here too. With a lot of other lesser-known trades and job programs. Silas Eugene McNeil running this place? Nope this place would be running into the ground inside of a day. But I would give him a week. I want to know what blackmail he had to cause this. He had to have something on the people here. Miguel De Le Guy is going to have fun getting it out of Regan."

Erin "Regan is as tough as they come Johnny."

Reve Johnny "Yeah, but he hasn't dealt with Miguel yet. He going to wish he never had too."

Erin "Oh…He is that good and tough?"

Orville "He has been given the rank of Templar. His family have 36 generations of templars in them. So, he can arrange things most other couldn't nor wouldn't do."

Stoner-Boy "Don't worry, he will be rather gentle with Regan. Regan will crack." As they all look at Stoner-Boy with a questioning look.

Tania "Now, how would you …." As Orville interrupts

Orville "Don't worry your pretty little head, Tania. I trust Stoner-Boy's words in this. You don't want them to run the school either?"

Stoner-Boy "Nope, But I do want our usual president back. He has the most patience in dealing with the student body. Also, he is the most benevolent president we ever had here. The place is in chaos when he is not around. It becomes more orderly when he is back. But there is a lot of learning and fun here. But this will get him back sooner. I dare say he will be back in a day or two." As the girls and the Women look at him funny. While the men simply trust his word on these things.

Orin "Well that was great, can we go home now?" As everyone laughs

Tania "No young man, you're not getting off that easy. These girls are part of the clean up crew. I know they were involved somehow in this. As for Rodney, he is working on cleaning the north yard." As she looks at the Von Weib girls.

Colleen "Well it's us showing Orin around to his classes. Or Virginia showing him around? Which do you prefer Erin?" As the girls and Wihelmine smile. Tania gives her a cold scowl to Colleen. Collen smiles with her sisters. Making it all Erin's decision. However, Orville chimes in.

Orville "Tania either, you allow one of the girls here to escort him around. Or I'll have to leave it to Stoner-Boy or Rev Johnny here. I would prefer one of the students showing him around. But I would prefer that his mother chooses his escorts right now." Tania looks more annoyed than ever.

Erin "I would prefer Michael Joseph Wolfsen. He seems like a nice fellow. So, the girls will help him out this evening for the classes this evening. Does that sound fair to all of you?" As the girls smile with joy. Wihelmine also smiles with joy. Rev Johnny and Stoner-Boy simply smirk. As Orville has the biggest grin imaginable.

Orville "Well, I can get him to help you out. But right now he is sparing with Luke over there at the moment." As they look at the two having a war of words. Seeing who could saber rattle the best.

Rev Johnny "Well, I can show him to his classes and the layout he should know for his classes. This way he won't get distracted. Also, we can go over a lot of things during his mid-day break. The siestas are good for a lot of things." As the women frown at the idea. They see that Both Michael and Luke are still arguing over something. Then Matt Jones approaches them.

Matt "Hey Orin! How are you doing? Anyone going to show you around?" As the rest of them see Matt as a savoir of sorts.

Tania "Hello Mathew, it's been a while. How do you know Orin?"

Matt "We met yesterday. Now that the prank wars have started. Also, seeing the new President ousted in record time. Boy did a lot of people lost a lot of civil bets here. The orientations are always fun here."

Tania "Well, Matt your offer is kind. But Some of us would rather have Orin escorted around with more reliable sort of person." As she looks at the others.

Rev Johnny "He's as good as anyone else here Tania. Matt is good role model to act as a tour guide. And show him around the campus. He knows the campus like the back of his hands. As one of the Leaders of the engineering clubs and a few more. He knows the layout better than most people. He also knows the tunnel entrances and the rest of the ins and outs of this place. Besides, you're not still angry that he beat Rodney in the fantasy games last year, are you?"

Tania simply smiles "No, of course not. If there isn't anyone more qualified here?"

Matt "Come on Orin I'll get you to the first class. There are no bells here." As he puts his arm over Orin's shoulders and walks him out of the auditorium.

Wihelmine "Not so fast there Matt. I would like a few assurances. My Daughters will escort him around at night. Is that fair to you?"

Matt "Sure, not a problem. I wouldn't dream of it, Mrs. Von Weib. Anything else?"

Wihelmine 'Yes, no recruiting him to the clubs. He's not ready for that yet. Also, introduce him to the hockey coaches. For the mid-season tryouts for the JV team."

Matt "That is fair too. Besides, It, would be fun having him try out would be cool for him and us. So, anything else?"

Orville "Nothing else Matt. I'm happy that you have obliged us with your help. Just allow Orin to sit in your club without, joining. As a personal favor to me. This way he can see what he will get himself into later on in time. You have other clubs he is interested in as well."

Matt "Well It's the War Scythe 90K club. We play matched twice a week. Along with the art club and comic book club. Orin is into all of those things. And much more in hobbies in common."

Matt "Sure, not a problem." As Matt escorts Orin to the first of his classes

Orin "Still trying to figure out this place. Discovering how big it is"

Matt "It's going to take a few weeks for you to get acclimated here. I didn't know you played War Scythe 90K."

Orin "Sorry, we didn't get a chance to go over everything. I'm just trying to get used to the insanity around here." Matt laughs.

Matt "Orin, you're going to get used to the crazy things that happen around here. What is your opinions on homo-superior?"

Orin "Well, I think they exist. Too many stories about magic, sorcery and different species. Why do you ask?"

Matt "Well we talk about that all the time in the comic book club. Also, the science fiction club too. Also discussing the War Scythe 90K's lore. In its creation and how it effects the rules depending on the lore and the rules with he game. There are players that love the lore more than the game."

Orin "Well the lore is interesting. But it's a game where the lore helps you understand the pieces of the game better. Moving them correctly on the board. The lore is a codex how to use the pieces properly. Then you can use unorthodox strategies to move the pieces for victories. There isn't no such thing as a useless piece."

Matt "Oh...So, the people who concentrate on the lore. Are trying to recreate the codex properly?"

Orin "Yes, but there are three combinations of the codex. I know all three of them. But the person who taught me how to play shared the first combination. I helped him figure out the second and third combination of the codex. After figuring out the other two codex's, I tried the combinations. Then I was able to move the pieces as specified in the lore correctly. Once I could do that. I was winning the games more often."

Matt 'Wow...Are you free this evening after classes?"

Orin "Yes, I am free. So, you want me to bring my pieces over?"

Matt "Not necessary, we have all the pieces for forty comic book shop inventories."

Orin "So after religion class to sit in or to play?"

Matt "I want to see you play. I have a funny feeling that its going to be good."

Orin "Here is the math class. Staying here or sitting in the class?"

Matt "Hanging out here. But I am to show you around until the siesta starts."

Orin "Okay cool" as he enters his first class. After the first set of his classes. He has his first siesta. Then he walks to the Shopee. As he opens the door, he sees boxes upon boxes. It's shipment day. Receiving it will take its time. As he see's Tania, Pauline, Xenia, and Kathy bustle around in the cramped spaces. Kathy sees him and wave him over to her location.

Kathy "Orin put you books and stuff on that table. And help me open these first five boxes. And I'll show you how to take in the new inventory." As Orin puts his books on the table and takes off his jacket and is about to roll up his sleeves.

Kathy say "Oh…here is a shirt and pants here's. The changing room is over there. You don't want to ruin your uniform. Sorry I forget the school keeps neatness to military standards. The changing room is over there, with a set of sneakers for you too." As Orin walks to the changing room and changes his clothes. He goes out of the room and walks to Kathy.

Kathy "Good. Now here are the sheets. The code describes the item. The box in the row has a number of said items. The boxes below it is where you input, he actual numbers. If it the right amount you input the right amount. If we are over, you put plus and the number. If we are short. The you put a minus and the number. Do you have any questions?" Orin nods no thinking simple enough.

Kathy "Good, now I'll split the paperwork in to four quarters. Here is your quarter. And the rest of us has the other paperwork. If you find items with no paperwork your ask for us to check if we have it. But the boxes are numbered. So, it shouldn't be an issue. Doesn't mean it can be an issue." Orin simply nods in acknowledgment and gets started. He sees that the siesta is four hours long. He wonders how long this will take to finish. As he is doing his work and going through the boxes. Accountign for the t-shirts, the games, and the trade paperbacks and hardcover comics as well. Also, all the new Japanese comics and merchandise. Listed as merch for short. As he is almost done recording and finding room for the items, in its proper place. He noticed that Katy put the boxes in the sections of recording. Once the boxes were emptied and broken down. The Shopee is getting bigger with space. As he finished with his share of the paperwork Xenia walks up to him. Speaking with a Russian accent.

Xenia "Wow, you work fast and precise. Like your mom. Can you help me out with my section for a quick moment?"

Orin "Sure, after that may I Start my homework. I'd like to be ahead of it than behind it."

Xenia "Don't worry it won't be that long. Just need another set of hand moving this onto the shelves that a bit high." Orin nods with the meaning Okay. As they move the net set of games in the front and the new section with swift speed and efficiency. Tania notices that Orin is working well with Kathy and Xenia. Pauline is checking this out and notice that the inventory check ins are done right. And less complaints about errors too. And this took half the time as usual.

Tania "Ladies, how long did this take?"

Pauline "It took and hour and a half. The dashing young man works methodically. And did the job right. What was your motivation?"

Xenia chimes "He wants to start his homework, so he won't fall behind too soon."

Kathy smiles "So he wants time here to study while it's slow. Good thinking on his part."

Pauline "Oh.. I like that. He's going to work out well. Tania. And we are finished here. Let the young man do his schoolwork. We'll help him out if he needs it." Tania smiles and sighs with relief.

Tania "Sure, not a problem. You can do the work right were you left your books. What time the second half of your classes begin Orin?"

Orin "I think 6:30 according to my schedule today? I know tomorrow it's 8pm." As Tania extends her hand as a silent gesture of hand me your schedule. Orin complies without hesitation. And she sees the schedule.

Tania "Oh…Yes, you do have an unusual schedule. I see your not messing around with the downtime for homework. I wouldn't either, which is fine by me. But yes, young man begin your homework. But you will be expected to stop when customers come in. Which shouldn't be a problem except on event days. Good thing no events are this week. But in the coming weeks you will find it hard doing the work during the siestas we have here." As Orin nods in acknowledgement and starts doing the schoolwork. As he is doing the work for the first hour. He is about halfway through literalizing that the work is going to get harder as time goes on. As customers walk in. He stops and helps them out. Kathy realizes that he has a knack of helping them out and recommending a few other things in the hobby shop. Xenia is astonished of his concentration about doing a task at hand. As he is finishing up his schoolwork. Seeing that he will do most of his work here. Relaxing and decompressing at home. Sensing a smart lad in him. Also knowing he can ask for help of the ladies here. Which he did depending on the subject. Utilizing three tutors does help him a lot. And the fact he is taking advantage of it is a good thing. Pauline notices that he looks at the exits and entrance. And other nooks in the shop. For possible exits and entrances. She realizes that he is looking around. Making sure no one leaves with good that they didn't pay for. Tania just stares at him and smiles as he does everything. Knowing he is going to work out well. As long he isn't overburdened with work and schoolwork. She sighs that that wont last long. But she knows in her heart he will make it. As she sees him working a Tal man about 6'4 230 lbs of lean muscles walks into the shop. The ladies just look and shocked. Xenia taps the table that Orin is doing his schoolwork. Orin Looks up and stops what he is doing and greets the customer.

Orin "I apologize for my tardiness. How can I help you this afternoon? Oh…My name is Orin."

The man chuckles "You didn't have to train this young man much Tania? Oh, My name is Devon Marcus Darquemune at your service young sir."

Tania "He is ahead of the curve. He is in all advanced classes in the school."

Devon "Really? You wouldn't be that Orin E. McNeil that is related to the recently, how shall we say sequestered president of the college would you? I know the old coot of our mayor was very annoyed that we didn't go through him as we should've. But then again, the man's office e is the park bench. We wanted privacy in such matters. Also, we didn't want to deal with that pot smoking filthy hippie of a preacher either." Orin looks at Devon with a quizzical look.

Orin 'Yes, I am. I just don't get along with Silas Eugene. Attempting to take me by force and killing one of my friend's kind of does that to you as a person. My mother and I want nothing to do with the man in general."

Devon "Oh. My apologies, and he did get away with it apparently. Or he wouldn't be here. Hmmm…. Well, that old coot of your husband knows more that he is letting on. As usual, making us flinch. Dam that old coot, Tania!"

Tania "He keeps secrets for a lot of people Devon. So, if you all did this willingly behind his back. He is going to be on the warpath. No questions asked about that. Him exercising his emergency power like that. He more than likely knew what he did to this young man here. And Orville has taken a liking to him to boot." As Devon now sighs with a grimace on his face.

Devon "Great, this is going to be a lot tougher than we bargained for. Thanks for the heads up all of you. I was to know what set one would buy for a beginner of War Scythe 90 is good for a beginner?"

Orin "Hmmm, the basic set would be a good start. But the best expansion for the beginner set would fell bat brigade and the winged raft units as well. We have them right here." Devon simply smiles and looks with approval to the ladies of the Shopee.

Devon "I've been trying to get a straight answer out of Rodney for years on this subject. And this young man gave it to me in less than five minutes? Tania, keep this one happy please. My son wants to play. And now I've found a man that can teach him good and proper." Tania simply smiles.

Tania 'I'll try Devon, you can bring your son here anytime. But I know Rodney and Orin will be fighting for space or who deserves to be taught how to play."

Devon "Matt said that there is a new person coming into the tabletop club tonight for a friendly match tonight around 9PM. Just asking he wouldn't be talking about you?"

Orin "I asked him not to mention me by name. Because I don't know how everyone here would've reacted to that?"

Xenia "Don't worry Orin, despite Tania's favoritism. We do a lot of business with that school club. They always pool the money together and share prices. It's a good club to be a part of. The issue is they threw out Rodney because of his antics. The clubs he oversees are the ones he is still the head of. Or in the hierarchy of power." As she glares at Tania. With Kathy smiling and Pauline giving Tania a stern look.

Devon "So may I come over with y son and see how you play?"

Orin "As long as you just keep it between you and your son. And this doesn't leave the room. I do value my privacy."

All in unison "Of course we will keep our traps shut."

Orin "Anything else would you be interested in?"

Devon "Not at the moment but, thank you! Just asking what you were studying?"

Orin "Just finishing up my calculus problems now. And finished up my physics and chem homework. But I know it's going to get rougher as the trimester goes along."

Devon "yes, the school is intense. But our high school grads are four-year college graduates everywhere else. So, it is worth the time and effort. Our military college in one of the best in the world as well. So, a lot revolves around the school. I'll see you with my son tonight young man. Have a nice day lady!" As he leave the shop. Tania looks at Orin with a big smile on her face.

Tania "I know Rodney tends to scuff him a lot. But I've been wanting his business back for a while."

Orin "What did, or should I say didn't he do to this man's family?"

Tania "Well, I still don't know all the details to this day. But Devon wants to come back here. He finds Moon Dog's a bit rowdy."

Orin "We he is going to find out that I have an account there and my War Scythe 90k profile is there too."

Kathy "That is okay with us. You have your space and Rodney has his. This way we won't hear anything about space issues when you setup your campaigns here. Besides we have a studio here if you need to do your art projects in the back. Want to see it?" Orin nods yes. Kathy takes him to the back, and he sees the studio. It's small but adequate. The new tubes of paints and charcoal pastel chalks, pencils colors and regular. Brushes and inks and paper and canvases. As he sees the supplies.

Orin" Do you sell the supplies?"

Kathy "No, but people tend to give it to us. Because Tania paints herself. And she does paint the miniatures as well. She likes that aspect of the War Scythe 90k game. So you have a lot of supplies. That is Why Orville didn't let you buy too much. Because he and Tania have them here. All you have to do is let her know what your using."

Orin "Okay, I can see why Rodney now feels threaten around me?"

Kathy "Well, that and the fact of your family relations. He will always find out who he is dealing with. One way or another. So, he is very cunning. Give him a slight chance. He will get you into a lot of trouble. So, did you finish up your first round of homework?"

Orin "Nope I was almost..."

Kathy "Now get back to your schoolwork. We did promise you mom not to let your grades slip." As he runs back to the table to finish up his schoolwork. Orville walks into the shop. As Orville sees Orin finishing up the work.

Orville say to Tania "I just walked into Devon. He was usually apologetic to me about the incident of the incident at school this morning?"

Tania "Why, yes Devon was here. He introduced himself to young Orin here. Orin did explain a few things why he doesn't get along with his grandfather. After the explanations, Devon offered his sincere apologies. Stating that he has to back track a lot of things now. So Orin answered a few question about this game here. Orin explained to him. And now he wants Orin to tech his son how to play this game. Here in the shop. Or at the table top club when he has times from his studies."

Orville "Young man be careful. You didn't ruinanyhting. But now theyare going to be compliant with me about what happened this morning. Let Horatio and Jacob deal with everything else. He asked you if you were related to him." Orin nods a yes.

Orville "Good and you told him why you don't get along." Orin simply nods a yes.

Orville "Alright, that is good. Saves me a lot of trouble with the rest of the lot today. Also, don't give out too many recommendations for anything else outside of the game shops. O don't want to fall into the traps these families make."

Orin "Noted, I have to finish up my last few problems, so I am on pace for tonight."

Orville "Good, now I have to talk to Kathy and Xenia. May I have a word upstairs?"

Kathy "Sure."

Xenia "No problem."

As they walk upstairs to the upper offices to the shop. Orin goes back to his homework. After he finishes up his homework. He hears loud talking upstairs. He now notices that Xenia and Pauline and Kathy are downstairs. As he is looking up and hears more talking.

Orin "This is a daily occurrence I, see?"

Kathy "Yes, it is. You will get used to it. Don't worry, but he will ask you to walk with him afterwards to cool off. So, when he says walk with me. Don't worry Tania will let you do it. You walk with him. Tania has made promises however that she shouldn't have made. And because of that. You are in the thick of things here. Your father and mother and Orville didn't want that for you. You'll have to adjust sooner than you hoped for."

Orin sighs "What else is new for me?"

Xenia "Well, you have three gallery openings in the next three months. Don't forget those. The pieces are wonderful by the way. You earn some good coin from them. Also, Tania's ten percent off the top."

Pauline "Don't worry, all of this overwhelming stuff in the beginning will pass. You will get used to it. Besides I hear him coming down now. Good thing you finished your homework, and the shipment has been taken it. Rodney screws around too much." As Orville comes down from the offices upstairs.

Orville "Orin come with me." Orin simply follows him outside.

Orin "What is going on?"

Orville "I just found out the deal they made with your grandfather. And it's not looking good either. It looks like they have to return the money with interests. Which I am all for. Or give him what he asked for originally. Which Tania and I are against. The problem is that they already spent the money. Now they have to give him what he wants. Unless I get Jacob to bail them out. Which will drive Horatio nuts. With everyone else here. So we are heading for Horatio's right now and give him the 411" Orin and Orville look annoyed. As the head to Moon Dog's shop. As the enter the A&P to location set aside for Moon Dog's. The se Horatio with Jacob discussing things. They see Orville and Orin and wave them over.

Horatio 'What is wrong?

Orville "Gentleman, with out going too deeply into details. The arrangement was made, and a lot of money was paid off to the families involved. And the money is enormous amount. It was the combined donations for all the renovations made to the building and the school too."

Jacob groans" Let me guess pay back with interest. Or give the bigot his way."

Horatio "Jacob, can you pay back with the interests?"

Jacob 'Well, I can but the old coot still owes me money. Knowing that I am buying the debt. I can officially keep everything because he owes me money and not pay him a red cent. But he families involved would have to pay me back. And it's a win, win for me. But The Darkmoon's and the split relations families that did give the money away will have to pay me. And I will collect from those muther fuckers. If I should be inclined to do this. What was the rest of the promises? Besides entrance into this community Orville?"

Orville "Lock stock and barrel custody of Orin here. And a change in his schooling to the military Academy area. And all of his father's cronies including you and Horatio run out of town. Which includes Miguel De Le Guy's family as well."

Horatio "Why that god dammed asshole mother fucker. I have the right mind to hog tie him to a post and whip him as if he was a dirty rotten negro who escaped his master back in the day."

Jacob 'I'll help you there Horatio.'

Orville "So, you'll give me the loan then?"

Jacob "No worries, Orville. He isn't getting a red cent back. The legalities will have me win. I just don't know Horatio here is going to like that I technically own this whole dam town now."

Horatio "Better you than him. He is a true savage. At least you're an educated savage."

Jacob laughs "You're right about that one. But I'll screw over the Grand Ferret good and proper now. Anyone want to see?" Orville and Orin and Horatio raise their hands.

Jacob "Good no time like the present. Want to bring your mom along Orin?"

Orin "Yes!" with a smile on his face.

Jacob "You do have the papers ready?"

Orville "yes, I do. Horatio you're the notary republic." As Orin witnesses the transfer of the debt to Jacob and how he finishes up the paperwork. They walk to the military stockade. Picking up Erin so she can see this site. As they walk on over to the stockade. They run into Johnny and Stoner-Boy.

Stoner-Boy "Now what do we have here?"

Rev Johnny "I don't know but Silas isn't going to like it. Neither will Regan either."

Jacob "Don't worry your pretty little heads here. It's going to be a very civil conversation." As Jacob approached the door to Silas's cell and gives the nod. The door opens and Silas is sitting with a grin on his face."

Silas "So, they ae going to give in to my demands?"

Jacob "Sort of. They are paying he debt. But since I bought the debt. There is a snag about me giving you the money. Because you owe me three times the amount you gave them. So I am keeping the third you were supposed to give me as your money back. SO You are leaving with one third of our debt settles. The rest of them will pay me back. But you still owe me money. So pack your bags and fucking leave here. The rest of the families will have to deal with me Silas Eugene McNeil!"

Silas face palms "Orville went to you?"

Jacob "Yes, he did. And he remembered that you did owe me money. So, this was the perfect way to get a third back. Kick you out, and have your coffers emptied out a little bit. It will take you time to replenish them. But you'll be out of here. And you have to go through all the proper channels again. Also, you have to pay the erst of the money you owe men too."

Silas Eugene McNeil "At least my daughter and grandson isn't here to see..." As his voice trails off. He sees his daughter face with his grandson with a smile.

Silas "Jacob, may God dam you to the deepest depths of hell and the lake of fire to boot!"

Jacob "May the great spirit drop you there first so I can laugh at you as you fry! Now Miguel, would you mind escorting these miscreants to the nearest exits of the town. And put all points bulletins of them not entering without the tribe's explicit permission. And that the mayor must ask for the tribe's permission to let them in. Also state until he pays the debt to the tribe. He can't hold any office or donate money to any the charities, school, or societies. I think I covered everything in these matters. Now make sure that the door hits them on the ass as they leave Miguel"

Miguel De le Guy the 36th smiles "Of course Chief Jacob Gator-Star. I will be my distinct pleasure to do so. May I begin with Mr. Regan first. I haven't finished teaching him proper manners sha we say."

Jacob "Sure, be quick about it, however the longer they stay the more opportunities they will get."

Miguel De Le Guy The 36th "Nope just Mr. Regan. I'll throw the rest out good and proper. He will stay to be a mind lesson in manners and respect Mr. McNeil."

Silas Eugene McNeil simply nods and looks at Jacob "You'll regret this you stupid injun."

Jacob "Now, now honky cracker jack eating corn fed white boy. Go sell your snake oil somewhere else. No one wants you here. And Now I have taken the liberty of getting a third of the tribe's money back. That you do owe. Now the other two thirds will be easier. You God dam savage. Killing innocent people for the sport of it. Terrorizing small children. Getting away with it time and time again. Your northerners are worse that the old southern gentlemen here. Oh yeah, I forgot. They migrated up north while the of the northern gentlemen migrated down south. Tax burdens and all. Funny how history is. Don't you think Silas?"

Silas just sneers "Jacob, this isn't over. Not by a long shot!"

Jacob "Miguel, make sure they leave as instructed. And make a good example of Mr. Regan as well."

Miguel De Le Guy the 36th smiles "Yes, master Chief Gator-Star. I will do that just for you."

Silas sneer at Miguel De Le Guy "Race traitor. You'll burn for this."

Miguel De Le Guy the 36th "I know better to mess with them. I do know better. Then again you don't know better Silas. I'll be more than happy to teach you. If he wishes it?" look at Jacob.

Jacob "no need, Mr. Regan will be enough of a lesson taught, okay?"

Miguel De Le Guy The 36th "Sure, no problem, master chief."

As they are now escorted out of the premises. Jacob directs traffic. As the people are moving out of the military installations. Being told the basics. Also informing them without the proper invites now. They can't enter the town. Also informs them that then penalties will be severe. AS this is done. They leave the stockade. Orin and Erin are feeling happy. Orville can't wait to tell the idiots that they owe Jacob money. Horatio can't wait to laugh at them. And Orville escorts Erin and Orin back to their jobs. While this is happening, Xenia runs towards them.

Orville "Is it true that you got the old coot out of town, and he is pissed?"

Orville "Yes, Jacob put up the money. And he owes Jacob money. So, he didn't get a dime back either. Now as per the court order. Once Jacob receives a form of payment. The Old coot must pay the rest of it. So now the old man has a ton of issues. Now he has to pay Jacob back. And he none too happy about it. Also, the rest of the families have to pay Jacob back the notes he bought out. They're not going to be happy about that either."

Xenia "It's okay, at least it's Jacob and not that idiot. The families will pay Jacob in installments. As long as they can do that. That will be up to the tribal elders and the monthly payments. Jacob will work that out with them. The dam fool called Jacob and Injun before he left."

Xenia "Stupid yankee coot."

Orville "Agreed, now that I am returning the boy to his work. Knowing he finished his homework. Doe she have anything else to finish at the job?"

Xenia "Not really, but he hasn't eaten anything yet. And the siesta is almost over."

Orville "True, get the boy some grub on me. And make sure he is ready for the late afternoon and evening classes. The Weib girls are escorting him today. But they would love to know what happened to the so-called Grand Ferret and Mr. Regan. I believe Orin has two a night. Am I correct?"

Orin "Yes, my art classes and my Religion classes."

Orville "Good, now get your lunch and get a little rest and go to classes. And don't forget that tabletop match you have tonight. Don't worry, you are doing a fines service for the Shopee. Devon is a good man. As well as a good father. So, play well tonight. And don't piss off Matt too much in the match."

Orin "Okay, I don't know what format yet." As he nods. Xenia takes him to the Mucho Macho Taco. As he enters the place. Hearing the music of the mariachi band play and the seeing the portions of the food

Andersonville

that was served. His eyes widen. Xenia drags him to the takeout part of the restaurant.

Xenia "Do you want a chime changa?"

Orin "ah.. yeah sure?"

Xenia "This is the first time here?"

Orin 'Yes, I though this place was an urban legend."

Xenia laughs "Nope, it isn't the portions are huge. And the décor is fun. But depending on the day the attire is rather shall we say flamboyant."

Orin "Who needs a strip club when you can come here?"

Xenia laugh "Yeah, tell me about it. Also, the food is good too. So, do you want it to be pork, chicken, cheese, or chorizos? Or do you want the supreme with all the meats?"

Orin "I'll take the supreme with all of them with the works and guacamole and sour cream."

Xenia "Wow, you do have tastes. You hear the man. I'll get my usual please. Rather short on time. After the order was placed and fulfilled in rather good time. They go back to the game shop. As the enter. Tania is having a screaming match with a few ladies about the stunt Orville pulled. As Orin hears what was said. He decides not to listen anymore. He just slides to the table Xenia guided hm to. He simply eat his chime changa with his drink. He did enjoy it. As he was eating his food, he noticed the time is growing short. AS he finished up his food and washed his hands. He changed back into his uniform and was leaving the Shopee as the other ladies finally noticed him leaving. As one of them was about to say something.

Kathy "Hurry up you are going to be late for class." Giving a thumbs up.

Orin "Thanks leaving now bye all." As he races out of the shop. With a sigh of relief about the drama what ensued. He wonders how often he going to deal with such things. As he walks to the school. He bumps into Luke. As Luke decides to catch up to him. Luke taps his shoulder.

Luke "Why are you in such a rush?"

Orin "I just finished up my assignments. I like to stay ahead of the curve. Is that a problem?"

Luke "Nope. I admire that. You know that this is the fastest way to the studios right?"

Orin "Yes, I have the art class now, then religion at the end of the night. I'm a bit too busy Luke. I have to run."

Luke "I see that, want to hang out a bit tonight? I'll be at the tabletop gaming meeting tonight. I hope to se you there? It's a big night. The first of the trimester. We have casual games there. No leagues, just fun times playing the games there."

Orin "If I have time. But If I don't maybe next time."

Luke "Says sure no problem." As Orin moves forward to the building for the art classes. Drawing the human form. He arrives to the studio classroom. AS he is sitting in the room. Managing to get his seat. The instructor has the class sit in the places assigned to each student. As they sit and get the supplies read awaiting the model. He sees Virginia walk in the room with a robe on. She smiles sat Orin and waves. The class is now looking at him. He simply ignores her as he gets the paper ready to draw. As he looks up and sees Virginia disrobe and smile sat him. As he begins with the rest of the class to draw her. As he is drawing her. He hears a voce in his head again. But it's Virginia's voice "Wow he is doing a good job ignoring me. Or is it the fact he is concentrating on the assignment of doing the portrait right. I do trust him to do it right. Well, I'll see the results in an hour from now." As her voice fades. As the hour finishes up. Everyone has to submit the work finished or unfinished to the class review. As well as the model. As everyone's work is scrutinized for the techniques. His drawing had the least complaints of the bunch. He got more compliments from the other students and Virginia.

Virginia "I must say that the best drawing anyone has ever done of me. I'd say there isa quite few who couldn't do better."

The instructor. "Orin you got an A. I'll come up with something better night after tomorrow. Now class is dismissed." As everyone collects their things. Virginia taps Orin on the shoulder.

Virginia "Orin, what class do you have next?"

Orin "Religion with Rev Jonathon Kingsley. Why do you ask?"

Virginia "Oh…Well, you better get going; he hates it when people are late discussing the word." As he leaves the classroom, he notices that Virginia is still naked. As he pays no mind. As he enters the next classroom. He sees it's empty. As he waits one of the Weibs enters the room. It's Colleen.

Colleen "Sorry I'm late. I had to get a few things done. And we had to avoid Tania coming up with bright ideas." As she sees the drawing of Virginia in his portfolio. As Colleen, grabs the picture. With the grade marked as an A. Colleen looks at Orin.

Colleen "Dam you are good. He never gives an A unless you are gifted. And I have to say you got her down pat too. She was flirting with you to by the expression of her face. Well, I'm jealous that you do any of us yet. Now I want you to do that. Come On I'll walk you to class. Anywhere else you have to be tonight in here."

Orin "Ah. Yes, the tabletop gaming club. I have a friendly match of War Scythe 90k with Matt tonight?"

Colleen "Wait a minute, you have a match with Matt tonight?"

Orin "Yes, I do have one. He says it's a friendly match. But I do not believe in friendly matches. In this game the matches ae never really that friendly."

Colleen "We five have to be there. We are fans of the game. But we are not really good players. Why doesn't anyone else know about this in the school?"

Orin "I asked to keep this quiet for now. Once the results come out. I can't help that."

Colleen "True, well I'm in your class. So are the rest of my sisters. The tend to skip Trimester of this course. But I think this year. We might actually get a grade." As Colleen chuckles. As they enter the class. Colleen sits Orin next to Cassaundra, Rebecca, Rory and to the other side of him is Colleen herself and Rachel. Reverend Jonathan Rodrick Kingsley walks in. Seeing that it's the six of them. He simply cracks his knuckles.

Rev Johnny "I guess the lot transferred out of my class."

Saundra "Well, you are notoriously harsh on the readings. But anyone that know you. You ask us for our interpretations of the texts. Knowing that it changes per interpretation."

Rev Johnny "That is too true about me. But hat is how I know you read the material. So I ask the first question. DO you all believe that God exists?" The six of them raises their hands. Slowly.

Rev Johnny "Okay that is a good start. Do you believe its Jesus Christ?" The five of them now have blank stares in their faces. And look to each other.

Orin "Well, I do believe he existed. I do believe he was using a form of civil disobedience to Caesar and the other Jews in the texts. But I'm not sure he is God in human form. How should I know that without any doubt's sir?" As the girls' cringe with his answers. Expecting a blast of outrage. To their shock Johnny laughs and smiles.

Rev Johnny "Well Orin that is a really good set of answers to my questions. So, I do like the answers you have provided. Jesus was antiestablishment. Because the establishment of the time was the issues. Romans took over Israel. The Israelites were a form of emotional bondage with the roman empire. Also, some were in physical bondage as well. They were also drowning in sinful activities with the Romans. They were waiting for what? Do you have an answer Becca?"

Becca "Says, well they wanted a warrior king to return. And free them from Roman influence."

Rev Johnny "That is correct Becca. Good job. I see the six of you actually read the books assignments. Saundra what else can you tell me of the period?"

Saundra "Well, typically the Romans treated the Jews as second-class citizens. Because the Jew had as they Romans believed a stuck attitude towards there conquerors. It feed a lot of malcontents between both parties of people in general."

Rev Johnny "Wow, that is good and correct Saundra. Now can anyone answer me this question. Do you believe Jesus is God?"

Orin "I do believe he is God. But my faith is shaken, because why would he let bad things happen to himself and others? That is what shakes my belief to the core." As the girls nod in agreement with Orin.

Rev Johnny "Oh…You suffer the issues that most modern Christians do. How can our faith be affirmed? Well, all I can ask this question. Did you all receive the gift of the holy ghost? This is a yes or no answer." As the six looks at each other they nod in agreement.

Rory "I can speak for myself and my sisters. I have yet to receive as you say the gift of the holy ghost. How does one know if they have received it?"

Rev Johnny "One way is the ability to speak in tongues. If you read Acts. They speak of the day of Pentecost. With the manifestation of the holy ghost upon the Apostles and the initial followers. It's a different sensation for each person. But I say once you receive it. You are a changed being. Once you do receive it. You know the difference between those who have it. From those who don't have it. The attitudes are as if it was night and day. So, with a general overview here. Have any of you received the gift yes, or no?" As they look at each other.

Rachel "I can speak for my sisters and I. We haven't received the gift. I'm not sure about Orin here."

Orin "I have yet to receive such a wonderful gift myself. I do not think my mother has either when I think about it."

Rev Jonny "You mother has received the gift a long time ago. She hasn't communed with the holy spirit for a while. That is her problem. She is taking step to remedy that. As for your answers. I am glad you didn't lie to me about it. This gift has no half measures. The more half measures. The more the Devil works doubts that Jesus is God. Also, this gives me a chance to help you accept the holy ghost. And accept Jesus is God. Now we go on to ask what the gospel of the Psalms means to you?"

Orin "I like the idea that David always asks what he did wrong to God. And yet he still praises him. The fact that he takes personal responsibility."

Rev Johnny "That is one way at looking at it. But you missed so much. It looks like you speed read through the Psalms Orin. There is plenty advice in there for different situations."

Orin "I've only read 40 chapters of it. I haven't finished it yet."

Rev Johnny "Oh that is different. You're not all the way through it yet. Well, that explains your answers for now. It gets more profound as you go along the reading of Psalms. You will get it. Now lets us discuss Acts for a little bit more." As Rev Johnny goes over half the book of Acts. The time breezes by fast. As Johnny Says "Now finish up Psalms, Acts and Start Judges too. Have a good night, all? Orin would you mind coming over here for a moment." As Orin walks to Johnny. He sees the girls keeping an eye on him and Rev Johnny. As the leave the room.

Orin "What is up?"

Rev Johnny "Well thanks to your grandfather too many people have taken an interest in you. I don't particularly like it. So be careful, the clubs are back door entrances to the societies. So don't join officially any of them. I don't care what Tania or Wihelmine say about it. Listen to Orville and I about these clubs. I know the girls are on the same page about this one. So be careful. There is a lot of your grandpa's people around here too. I don't know for sure. He left with a whole lot of crows. And What Miguel De Le Guy did to Regan. Well that isn't going to go well for anyone."

Orin nods "Okay, I'll my eyes peeled. Nothing new for me."

Collen walks into the room. "Come on Orin you're going to be late for that appointment."

Rev Johnny "What appointment is this?"

Orin "The tabletop gaming club. Just visiting it tonight. Should I cancel?"

Rev Johnny "No. let me come along. I want to see what is up." As they make It to the club area. Johnny and the girls see the tabletop club. AS the enter the room. Orin's eyes widen. They have every piece ever made for the game. Including the special edition play sets. AS he looks around. Sandra is leading Orin to her favorite pieces of the game. While Rory shows the pieces that are her favorite. Colleen shows him here favorite landscapes. While Rachel shows him here favorite mechs. Becca simply yawns and show her one and only favorite piece. Now that Orin is looking around. Luke and Matt walk into the club area with Michael. They see the girls with Orin and Rev Johnny.

Michael "What brings you here Rev Johnny?" Smiling to the Reverend.

Rev Johnny "Not much wanted to see this club's Hussle and bustle for a change. How are your studies going Mike?"

Mike "They are going well. Why do you ask?"

Rev Johnny "I didn't take you for this club?"

Mike "Oh.. I used to play. I love playing against a worth opponent. Because Rodney cheats a lot in this game. A lot of us old players barely come inhere anymore." At the corner of there eyes they See Devon Marcus Darquemune enter the room.

Rev Johnny "Why is he here?"

Mike "Looking for someone to teach his kid again. He doesn't like the atmosphere in Moon Dog's Too many people for his taste. Which I don't blame him. However, here is a bit different. The atmosphere is a lot nicer." Devon approaches the men.

Devon "Hello Michael, and Jonathon. How ae the both of you?"

They reply in unison "We're just fine and you?"

Devon "I'm doing well, very well tonight actually." As he smiles, which worries Rev Jonathon R Kingsley. As he decides to pass along pleasantries. He moves to the girls and Orin.

Rev Johnny "Orin, what did you get yourself into?" Pointing at Devon.

Orin "He came to the shop and asked a few questions about what sets a beginner should use. I provided him the answers he sought. Tania was elated. Did I do something wrong?" The girls and Johnny groan. Looking all around the closed in area.

Colleen "Devon is the executive vice president in the school. He is always looking for War Scythe 90k players to teach his children. As a rule. We don't give him information about how to play. The kids don't really want to learn. But their father insists upon it. Because the quarterly tournaments are a big thing here. So, since no one gave you a heads up. It looks like how well you do. You're going to be spending a lot of time here. Which a lot of people won't like. Spending to teach people how to play. It's one of the big rules here. You don't teach here. We make an exception for one. We make an exception for all. So he wants to see how good you're at the game." Johnny just rolls his eyes.

Rev Johnny "Now, I must talk to Tania. He sued to shop there all the time. Now possibly getting his business back. She didn't give you the full story and shared stories either I take it."

Orin nods "Well, it's too late now. Is it this busy on the first night?'

Saundra "Yes, it is. It depends on how the game runs. There is one match tonight. It's Matt and a mystery player? Now wait a minute, you're not the mystery player!?" Orin simply nods yes.

Rory "Dam boy, you're attracting more attention than you think!"

Rachel "Look Orin, keeping a low profile here is a bad idea. All it does is attract more attention. You made this an event. Not realizing you did do that." Orin whistles in concern and dam he screwed up big this time.

Becca "My suggestion is, throw the match. This way no one wants to play with you. Make an obvious mistake with Matt. But make it as a slight mishap instead. This way people will know to leave you alone. If that is what you want." AS she finishes the statement Stoner-Boy is right behind them.

Stoner-Boy "Now son, I suggest you play a fair game. Also, if you lose. You lose but do it with dignity. This way people will leave you alone and trat you with respect. Don't you agree Johnny?"

Rev Johnny "That sounds like a plan. Make it a low key match if you can? How good is Matt?"

Mike "He is very good. Luke and He play all the time. But that is why Rodney and Matt, and Luke are rivals in this game. The three of them play at Tania's shopee. But the rest play here or at Moon Dog's. We prefer Horatio's place because we can dress down and enjoy ourselves. So you are going to be playing there Orin?"

Orin "I have an account with Horatio. Preceding my entry here."

Rev Johnny "Okay! Cool not too bad. Good thing the club spaces are closed on the weekend?" AS he eyes the girls. The girls simply smile.

Orin "Should I ask now or later?"

Becca "It's a story left best for another time. Just do your best with Matt Orin."

Matt walks up to them. "I've taken the liberty of setting up all the pieces needed for this as per the random rules of the game. With randomized pieces. Is that to your satisfaction?"

Orin responds "sure." As Matt leads him to the preset board. Mike, the girls and Reverend are scared. AS they see the setup know as death plasm field. It's the most notorious setup in the game. It's the hardest landscape to navigate you armies through. The units as well. As they begin to roll who goes first. Matt rolls a 13 on the twenty sides die. Orin rolls a 19 on the die. Matt just shrugs. S Orin concentrates on the board and the pieces. The object is to obliterate the other pieces or make him or her surrender. As Orin studies the pieces he has and what Matt has he begins with an odd move. He moves his heavy mechs in the left flank. Matt does a double take. His eye narrow. He decides to move his heavy batteries into a safe position. They roll again and pick up a card each. The cards are ability modifiers. This helps in the damage step when actual combat occurs.

Matt "Very unusual beginning. Don't you think?" As Luke just ponders on what is going on. Devon just rubs his chin with a smile instead.

Orin "The day is young so to speak." He moves his light armor troupe to the right flank now. And sees Matt do a double take. With Luke draw dropping. While Devon is smiling.

Devon thinking to himself "Either he is stupid or quiet clever. Or just plain old mad. My son can learn a few things from him. Even if he loses. I want my son to hang out with him. He would be a good influence. I have to run it passed Orville though. But it will be worth it. And even Rev Johnny."

As they see the fist set of moves Matt wonders what he is up to. Matt thoughts "Well he purposely but his weaker forces in the right flank. Most people would us them as pincer to drive up the wedge. What is he thinking? The mechs are out in the left flank where they would be useless. Now I'll teach this young lad a lesson inn tactics." Mat moves his main forces down the middle. In range for an attack in the next role. While this is happening the Weibs are trying to figure out what Orin is doing? Saundra then figures it out what Orin is doing. As she think is to herself "I've seen only Totowa and BoMach pull this off before. If so, Matt is going to be surprised with Luke too. It's also a very simple combination of cards too. With rolls of 3 and above to clear the field and the command center." As she whispers to her sisters what Orin is up to. The Weibs simply notice that Devon is realizing the same thing. All we wait is now if Matt takes the bait.

Orin simply plays the following cards in a row. Hyperlink, super link and quantum link in that order. Which allow unlimited free movement in the field and 19 rolls in the round. Also unlimited draws in the same round. Mat and Luke jaws drop! Luke thinking to himself" Wait a minute with that he can have constant first opportunity attacks for 19 rolls plus his three standard rolls. What is doing? These are legal combos too. "As his eyes narrow. He realizes "Oh crap, this the fabled phoenix gambit. He will run a constant loop of damage and movements if he has the right rolls of 3 or better. But he first three rolls make all the difference.

Orin Moves the pieces into place with his unlimited free rolls. He plays the carrier card for seven rounds of quadruple the firepower of each piece. He surrounds Matt's forces and begins the attack roles. He rolls a 17, 13 and a 20 for his first three roles. The look on Matt's and Luke's faces are priceless and in shock. As he deals the constant damage with the first three rolls. He was able to wipe out Matt's pieces in the first three rolls. He second three rolls were a 9, 5 and 10. Ensured he captured the encampment intact. With all the equipment and converted. Rolls second and third now academic. But needed to reconstitute the forces form the carrier as per the rules. As the rolls progressed and all the new pieces were on the board. He has the whole field covered and as he crowds watches him move the pieces as if they were dancing around the field. Luke and Matt started to laugh hysterically. As everyone including Orin is watching them laugh hard. Devon has a great big smile on his face. AS the Weibs jaws simply drops. Reve Johnny thinking to himself 'Now I know why the old man wanted him so badly in the military college side. He's a tactical genius."

Orin after finishing up the turn he says "Orin, I think that is game? Any objections?" As the room roars in laughter. Matt walk up to him and shakes his hand. Luke Shakes his hand too.

Luke "I'd hate to think if you had your favorites pieces out there. Knowing that you can pull this one out of you hide."

Matt "I heard stories about that gambit. I never thought I'd see it done. Laughing hysterically about I was the poor sap that triggered."

Orin "You all did set up the board. But there are forty-five ways to pull that off. But it depends on the Terran used and all of the other logistics of the space." They booth look at him and jaw dropping.

In unison "There is forty-five more ways to do this depending on the terrain?"

Orin "yes there is." As he stayed calm and cool about it."

The Weib girls rush him and hug him as say in unison "Wow that was great! The last two we saw pulled this off were Totowa and BroMach!"

Rev Johnny "Well done young sir. Well done. Now you have to go home all of you and get some rest."

Orin "Who are they?"

Colleen "We'll talk about them another day. Sort of a sore spots really."

Orin "Okay, no problem here." As Devon approaches Orin. Jonny intercedes.

Rev Johnny "Now let the boy rest Devon. He needs to do his homework and other duties before he can teach your boy. And a few things need to be run by Orville first. You understand that?

Devon "Sure, you're about that. But he was brilliant with this. It's one of the hardest things to pull off."

Rev Johnny "yes, I know. I only know a handful of people that can pull that off. So, I'm inclined to give the boy his rest.' As the crowd leaves. Orin walks with the girls to home. As he sees Orville walking towards him.

Orville "I hear you are cause quite a uproar?"

Orin "Nothing in particular."

Orville "Ah.. Modesty, something I enjoy and never get enough of. Wiping the floor with Matt like that. Rodney wished he was there. But he is happy you will be playing at Horatio's instead of the shop. Different tiers in the shops."

Orin "There is a but going to happen is there?"

Orville "Well, its about Devon and the fact h wants you to teach his son. How to play the game proper."

Orin "I've taken the liberty of declining his offer for you. For the reasons he was one of the ilk that tried to put your grandpa in power here." Orin looks at Orville and smiles.

Orin "Thank you for doing that. Rev Johnny didn't want me to have any dealing with him either."

Orville "That is good. Also, better that you are heading our advice on this matter."

Saundra "We told him it was a bad idea too, Orville." As the Von Wieb girls smile.

Orville "Thanks girls for the advising him like that. Don't you have classes tonight?"

Rory "They don't begin until next week. More Moonlight instead of sunlight."

Orville "Of course, well thank you all. Now you get home and study. The next few weeks are going to be rough." As they go to there perspective homes. Orin just falls onto the bed. As he dreams. He hears the girls arguing over petty things with their mother in his head. As he drifts into sleep. He feels his body being touched. He wakes up and he noticed that he is in his boxers and that Virginia is looking over him.

Virginia "I took the liberty of letting myself in.|"

Orin "Virginia!" As he sees the Von Weibs outside, on the balcony sneering at here.

Virginia "Oh.. Hi ladies!" As she waves at them. The Door slides open and Wihelmine wiggles here finger as in come over here.

Wihelmine "You have been told by his mother not to do this crap. Now knock it off and get out now!"

Virginia "Well, I thought it would be nice to congratulate him on his win." As she smiles.

Cassaundra "Now you little two-bit slut! I don't care what Tania promised. He has the right to choose whomever he dams well pleases! Now get out! Before we get his mother here to beat that tiny prissy ass of your out of here! We promised not to do this level of crap to him." As Virginia walks on the balcony. Wihelmine signals Orin to lock the sliding door. Orin does that. Virginia looks coldly at Orin now dealing with the Weibs on the Balcony.

Wihelmine "Now young lady. We are going to say this once. Unless you want to be purged from this house. Leave as you are. I'll Deliver your clothes back intact. Now let the boy sleep." Now Virginia look around and says "Can I have my clothes back now?"

Wihelmine "Nope you're walking home just like that. With explaining why, you are walking home just like that." As he sees Virginia using the ladder coming down. Collen signals Orin to find her clothes. As Orin finds them and puts them in a bag. He Slides the door just enough to put the bag out. The Weibs simply smile at him.

Rory "You are such a good young man. Is she frightening you again?"

Orin "Actually yes, they last time things like this happened. My Grandpa was almost successful in kidnaping me."

Wihelmine puts her hand on her mouth 'Oh my...We will take the clothes back to her later. But we will tell your mother what happened.

Now go back to bed and keep this door locked. AS Orin turns around to heed the advice, he hears a whoosh. He doesn't bother turning around to see if all f them left or some of them stayed. He was just tired and wanted some sleep. As he went back to bed. As he drifts back to sleep, he wonders how things are going. As he floats in bed. He hears a voice in his head "You've done well today. But I'll be home soon. But I agree with the girls and Orville. Virginia is a problem. And I'll have to deal with Tania in this matter." So just relax and take rest. This will be your new normal and enjoy the rest you need. Tomorrow is another day." And with that Orin wakes up and sees Saundra on the balcony before sunrise. He can tell with h twilight apporching. He walks outside on to the balcony and sits next to Saundra. She turns with sad looks in her eyes. As If she is about to cry.

Orin "What is it?"

Saundra "Well, you have been sold up the river essentially. Your mother doesn't realize it. But around here there are arranged matches that are in place. Tania made one with you and Virginia. My mom discovered the deal was made. You mother didn't agree to that level of the match up. But Virginia's parents aren't going to budge on this. Orville is trying to stop it. Good thing Jacob agrees with Orville and my mother on this one. So, it's going to be a pain the next few months. We were told not to get involved with you. The problem is that we don't want to leave you yet. We are a distant bunch Orin. It's rare that we smile at all. You have made us smile now, two days straight. Our mother is happy that we are smiling. But we have to wait for our father to return. But we now know that the missions he had to do, kept us from him. And why our mother left him for it. We like being happy. Now I suggest you go back to bed. Your classes are in the evening today. And you have to work at the shopee today as well."

Orin "Will I be able to hang with you all in school?" Saundra smiles.

Saundra 'Well, she can't stop that now, can she? Nor us hanging out on the balcony either? Get some more rest. We'll talk later on in the day. Night, night sleep tight. Want me to sing you a song to sleep?" Smiling sheepishly now. As Orin turn arounds and head to the bed. He looks up as he sees her waving goodbye for now. As he closes his eyes, he sees her evaporate before his eyes. And hears a whoosh. Now he's seen it.

Boy are they fast. Now he wonders with some of the odd questions he heard yesterday. As he drifts to sleep, he thinks to himself. Grandfather is making his moves on him. The societies in this town are making moves for grandfather's behalf. Now the town locals want a piece of my hide in one form or another. Arranged pairings. And father is going to be here soon? What a first day of school.

CHAPTER 13

Day to day life in Andersonville

Now much of the days have gone like the first day of school. Not as Hectic. With work in the classes piling up. It's been three weeks since the antics of the first day of school. Events from the Homecoming dance through the tournaments of War Scythe 90k. Go along as the day blur into the mundane. Things are not as what they seem. At least to Orin's thinking. There are days he see people floating or hovering a few feet off the ground. When they see or thinks h notices them, they come down to the ground and look around to see if he is going to make any comments. As he walks back to the shopee. Tania gives him orders to fulfill and do inventory on a weekly basis. After this for a few weeks and doing his homework. Virginia makes her daily appearance at the shop claiming him as hers alone. Because he is bored and doesn't want to piss off Tania. He does engage in conversation with Virginia. For time to time. Today three weeks later is one of those times.

Virginia "What do you mean you don't want to go to the homecoming dance?"

Orin "It's not my thing. I'm sorry you feel that way about it. I just don't want to go."

Tania Chimes in "Orin, now you just have to go."

Orin "Nope, not interested in going. Besides I just want a slow and peaceful night for a change. Do a little recreational reading. Enjoy life's other pursuits. What is wrong with that?"

Virginia glares at him with Tania. Virginia speaks "Now Orin, you don't want people getting any of the wrong ideas about you now?"

Tania "I happen to agree with the girl here!" as Orin looks at both of them wondering if he shouldn't have engaged in this conversation today. The dance is this weekend after all. He does know that Virginia bought a special dress for the event. Tons of men asked her. She declined because she stated that she had a date. Meaning it was going to be with me. Whether I liked it or not. The Orville walks into the shopee.

Orville "Orin, good! We need to talk for a bit. If you ladies would allow me some time with the boy?" Tania dismissably waves her agreement with it as Virginia is really angry with this set of events.

Virginia "Now you old coot. Don't take too much time with him. He still has to decides about where to go after the dance." With a red-hot look at Orville.

Orville laughs "Honey, Only Tania can give me that look and make me tremble in my feet. As you can tell she didn't do it. So, you're out of luck here. Come on son we need to talk about your relations here in private." As the walk out of the shopee. They walk to the closet coffee shop and talk. As they enter the shop and grab a table.

Orville "Did you eat lunch yet?"

Orin "No, not yet."

Orville 'Good, I'm buying so it'll let Virginia know she has to leave the shopee and stop harassing you." As the order the food they are going to eat. Orville starts off to speak. Until He Sees Xenia walkin.

Orville "Will these women ever leave me alone to talk with you. A moments peace is all I ask. Is that too much boy?" Orin smiles and snickers.

Orin "Apparently yes old man. Not leaving us be for five minutes."

Xenia "Are you buying him lunch Orville?"

Orville "Yes, Xenia why?" She smiles at him.

Xenia "Good, that dammed adolescent child won't leave this poor boy alone. And give him a moments peace. If I'm interrupting, I'll leave." Orin and Orville smile.

Orville "you can join us, Xenia. It will be a slight relief. From Tania schemes and love setups."

Xenia "You ain't kidding there. Saddling you poor dear with that one! Virginia Tepes Darkmun. Worst pairing ever!" As Orville and Orin smile.

Orin "What was it you wanted to talk to me about Orville?" Waiting on their meal as Xenia finished her order.

Orville "Now son, you have to go to that dance. And weather you like it or not. Virginia is going to be your date." Both Xenia and Orin groan in disbelief.

Xenia "Why her? Of all women her! I would rathe see him with one of the Von Weibs instead. They get along better. In spite of the spats, he gets into with Saundra. And they have been epic ones of late. I never seen any of them lose their cool like that since BroMach and Totowa left here." As Orin raises an eyebrow with the last two names mentioned. The food arrives. As they eat their perspective plates. Orville decides to go back on the point of contention with the upcoming homecoming dance.

Orville "There ae three dances a trimester. Homecoming, Prom, and Coming out dance party. To be invited to one is normal. You, young man has been invited to all three. Which means you must make all three play dates. Preferably with the same young lady. Now, Virginia has claimed rights to you. Has anyone else claimed rights to you? I need to know that now!"

Orin "I would say Cassaundra Von Weib has in her own way. But because it's Virginia Darkmun. It complicates matter a lot." As Xenia smiles as Orville groans.

Orville "Now I must talk to Wihelmine about this. The Darkmun's like you. They want you into their clan so to speak. Despite the new branch, it would make. Just to see have far the relationship has gone into."

Xenia "I told Tania making promises here was a bad idea. But does she ever listen.. No!"

Orville chuckles "Now Xenia, what do your other sisters think of the pairing?"

Xenia "To quote Pauline. They get married. It's goingtop be such a blood bath between them and the rest of the Ulberg's that there isn't gong to be Darquemune left. Let alone the offshoots of the clan. To quote Kathy. They get hitched. It'll literally be a gun point. Knowing the gun will be in the church right behind his head. And the he will kill the poor wretched girl on the wedding night. Having help of the Weibs to perform the homicide successfully hiding the body!"

Orville "Dam! That is harsh. And Tania still refuses to listen?

Xenia "Well, yes because the deal she is trying to fulfill is taking precedence. That is the problem with the situation here. Orville, she isn't going to back down unless something happens to change things a lot. And that is gong to take a lot of intervention here."

Stoner-Boy "You'll worry too much. Let the boy skip the dance. Make sure it's the best decision for the boy. They aren't taking to each other. There isn't chemistry. Just say he already has a date. I know Saundra would love to go with him. Talking hte girls to show up would be easier said than not going. Sorry to interject here Orville."

Orville "Okay, Stoner-Boy I'll do just that. I'll talk to Wihelmine about this. I am going to have my hands full. Aren't I Stoner-Boy?"

Stoner-Boy "Not as much as you think. Now I got to go." As he leaves the coffee shop.

Xenia "you do know I can arrange that. Easily. The girls haven't had a proper homecoming date yet.

Orville "I'll talk it over with Wihelmine. She is going to love this idea way too much. I know Erin hates Virginia. But I don't know why?"

Orin "Easily, said. She hates the idea that she thinks she owns the house her and me."

Orville "Oh, well that would piss off Tania too. And that attitude would make a lot of other people angry. Well, I can work with that. But Wihelmine, would like a dinner in your place with your mom first before agreeing with any of these plans. Meaning you too have to invite all six into your home."

Orin "Well, mom has to be okay with that. But I can convince here. But it has toi be done this week?"

Xenia 'I would do it tonight if I could. Just to get it over and done with. But best do it in the next three weeks. Give Erin some time to get things ready for the show so to speak."

Orville "I'll be there for the dinner to make sure everything goes smoothly. Is that Okay with you Orin?"

Orin "Uhm… Sure, no problem. Why do you have to be there?"

Orville "Just so Tania understands that someone she can trust doesn't bet the far in here eyes. Okay?"

Orin "Okay, that makes sense. No problems here. Any special setup I have to do for them?"

Orville "Yes, but I'll take care of it. Let me talk to your mom about it. No worries?"

Orin "Nope no worries at all." As they finish the meal. And leave the coffee shop. Orville decides to take Orin for a long walk and talk. As they round the corner to the park bench. Where he tends to do most of the town's business.

Orville asks Orin "So do you love Cassaundra?"

Orin looks at him strangely "Well, yes, I do. She is a good friend and confidant. She has told me things. That she doesn't tell her sisters or mother. I tell her things too. That I don't share with just anyone. She is the closest friend I've had since Anna. Who have I left in London Ontario to move down here? Aster not making it to the JV team here. Having Slava still honing my body to a well-oiled machine to play hockey. Saundra has been at my side. So yes, I do love her. Question is does she love me? I don't use the l word around here. I know she is scared. I just don't know why she is scared."

Orville "Well I know some of the things that is wrong with here. But it's best you find out on your own. From her telling you everything. Not hearing it from someone else."

Orin "Your right about that. But I am patient man."

Orville "yes you have to be that way with women?"

Orin "Anything else I should know? That I'm not supposed to hear from them?"

Orville "Nothing that comes to mind that is public knowledge that you don't know about. However, there is a lot of things you should be made aware of. It's not my place to fill you in. Neither is it Tania's either. So, what family business you refer to."

Orin" The Darkmuns' clan's involvement with my grandpa?"

Orville "Well, its worse than I expected. The money trail is very bad for the families involved. The money and the transaction were bought and paid for a peace. A Peace I would never agree with. Because I couldn't trust the man with the money, he promised them. After the stunt I pulled.

Getting Jacob involved making him pay the rest of the money he owes Jacob's tribe. Once he finishes paying Jacob his money. He won't have a pot to piss in. But the rest of the families involved. They must pay Jacob the interest payments. The families are just plain ole enraged. Now that they must pay Jacob. And now Jacob is running the table in the town's business. Only Horatio is happy about that. And most people thought Horatio would be angry about that. No one wants an American Indian running a prestigious ton and school such as ours in north America. Now Jacob is running the show. All the changes in the programs. Things he's been trying to push for years now. And the president will be taken off active duty when he returns this trimester. Sometime in this trimester. Running the school as he should do. Also having the military cadets mixing with the civilians' students is a good thing too. So, the civies know that they have to perform their duty and defend this country. As conscripts or volunteering in the militias."

Orin "So, the fact Jacob is running this town. And Horatio is backing him up? They are stunned?"

Orville "Yes, they are. And it's going to get worse for them before it gets better. Now anything else you want to know that is public knowledge?"

Orin "Devon is hanging around the shopee again. Trying to secure my services. And Tania said he should talk to you? So, what should I say if he conners me? I find it unlikely, but probable."

Orville "Well because he did get himself involved with your grandfather. I prefer a safe distance between the two of you. Unless he wants Miguel De Le guy watching over the two of you?"

Orin Laughs "Yeah that is going to be a sight to see. But he wont get away with it. He would rather wait. Instead of letting Miguel watch us in the lessons of War Scythe 90k guides."

Orville laughs "Yes, that would be hilarious." As they walk back to the shoppe. They See Tania with arms folded. With a icy hot cold look on her face.

Tania "Now, you boys know how to ruin a girl's parade!"

Orin looking innocently "What do you mean?"

Tania "Well, you were supposed to go with Virginia for your tux fitting."

Orville "I'll take care of that. No worries there."

Tania "She was going to pay for him to have a proper dinner jacket. For other events this trimester."

Orin "Oh… How many events was I listed to go to with here?"

Devon chimes in "Well usually it's three events. The rest are optional. But in your case, you were selected for all thirteen events. I should know, I am hosting ten of them."

Orville "Oh… You have invited him to all thirteen!?"

Devon "Yes, Orville we did invite him to all thirteen events."

Orville "Dang knabit! Tania, what did you do?"

Devon "It wasn't her fault. It's Grand Ferret's fault. Part of the deal was to pair up Orin with one of our own."

Orville "Well, that deal is null and void Devon. Because Jacob has to chime in on that deal. And if Jacob disagrees with it. Then the deal is done for."

Devon face turns chalk white now "We didn't think about that."

Orville "You're dam straight you didn't consider that." As a voice behind him says.

"Now, now Devon. Jacob isn't going to like that part. Because he is rather fond of the boy. As I am fond of him too. This pairing isn't working out" as they turn, they see Horatio speaking to them about the situation. As Orville smirks with Orin.

Horatio "However, young man. I must insist that you attend all thirteen events. Also, I will escort you to all of them. Jacob is working hard to make all appearances. As you should as well Orin." As both Orville and Orin groan.

Orville "What are you two up to Horatio?"

Horatio "Well, there are a whole lot of deals that are being made. But the boy needs to make his presence known to the families. So, if he doesn't have a match pairing. That is fine with us. But he has to show up. And make his presence known to the families. Sorry son. This is happening sooner than later. If you don't want, he gist of a tux from the Darkmuns'. I understand. But you need a tux or two for these events."

Orville "There isn't a way to talk you two out of this. Is there?"

Horatio "Yes there isn't a way out of this. I'll explain it later gentlemen. Orville would you please escort the young man to the Taylor's shop. SO, he can be properly measured for a tux." As Orville and Orin look at each other. With a look Better Horatio than Virginia or Devon. They go to the Taylor's shop. As they walk to the shop. The hear Horatio yelling at Devon and Tania. Orville just nods and shakes his head. This isn't going to end well for us is it looks.

Orin "Well better Horatio than the other two?"

Orville "There is a deeper game being played here. And you're a major piece to be played here. It looks like you go t roped into a black op here. Now I'm getting why Jacob is doing these things. Great, even your father wouldn't approve of these things. He might use Virginia as an asset. Just to get close to the targets."

Orin "Oh…Great, mom isn't going to like this. Can we turn him or Jacob down on this matter?"

Orville "Maybe I can Rev Johnny to help you out of this mess. Maybe Miguel De Le Guy the 36th to use one of my favors in this one."

Orin "I wouldn't count on it. From the look Horatio has. There is something amiss here. Let's go and get my measurements."

Orville "Yeah, you're right about this. Let's get this done and talk to both of them after we get the tux's"

As they enter the shop for the measurements. They see Virginia with a huge smile "you too are back?! Let get this started!"

Orin "Now, wait a minute here. I'm not accepting you purchasing my Tux's. I want to feel comfortable in it. I'll go with Orville judgment here. Not yours Virginia!" As she simply nod with a frown on her face.

Orville "Virginia, please, don't make this harder on him than it already is."

Virginia nods "Okay. May I watch while you two choose?"

Orville "Sure, why not" Looking at Orin as in don't challenge this decision. Then his mother enters the shop.

Erin "Young lady you behave yourself. Orville, if my son feels the slightly uncomfortable. She is bounced from this shop got it!"

Orville "Yes, I got it." As Erin leaves from her break and he glares at Virginia. Virginia puts her head down in acknowledgement. As the measurements made with the jacket and the pants and the length. Taking the time with the Tux styles. And the final decisions were made. Virginia was very civil with eh choices. Orville liked the fact that Orin choose sleek and elegant looks. More in the vein with Sean Connery or Roger Moore's James bond looks. The four Tux's are not bought and being made. The first one will be ready in two days. The rest will be finished in about a week or two from now. As they leave the Taylor's shop. Orin walks to the game shopee. He walks in and picks up his books.

Tania "I'm sorry Orin. I didn't want this to happen. But I have to depend on these people to keep the businesses running."

Orin "I understand that, Tania. But I am not a resource that can be sold or bought by people. I wish more people understood that. I just want to learn. Develop my talents. And perhaps fall in love. And find the right women for me. Not people forcing women on to me. I need to feel that its right for me. Not right for everyone else." Tania puts her head down and sighs.

Tania "You're right about that. I should listen to my sisters more often. Sorry, what would you want to do now?"

Orin "I'm going home now. I have a half day today from classes. I can do some artwork at home today through the evening. I just need to be alone for a while."

Tania "Could you do a portrait of me this week?"

Orin 'Sure, I can do that in the studio here. But I would prefer Orville watch as the work is being done. Just in case something would go awry."

Tania "Sure, that isn't an issue. Can we do that today?"

Orin 'I need to decompress for today, Tania. Later on, the week. Maybe." As Orin leaves the shopee and walks home. He is stopped by Matt and Michael.

Orin "What do the two of you want?"

Matt "Jacob sent us. He wants you to meet him at Moon Dogs right away. Are you free now?"

Orin "Yes, lets go. Before I decide to change my mind." As they go to the A&P where Moon Dog's is located. As he enters the market. He waves high to the workers in the market. Where he usually buys his food and other items for the house. As they make there way to Moon Dog's they see Jacob in the rental space. Jacob waves him over.

Jacob "Sorry for making you go to all thirteen events. But this is the best way to find out what is your grandpa is up to. He did agree with the pairing with you and Virginia. But I need you to help find out what is going on here. Because I don't want your grandpa's ilk here. I know both of your parents won't approve of this. But we have no real choice here. That is why Horatio is escorting you to these events. Also, one more thing. Will you please treat Virginia more civilly? I'm not asking you to lead her on. I want you to be a Lil bit nicer to her. Just a smidgeon bit nicer. Is that too much to ask. She is the cog to get us the information we need."

Orin "You must run this passed my mom. I know she going to hate it. But she will see the necessity of it." Jacob groans but understands the necessity of it.

Jacob "I was hoping not to let her in on this."

Orin "True, but if she finds out from a secondhand source. The she will end it right on the spot."

Jacob "Yes, You're right. We need to let her know what is up. Let me go to her job and explain the plans here."

Orin "Good luck, I know you're going to need it."

Jacob "Now we need you to be nicer, and I'm not sending you in there alone either. You won't be alone either. But I can't tell you the whole picture. Horatio and I will have it. Not even Orville will have it. Now I will give you the first event. It will be the homecoming dance. And I hear you are making alternate plans."

Orin "Yes, I am. But you are going to talk me out of them right?"

Jacob "Nope, wouldn't dream of it. They will think something is up if you went with her. I want an outrage from Virginia. To be honest outrage. Something she can't doubt. Who is the alternate date so to speak?"

Orin "Well I was thinking asking one of Wihelmine's daughters. Didn't narrow down which one or all of them."

Jacob smiles "Perfect. As them all out at once. This will be more perfect. It'll make it easier in the coming events for Wihelmine's help later. Now go and ask them out ASAP. And tell then it is to piss off Virigina Darkmun. That should be motivation enough. Now get going. I will let Orville know what is going on for now. As well as your mother. It's going to be a big fight. But I can handle it. I need to let Rev Johnny know too." As Orin walks home, he notices that the sun is going down later. He enters his home. He walks up to his room. And decides to draw a bit waiting the sun to come down. Aa he is drawing, and the sunlight goes down. He hears a massive swoosh on the balcony. He looks over to the sliding door. He sees all five Weibs girls on the balcony. Dressed in their school uniforms.

As he walks out to the balcony. The girls are surprised that he came out so soon.

Orville "Ladies, I need a huge favor from all of you."

Saundra "What type of favor?"

Becca 'You're asking me too?" With a quizzical look.

Rachel "This is going to a huge one, isn't it?"

Rory "This is going to be fun?"

Colleen "You sure you want to ask us this? Our mom may ask one in return for or help."

Orin "Well how badly do you want to piss off Virginia Darkmun?"

As the girls rub their hand with mischievously "We are in!" In unison.

Colleen "What do you have in mind?"

Orin "Well this is going to come off as me being a pig."

Saundra "No hush boy. We know you're not a pig. We are strippers for crying out loud. You treat us with respect. So please tell us what you want out of us. Pissing off Virginia is a past time of ours."

Orin "Well I need to take all five of you to the homecoming dance to piss her off." As the ladies' jaws drop. They smile and start crying. He notices that the tears are red.

Becca "You want to take us to homecoming?!"

Rory "You really want to start up that kind of ruckus with us in your arms?"

Rachel "Oh… I'm in all the way!"

Colleen "I should kiss you now young man!"

Saundra, Smiling and crying "Absolutely, we are all in. No one hasn't asked us to go to one ever! But our mother would like to have a nice long chat over a meal with your mother in this case."

Orin "Don't worry the invite will come in soon. I don't know how soon. However, I know it will be sooner than you all originally thought." The girls give Orin a group hug. They can't wait to buy their dresses.

Saundra "You will never forget or regret this Orin."

Becca 'I will best my best behavior for this Orin."

Rachel "Did you get the tux yet?"

Rory "I know he has one on the way by now. Orin is prepared like that. We have gowns for these occasions. We have a lot to go through here sisters." As she looks at her sisters

Saundra "What is going on Orin?"

Orin "All, I have to say is that this a big operation about my grandpa. And I have to go through all thirteen events. But I need help. Horatio is escorting me to these events. Jacob will have help there too. So, this is all I can say. But I have to start treating Virginia civilly after homecoming. Not too civilly. Just civilly enough that people won't notice too much."

Colleen "Oh, but we are going to have so, much fun with this girls." As she winks at her sisters.

Saundra "Oh.. Yeah, we are going to have a fun times with these events. Mom is going to have some real fun with this."

Orin "Well, I will have mine tomorrow afternoon. And your dresses will be ready?"

Saundra "Oh…We have the gowns. Don't worry about that. You will be the envy of the who school." Orin hears the doorbell. As he looks at eh ladies with a look I have to go.

Colleen "Now, you go and lock this door behind you. We'll be fine." As Orin lock up and walks away from the balcony. He heir's another whoosh. He doesn't bother looking. He knows they are all gone now. As he opens the front door. He sees it's Rev Johnny at the door.

Rev Johnny "May I come in?"

Orin "Sure, Rev Johnny?" Orin bid him entry to the home.

Rev Johnny "What type of bullshit that Jacob talked you into this time?"

Orin "Well, it started with Virginia wanted me to take her to homecoming dance. And that I am booked solid for the thirteen societal events of the trimester. That I must attend all these events. Weather I like it or not. That Horatio is escorting me to said events. Also, that I must start to be a tad bit nicer to Virginia. I think that covers it." Rev Johnny face palms and realizes, what is going on here.

Rev Johnny "He's really going through with it. His plan to get to the bottom of the rest of the promises they made with your grandpa?" Orin simply nod in acknowledgment.

Orin "So, what mess I got myself into with agreeing to go along with it?"

Rev Johnny "Well, you're going to inadvertently do what your grandfather wanted. But, not in the fashion he wanted. Meaning you're going to do somewhat Tania envisioned here. Which will ensure the wraith of Rodney." Orin whistle's

Orin "Great, he and I haven't been getting along of late. And I know he's been passive aggressive with me about it too boot."

Rev Johnny "Yeah, and that is when he's the most vindictive about things. He does do things for Orville. But he has a special knack for them. So be even more careful about it. And be on your guard. So, who is the alternate? For the dance. She has to be as engaging to the eye as Virginia?" Orin looks sleeplessly at Rev. Johnny.

Orin "well I did go over this with Orville and Xenia. They agreed to the idea. I am taking all five Web sisters to the dance." Rev Johnny jaw drops with the shock. Then his eyes fill with rage, Orin never seen him angry before. His mother warned him about his temper. Meaning that he has one.

Rev Johnny "You did what!! You didn't ask them already! Do you at least know what little is going on?!"

Orin "Just the little I could tell them. Not everything, because Jacob needs them for the other events." Rev Johnny simply face-palms again.

Rev Johnny "Terrific! Your dad isn't going to like this. Your mom is going to like it even less. Who is going to break it to her?"

Orin "Jacob is going to do it."

Rev Johnny "Well I think he did. And she isn't handling it well. That is why there was a blow up at her job an hour ago. They adore her. But if they knew what was going on. They would be more sympathetic."

Orin "What happened?" Now worried more than ever.

Rev Johnny "Don't worry. It's owned by Tania and Orville. So they were there. Great, now we are in the crap now. These families and their drama. But at least the home coming dance will be fun and eventful." As Johnny makes his way out of the house. Erin walks in with a harsh look in her face. As she glares at Johnny passing through. Johnny returns the glare with a sympathetic look. She simply sighs and is resigned to the next set of actions that are about to transpire.

Erin "Young man, you're in it deep. And there is no way out but to go through it. So, here is the plan…"

CHAPTER 14

Homecoming Dance

Erin "you did what!?"

Orin "Well it was Xenia's and Orin idea to ask all five of them. And I did do that all at once too. You should've seen their faces mom. They were crying. I think outside of their parents and close family members ever saw that site."

Erin face-palms "Yeah, they had a rough life. The fact that they do like you. And that in spite of everything. You asked them to homecoming. Wihelmine says they never been to any o f these dances with anyone they liked. So, I am happy for them. You did give them a heads up?"

Orin "As much as I could. Explaining to them it's part of pissing off Virginia. Also, that I have to be a tad bit nicer to her. Also, I have to tell her that I asked all five of them out to this as my dates. Yeah, I know this isn't going to go over well. And we have to invite Wihelmine and the girls for dinner. Orville will be here for that"

Erin simply smiles "they have a temper, sure. But they aren't as bad as people say. But then again, the rest of the lot is a different story. How are your dance steps son?" As Erin smiles at her son.

Orin "Dancing is still not my best suit mon. And this is three days before the dance. I am ahead of my classes. Except religion. Rev Johnny keeps piling up the work. Then again all the Weib sisters are with me too. So I think it's because they always managed to skip out on the classes."

Erin "Now go to the shopee. We have to prep your dance moves for the event. Since you are ahead in your studies. I can muster up a few dance partners for you." As they walk to the shopee. The see Wihelmine in the street. As she waves, they wave back. And she walks to them with intention of getting answers from them.

Wihelmine "Why it's the both of you. We must talk a bit now."

Erin smiles "Yes, we do. How about over there?"

Wihelmine "Oh… that is perfect."

Orin and Erin walk to the table as they site with Wihelmine.

Wihelmine "Now is this right that you asked all five of my young ladies out to the dance all at once?" As she has a devilishly smile on her face.

Orin "Ah.. yeah I did." Looking sheepishly

Erin "Yeah he just told me this a few minutes agon." Smiling

Wihelmine "Ah.. And you doing this just to put Virginia in her place?" As her smile grows wider as her eyes light up with joy!

Orin "Ah… Yes, but there is a lot going on that I don't know about and.." As Wihelmine simply brushes off the rest of what Orin's about to say. Wihelmine smiles bigger and wider than before.

Wihelmine "I don't need to know the sordid details. I will find them all trust me. Then again so will Tania and the rest of the Darrquemune's and their offshoots in the family tree. Just too dammed many of them here. Any chance I can get to put one of them in their place is fine by me. But providing my girls a chance to put their so-called golden child in her place. Now that I say its priceless endeavor for me." As her smile grows bigger and she holding a laugh in as hard as she can.

Erin "Well, yes we have to see Tania about a few things right now." Wihelmine smirks

Wihelmine "About what pray tell? If may know."

Erin "Well, Orin isn't a good dancer and he needs to brush up on his steps. So…" Wihelmine cuts Erin off with her hand.

Wihelmine "Don't go to Tania for this one. Rodney will botch it up. I'd rather have the boy learn from one of my other ladies outside the club. Than, let Rodney have the chance to botch it up. Did you tell them why you two were going there now?"

Erin "Ah.. no not exactly."

Wihelmine "Good don't mention it then. And don't le them figure out he not good at all. I'll take care of this for you. It would be my genuine pleasure to teach the young myself if I have to. We'll whip him into shape. We want to succeed in these endevours." As Wihelmine smiles.

Orin "Mrs. Weib, we need to go before they get to curious about the hold up."

Wihelmine "Why, yes of course. Tania is hopelessly paranoid when me and the girls are involved. Then again, you haven't seen us angry yet. So, I know you will. I just pray you don't run away from us when you do."

Erin "We have a nasty temper too. So, we are understanding of bad tempers."

Wihelmine smiles "Thank you so much for understanding us!"

Erin "I'm a single mom too. You have five compared to my one. So, life isn't what is cracked up to be." Wihelmine simply hugs Erin.

Wihelmine "Now you too get going. I'll see you later tonight young man." As she walks off smiling.

Orin "Great, now what do we do?"

Erin "No be quiet. It'd be alright. You do have art supplies there right?"

Orin "Why, yes but oh no you got to be kidding me?"

Erin "No, choice in the mater do a good charcoal piece for her. Don't worry Orville is going to be there." As they enter the shopee. Rodney just glares at them. I think he found out. Now as the make it to the back of the shopee. Xenia and Kathy and Pauline are smirking. As Orville and Tania are arguing.

Tania "Why did he have to ask one of them. But asking out the entire lot! Wihelmine is going to be on fucking, cloud nine. That a man would dare to ask out all five of her ladies."

Orville "Tania, he not taking to Virginia. And she is being downright incorrigible to the lad. Also, the bad dealings made with his grandfather is provoking a lot of tension here. So, we have to find out how deep. We promised a lot of people that hunters weren't allowed in here without the proper vetting. And that takes years into the acceptance letters. No exceptions to the matter. The boy doesn't know what hunters can really do." As they make their presence known. Orville gets his composure with Tania as they smile and Say "hello there" Off key, because Orville was the off by a few seconds.

Orville "What can we do for you tonight?"

Erin "Well actually I want Orin here to sketch your wife as requested. I'm here for emotional support. He did want you present for the sketch."

Orville Smiles, you are a good man Orin. Hmmm.. what type of sketch you want my dear?"

Tania smiles "Well I wanted to do it in the nude. But because…"

Erin "Now shush young lady we are here to make sure not funny business happens okay."

Tania and Orville simply smile and say "Okay, you do have a point" in unison.

Orville "What are you going to use?"

Orin "Charcoal, sir."

Tania "Oh.. my, it's going to look beautiful!" As Tanis disrobes ad the setup in the studio for the portrait. Orin pulls the charcoal out and the drawing board. And begins the sketch. As he is Drawing Tania. Xenia, Kathy and Pauline check his techniques out as he continues to draw her properly. Orville simply smiles in satisfaction. And then he notices a few things in the portrait and keeps them to himself. But Tania's sisters are like to ask questions.

Pauline "Why are you drawing that?" as Kathy nudges her to keep quiet.

Orville "Why are you doing that son?"

Orin "I always put a little of my imagination into the charcoal pieces. Is this unacceptable?"

Orville 'No, no, your have a keen eye for such things young man. This is very befitting of my wife." As Orville thinks to himself. "I wonder if the boy can hear us now. If you then it's not much time left before he comes to age." As Orin continues to draw Tania. Erin just talks to the other ladies in the room and Tania sparingly. Once the sketch is completed. And shows Tania after she gets dressed the finished product.

Tania blushes red. "My, word you did capture my essence correctly. If I do say so myself showing the Orville and her sisters."

Erin "Yes he is quite good at what he does. "As she smiles.

Tania "Yes, he is. I'm definitely keeping this one in the back of the shopee. You don't mind Orville. Out of site from most people."

Orville "Yes in the back of the shopee. Out of site as much as possible if you don't mind. Bad enough I have to sleep on the bench outside. People see sights of me they shouldn't have too. Thank you ever so much for letting me stay a few nights a week Erin, by the way."

Erin "No worries, Orville. Happy to help anyone in need. Now if you will excuse us. I'm taking my boy out for dinner." As they leave the shop. Rodney bumps into Orin. Erin doesn't like the bump at all.

Rodney "You know you're playing with fire boy. And I will get my pound from you. And don't worry about it. I'll get it by hook or by crook." As Orin sizes him up and smiles.

Orin "Rodney, never get me angry. You're not going to like me when I'm angry. And when I'm angry. She is enraged. And you don't want to deal with my mother when she is enraged. Not even Tania can protect you from her rage. And for the record. I really don't want to do this. But I'm being forced to do it. So, I might as well try to enjoy myself a little. Where is the harm in that?"

Rodney simply sized up Erin and realizes it's a bad move right now "Okay boy, you're right about this whole affair. It does stink to high heaven. But you better watch your step around here. Because, If I collect. I will collect in a manner of my choosing. So, you better watch yourself."

Orin "I'll be very careful as the situation demands. Is that fair enough?"

Rodney nods with the whole shoppe as witnesses "No, you should've taken to Virginia. Life would be much simpler for you. But you have been warned."

Erin "You cause any trouble to my boy young man, you are going to wish you would be dealing with just my father. Understand that?" Now Orville steps in and glares at Rodney.

Orville "Rodney that is enough. If you do any harm. I will let the people you did wrong to have your hide despite what Tania says. And it's been a long time coming. Too much is at stake this time around. So, knock it the fuck off." Rodney simply back down and smiles with a look in his eyes. I'm going to git you sucka.

CHAPTER 15

Dance lessons

As Erin and her son Orin finish dinner. They make there way to the outside of the club. Wihelmine is outside with the girls. And she notices that they are still in their uniforms. AS they approach them. The young ladies are all smiles. As they come closer Wihelmine waves them in another part of the building. Which happens to their home.

Wihelmine "I've taken the liberty of opening the dance hall in the house here. I got the sound system ready and all the music form the 60's through the current. Ball room dancing jazz, rock n roll. All the good stuff here in vinyl too. Nothing like haring the pop of the needle on a record. What is the mater you two?"

Erin "Rodney know what is going on and he gave a warning to Orin about getting his pound of flesh."

Wihelmine "Well, I'm not surprised. Rodney has a thing for Becca. Becca does things in self-defense. She can be mean about it. A little to mean I'd say for my tastes. But Rodney, does have genuine feelings for her. The issue is when she saw Rodney in the full moonlight so to speak. It was a turn off. But I would worry a bit. If's he determined to get you. He will do it. Does Orville know?"

Orin "He did it in front of Orville and Tania. Orville said if he does anything he'll let the town get him for all the things he done to them."

Becca laughs "Well, that will be a site to see." As she laughs

Wihelmine "Now Saundra show the good las how to do a waltz." As the music chimes in Saundra extends her hand.

Saundra "Come now I wont bite that hard." As she giggles. As he approaches her and as she places Orin hands in the right spots. Not to low and not too high either. As the pace is slow and deliberate. Saundra notices the problems Orin has right away.

Rory "Wow, he wasn't kidding. His Hand eye coordination is beyond perfect. But dam he has the worst two left or right feet I've ever seen. Ouch!"

Wihelmine "I've seen worse than this Rory. Also he did warn us about this too. Which makes it all the more fun. We'll whip this poor young man into shape. By the way how far ahead are you in your studies young man?"

Orin "Well, I'm three weeks ahead. But is because I'm so used to moving around like that."

Erin 'Yes we've moved a lot in the last minute and at the last hour a lot before."

Saundra "Oh.. that explain a lot. And why the two of you look at you're surrounding a lot. But knowing who you are related to. I don't blame you all one bit."

Erin "Thank you dears, you have no idea I appreciate you six for all of this."

Wihelmine "Now, you are the first set of neighbors in a while that really wanted to get to know us." As Orin looks at Wihelmine, he notices fangs for a split second. And they are gone.

Erin smiles "No worries, I'm glad we are in such good company."

Rachel "I have an idea. Let's work with another sort of dance that requires him to use his hip instead." As Rachel extends her hand to him. As he accepts. Let's do simple sliding from left to right. As her sisters get what she is trying to do. They follow suit. As their mother s watch with pride and joy. To see them working on the moves on the floor and how slowly Orin is getting the moves. But he is smiling as he is learning and laughing with the girls. But he notices that sometimes their eyes go to gold. Other times Back and forth. As the hour he noticed the ears have point and they disappear. As the hours pass into daytime. He finally go the waltz down with the other dances.

Wihelmine "Now ladies and gentleman. We must take a break. You mom is tired Orin. We'll see each other tomorrow night. Same time, take your mom home and let her rest. She has the day off right?"

Orin "Well, yeah Orville insisted that she has the next three days off. She been working a lot of late. Then again so have I" As he sighs in relief. AS he waves goodbye for now to the ladies of the house. They all are smiles and wave night, night so to speak. As thy walk across the street and enter the home. They see Orville alone in the house.

Orville "Having the ladies teach him how to dance across the street huh? Smart move by the way. The two of you. Rodney won't screw that up now. Tania will be hurt but not disappointed in the two of you. Since Rodney is on the warpath. He usually stays at the shopee during the dances. Because he can't go with Becca or any of her sisters. So, he is extremely jealous now. The girls know what happened in the shopee?"

Erin "Yes, they do. The just rolled their eyes. Wihelmine just sighed with disappointment. Explaining what Becca does is out of self-defense. And that she is downright mean about it. But Rodney is a whole different matter altogether."

Orville "Well, that is true about Becca and her sisters. The issue is that too many people have laid claims on them in the past. Well, it didn't work out well wit them. Things just simply didn't take. Luke Tepes Darkmun is another perfect example. He is in love with Saundra. The problem is he driven would be suitors out of here and fast. Once he sees you with all five of them on the dance floor. It's going to be real trouble fast. So, the chaperones in the hall are set. With Horatio Jacob and Johnny and myself there. But that doesn't mean things won't go awry."

Erin "Will I be there as one of them? I Know Wihelmine will be."

Orville "That is even better. Makes my life easier. Now get some rest. You're not working he next fe days. I'm trying to keep you two apart for now. I can't do it forever. Until he cools off a bit. But he will needle you at every turn."

Orin "It's okay. I am used to it by others. But he seems to have a hatred for me?"

Orville "Very perceptive. It's because, he can't slack off anymore since you were hired. Now he must put in elbow grease into everything. Now that he must work. He's nothing but angry and jealous. So, he is gunning for you now. But he has to wait for his shot. So, be very Leary of him now. No matter how nice he is." With that Orville shows himself out. Now two more nights of lessons. After the last night of lessons. Orin is set for the dance. He has the corsages set up for the ladies. He picked them up earlier in the day. He got his Tux and is walking across the street to pick up his dates. He is now nervous. He wonders how stunningly beautiful they will look. AS his mother smile sand says "Don't worry. It's going to be fine" As they approach the door to the house. They ring it. Wihelmine answers the door.

Wihelmine "Oh…You're here!" You can tell she is so happy in her eyes. As she gets things ready. She realizes the corsages in his hands. Each specific to each of her girls.

Wihelmine "Oh… My, you did come prepared. And it's their favorites too. Each individual one of them. Is that a clip on?"

Orin "Ahh.. yes. I don't know how to put on a proper tie so to speak."

Wihelmine "Now, hush boy I have one here. And may I say you dashing in that tux. The girls are gong to love it. Wait here." As they wait he sees the ladies coming down in their gowns. All sleek and colorful in their own way. Rory, has a hunter green strapless gown showing most of her back and her hips off. She fills it nicely. While Becca has a nice blue with spaghetti straps showing her chest and hips off. Rachel comes down and hers is a nice pastel orange. Showing her hips and chest off. With eh straps on her shoulders below the collar bone. Colleen comes down and she is wearing a gown with the slit wither legs showing and her hips and chest showing a bit and its sky blue. Now Saundra comes down in a nice red gown. Fitting very close to her form. Showing all her curves as she twirls around in her gown. As they wlk up to him. Saundra has his tie.

Saundra "Come over here young man. I'll do the honors for this moment." Aa Orin steps forward and allows her to tie the bow tie properly. As she finishes this properly.

Becca "Wow, you look absolutely skirmish. A meal to be had." And a elbow to her left gut.

Rory "Now, now we are all going to have us some fun tonight. The girls are just going to be mad with envy."

Rachel "Well, it's going to be a night to remember."

Colleen "Now let's go and rip it up!" AS Orin puts the corresponding corsages in each o f them. The ladies actually blush as Orin simply smiles. He notices that their mothers are smiling too. Once all is set.

Erin "Now let's go to the party!" AS the lever the house. Orin notices that someone is lurking in the shadows. He can't make out the figure. As he taps Colleen, Saundra whispers "That is one of the Darquemoon's. They keep watch over house a lot. It's one of the reasons why we like the balcony so much. So, we can keep an eye on them. Just relax, they don't dare send anyone to keep a eye on your place. Evers since Virginia was told walk naked home." As she giggles on that punishment. As they leave and head tot eh main dance hall in the school. Orin notices activity in the game shopee. Rodney is there. With a harsh cold look on his face. Yet he smiles and waves. Orin now feels a cold shiver down his spine. As if someone walked over his grave. As the go through the gates and the ahllways. Getting closer to where the music is. They produce the invitations to the dance. The people receiving them are doing quadruple takes seeing who he has as dates. As they enter the closed off area before you can come in to the hall. The door opens and the people are there dancing away and they notice him and the ladies walking in with smiles on their faces. They arrived at homecoming dance. And they are here to perform. Not play.

CHAPTER 16

The storm at Homecoming Dance

As they break into their own grove. The ladies and Orin are dancing up a storm. Putting the rest in the hall to shame. However, some are keeping up wit them. As the girl alternate depending on the music as the dace around him. There is a certain woman with a gold dress and high heels breaks through the lines and taps Orin on the shoulder. At this point he is dancing with Saundra. Her smiles fades as if a mother defending her cub "Don't turn around. It's Virginia she said." Following Saundra's lead. Orin doesn't turn around at all. Instead concentrates on dancing with Saundra. When the times comes to alternate, he alternates with Becca. This raises a lot of eyebrows in the floor too. Virginia still taps Orin on the shoulder.

Becca "She still there and don't turn around and keep dancing "Orin responds to Becca's warning. And continues to move through the motions. He actually enjoying that he is dancing with the girls. And he is holding his own with t hem too. At this point Virginia taps again when he alternates with Rachel.

Rachel 'Don't turn around she still there. And she is blood red with anger now." As he nod sin acknowledgement. Keeps dancing away from Virginia. But she stays close enough to them. As the floor moves around and people are coming in and out of the floor. He alternated with Rory now. As they practiced. Virginia Taps his shoulder again.

Rory "She is at it again. Now her eyes have a piercing stare of hot cold rage." As Orin Acknowledges Rory, they keep dancing. As Virginia keeps up with them. Colleen alternated with Rory.

Colleen "I have an bright Idea. As they dance just follow my lead." Orin Just nods with the plan. As he finishes up with Colleen. Wihelmine decides to cut in on the fun. This raises all the eyebrows on the stage. Virginia now is incensed. She taps vigorously on his shoulder.

Wihelmine "Boy is she angry now. You're going to like what next Orin" AS Wihelmine smiles. As he finishes off the dance wither she alternates with Erin, his mother. Virginia is at a pause and doesn't know what to do next.

Erin "Okay this is a sight if you ever wanted one. She is shocked to her core and doesn't know what to do now.

Orin" So still don't turn around now right?"

Erin "Right you are boy. Oh.. Boy Tania is walking in." As the alternate with her. Virginia taps on his shoulders again very impateiently.

Tania "Would you mind giving the poor girl a chance. Just one dance." As he looks at his mother, Wihelmine, Saundra, Colleen. Rory, Rachel, and Becca with give Tania what she wants look. But they death glare Virginia to make sure she understands. That it's a sympathy dance. Nothing is going to come of this dance. Virginia just lifts her head and taps Orin's shoulders one more time. So, Tania lets Virginia cut in. As he lets Virginia cut in.

Virginia "All this trouble to get one dance out of you!"

Orin "Virginia, I'm not in to you. Would you please stop it. I've been nice about it. Just leave me alone. I don't care what Tania thinks on this. My mother's say is final in these matters."

Virginia "Oh... you don't get it boy. You've been bought and sold, by your grandfather. It doesn't matter what other people say. Your mine now. And I'm not letting go. It doesn't matter what Jacob says either!"

Orin "What do you mean bought and sold?"

Virginia "Well, you grandfather made certain assurances, that his blood line mixes right. Also that the union of the families will be cemented in matrimony. So weather you like it or not boy. You are mine to with as I please." As the waltz continues the ladies across the room have a look of shock. This includes Orin's mother and Wihelmine. Virginia

Orin "Well, my father will have to give his blessings too Virginia." As he snickers.

Virginia "Funny he isn't here!"

Orin "True, but he does have his proxies."

Virginia "Really, prey tell, who are they?"

Orin "Well, let us see… Orville, Horatio, Jacob and lastly not least Rev Jonathan Kingsley and Stoner-Boy. That about covers it in a nutshell! So, what about Jacob interference that doesn't count for anything?" Virginia gives Orin and Icy cold yet hot look. Tania, covers her mouth and realizes that Orin's father went to such lengths to protect his son from the families in here. Until his arrival, no contracts to be made on him. Wihelmine, Erin, Saundra, Becca, Rory, Rachel, and Colleen simply smile with that revelation. Knowing that he couldn't be sold to any family without Orville's or Jacobs's, Rev Johnny's, Horatio's, and Stoner-Boy's consent! As the waltz continues.

Virginia "You're pretty good for someone who claims to have either two left feet or two right feet?"

Orin "Well, I had help. They were good enough to ensure I wouldn't embarrass them on the floor. The price of the lessons was, that I had to take all five of them to the dance. Which I didn't mind at all. But this was levied after I asked all of them out at once." As he smiles at them. And the ladies smiles back waving at Virginia. And his mother and Wihelmine waving to Virginia and pointing to the clock that her time is almost up. Virginia is now incensed with rage.

Virginia "Well, now I'm going to have to teach you a lesson in proper manners little boy." She stomps Orin foot with her heel. The she slpas him across the face. Paint brushing him with the slaps. Hits him the solar plexus knocking the wind out of him. Then she slaps him in the balls. With he final hit he begins to bend over. As She goes for the final strike. Collen grabs one arm. Becca grabs the other arm. Rory grabs an ankle. While Rachel grabs the other ankle. And Saundra pull Virginia head back by the hair. Walking her to Erin and Wihelmine.

Erin "Now, no one does that except myself, or his wife. Which last I checked. You happen to be neither!"

Wihelmine "You would let his wife get away with that?" Holding her heart with a smile.

Erin 'I taught my boy to be a gentleman. So, If his wife did that. It would be for a good reason. Like abusive behavior, physical or emotional. And in this case. He was clear and blunt about his likes and dislikes."

Wihelmine "Well, you do have a point there. And to intentionally incur the wrath of my girls like that. Is really bad ju ju." As she smiles at Virginia struggling as she is being held by the Weib girls.

Tania 'This is a really bad misunderstanding here.." Orville walks up with a very angry look.

Orville "Tania! Don't, just don't say another word! You know the contracts like these have to go through proper channels A. B, his parents have to be made aware of the proceedings. C, they were not involved in the proceedings. D, whatever was made was null and void when we threw out his grandpa!" As he is flustered and red in the face.

Horatio "Now Tania, at least one of the proxies had to be involved in said matters. And since they went out of their way not to have any of us involved. Well, that void the contracts. And the Darkmuns' and other I the offshoots lsot a lot of money power and prestige in this mess. Jacob is too busy collecting for their screw ups this time. And he is collecting with a smile on his red face!" As Virginia struggles. Erin slaps the crap out of her. And offers Wihelmine a few turns as well. Wihelmine doesn't pass up the chance either. And finishes her off with the slaps. Between both of them they seem to be excessive.

Wihelmine "Those extras were for my girls who worked really hard teaching him how to dance like a proper gentleman. Now girls, would you please take out the trash?" The young ladies simply smile.

In unison "Yes, mother dearest!" As the hold her up and find the nearest trash can. They stop and wonder how to put Virginia in the can. Thinking of how to do it right.

Saundra" Sisters, like all thing. We should do it headfirst." They smile as the put Virginia in the garbage can head first with her legs sticking out wiggling trying to get out of the can. However, unbeknownst to Virginia they tie the can to the doors so it won't fall. So, the crowd sees her legs frantically. Wiggling around the doors. But unable to topple to the ground. Luke walks over and unites the can and lets it topple tot eh ground. As Virginia backs out of the can. Realizing the girls poured the punch and other things in the can. To make her appearance worse. Where Devon walks up to the Weibs.

Devon "For the sake of a peaceful ending. I must ask you all to leave. Which includes Virginia as well. Luke take her home. Now!" Luke and Virginia obey in protest. But Luke has a nasty look for Orin. While Virginia has the look of, you're still mine by hook or by crook. You are mine. As they let the cousins leave first. After a few minutes Orin and the his party leave the hall. Escorted by Horatio. As the Weibs split from Orin and Erin and Horatio. The Wiebs give Orin a kiss on his cheeks. And Saundra just gives him a deep kiss.

Saundra "It was a good night. The best tiem I've ever been kicked out of a dance. And boy was it worth it!" Wihelmine smiles at the site.

Wihelmine "Come now girls. We have to go to work now. Because we got thrown out. But it was sure worth it." As Wihelmine cackles like a hyena. As they part ways. Horatio wants to talk to Orin alone.

Horatio "Erin do you mind?"

Erin "Not at all. I'll be home. Don't come back too late." As they walk towards the shopee. They notice the lights are on. Horatio starts feeling woozy. As is passing out. Orin isn't affected by anything he can clearly see. As he approaches the shopee. He see Rodney and a few others.

Rodney "Perfect timing. Have you ever played GURPS rpg tabletop before?"

Orin 'Nope, why?"

Rodney "We need a seventh player. And you have been elected to be the seventh member of the party. Come on we'll show how to roll up your character"

Orin "What about Horatio he is passed out?" A Rodney and company pull Horatio into the shop. And lays him on the couch.

Rodney "Don't worry, it'll be fine. He just tired. Now lets roll you a sheet. And get you into this campaign. It'll be a night to remember. Here drink this before we start. It's tradition." Orin hesitates about it. But Matt is there to convince him it's nothing he should worry about.

Michael is there to calm his fears about the drink. As Orin drink the brewed drink. He feels dizzy and yet lucid. Then he feels fuzzy all over.

Orin 'What did you all give me?" As they smile and say "Welcome to the game Orin."

CHAPTER 17

Critical Botch, Nat 20's

As Rodney shows Orin how to roll a character in GURPS. Orin head feels very fuzzy. Not knowing what was in the drink. He feels somewhat dazed. He is confused. As Matt shows him the functions of the dice. Which is meant for the uses in weapons and items. As he is getting the information down. He feels his head going fuzzy. As Rodney is dispatching the mission based on the roll of a D 20 dice. A twenty-sided dice. Now the rolls for the mission take place.

Rodney "Well now we'll begin our LARP session. This all takes place live and with the mission you roll. One through twenty is the missions and it's parameters." As everyone looks nervous. Because these are all real missions with real consequences. And these characters are themselves. Not off shoot of races. Now the fuzzy feelings are getting worse for Orin. He is trying to figure out how to break the fog. He just can't do that. Neither can anyone else he can sense. Michael and Matt are trying. However, they appear to have no such luck. As Rodney is holding court so to speak. Now he speaks to them directly.

Rodney "Now as High grandmaster of tabletop games here in Andersonville. We now Start the quarterly GURPS one night campaign. Now as usual, we roll for our missions. And the parameters of each mission. What items are in play for each mission. And how much help from GOD you will need and get with your corresponding rolls." As each of them roll. The missions are based on how much mischief you can cause in the evening. So depending on the mission. The items in use are specific to the mission. But no ones knows what mission they will get. This is how he causes all that trouble. He spiked the drink with a hypnotic effect to people. I must be that Orin thinks to himself. Man, he did say he would get me for something. And now this is his chance. And he's not letting it slip through his fingers. Matt rolled for his mission of mischief. He didn't look too hany about it either. Michael rolled and was content and relieved that it wasn't too crazy apparently form his facial expression. Now it's my turn Orin thinks to himself.

Rodney "Orin its your turn to roll for you mission." Orin rolls a one. Rodney's jaw dropped tot eh ground if could do that.

Rodney "Roll for your items." Orin rolls natural twenty. Five times for items, objective, and finally the blessing of his GOD for guaranteed success in the mission requirements. Rodney face-palms himself. Pondering on all things. He guaranteed he would get away with all of these things. And now Rodney know he has to accompany his for the success of all the rolls. Rodney looks upstairs as if fate had intervened in this case. Or the fact that chance took over where fate was too busy. Or maybe karma had a role in this.

Rodney "Your mission is to mark a vampire. And I know which vampire you will mark." As Rodney smiles at the irony.

Orin 'Which vampire?" Rodney smirks.

Rodney "Oh… I know the one to mark. And it's well deserved. You have to use these silver fangs and this silver cross to mark the vampire in this mission. Don't worry it won't be permanent. But he mark will be funny to see." As he leads Orin to the intended target. The room gets all smokey and fuzzy and they are in a strip club. He can't make out where he is in the club.

Orin "Is this one og Jacob's clubs?" Rodney, nope but it's nothing to worry about. Orin really worries about it now. If there is a fall out of said vampire. They are both in real trouble. As Rodney compels Orin with all the spells at work.

Rodney "To complete the mission. Once you see the dancer sticks her butt out of the beaded curtain. You are to bite her on the left cheek with silver fangs and slap the silver cross on the right cheek. Got it?" Orin tries to resist. But he can't for some reason. As the moment of opportunity arises. The dancer has her butt out. As Orin approaches, he hesitates. Because the butt really looks familiar. But the drink and all the spells and drugs apparently in it. As he bend down and bites on the left cheek hard and slap the cross on the right cheek just as hard. Everyone in the club hears a scream. And Rodney pulls Orin out of the club, without fail. He smiles with a sense of satisfaction.

Rodney "My GOD!, I finally got her!" As he is dancing the jig in the street. He sees Becca.

Becca "Rodney, what have you done this time?" Rodney's jaw dropped. And he tries to recover. Becca notices that Orin is out of sorts.

Becca "Rodney you didn't give him witches brew?!" Looking very angry with him.

Rodney 'Nope, Matt gave him the red dragon's recipe of that brew." As he is worried now. Because she now knows that he setup the hazing speel to knock out certain people in the surrounding area of the shopee.

Becca "Rodney, if you got him into one of your GURP's LARP sessions" Rodney has a wary smile of admission on his face.

Becca "Last time you did a mess like this a whole parish paid for it! Who was the intended target?"

Rodney "I'd rather not say."

Orin "Becca, I'm trying to fight this off here. What happened to me?"

Becca "Let me get you to the club. Where is Horatio?" As she walks Orin to the club. Rodney twiddles his fingers. And the silver fangs and the cross are gone.

Orin "He's laying down in the shopee."

Becca "Of Course it's their monthly card game tonight. No wonder he could get away with this. I'm impressed that you can fell something is wrong. Also fighting the effects. I hope you didn't do anything to stupid." As they approach the club. Becca sees a commotion there. As she approaches, she sees Saundra laying stomach first on the stretcher.

Saundra see's Becca "That is the last time I'd take advice how to treat a customer from you. As usual sister you break it and we end up paying for it!" As Becca moves Orin closer. To their dread they see a bite mark and a cross imprinted on Saundra's ass.

Becca "Orin, I think I know what he made you do. And I'm deeply sorry you got caught up in this. Knowing what he did to you. I'll bring you to Orville now. And we'll get you out of this one." As she walks Orin to Orville.

Wihelmine "What are you doing come over here now young lady." As she drags Orin to her mother. Wihelmine sees it in his eyes. Knowing the lights are on. But no one isn't exactly home in there.

Wihelmine "Let me gues Rodney right."

Becca "Yes, he was very happy about something he accomplished. I just don't know what he did. I'm not sure eve he knows what he did. For sure, but I have a good guess. Once he saw me and went pale really fast, really quick. But he then admitted to giving the red dragon potion. And that is why he is like this. However, he is fighting it."

Wihelmine "Okay take him to Saundra and let her see. It will make it easier on her. Then Take him to Orville. And tell him of the confession Rodney made as well. As Becca takes Orin to see Saundra. He looks closer at Saundra. He notices fangs pointer ears and gold eyes. And Saundra sees him.

Saundra "What happened to you!"

Becca "Rodney made sure he drank red dragons potion. And lured him to one of his GURP's LARP campaigns. No one was watching him. So he made his Trimester move. Figures it would be homecoming."

Saundra with a look and sees a drop of blood on Orin's lower lip "Now lets see what we have here?" As Saundra swipes the blood off his lip and tastes it. He eyes widen with shock and horror and some relief as well. And wonders why he isn't dead.

Saundra "Becca that's my blood mixed with his saliva. He did this to me. Rodney didn't realize it was me. Nor did he realize that, Orin could survive our blood." As Saundra's eyes narrow.

Becca "What does Virginia know that we don't. Take him to Orville and let him dispel it with the memory back. We'll teach Orin a hard lesson in who to trust. Meaning the person Rodney complled to give him the drink. But, sighs we can't let Orin of the hook either."

Becca "Yeah I know. I don't want to. But it must be done. Mom won't stand for it because the families won't let her get away with it. I'm sorry, but we have to be a little mean with you, for the time being. But you will understand, soon enough." As she waves Becca off to the old man in the bench. As they approach the park bench. The Darquemune's are complains on what has transpired in the night. Orville dismissing them as repentance reprisals of the evening. They complain until they see Orin.

Devon 'What happened to you boy?"

Orville "Now Devon, get Owen, Malcom, and the rest of you dammed hyenas out of here. I'll take care of the boy." They all leave. But with looks as they leave. Wondering if they can hear anything.

Orville "Now get, all of you now!" They begin to disperse fast. As Orville checks the boy out. He asks what happened. Becca tells him all the details. Orville simply face-palms.

Orville "Now you all want to know how he survived. When this gets out. Virginia is going to be more determined to bond with him. The problem is it may already be too late. All we can do is delay it for a few months. But now he must go to the coming out dance. No way out of that one now. Dam you Rodney. I can break the potion. But he will remember everything down to the things he saw. I can chalk it up to the ingredients of the potion. But the time is coming sooner than later. And his mother's hopes are going to be dashed forever now. Let alone his father's. He will have to pay a bone your mother will decide."

Becca "We want it to slide this time. But it's not our decision now is it?"

Orville "you are correct there. But I'll do my best. But Rodney won't pay a dam thing. Tania will see to that. But will they let Orin and the rest get away of being the victims here. Now that is the issue Becca. I know that Saundra isn't the very forgiving type. But the boy will man up and take what you five will give out. But as for the families. He may not be so lucky. I just may have to give in to Virginia's demands. Or at best two of them." Looking sadly at Orin.

Becca "Don't worry about that right now. Rodney knocked out Horatio as well. And that isn't an easy feet."

Orville "You're right about that. Now let's fix up the boy." After Orville gives Orin a drink the fog subsides. And a look of horror is on his face.

Orin "What did I do? It's all a heavy fog."

Becca hugs Orin "Don't worry we forgive you. We just have to figure this out. Okay?"

Orin "Yeah, but it wasn't just me. He hid his tracks pretty well."

Becca "Yeah but he confessed it to me. And everyone knows I never lie about his antics."

Orin "But the trust is gone." Looking down sadly.

Becca "It's not gone. Nor is it shattered. My mother saw you under the influence of what Rodney gave you through Matt Jones right?"

Orville "well Matt wasn't in control of his faculties either. Now go face the ladies and they will decide what to do with you." As Becca takes Orin to the hospital. Over the corner of Orville eye is Stoner-Boy smiling.

Orville "What are you smiling about?"

Stoner-Boy "All according to my father's plan. After all his house has many rooms." As he whistle's and walks off. Orville, his father has a weird sense of humor. That is for sure. Then again, it's way over my head too.

As Becca and Orin tell Wihelmine what transpired. Rory, Rachel, Colleen, and Saundra are fuming with Rodney. Because Orin came right away to tell Wihelmine. She isn't angered by him nor are his daughters. The hug him and kiss him.

Saundra "No hush stop crying it's going to be okay. But we must be a little bit mean for appearances sake. But it wont last long. A fortnight would suffice mother?"

Wihelmine "Yes that will do. Under one condition. And that old coot better comply with this one. You smack Rodney as hard as you can. With whatever you can use or muster every day you go through your hazing." Orin simply smiles and nod with a yes. And in his eyes, Tell this story, He will get it. You better put bets on it.

As they walk back to their perspective homes. Wihelmine bumps into Orville. And explains the conditions of the punishments. Orville smiles and completely agrees with her punishments. But the school has to know these types of events are taboo here. Wihelmine agrees, but Saundra has to agree to it. With a facial expression conveys the issues. Sandra gives the respectful nod in agreement. Now with that settled. Orville walks to Orin.

Orville "You got ten days of hazing by these ladies. Those are going to be the ten toughest days of your life now. And you got off lucky.

Coming to her directly without having me there. Showed her that you truly love and respect all of them. And the fact you're not belly aching over this either. Now hitting Rodney every day at work. Is the only place to do it. So the other ladies have to tell Tania. Either she lets you do it. Or she and Rodney is going to get the hazing of a lifetime. Nothing I can do to protect her nor him here. Because you are taking it like a proper adult." Orville smiles at Orin with pride. Now you go to bed. We'll continue this in the morning. It was a sure humdinger of a homecoming dance!" As Orville walks back to the bench. Orin sees his mom. She already knows what transpired. And the punishments that are being handed out. Even to the victims of Rodney's antics. She smiles at Orin with pride.

Erin "These two weeks will fly by. Besides, I have a few things you can use to hit him with. And don't worry. Horatio is going to be there to ensure he gets hit. By hook and by crook."

Orin "He's that angry!"

Erin "Oh…He's enraged!"

Orin "Oops… I bet Jacob wants a piece of Rodney's hide?"

Erin "He certainly does want a piece. No one does that to Horatio but Jacob!"

Orin "It's been a long night. Can we turn in now?"

Erin "Why, yes we can. We can go over this in the morning" As they go into the house. Orin gets ready for bed. He hears a whoosh. And see all five of he sisters on the balcony. As he opens the sliding door.

Orin "I thought it would be later that you would be visiting me?"

Saundra "Well we figured one nice evening before we start tomorrow on you."

Orin "Thanks, I feel really rotten about this."

Rory "That is why we feel bad about this too. But eh families want this done to all of you. But they won't know until is probably done that Rodney is actually getting punished this time around. So, everyone saves face. Meaning he will be caught this time around. And you're the one going to administer it."

Colleen "We'll help out your mom on the bright ideas to use."

Becca "That sap won't know what hit him." With a sad look. As she didn't want it this way.

Rachel "He'll get his for this. It's not the first time he did this either."

Orin looking sad "I know we are better than this. But I want this done and over with. So no more sick games or retaliation after this. Unless provoked okay?"

The Weib sisters "Yes Orin, your right only in response." Looking dead at him sincerely meaning it. This sends chills down his spine.

Orin "Okay should I know the details? Or should I be surprised?"

Becca 'Surprised works best. But we will tell you how to take him down!"

Orin simply smiles "Okay tell me before I go to the shop. This way he can't anticipate what is up." The girls smile and give the thumbs up. As he returns to bed he hears the familiar whoosh. And they are gone again. Now al he has to do is survie fourteen days of hazing. And returning the favor to Rodney fourteen days on a row. No easy task. But it's going to be worth the time and effort. Now he sleeps for a better tomorrow. He is smiling as he sleeps.

CHAPTER 18

A fortnight of Hazing. And a dinner with the Weibs

The fortnight begins with a student body gathering. About the activites don suring and after the Homecoming Dance. As the presenter shows off each victim. Either cheers or boos were made. It was surprising how many boos there were. Virginia got a lot of heat with boos. She looked Mortified about it. No one laughed at her in the dance. But this made it clear that she was in the outs with a lot of people. As each victim made their complaints known. It was Saundra's turn. As She walked up in the front of the crowd. She simply took off her panties turn around and bent over and lifted her skirt. Showing of the bite mark and the cross imprinter on her perfectly shape butt. She twist slightly and smiles. The smile was playful, however the icy cold look in her eyes told a different story. The story when I get who's responsible for this is going to pay. The crowd simply laughs at the marks. The Weib sisters are furious now. Orin barks out how this is an outrageous, that things like this happened even to Virginia. To she he was not a hypocrite. As the first day of hazing will begin. Orin thinking how the pranks would start. He fell victim to having his looker opened. And shaving cream in it. But he noticed that his books were intact. But not his clothes. And when he would go to the shopee, he would give Rodney a right cross with brass knuckles to start. Knocking Rodney the fuck out on day one. Day two, the haze was that all of Orin's clothes were dumped into the pool. The next day Orin used a crowbar to knock Rodney out again. He did it in front of customers too. Tania wasn't happy about it. Bit she had to let it slide. As the hazing intensified the more brutal the beat down he gave Rodney. As the final week approached to the final day. Orin had a twisted idea. That he only shared with Horatio and Xenia. They agreed with the plan. But getting done would be the finale of the hazing. Which was good for Orin to do. He does have his mother's mean streak and it's was going to show with gusto. The last haze was covering Orin with paint and plaster dye tar and molasses. This made his final beat down on Rodney worth it. He set up for Friday night. He setuo a special sale at the shopee. Where if you spent 500$ 1000$ 1500$ you would receive a special gift. He told Orville to act like a barter in a carnival for this prank. As soon he got into the shopee and changes his clothes for something cleaner. Tania walks in.

Tania "Dam those girls really did a number to you for their final hazing." Orin simply nods in acknowledgment.

Tania "I don't like this side of you Orin. Please say a word."

Orin "Just one more beat down Tania. Just one more beat down. It's going to be a big sale day." As he plots the moves he needs to make. As he walks into the main shopee floor. He see Rodney. Rodney cringes, and stops.

Rodney "hey what gives. You stopping for today?" As his smiles comes back.

Orin 'I'm tired today. The last prank took everything out of me." Which is almost true almost true. As he gives a tired look. Now Rodney relaxes. As Rodney gets into reach. Orin sucker punches him and hog ties him like a piece of cattle. He then raises Rodney up like a piñata gaging him. As the customers come in they and Tania see this.

Orin "Now you free gift is when you spend 500$, 1000$. 1500$ is a whack at good ole Rodney here. 500$ 1 whack, 1000$ 2 whacks, 1500$ four whacks. This also includes preorders as well. But these preorders must be paid in full. No refunds." Now the crowd runs in and out of the shopee with eh news spreading like wildfire. Orville as a barter is making sure that the free gift was worth it. Not knowing all the details at first. When Rodney eyes open, he is humiliated as it is. However, what he discovered was even worse. When he hears the details again of what is going on. There is a line that wraps around the game shopee four times over. Everyone at least spending 500$ or more. To make each tier. As Rodney's body is pull up and down. As everyone gets there, whack in on him. Orville walks in and sees what all the commotion is about. He sees the commotion and looks at Orin. Orville simply smiles as Tania looks upon Orville with horror.

Tania "You're not going to let the lad continue this, Orville?" Looking compassionately to him.

Orville "My dear wife. It's been a long time since I have disciplined this lad myself. Now, I need to pay my money for the four whacks. What can I buy for 1500$? Wait a minute that new uber special edition War Scythe 90k set with all the new and limited editions pieces." As Orville purchases this set in particular. Knowing the other will be a prize for the tournament. As he pays the 1500$. Rodney is scared out of his mind. As he gets the stick. Wihelmine enters the shopee.

Wihelmine "What is going on in here?" Then she sees Rodney and she laughs.

Wihelmine "How did you do that and what are you doing?" as she is still laughing about this one.

Orin 'Well if you purchase 500$ in merchandise. You get One whack at him. If you sopend 1000$ you get two whacks at him. If you sopend 1500$ you get four whacks on him." Wihelmine laughs hysterically about this. She falls on her ass laughing this up.

Wihelmine "Orville you're allowing this?"

Orville "Hell, woman I've paid 1500$ for four good whacks!" Wihelmine is laughing harder now. To the point of hickups. Her Daughters arrive. They see the site before them and laugh. Once they hear the prices and the number peer whack for each interval. They laugh even harder. Then they and their mother pooled money together. So that each one of them would get four whacks each. Jacob and Horatio arrive and paid the 1500$ for their whacks. Tania tries to stop this. But her efforts are in vain. Because when Miguel De le Guy the 36th arrived. He has his money for his four whacks too. As everyone sizes up for the four hits. Rodney mutters something, that the girl and Orville could understand. Saundra asks Orin to lower him just right. As she lifts her skirt and shows off her marks to Rodney bending over and a slight twist with a smil on her face. And her eyes with a hot satisfaction on what is going to transpire. She asks Orin to lift him up and asks to play with the rope to making sporting. But she hit the make for times in a row. And she broke her stick doing them. Wihelmine takes her turn but save one whack. Orville takes a turn and saves one whack. Jacob takes his turn and saves one whack. When Horatio goes up. He asks Orin to make it challenging. As Orin complies with the request.

Horatio "Now Muther Fucker this black man going to teach you respect!" As he whack Rodney three times he saves the last whack. Now Erin enters the room. She sees the spectacle and laughs at everything. She laughs so hard she is getting the hiccups too. And then Orville hands her the stick.

Orville "We four saved one whack just for you each." Erin smiles

Erin "Now Orville, Jacob, Horatio, and Wihelmine. You really shouldn't have.

Horatio "But my dear young lady we surely insist!" As Erin smiles She winds up and hits Rondey harder than Saundra or Orville or Horatio combined Four times. To hear him groan.

Erin "Now that was fun cut him down now Orin. Everyone did get their whacks in right?" Orin Nods a yes. As Erin walks to Tania with eyes we need to talk.

Tania "Was this necessary?"

Erin "Unfortunately yes, it was. AT the rate he got away with things here. Your lucky my son didn't come up with something on his grandfather's level of being just plain ole vengeful behavoir. This is more of his father's tune. Be thankful he restrained himself with this being the final haze on Rodney. And Boy did everyone take their shot at him." Tania ushered her head down. Knowing the money, they made today would pay the medical bills five times over. But the poor boy's confidence will be shattered for some time now. After Orin, lowered him down and untied Rodney. He bends over and whispers.

Orin "This is what happens when you try to play games with me boy. I know whole shit load of games. I don't like using them either. Never ever make me feel the need to do this level of shit. Do you understand boy?"

Rodney 'Sure, I understand crystal clear. I won't do that again nor anything things else on that level again. Unless asked by Orville himself."

As he is looking at Orville. Seeing Orville smiling at the both of them. Orin Helps Rodney up and takes him to the dressing room. They decide to close the shopee for the evening. The ladies going over the sales made for the day. And boy did they make a lot of money. As Orin and Rodney leave the shopee. They see the Weibs waiting patiently for them with his mother Erin and Orville, Jacob, Horatio, and Rev Johnny. As they walk towards them. Rodney is limping a lot. With grimaces with each step. Knowing it'll takes days for him to recover. As Rodney walks over to Orville he simply sneers at the old man. This was a bit too much look in his face. The Old man simply slaps him. With the look don't make me do this again boy.

Orville "You broke your mother's heart here. Making your cousin do this. So don't make us do this again you hear!" Rodney simply nods.

Rodney "You're right I won't do this again without your permission father. But I have a reputation to uphold as the main prankster here. I can't let anyone take my title now?"

Orville "Who would want to here. You just pissed everyone off One time many Rodney. The families go involved this time around. The victims had to pay a boon to those you manipulated to as well. As in there agreed reprisals. Knowing that you used the hypnotic drugs and psychedelics in the drinks. So, they felt bad for it. And Only Orin got his pound of flesh so to speak until today. The simple brilliance of the plan. Appeased all the families on this one. Because the boon of the money your mother got was the payment she would've gotten. Now your cousin here is the big man on campus. And the funny thing he doesn't want to be the big man on campus. He just wants to do his work and find a good paying job and not be hassled by anyone." As Rodney looks at Orin and smiles.

Rodney "You're a worthy opponent. Never say any of it coming. Is that how you play War Scythe 90k?"

Orin "Yes, but I deciphered the codex in the lore. Once you do that it's easy to maove the pieces around effortlessly." Rodney's jaw drops.

Rodney "There is a codex! I thought it was a hoax or a long lost myth."

Orin "Nope it's real. But boy is it a pain to collect and decrypt. Once you have the completed cyphers. You can stack the moves easily."

As Rodney looks upon Orin very differently now. Rodney gestures to Horatio.

Rodney "He's your top player isn't he?"

Horatio 'Yes he is. He has beaten a lto of top players in the online version and the table-top as well." As Rodney looks at Orin.

Rodney "Can you beat Luke?"

Orin "Most likely. But he tries to get to see my matches at he clubs. I don't like the atmosphere in the school. Moon dog's or the Shoppee I prefer. But not tonight. I would like to see Tania cool down a bit first." Rodney looks around with a look of silent agreement with that one.

Rodney "Yeah that is a good idea. Now I am going home to bed. And no more pranks with you six. I've learned my lesson. But I will uphold my title. Just not with you all!" As he walks off. Erin gestures every to go to her home for dinner. The Weibs accept with everyone else. As they walk home. Saundra is holding Orin's hand. At the steps of the home. They see Luke and Virginia tepes. They have food with them too. Wihelmine gestures a truce so to speak with her hands. Luke and Virginia agree. Erin isn't happy about it either, so are the other men in the party as well. The girls are just keeping the peace for now. Because Orin made a spectacle worth of Rodney and got away with it. Tania couldn't say a word about it. As they let the Wiebs stating that each one individually is invited into the home. They set up the table. As the rest of the men setup the food. However Orin is told to stay at the table. While they server the food.

Luke "How did you come up with that? It was brilliant. Simply brilliant. Outsmarting him like that. Rodney gives me a run all the time in games. But you, you have a real talent Orin." Orin nods.

Orin "Thanks, no big deal. He doesn't know me that well. I took advantage of it."

Luke "well, yes that is true. We don't know you that well. So, you are the local wild card. Keeping people on their toes. But he Weibs know you well now, don't they?" Orin simply dismisses the question with a look.

Orin "What are you getting at Luke?" Luke jaw just drops. As he sees the girls exploring every nook and cranny in the house. Seeing the unfished works with the finished works.

Wihelmine "Wow, your artwork is amazing. Now I know why Tania has those gallery opening for you. You must make a bit of coin now?"

Orin "I make a humble living off it. But I need the day job to keep going."

Rory 'Absolutely, right about that."

Saundra "I really love the etchings you do. They are nice."

Colleen "The paintings are vibrant."

Becca "The charcoal drawings are fantastic!"

Rachel "I do love your quick sketches too Orin. You have a very good eye for details"

Orin "Thank you all ladies. I appreciate it very much. I just want to enjoy a good meal and get some sleep. I know for some of you this is more like breakfast."

Saundra "True, but we like it here." As the food is served Orin notices little twinkles at the Weibs plates and Johnny's plate too. As they eat Virginia decides to chime in now.

Virginia "Now with such a performance. You must be ready for that coming out dance in a few weeks."

Orin "Nope, I'm not. Nor do I want to go. Horatio, that is one of the ones I can skip, right?"

Horatio "Says, actually that is the only one you can skip. And it was informed that you're going to that event." As he smiles

Luke Tepes Darkmun "Ordinarily you would be correct. However Vladimir Cristopher Darquemune is requesting that he attend this one. Since how he made a spectacle of Rodney. He really impressed us with that. And Vladimir wants a meet and greet. We are here to secure that. And we aren't leaving without an yes." As the rest of the table looks around.

Wihelmine "Luke, Vlad will have to no for an answer. Or if he must go the Von Weibs and their nana will be in attendance. That is the only way you're going to get a yes. And also the Lupins must be ther as well as the Ulbergs and the Woldson's with all the offshoots." Wihelmine simply smiles at this point making Luke and Virginia squirm.

Luke Tepes Darkmun "Well, that is a big guest list. Having your mother show up Wihelmine. Is that wise, she isn't well regarded." Looking scared now.

Erin "Now as Wihelmine said that has to be the guest list. Which includes his father as well? Not one must be absent in these matters. I mean not a single one must be absent. The exception is my father he can be absent. If he is there or any other of his representatives. We are leaving promptly. Any other questions. These are the conditions. The riverboat fiasco earlier this month was not a happy event. As I recall. Having my son gamble like that. And he actually winning it all. Just for your family to renege on the deal. And the whole ot of you were cheating except him. Good thing Horatio and Jacob took care of that." As rev Johnny glares at Jacob for that one.

Jacob "Alright Johnny, I made sure that won't happen again on the river boat. At least without his parents present. But he was gambling on Horatio's behalf." Looking innocently.

Horatio "I do believe when we entered you said, and I quote you Jacob. I've taken the liberty of converting you cash into cheeps." As he dismissively waves his hands.

Jacob "It's not my fault you're a horrible card player. But you boy Erin is adam good card player. You must have taught him how to play!" Erin snorts

Wihelmine "Now those are the demands. If one person is missing, then it's done and over with. I will not have her boy displayed like a mare in a show. You've done it too often with my girls. And it was nothing but trouble ever since. Now take it or leave it you two." As the two look at eachother, and nod in agreement.

Virginia "Only his wife or mother tells him what to do Wihelmine. But in this case, he'll make an exception. For this exceptional young man. He likes the fact he doesn't flaunt it. He adores the fact that he doesn't squander it. So the deal is satisfactory. Now Luke we have overstayed ore welcome. How did you Wieb Ladies like the food?" The Weibs looked at eachother and said in unison "It's was scrumptious." And glare at them to leave. Luke and Virginia Take their leave. As they leave Virginia blows a kiss to Orin. The Weib sisters just sneer and hiss at her.

Rory "Next time I think we should do more than put her in a garbage can!"

Becca 'I agree that cunt deserves a arse whooping."

Erin "Now you're insulting all the cunts out there. The ones I have met had some but not much common sense."

Orin "Definition of cunt. Acronym Can't Understand Normal Thinking/Things. In spite of gender apparently I'm surround by them!" Everyone laughs at the table.

Wihelmine "Now I wonder how to this young blush?" Erin's smiles
Erin "I know how and whispers in her ear."

Wihelmine "Really! Can we do that? I want to see this site. So do the girls."

Erin "Sure, Orin I want a sketch done of us ladies in the nude. Now!"
Orin starts to blush 'Mom, do I really have too?'

Wihelmine "You heard your mother now." As they go to the couch. Getting ready for the sketch. Johnny just gives Erin a death glare. Erin simply sticks her tongue at Johnny. As the ye set the scene in the couch. And Orin does it with charcoal. He swiftly draws the scene out precisely and acuratelt the scene in question. Blushing the entire time.

Wihelmine "He walked Saundra back to the club one night. And she tried to flirt with him really hard. It didn't phase him one bit. Seeing him blush like this is fun. But how comes he doesn't react to people naked like that." As a though goes into Wihelmine head. It's Becca "Mom what are doing. We couldn't compel him. It took a powerful potion and he was still fighting that off successfully apparently. That Rodney has to use a few spells too. He just to strong willed."

Erin "oh... that is simple he grew up in a nudist colony. He's seen fully developed Men and Women since he was four. So, it's natural sate of being for him. So he tends to dismiss people trying to dress sexy to impress him. Since your Daughter are exotic dancers. Showing up half naked on the balcony. It doesn't really bother us. I think people around here would have a problem with him being a nudist at heart." Wihelmine simply smiles

Saundra "Oh.. that makes perfect sense. It's just a human body's natural form to him. This is art. But drawing you naked Erin that bother's him"

Wihelmine "Now ladies, let the poor boy finish. It's understandable, he believes it as GOD intended it to be. He hates that there are too many perverts out there to ruin it. Which I agree with his lien of thinking. He looks upon you as woman. Not sex objects. Virginia looks upon him as a sexy toy and nothing more." After he finishes the sketch. And Passes it along.

Wihelmine "May we keep it out of prying eyes please?"

Orin 'I do trust you with that Mrs. Weib." Wihelmine smiles

Wihelmine "You're the only one that gives me the proper respect here boy. I will cherish this. But I have to keep it away from nana. She go nuts over this. Not eh way you expect. She can be worse than Tania!" As the girls leave through the back to the club. Orin pounders what is going to happen next. Wihelmine mentions to mom how all the girls tried to seduce him. And mom gave her the answers. My is a little too comfortable with Wihelmine. He wonders why? As the men leave the house. Rev Johnny talks to Erin.

Rev Johnny "Erin, you're playing with fire with the Weib's just be careful. I have to tell you the last time a similar event happened like this."

Erin "Supposedly, she took out on an entire parish."

Orville "Yes she did. Just not any parish. She took it out on Johnny parish." Erin looks at Johnny and puts her hand over the mouth. She stares at Johnny and starts crying.

Erin "I'm so sorry. I should've guessed it earlier."

Rev Johnny "The girls are good eggs. Wihelmine is still a little confused. It's not what happened to Rodney wasn't undeserved. But now he is attracting too much attention."

Erin "well at least his Father won't be there and it ends there."

Jacob "Wrong, He will be coming back the day before the event. That is a hard date. Because he makes that event. Nana being there is the wild card. And she might just show up." As the lot of them simply sighs.

Orin "Great, better get that last tux. It's going to get some use after all." As he walks up to his bedroom. He notices that the girls moved things around. And he actually likes the changes they have made. As he opens the door, He sees them in his room.

Orin "You did hear them down there?"

Rory "Yes, we did. And it sucks."

Rachel "Now we are hedging a bet. Hoping Nana isn't coming." As becca is walking naked through the room.

Becca "I would say run. But there isn't anywhere to run to. Vlad wants to see you. You see Vlad. Only one person that can tell him to fuck off. He isn't here now." As she puts on the black see through blouse.

Colleen who is half naked now, "Wait a minute, how about we discourage two or three of them to go. They would understand, right?"

Saundra who I still naked laying on Orin's bed "That won't work now. And we do know it. Embarrassing Rodney like that. Put him on the map here. Now there is going to be more than the usual spectacle. It's going to be special this year. Now Orin is here to be bought and sold for in the society circles here. And Vlad does dote on Virginia, a lot. So she has the high bids at the moment. So does Carrie, Margaret, Cassidy, McKenzie, to name a few." As she looks down with sadness.

Orin "we'll figure something out. There got to be a way out."

Rory "I'm not sure there is. Nana may come, because it's her Trimester visit. She is due for one. She always does come during the coming out parties. In the hope there is a suitable male in her eyes for us. So is always disappointed in the turn outs."

Colleen "Not this year, however. That if she comes."

Rachel "Oh.. that is right. She would want to give him the once over."

Becca "dam, you're right. And she is the harshest judge amongst them all."

As they leave his room. He leaves the door unlocked. So, they can freely get there things. He doesn't mind them coming and going. He feels safe with them. Now another party he has to go to. But there maybe a chance he can ditch this one. Slight chance, but a chance. He decides to go to sleep.

CHAPTER 19

The coming out party and Grand Prix War Scythe tournament

As everyone is getting ready for the coming out party. Orin is getting nervous over it. The guest list is confirmed. Except two hold outs. The hold outs are Nana, and his father. If one is a no show. Then he can skip it. But he has a funny feeling it won't be that way. As he goes for the siesta. He sees Rodney at the shop. Rodney is doing his job now. And he's seem happier about it. The tournament is coming up.

Rodney "You look terrible? The Party right?"

Orin sighs "Yeah, it sucks, doesn't it?"

Rodney "Yeah it does, but for the women is equally as bad too. but this year you are the star attraction. So how is your ranking in War Scythe this tournament?"

Orin "I'm in the top 3 in the world. How about you?"

Rodney "I am in the top five in this region. But you and Luke are my real competition. But If I lose to you. I wont mind. You won't disrespect me like that. Luke, I want to see his ass handed to him however. Dam the qualifier is on the coming out party. Oh.. Dam Vlad wants to see you play. Shit man, he hosts the games in the coming out party. He usually has the best talent there. That is partly the reason why he wants you there!"

Orin "So we are both hosed."

Rodney "Yup pretty much. Since Tania and Horatio are going to be there. Oh, dam it's the grand prix format. Win as many rounds as possible and games in the set time limit. Vlad picks the set for each player too. Dam them all to hell."

Tania 'What are you too talking about?"

Orin "rodeny thinks Vlad is running a grand prix format in War Scythe 90k at the coming out party for the players." Tania simply smirks

Tania "Rodney it took you this long to figure that out? I'm disappointed in you. Orin I can understand, but you?"

Rodney "My head still hurts from being a pinata" As rubs his head.

Tania "Now we are in the shit. Nana is here?"

Orin "How do you know Tania?"

Tania "We women know things son. In time you learn to trust it." As Orin just shrugs.

Rodney "How are you going to beat them?"

Orin "As usual by the seat of my pants. It's all about how you move the legions and the races they are in the game. They each have their own specific abilities. If you stack them right. Well you can clear the board in the first five rounds. If you, do it wrong. Then the game is a long one. It depends on who the player is." As he scratches his head. Trying to figure out how to get out of this one. Erin walks into the shoppee.

Erin 'Hello Tania! Hello Rodney! How is the head Rodney?"

Tania "I'm fine, and he is fine. It still hurts for him to think. Then again I think that is why he is doing so well in the shopee here." As Tania laughs

Rodney "It'll get better. What is up Ms. McNeil?" as Erin smiles

Erin "I have bad news for Orin here. Wihelmine's mom arrived last night. And His father arrived this morning. He is living on the campus right now. So, you have to go now. The Tux is ready. Also, he must tend to a few more things in the school before he meets us at the event. At Darquemune's Castle point." Orin looks devastated. He really wanted to skip this one. Everyone is closing shops for this event. So, I don't know why it's this big."

Tania "He is hosting the War Scythe 90K regionals in his home. Anyone who is anyone comes to that tournament. You can make bets on any player too. Honey you won't stop the betting. But you can have two people sponsor him. So, he won't be responsible for the money. I bet Jacob Gator-Star and Horatio Tiberius LeClaire are his sponsors for this event. As I sponsor Rodney every year. So I'm looking forward to these two young men clearing the clocks out of the other players. Especially if it's Luke. The boy needs to be taken down a few pegs." As Orin graons about he Tepes offshoot of the Darquemune's. He simply can't figure out why the Tepes middle name is all over the family tree and offshoots. As he tires of these details.

Orin "Tania, may I go out for a while and clear my head. I'm fisnihed my homework and my projects ahead of schedule. I would like to enjoy the day if I can." Tania smiles

Tania "Sure, my boy. Just go out and see Orville. This way you can still get paid." Orin takes the advice and walks to the center of town to Orville's park bench. He isn't seeing anyone and it appears he is sleeping. Orin knows better. He just resting his eyes. Orville loves to watch people and what they are doing. As he approaches the bench. He whispers

Orin "Am I interrupting anything."

Orville "Nope not a dam thing. What is troubling you boy? The gathering in tomorrow night?"

Orin "Yes that is what is troubling me. Any advice how to proceed?"

Orville "Yeah don't be a no show. Also be nicer to Virginia while you're there. Three, win the tournament. I know you beat Rodney with ease. It's Luke Tepes is going to be the problem. But kick his ass. The boys and I have a lot riding on you. You'll do fine. Just keep following the prophesies about your life. And all will be fine." Orin triple takes.

Orin "I haven't told you about those dreams."

Orville "You didn't have too. The man that gave you those dreams told me. You should go and talk to him more often. Then again, he is hard to catch up with. But follow the smoke and you'll find him. He told me to bet on you. Every time I follow his advice. He's been right. So, he never fails me. I do believe in what he is saying too. I used to be too wrathful for my own good. Or do you want to find him together?" Orin decides on the latter. As they go around to find Stoner-Boy. Stoner-Boy finds them in the middle of the park.

Stoner-Boy "My, my what do we have here. The man that humbled Rodney. Orville and Tania never thought they see the day. It's a shame it had to be that rough. Then again you have to be that way to straighten someone out. What can I do for you two today?"

Orin "You're that said I would win the tournament. I don't want to play. I don't want to go either."

Stoner-Boy "The board is set. You must play, or things will go horrible wrong for you. The dies are cast. All I can say if you don't go. Your grandfather wins. And you'll be lost. And your mom won't recover from this either. She won't go over what happened last time he tried to intervene. It really hurt her too much. I don't want Silas Eugene McNeil here. So you have to drive him out of the town by winning the tournament. Besides I'll be ther too. Don't worry about Vladimir. I always get passed his guards easily. Now boy toke up and drink the water. You will be fine calm cool passive. With nothing to worry about." As he passes the bong. Orin opens the top. And a lot of smoke is coming out. As he tokes up. His eyes roll and he is calm cool collected. And then he drinks the water and he feels even calmer and more at ease than before. Like something washed over his spirit and he sees the same vison again with he girl in the white dress floating all over town in triumph. As he comes down gently from this vision, he looks at Stoner-Boy.

Stoner-Boy "You'll miss out if you don't go. Just prep for it. Wipe the floor with the so called rivals you have here. Go there to play and put some more people in their places. But be generous with your victories. Be kind to them, that cross you with ill feelings. And for clarification. The girl isn't Virginia. So you don't have to worry about that. But you will still have to contend with her while you live here, understand?" Orin simply nods yes.

Stoner-Boy "Now go be content and win. By the way your father is right over there. Walking around. Go and talk with him. I know you too need that. Orville escort him there so he doesn't miss his moment." As they approach Owen's father. He sees he has silver hair now. He's tall, and still solid. As his father sees Orin. He simply smiles and cries. He runs and gives him a hug.

Owen Ulberg "Now let me take a good look at you. Wow, you have grown quite a bit. I know missed too much. How much have I missed?' As tears are flowing down his face.

Orin crying now "Well quite a lot. I don't know where to begin?"

Owen Ulberg "Well how about he past trimester? Let's begin there. And work our way down." Orin goes over the past trimester. Filling his father in all the details, that Orville, Horatio, Jacob and Rev Johnny might not told him. Owen Ulberg is crying with tears of joy. Hugging his son.

Owen "Wow, you do have an interesting life here. Also, I'm very happy your mother and you made good friends of the Von Weibs. They are a tough but good bunch. They just got the shaft a lot. But I am proud of you. But what Rodney made you do. I would have knocked his block off. No matter what Tania might have said. But got the town to pay for it and give him a once over. Now that is priceless. But I can't let you do that in school Okay?"

Orin "It's Okay dad he's calm now. But he won't mess with me again." As Owen hugs Orin one more time.

Owen Ulberg "Now go home rest up. You have a big day tomorrow night. I have to visit Wihelmine and her daughters. I need time to catch up. Long story but worth the time once heard. I told your mother a lot about them. But not everything. So don't try to pry too much. Take him home for me Orville. And also keep and extra eye on him for me." Orville smiles.

Orville "No worries president Owen Ulberg. He will be safe." As they part ways Orin feels at ease now. Orville walks him around town. Letting the boy soak it in. That his father is here. And that he has a lot of work with everyone in his life. As they go throught he stores looking and walking about.

Orin "You had to do the same with Rodney?"

Orville understanding the pretext and sighs "Yeah, I did. The same with your father too. Being his grandfather and all. Yeah, I know I still look young. But I'm older than most people think. But, being the Mayor has it's responsibilities. That always outweighs the privileges. So he gets it now. As you do. You are a responsible young man. You have been made into one very young. Now that you are enjoying life a little. Your father is ecstatic. He knows it's a bumpy road. He just making his time with the people he loves. Rodney just rejects my attempts. He is happy you provided me the discipline you provided. Tania know it straighten him out. But he also knows that spare prize set is coming to you. Because you were a man about getting the punishment from the girls. And that you took it without a gripe about it. Wihelmine, wanted to know what you would do to Rodney. And your final solution what shall we say, was rather unique."

Orin "It also had the virtue of never having been tired before."

Orville smiles 'Yeah, that is true too. Xenia helping you out was a big surprise too. That shocked Rodney, that his aunt's approved of it. Meaning Tania had to shut her trap about it. And not yap continuously about it." As Orville laughs about it more. As they walk back to the shopee. They Hear Owen and Erin argue a lot. And it's about how much time he gets to spend with Orin too.

Orin "Maybe we should go through the back and let them have it out. She does have a lot of pent up angry towards him."

Orville "Young man, discretion is the better part of valor." As Orville gives the thumbs up. AS they walk to the back. Xenia is there with the hung-up Uniform and Orin's books.

Xenia "I didn't think you would mind?"

Orin "Not at all, makes life easier. Thanks!"

Xenia "I punched you out of the rest of the day. So go and enjoy the day."

Orin "I'll probably sleep it away."

Xenia "Yes, you should. You have a big night tomorrow. You should have a lot of strength for it. I'll be thee rooting for you and Rodney. But Rodney wants to see you play and beat you straight up too. But you two will do great. If you wipe that smirk off Luke's face." As she smiles and give him the rest of his things. Orin walks home with Orville. As they enter the house. Owen gestures Orville to make use of the house. Orville jumps at the chance for the shower and the spare bed. As Orin walks upstairs. He sees the Weib girls in his room with the curtains drawn to not allow sunlight. Sandra in on the bed reading her last bits of the assignments. While Becca is laying on the floor naked reading the book she going to be quizzed upon tomorrow. Rory is sitting at the desk reading and writing notes for her test. Rachel lying on the floor reading her last assignments too just wearing a shirt with he legs up. And Colleen just reading in the easy chair wit her legs crosses wearing her bikini. As Orin approaches the bed.

Orin "Can you simply move aside Saundra I just want a little sleep." She smiles

Saundra "Of course, you don't mind that we are here?"

Orin "Nope, you five have always treated me with respect. No worries. And you five took the time to get to know as well." All of them smile with thankfulness and appreciation.

Colleen "You're having trouble sleeping?"

Orin "Yes, I am."

Becca "Hush now slip out that carp and into your boxes boy." As Saundra undresses him and put him into his bed. She smiles.

And the girls sing him a Lullaby. As they sing, he falls into a deep sleep. Orville peaks to see what is going on. He simply smiles at this loving site. As the Weib girls put their friend into a deep sleep. As they look and see Orville simply smiling at the cute site.

Orville "If you're mothers' and nana saw this. They would be so proud of you five. I'm taking a nap here. So, don't do anything that this old man wont approve. By the way your father is here as well. Just to give you five a heads up. Just give the man a little time as he requests. He does love you five and your mother too. It's just nana and Wihelmine, have issues with the societies here concerning about you father's blood line. They just can't stand that."

Colleen "Wait a minute, we haven't heard this before?"

Orville "Yes, you haven't. And that you five should've heard this before for a while now. And that your mother should've told you a lot of things too. And I told Wihelmine one day I will be forced to say a few things to straighten her out. Well today is the day. Vladimir Darquemune wanted your mother in the family. She choose your father instead. And Noni was proud of her for that. But he price that was paid was too high for both of them. Vlad killed your grandfather Orin. And made your father public enemy number one if a few places. And that he had to clear the majority of them out to come back home. So, be kind to the man. He just wants a relationship with you girls. If your mother doesn't want one with him anymore. He had to make sure it was safe with all of you." The girls start to cry now and hug Orville. He patsthen on the heads.

Saundra "What should we do?"

Orville "Give the times the man wants. He will have it. I'll make sure of it." As he walks down to the spare bedroom. Saundra just lays next to Orin hugging him as he is sleeping. The girls gather around the bed studying awaiting the sun to come down knowing that he is sleeping well.

Saundra whispers in his ear "Now, my special prince of the night. The time will come when you know everything here. I pray that you don't shun us. We love you that much." She kisses him on his forehead.

The next Evening

First we draw blood, then we party hearty. The Coming out Part for the eligible men and women young and old. If they wish,

Coming to castle point. Well, it's the castle in the other side of town. The Northwestern side to be precise. As the cars fill in for the event. All who come have the option to bring spare sets of clothes. Which Orin, and Erin followed the advice from Orville to take. As they see the rooms. They noticed that this caste was brought from Europe brick by brick. As they see the tapestries on the walls. Erin and Orin are astounded how everything is so authentic. As the look around. They see the Weib's Smiling looking perfect. And they see their nanna. As they approach Orin and Erin.

Wihelmine "may I introduce you to my mother. Annabelle Christy Von Weib." As Orin bows as a sign of respect along with Erin. Annabelle simply blushes.

Annabelle "Why you're are a vison. When the girls said that you were dashing and respectful. I though they were blowing cold smoke up my chimney! Let have a good look at you son. If' your mother doesn't mind?" Erin gives a smiling nod of approval. As Annabelle gives him a once over.

Annabelle "Why, this young man has yet to reach his prime. Oh.. This is a good thing. My Grand daughters tend to burn men rather fast. But ther were two that made the cut. You have heard of them?"

Orin "In passing. When they are ready they will tell me more about them."

Annabelle smiles 'Why, yes you are right about that. This dammed family has a knack of driving wedges and driving people away from loved ones. Do you play the War Scythe 90K?"

Orin "Yes, I do. And yes I'm in the grand prix tournament for the regionals here too."

Annabelle "What are the odds on you?"

Orin "Humbly Jacob Gator-Star has me 12 to 1 At the moment. The odds change with every round. But he wants to keep them at 12 to 1."

Annabelle "Hmm those are impressive odds. Now let this pretty gal help him out for better odds making. I'm sure I can get 30 to 1. Now ladies watch your granny work." As the girls giggle, knowing Noni will get that 30 to 1. As they make there way to the odds pool. They run into Jacob and Horatio and Orvilee. They See Annabelle.

Jacob "Annabelle! So good to see you!"

Annabelle "My girls tell me you need help making it 30 to 1 for our boy here?"

Jacob simply smiles "Annabelle, what is it going to cost me for this help?"

Annabelle "Nothing just one simple dance with the dashing boy here." The Weib girls and Wihelmine jaw drops for this one. They never seen their Noni so taken by a man before. What does Noni know that the don't?"

Orin 'It's okay Jacob I would have simply allow the request with out a problem."

Annabelle "Now, young man shush. I am conducting business with a good friend. He is to make sure no one cuts in besides my six little ladies. Their mother will always be my little lady." Wihelmine blushes now.

Jacob "Well, that is a price I can pay without recriminations. Since it's ok with Erin." Erin smiling a lot. Seeing that Wihelmine's mother looks so young to be in her 80's. She looks more like in her mid-forties and is stunningly beautiful.

Annabelle "Now lets get to work. I see your bracket is up first Orin. They got you in the low end too. Is this your first grand prix?"

Orin "My second. I did well last one. But I denied my placing because ethe other player had to leave for unexpected circumstances."

Annabelle "oh.. You're him then. Yes, I don't blame ya there. You want no doubts about the win. Now you go. We'll get the odds and I'm betting heavily on ya. Don't worry this gal still has a lot of fight in her!" As she smiles off. As Orin is escorted to the pit of the brackets. He sees Rodney. He gives him the look of clean house boy. As Orin give the same look back at him. Rodney has a thumbs up. As he rounds begin the odds are fixed up to the final round. Orin sees his odds. And dam Annabelle talked it up to 80 to 1. Now as the pieces are given randomly per round per player. Orin grabs his set. And his opponent grabs his and the battlefield is set. They now put the pieces on the board. The coin toss has been made. Orin lost it. But that doesn't matter to him. He sets the pieces in play according to what he has. He has the goblin mecha legions. Not bad draw, but the cards he has with dice is all that counts. As he sees his opponent set up his legions. It gives him the time to setup accordingly. As the round officially begins. Orin was able to counterstrike in the first move and do a board wipe. And capture the bunker in the second move. His opponent jaw dropped and looked at him with a deathly glare. As the night proceeds. Orin was able to move up the ranks swiftly and steadily. Approaching the final four of the night. After his semifinal was done. The final judge would be Vladimir himself. As he looks at him. Vladimir is apparently having a bad night. People are having trouble paying out the bets apparently. Which means Jacob and Annabelle are cleaning the clock out with winnings. But the odds can change in the final round. Now it's up to Rodney and Luke Tepes to finish. It was a fun match to watch. But Luke squeaked out he final blow with his final role. Rodney looked at the board. And Rodney glares at Luke. Rodney has been played. And he doesn't like that Luke is merely toyed with him. As Rodney accepts his third-place trophy and prize. He walks up to Orin.

Rodney "Orin, he is worried. You have this. His people have been watching you closely. They gave you what have been know as the worst pieces in the game. And you still wipe the floor with their players. They've lost a lot of money tonight. Its all riding on Luke now. Final round you have the option of requesting the pieces you want. I would take it. And get him good for everyone that lost tonight. Go kick his ass!" Orin Smiles

Orin "Oh... I will, but it's going to be epic. Don't worry watch the show." smiling at Rodney. Rodney simply smirks. He doesn't know what he has in mind. All that he knows that Luke Tepes is going to be blindsided but good.

As they set the final battlefield up. With the obstacles and array of other pieces. It now comes the time to choose your pieces. Luke Tepes chosen the Valkyrie legions. The full set. As it's the most powerful contingent of the sets. Orin looks over and decides to make a mixed legion set instead of a pure set. He chooses, the dragon brigade, the warthog units, The sprite platoons, and the wolfen vanguard. Notably the worst pieces of the entre game. The crowd is in shock. All but Rodney, Erin, Annabelle, Wihelmine, Saundra, Becca, Rachel, Rory, Colleen, Orville, Jacob, Horatio, Owen Ulberg (Owen is a common name in this town), Rev Johnny, Xenia, Pauline, Kathy, And Stoner-Boy. They simply laugh with everyone. Because they know something is admiss here. And they know the odds are not 150 to 1. Vladimir looks at Orin's choices compared with Luke Tepes.

Vladimir "Now son, you can pick better pieces?"

Orin "You've been stacking the decks all night. It wouldn't be fair to actually play fair now, would it?" Vladimir has a shocked cold icy warm look on his face. And he smiles.

Vladimir "I'll honor all the best and the words spoken afterwards too. Only if you win boy. But I doubt that, because you have the worst pieces in the game. But, you do play by the rules really well. But know this your are right. It's a rigged game. It doesn't need to be. But my dear Virginia and Luke wants you in the family. If you pull this off, I will also. But I honor the best and conditions of the winner. Good luck, you're going to need it."

Orin "Thank you sir for all your support!" As Vladimir walks away from his spot. Orin checks the cards and the pieces. Making sure nothing is missing. As he sees the setup Luke makes. He sets the board accordingly. The coin toss was replaced by twenty sides die roll. Luke Tepes Rolls a 16. Orin roles a 9. Luke goes first. Orin hope he does the classical gambits here. It makes it a lot easier. Luke Tepes performs as the classical player. Comes out with strength and cover. Poor boy, he made too many mistakes. For the unorthodox player. He setup the conditions for a total board wipe. And if he is stupid enough to mount the attack. It's all down in one shot. Luke takes the point of opportunity to attack. This is what Orin was waiting for. He plays the counterattack card for the free movements needed. Stacking with the safe heaven card to buff the defensives, plays the relentless assault card for 12 times the counter attacks with two free bonus action. Coupled with gravity wave card, which allows 8 more attacks. Al now it's need is 3 die rolls of 3 or better to wipe the board. He rolls 18, 13, and a natural 20. He clears the board in one shot including the bunker. He plays the carrier support card as well. To block al coms to the group and reinforcements for the game. The expressions on Luke Tepes face were priceless. The crowd is in stunned silence. Vladimir Darquemune is stunned and astonished by the victory. And the people rooting in Orin's corner simply laugh hysterically. Winning the bets, the money and cleaning the house out. And he did this all with he worst pieces in the game. Luke tepes loks to his kinsman and is speechless. Vladimir composes himself.

Vladimir "the winner and the new Regional champion of Andersonville Orin Ezekiel McNiel! I will honor those bets boy and whatever you incline to wish for the dance tonight. But you will be put on stage to be bought and sold. There isn't a way that old coot can talk you out of that practice tonight!" Orin looks dismissively

Orin "I believe you're not in a position to negate this. But you will try."

Vladimir "Oh…you're right about that one boy. I will try to get my way. And I do get my way." As he storms off awarding him the first-place trophy and the special edition Valkyrie sets. Orin walks to the group. They're all smiles except Orville.

Orivlle "What did he say?"

Orin "I'll be put up fpr show later tonight. And I will get my way boy. Just you wait."

Wihelmine "With what money? We cleaned them out!"

Annabelle "No so fat daughter. He still has old rules he can use. He will use them tonight. Or it's all out war. Don't fret young ladies there is a way out of this just yet."

As everyone is not getting ready for the formal. Owen Ulberg and Orville are in tense negotiations for the dance. And the final verdicts are made. As Owen walks up to his son.

Owen Ulberg "He threatened all out war. But he got his way. But not all his way. You still get to choose who you desire. However, she has to brought out by her father or her father's proxy. So don't worry. You'll have a nice time. Tonight, and remember to give Noni her dance first alright? She is a very nice woman. A woman you want in your corner. And trust me she is in your corner. She is having a grand ole time tonight. So get dressed and your mom will bring you out. I have something to attend to." As Owen Ulberg leaves to his duty. Orin walks to the dressing room and gets ready. Colleen walks in.

Colleen hugs him "So…You're going to be sold?"

Orin "Not particularly, I have an assurance of sorts."

Colleen "By, whom?"

Orin "I don't want to say right now. Too many prying eyes and ears."

Colleen "Yes, you are right about that. Saundra is in tears now."

Orin "You tell Saundra don't fret. Everything will be okay."

Collen smiles with a very doubtful look. As the he is lead out by his mom. The order of appearance is alphabetically listed. Some have already begun the dances. When Orin is introduced. He is in the middle of the card of men. He walks up to Annabelle Wieb.

She smiles and accepts. As the rest of the Weibs are there except Saundra.

Annabelle "Well I'm surprised I was your first choice tonight."

Orin "My father said make sure you get yours in. I don't see anyone else just yet either. So it's your luck day young lady" Annabelle blushes

Annabelle "You sure know how to make a woman blush, I heard what it took you to make you blush. It takes a lot to do that now. Doesn't it?"

Orin "Yes, it does. But it takes a lot to make me jump when people crack the whip."

Annabelle "All, too true there. You remind me a lot of my late husband. Just like you are cunning, dashing, and full of faith." As she sighs

Orin "You do miss him terribly." Annabelle smiles.

Annabelle "Yes I do, Why the young ones are so young and thoughtful. I wonder how you would make a good husband for the right woman. I dare say, my granddaughters would be the best match for you.

So, which one do you like most?" As Orin feels a tinge in his ear. As he sakes his head off. Annabelle simply smiles with a impressed look.

Orin "Sorry, about that. I had a slight headache come over me."

Annabelle "It's okay, dear. You are a worthy man. To have the attention of so many people. You are a good young man. Why did you have to be so young?" As she smiles as they next round of men and women go around. Some of the Darkmoon's Orin did dance with the Lupins as well. As he passes through the floor. Virginia decides to atemtp to cut in and Annabelle beats her to the punch.

Virginia "Nana your too old for this!" And Nana smiles

Annabelle "No I'm not to dance with a kind gentleman." As she glares at Virginia.

Orin "Alright I'll bite. What is going on?" Annabelle smiles

Annabelle "First please call me Noni from now. Second, it's a bit of a surprise. But I know you'll like this surprise. You're such a man of great faith. Oh yeah, we are finally at the w's We should look over there." As they Look. They see Owen Ulberg escorting Cassaundra Von Weib to the dance floor. The gown is a white with lace and long. With slit at the left leg for movement. Owen is just not fixated with Saundra. SO is the whole room. The is a shock look with everyone. As Noni guides Orin to her granddaughter. Luke attempts to make his way. But somehow, he trips on his feet. And sees Rodney smiling as a job well done look on his face. All the men begin tripping except Orin and Owen. After Owen finishes the dance with Cassaundra he looks at Noni and smiles.

Owen Ulberg "I think this young lady wants to cut in." As Noni smiles

Annabelle "Absolutely, he's all hers now!" As they switch in unison. Orin looks astonished. And is at a loss of words now. Saundra now concentrates hard. A voice says in Orin's head "Tell me everything." And he looks deeply in her eyes.

Orin "Whay is your voice in my head? It's not eh first time I've heard it. And why is it that sometimes I see point in your ears? Also, what do your eyes change into gold sometimes too. Also why do you have fangs?" Saundra puts her fingers on his lips. And she smiles, looking at the crowd with a mischievous look now. Luke is furious, Virginia is equally furious. The rest of the gathering is curious of what is going to happen next.

Saundra "Once revealed, you can never go back to the way it was before. Are you sure you want those answers?" Orin smiles.

Orin "Well I'm going to find out anyway. Too may things don't add up here. I keep my mouth shut. I just let it slide. But the truth comes out. No matter how you hide it." Saundra simply sighs in resignation. She is afraid of the possible shock to his system.

Saundra "Alright I'll show you." She lets her transformation of her face begin. Her eyes glow gold. The points of her ears grow full. And her fangs are showing. As their dance continues, the crowd puts the hands over their mouth except the people in with the Ulberg's and the Von Weibs, they smile at this.

Orin "You're so beautiful, you have nothing to hide from me. I don't know what I am honestly in this town." He Kisses Saundra. The Ulberg's and the Weib's cry tears of Joy. And he notices that his feet aren't on the ground. As they float to the music. They hover out of the castle. As they dance the night away over the town. Just looking into each other's eyes. Holding on to the movement. Simply smiling and laughing together. No words just the dance. As Saundra hovers down to the ground. It's in front of Reverend Jonathan Rodrick Kingsley church. Rev Johnny is opening the doors for the nightly bible study and sees them. He simply waves them in. Now Orin sees that Rev Johnny has the same marking of fangs as Saundra. HE sees the rest of the vampires in mas around the church grounds.

Rev Johnny "Ah.. my two favorite students. Having a good time. Want to hear the gospel of the lord tonight?" As they both giggle and smile.

Saundra "Sure, why not dear." As he holds Orin by her side.

Rev Johnny "Just wait, I have to tell the other where you are." Th a voice from the crowd.

Vladimir "Just wait one cotton picking minute. He needs to be turned now!" With an angry look in his face with the worst intentions imaginable.

Rev Johnny "Now come on Vladimir. They are to worship the lord Jesus." As he hold a cross in front of them. Al the vampires hiss in pain and flee the site. Orin does a quadruple take. Noticing that Saundra and Rev Johnny are unaffected.

Rev Johnny Laughs "Lord Jesus forgive, me. But I do love doing that to those unbelieving, denying creatures that disrespect you. Even though you have proven to them multiple times you do exist! And you are wondering as I'm waving the cross around why she isn't affected. It's because the gift of the holy ghost id for the fairy folk as well. And the accursed fairy line as well. Saundra is a true believer. So is her mother and the rest of her sisters. You should se how they react one I mix holy water with blood. It's hysterical the reactions to this." As Rev Johnny guides them into the church. The rest of the gang arrives.

Orville "To quote this correctly. If that god dammed preacher flashes that infernal cross again. I will find a way to rip his head off. Just delivering the message." As Rev Johnny and he the rest of them laugh.

Annabelle "Well didn't you spike his blood once?"

Rev Johnny "I have the right mind to do it again. Seeing him vomit blood for a week was so funny. I think I have six helpers in this endeavor?" Looking at Orin and the Weib girls.

Erin "You're as spiteful as Joshua. You shouldn't try a calming them instead?"

Wihelmine "Erin, this is my fault. I did turn them in a fit of anger. And Vladimir did help me with the turns. So, he tends to be spiteful to them. He puts up with me because he has heard the full story why he does these spiteful things from time to time. Is the subject about not having righteous rage tonight reverend?" Rev Jonny looks down in shame.

Rev Johnny "Yes, Wihelmine it is. Let's go in and hear what you have tonight." As the group enters the church. They hear a roar of welcomes and happiness in the building As the sit in the front row.

Virginia enters the church "Now before you get all too happy here. I must announce that the boy must be turned immediately. And to formally join a covenant. And it's up to the covenant for whom he associates with. And who he is bonded with too. So, turn him right now Saundra and you too pick a covenant as well." As the church sneers, at Virginia.

Owen Ulgerg "Look in six weeks is Orin's Birthday. His seventeenth birthday in fact. Let him enjoy the sun day-walker. After all the Tepes are all day-walkers. SO let him say good by to the sun. And he will be turned as per the Vampire rituals. I do believe this is her first turn s to speak. After all, she is a natural born vampire. I'm asking for a temporary stay of execution." The crowd is looking at President Ulberg's suggestion. With a shocked look on their faces. But Orville steps up and waves off his hands.

Orville "He's right to ask for the temporary stay of execution. Also, Virginia is a day walker. And the Tepes Darkmun's have the right to demand his turning. But he boy has noticed too many things in this town for the past trimester. And he kept his mouth shut. And went about his daily business." And the crowd calms down. Virginia looks at the mayor with rage.

Virginia "Well, my lord earl Oberon. We mere day-walkers and the other vampires want it done now!' As the crowd shocked that the young lady called Orville by his Fairy name.

Orin "Just asking Orville is the bench your throne?" Orville smiles

Orville/Oberon "Why yes son it is. The castle in the other side of town is mine. But Tatiana lives there now. And her sisters, the fates." As Xenia, Pauline, Kathy wave. Rodney waves too with a smile.

Orin "Rodney is Puck. Then who is Stoner-Boy?" AS the rest cough.

Orville/Oberon "Well I know for sure, and the Tatiana's sisters know for sure. But if he feels like revealing it to you. He will do it. But when the time is right. Now, Viriginia eitrher you're going to listen to the sermon. Or you will have to leave. And no one interprets the laws in this town. Except the Lord Jesus Christ or me. Since Jesus isn't here in the flesh. Since he isn't here right now. So, Virginia you must bow to my judgement. So, I say she turns him in six weeks. And that is final. And as for the coven he joins. It's his decision to join whatever coven he wants. Or if he doesn't want to join a coven that good too. So, either hear the sermon. Or get the hell out of this church of our Lord Jesus Christ! Sorry if I stepped on your toes Reverend."

Rev Johnny "No worries my lord Oberon. I couldn't have said it better myself. Now lets us begin with a prayer. Lord Jesus, thank you for bringing all together this night. We are here to for your wisdom and guidance. We are here to study the word and work in your accordance to be better children in your eyes. Please make us receptive to your word. Please drive the pettiness out of our hearts, please drive out he demons that prey on our brother and sisters. All glory lord is in your name. Please give us the clarity to serve your word and you. Amen." As the crowd finishes the prayer. Johnny begins the Study. As he looks upon Orin and Saundra. They look so in over with each other. And Saundra's sisters with Wihelmine, Tatiana, Oberon, Jacob, Horatio, Owen and Wihelmine smiling. As he preaches the word of the day. And the need to let go your personal vengeance. How it releases you form the hold of the devil. As he referred to Psalms, Acts, judges as he is preaching the word. Orin feels happy and loved for once. As Reve Johnny finished up the study. They all leave the church and realize it's almost sunup. AS they part ways for the time being. They enter their perspective homes. AS Orin walks up to his bedroom. He is met by Luke and Virginia.

Luke 'It wasn't easy breaking in here. Don't worry I believe Rodney can fix it for you." Looking icy hot colds look.

Virginia "Since she never turned anyone before. No telling what you would go through. At least with me you would be a day walker instead of a full vampire. So, I urge you reconsider and take the vow of silence of our kind. Also marry one of the Tepes bloodline. That is for your own protection." As Erin walks into the room.

Erin "Now you too. Ge the fuck out of my home."

Luke "He's making a big mistake here. You don't understand what you both getting into."

Erin shows her mark on her shoulder "This mean I am a huntress of the first order. I know what your kind is all about. My husband told of this place. But he did warn me about the politics of the covens. My father attempted to join your covens. And it all went to the crapper. So, you two get out of this house now! And tell Vladimir if he wants something right. He better do it his dammed self. Also, one last thing. He has to go through Oberon and Titania first bout these matters. And now get out, before I decide to figure out where he rests. Or should I give you a few scars that won't heal for good measure!" As Luke and Virginia are in shock of the revelations been made here. The run out the balcony and glide down gently to the ground and run home.

Erin "Orin get some rest. You have six weeks to enjoy the sun. Also, I do approve of your Saundra. She went out of her way to understand you. Like you went out of your way to understand her. She has become your best friend. Sad that Anna isn't her to see this. But your seventeenth birthday is coming fast. As she opens the curtains. Sleep with them open during he day. You won't be able to enjoy the sun." As she kisses, her son on the head. As Orin looks at the sunrise and decides to watch it. He is going to miss this. He now wishes Saundra could see a sunrise herself without dying. It's such a beautiful site to behold. Now he is beginning to understand Virginia's pleas. But his decision has been made. Six weeks he'll be a vampire.

CHAPTER 20

Six weeks later....?

For the past six weeks. Orin now sees everything that looked strange suddenly made sense. He starts to be more outgoing with people. Some give their condolences about the upcoming turn. He assures them he will be fine. But they give him pointers for the first couple days. As he walks out into the sunny streets. He bumps into Rodney.

Rodney 'Ready for the big night? Ready to become immortal?"

Orin "Nope, I'll just wing this one. Is that so bad being honest about it?"

Rodney "Dam, you are more ready than most people. Why are you so calm?"

Orin "I'm not sure, for some reason I'm at ease. But I am going to miss the sun. But I'm moving forward. So how is the trickster Puck today?" Rodney/Puck laughs happily.

Rodeney/Puck "You do amaze me Orin. One thing I should tell you. She hates werewolves. Most vampire hat werewolves. I just don't know why. Some consider it like mixing white people with black people. Back it he 1800's and half of the 1900's here."

Orin "Well it's good to know that. What happens when a vampire marries a werewolf?"

Rodney/Puck "Well, I don't know about that. All I know it's considered poor form in the covens. The werewolf community is okay with that. But the vampire community hates it with a passion."

Orin "Thanks for the heads up. SO where is Tania and Orville?"

Rodney/Puck 'Oh…you mean Lord Oberon and Mistress Tatiana! The are going over the conditions your mother imposed to the Darquemune's. They are truly scared of her. Especially when Rev Johnny confirmed her family lines. And the fact she does know how to hunt. And that she taught you how to combat nosferatu in all their stages in life. This made them squirm. Especially when the found out that her father is the head of the biggest hunter clans. So they are there to ensure your will be done my young lord."

Orin "Lord of what? You don't need to call me that."

Puck Laughs "Well Oberon will give you the title of lord after t ceremony with Saundra tonight. At the behest of Noni by the way. I'm finally allowed to call her that! You have no idea how long it's been for me to earn that right."

Orin "How long is fifteen years for fairy folk?"

Puck laughs "Well fifteen years is more like fifteen hundred years. She kicked him out of the castle for fifteen hundred years. Noni is twelve hundred years. Wihelmine is five hundred years old. And her girl are two hundred and ten years of age." Orin whistles long and hard.

Orin "Wow the argument must be vicious?"

Rodney/Puck "Oh.. you have no idea. So, you have ben gifted with the site?"

Orin "Apparently so. But I don't have control. So, it's kind of useless to me isn't it?"

Puck "Nope, ones gifted with the sight are knighted and given titles of lordship amongst the fairy folk. Because you are Truth Sayers by nature. Meaning that disputes are your responsibility now. Your job is to figure out who is lying he most. Or who telling the truth. Or finding the spells that hide things. Your types are the blood hounds so to speak."

Orin "Oh. Then I'll be doing courses at the CBI wings of the school now?"

Puck "Precisely. So, your job duties will become that of an interrogator and inquisitor for cases and crimes here. Sorry no choice of that being a job of your now."

Orin "I would've liked to spend the last day with them one last time."

"Are so sure about that?" Says Stoner-Boy

Puck "Stoner-Boy! What are you talking about?"

Stoner-Boy "I need to talk to the lad for the rest of the day. Don't worry he won't skip out." Puck takes his leave.

Orin "What do you mean?"

Stoner-Boy "This isn't the end with your relationship with the sun. The sun is always going to be there for your supernatural life. It does end. You will grow old. You will have children with her too. But enjoy the day. Don't feel like it's a drag. Just treat it like any other day!"

Orin "Uhm. Okay...I'll bite what is up?"

Stoner-Boy laughs "Well, this date has significance to you. Also there are a few things people have yet to tell you. But you'll find out tonight. Just look at the moon as she sized you up. All will be fine."

Orin "Okay, sure? Who is hiding something from me?"

Stoner-Boy "Oh...that would be Owen Ulberg himself. But the rest were told to keep quiet. He wants to tell you what is up before the night. But He won't be able to make it in time."

Orin "Another prophecy?"

Stoner-Boy "If you say so. It's going to be a night to remember. Enjoy life young lord of the land. It's always way too short. And Noni arrived before sunup. So, she will be here." Orin sees Stoner-Boy dissipate before his eyes now. And it was so fast. The wasn't a shimmer now. He discovered the shimmer is what you dissipate or teleport through the protection spells the Fairy folk erected in the town. So, this is the life fully aware and seen in all its glory, Discovering the supernatural mounts. Seeing dragons, unicorns, gargoyles, sprites, elves, goblins, Valkyries, saders, centars and many others. Now the strange things made sense. As he walks the town and waves to people everywhere. He now goes home and sleeps with curtains open. The ceremony will happen in a few when sundown approaches. He wakes up and showers up. He wonders if his senses of touch will be heightened. He has other questions, but hey will be answered when he is turned. So, after the shower. He made it to the forest at the edge of the park. He was told by Miguel De Le Guy that he has to wear this red robe. And only this red robe. As he is dressed in a red robe. The red signifies the blood of life. He looks at the Weib ladies. All of them were wearing black robes. Cassaundra's robe is black. Signifies she is the mistress of the night. As she walks him to a secluded part of the forest. She hears a ruckus from the other side of the forest. She hears Owen Ulberg wanted to say a few things to Orin. She disrobes herself. The she disrobes Orin. The full moon is out now. And Orin begins to fidget as she holds his hands as he is itching all over. She lets go of his hands as she wonders if this is a reaction to the robe. Puck wouldn't do this. Must be the Tepes for making him feel uncomfortable. As she sizes up Orin, she notices hair on his back. She never noticed hair on his back as she circles him, she notices that there is more hair in the front too. AS she looks upon Orin's face, she notices that his ears were getting pointy, and his nose stretches out and that his legs stretching out to a new length. And he is getting hairier and hairier as he grows taller. Cassaundra is now getting excited as she sees the transformation. Now Orin screams in pain. Orin howls and then her excitement.

Cassaundra "Yes, I knew you were special! This explains everything with the sight as well! Yes, you're a werewolf! You're a natural born werewolf! There hasn't been a natural recorded birth of your kin in One hundred years! Yes!" The she realizes what she just said. The feelings of excitement, happiness, and joy. These feeling turn into dread fear and terror.

Cassaundra "Oh shit! This is your first turn! Orin are you in there?"

The End?

CPSIA information can be obtained
at www.ICGtesting.com
Printed in the USA
BVHW051742170722
642355BV00004B/62